the
MEMORY
THIEF

the

MEMORY
THIEF

A NOVEL

Emily Colin

BALLANTINE BOOKS
NEW YORK

A Ballantine Books Trade Paperback Original

Copyright © 2012 by Emily Colin

Published in the United States by Ballantine Books, an imprint of The Random House Publishing Group, a division of Random House, Inc., New York.

BALLANTINE and colophon are registered trademarks of Random House, Inc.

Library of Congress Cataloging-in-Publication Data

Colin, Emily A.
The memory thief : a novel / Emily Colin.
p. cm.
ISBN 978-0-345-53039-4
eBook ISBN 978-0-345-53558-0
1. Life change events—Fiction. 2. Grief—Fiction.
3. Memory—Fiction. 4. Mothers and sons—Fiction.
5. Self-realization in women—Fiction. 6. Psychological fiction. I. Title.
PS3603.O438M46 2012
813'.6—dc23
2012020348

Printed in the United States of America on acid-free paper

www.ballantinebooks.com

6 8 9 7 5

Book design by Susan Turner

For Lucas, who stopped time.

And for my parents, who always believed.

the
MEMORY
THIEF

PROLOGUE

Aidan

When things go wrong at thirteen thousand feet, they go wrong fast. That frigid morning on the Eiger Nordwand, high in Switzerland's Bernese Alps, is no exception. German climbers call it the *Mordwand*—Murder Wall—for good reason: Since the first successful expedition in 1938, at least sixty rock hounds have lost their lives here. When Ellis passes out and the fog closes in, my first thought is this: The three of us are not going to become statistics.

I've been in similar fixes before: sick teammate, bad weather, big decisions, little time. I don't lose my head. I run down my short list of options, reject all but one as too risky. In the end we rope up, I toss some slings over an outcropping that looks solid, I lower J.C. and Ellis down. I want to get off the mountain, now. This is the fastest way.

Then it happens. The cornice collapses, overloaded with snow or just unstable. Down we go, all three of us. Rocks are everywhere and I feel like I'm in a pinball game, ricocheting off the face. I jam my axe in, trying to slow our descent, but we are going too fast. Now both of them are unconscious and I know that in every way that matters, I am alone. Again and again I jam my axe. It sticks, then it rips loose. Dimly I am aware that I am in pain, that I am bleeding.

Then I see it—a crevasse, gaping below us. We are headed right for it and my heart breaks into a sprint, fueled by a fresh spate of adrenaline. I try to get my knees up, to throw my weight on my axe. We have slid at least six hundred feet and I know from experience that arresting a fall at this point is near impossible, but my other option—giving up, letting all three of us hurtle into that icy maw—is not a possibility. If I die, I will die fighting.

The two of them go over the edge and fear clenches me. I dig in my knees again, throw my chest hard on the axe. It bites, and we stop. Below me, the rope jerks and goes taut.

I am alive.

There's no one else on this part of the mountain, and I know what I have to do. I know it instinctively, from years of climbing and more self-rescues than I care to count. Right now, though, I don't trust myself to move. I lie on the axe, pressing it into the snow and ice, trying to catch my breath. Blood runs down my face, into my eyes, but I don't dare raise my head. Even if I could, I wouldn't be able to see a goddamn thing: I am facing up the slope, away from where they've gone. I stare down at the reddening snow and I scream for them, as loud as I can. My voice echoes off the rock, up from the crevasse, mocking me. They don't answer.

I lie there, bleeding and screaming, for what is probably

about two minutes before I build the anchor, escape the belay, and make my way to the edge of the crevasse to see what has happened to my friends. But there is no way of measuring time like that. It feels like forever, and I have a lot of time to think. I think: I am alive. I think: This fucking sucks. I even pray, though to whom I'm not sure: the Catholic God of my childhood? *Daimones*, the mountain spirits that J.C.'s always going on about?

In the absence of a response from any or all of the above, I start thinking about Madeleine, which takes me by surprise. I think about how I would love to hold her, to breathe in her bonfire smell, to listen to her laugh. I think about her face after she caught me dicking around with Kiss Me Kate, how hurt she looked. This kind of introspection is not like me. When something's done, it's done . . . and it's usually done because I ended it, sorry to say.

I generally employ a conquistador's approach to matters of the flesh that would make Caesar proud: I Came, I Saw, I Seduced, followed by I Came Some More and Exited Stage Left. Relationships rarely enter into the equation, and as for love—bitch, please, as Roma is prone to say. I can get my endorphin rush somewhere else, thank you very much. But as I lie here freezing my balls off, it dawns on me—I miss Maddie. If I don't make it home from this expedition, her last memory of me will involve seeing me make out with a stranger. I'm not okay with this, I realize. Because I want to be with her. Still.

It's a dirty little four-letter word, and an even more appalling sentence. But I've come right up against it, here at the edge of the world, and I've got nowhere left to run. Holy denial, Batman. I feel this way because I love her.

I watch the blood drip off my face into the snow, I shiver, I shout their names, and all along I am thinking: I screwed up, big-time. I am slow on the emotional uptake and it has taken a near-death experience to bring me to this conclusion. I've spent so long trying not to feel, I've almost forgotten how.

The axe digs into my chest and my heart pounds against my ribs, an answering call. There's nothing to be gained from ignoring it, not out here with my friends dangling over an abyss and no help in sight. As long as I am talking to people who aren't about to answer me anytime soon, I might as well add her to the list. I close my eyes, I picture her face. *Maddie,* I say aloud. *Maddie, I'm sorry.*

ONE

Madeleine

SIX YEARS LATER . . .

On the surface, there's no reason for me to be concerned—at least, no more than usual. All Aidan says is "I think I'm going to try the South Face of McKinley again."

We're sitting at the kitchen table, me with a cup of coffee, him with a bottle of Gatorade. Gabriel is in his room down the hall, building something with his Legos. He'd gotten a big box of them for his fourth birthday, a mixed lot that J.C. scored on eBay. That was over six months ago, but they can still absorb his attention for hours.

Sunlight plays on the wood table, and Aidan runs one finger through it, tracing a rainbow of colors. It's an ordinary day, but still I feel a frisson of fear ripple down my spine. "Isn't that the route you tried last year? When you had to turn back?"

"Yeah, we were trying to do a new variation of the Cassin

Ridge, and the weather turned on us. It's been bugging me ever since." There's a pad of paper on the table, and he begins doodling something on it as he speaks—a face, it looks like.

"The one that's got that place called the Valley of Death?"

He looks up at me, his blond hair falling into his eyes. He needs a haircut, for sure. "That's the one. What's got into you, Maddie?"

"I don't think you should go." I've never said this to him before, and his eyes widen with surprise before they narrow in puzzlement.

"What are you talking about? Why not?"

"I have a bad feeling about this one. I don't know why, but I do."

"Don't be silly. It's an awesome climb. That was just freaky last year, about the weather. It shouldn't happen again. We got as far as the *bergschrund* with no problem—what?" he says, in response to the exasperated face I'm making over the rim of my coffee cup.

"You know I have no idea what you're talking about," I say. "English, please."

He rolls his eyes at me. "A *bergschrund* is a big crevasse near the head of a glacier. German for 'mountain crevice,' if you really want to know."

"I don't need the etymology, Aidan. Just the significance."

"'Schrunds can be a real pain in the ass," he says, crossing his arms over his chest. "In the winter, they're not such a big deal to traverse. In the summer, you've got snowmelt, so they're these big gaping holes."

"I just know there's a point in here somewhere."

"My *point* is, what happened last year wasn't a technical issue. We got across the 'schrund just fine. It was after that that the crappy weather set in." He unfolds himself and goes back to drawing.

My stomach twists. "I wish you wouldn't go. Can't you do something else? Go to Chile, or Spain, or, I don't know, China. Anywhere else."

"Relax, honey. You're getting all worked up over nothing."

"I'm not," I say, and even as the words leave my mouth I know that it's the truth. "I'm telling you, Aidan, I have a bad feeling about this."

"What, are you psychic now?" His tone is light, but I can tell that irritation lurks beneath.

"I've never asked you not to do something. I'm asking you now."

When he lifts his head this time, his mouth is set in a straight, obstinate line. "Don't be ridiculous."

I look down at my coffee, my stomach churning. "I'm not," I say again, my voice as stubborn as his.

"Yeah," he says. "You are." And he gets up from the table, spinning the drawing around to face me. Seen from one angle, there is his face. I look again, and there's the mountain, rising snow-covered against a cloudless sky. I stare at the picture he's drawn, watching the image shift from one form to the next. "Don't go," I say in a whisper, but it is too late; the front door slams behind him, and I hear the Jeep's engine rev as he peels out of the driveway.

We fight about the Mount McKinley trip for two months, a record. I argue with him, I yell, I plead. At night I wake from dreams where Aidan goes tumbling off the mountain, crashing to the bottom of a valley and landing, lifeless, in a heap. I dream that he is crushed by falling rock, that his Cessna goes down before he even reaches the glacier, that he steps on a weak snow bridge and goes hurtling into the depths of a crevasse. Then I wake up, my heart pounding in triple time, and look over at Aidan sleeping beside me, peaceful and still. *Don't go,* I say into the darkness of our room. *Don't leave me.*

Where this premonition of disaster has come from, I can't say, but it sticks. Aidan tries everything he can think of to make me change my mind, to "see sense," as he puts it. He listens to all of my doomsday scenarios and then, one by one, tells me why they're nothing to worry about. He teases me that we've changed places, that usually he's the irrational one and I'm the one calming him down. He makes jokes ("Denali? De nada, baby"), he makes J.C. come and talk to me. He gives me books about successful ascents of the mountain, emails me websites. When none of this does any good, he screams and threatens and throws things. He begs. And finally he retreats into a stony, stubborn silence, from which he emerges only to say, "I'm going and that's the end of it."

The night before he leaves in May, I lie in bed waiting for him to join me, and when he doesn't, I get up to look for him. He's sitting in the living room, in the dark. I can make out the dim shape of a glass on the coffee table in front of him, next to his lighter and a pack of American Spirits. He smells like whisky.

I sit down on the couch next to him. "Hey."

"Maddie," he says, and his voice is rough. He is crying, I realize with some horror. "What's happening to us?" he says. His voice breaks on the last word.

I move closer, wrap my arms around him. He is shaking, like he was six years ago when he came to tell me that he loved me, that Jim Ellis had died on the Eiger Nordwand and he blamed himself. "I can't lose you," he says. "I can't. I don't know what I would do. Tell me I'm not losing you, baby. Please."

Now I am crying, too. My tears mingle with his as we hold each other. "You could never lose me," I say. "I'm the one who's going to lose you. I know it, Aidan. I know I am."

He presses his face against mine. "I'm not going anywhere. I'll be back, honey. You'll see. I'll be back and everything will be fine."

"You can't know that. Look at what happened to Jim."

"To Ellis?" he says, sounding puzzled. "What's McKinley got to do with that? The Nordwand was a freaky set of circumstances, a whole bunch of bad stuff piling up at once. Ellis was sick. That cornice was shit. And then J.C. got knocked out. You know all this."

I don't know why I've got the Eiger expedition on my mind. Maybe it's the feel of Aidan's body trembling, the wetness of his tears. I don't think I've seen him cry since that day, not even when Gabriel was born, and it unsettles me. "All three of you could have died in the crevasse on that stupid mountain, not just him," I say, and shiver.

"But we didn't," he says, pulling away and wiping his eyes. I hear the familiar stubbornness line his voice. "I lost Ellis, true. I haven't forgiven myself for that. But I did the best I could. I built an anchor. I got us out of there. And I came back to you." He runs his hand through his hair. "It was a horrible thing, Maddie. But it also made me realize how I feel about you, after that stupidity with Kate. Those extremes—they're part of why I love what I do. I guess it's my version of a spiritual experience."

I roll my eyes, borrowing his bad habit. He sighs.

"Look, honey, there's a lot of guys who would be happy working a nine-to-five, or whose church is inside four walls rather than halfway up a cliff. But you didn't marry one of those guys. You married me."

"I know that," I say in a small voice.

"Are you sorry?" he says, turning his face to me. His cheeks are streaked with tears. He looks miserable, which is so uncharacteristic that it makes me start crying again.

"What kind of question is that?" I say, blinking my eyes so I can see him clearly.

"A real one," he says. "Answer it, please."

"No," I say without hesitation. "Of course I'm not. I love you for who you are. There's no one else I'd want to be with."

Relief flashes across his face. He stretches his arms up to the ceiling, brings one down around my shoulders. "Okay, then," he says, like everything is settled.

"But, Aidan, what if something like that happens again and you're not so lucky?"

His arm is still around my shoulders, and I can feel the tension seep back into it. He drums his fingers on the back of the couch. "If it does, then it does. That's why we get emergency training, so that we'll know how to handle tough situations. Skill and experience count for a lot up there. And I just happen to have a considerable amount of both. As do Roma and J.C. and Jesse." He wiggles his eyebrows at me, runs his free hand along my thigh.

I know he's trying to make light of this, to make me smile, but it doesn't work this time. "You can't control the weather," I say. "You can't tell the mountain what to do."

Aidan gives up on being charming and folds his arms over his chest. "Jesus, Maddie. Let it go, would you please? I'm getting on a plane tomorrow morning. I don't want to leave like this."

"So don't leave," I say.

"You know I have to," he says. "Don't make it worse."

I shake my head, and he takes my face between his hands and holds me still. "Have faith. You remember when I told you that, the first time?"

"I remember everything," I say, and it has the flavor of prophecy, like soon memories will be all I have.

"Have I ever let you down?"

"No, Aidan, but—"

"And I won't. Why can't you believe me?" He strokes my hair. His blue eyes are wet, the lashes matted. "Listen," he says. "I swear I'll come back to you, all right? I promise I will come home."

I know this is supposed to make me feel better, but it has the opposite effect, like he's shaking a fist in the face of fate. "You can't make a promise like that, Aidan," I say, my voice uneasy. What I really want to say is *Take it back.*

He holds his fingers to my lips, shushing me. "Don't worry, Maddie, okay? Don't worry, honey. Don't worry." His mouth takes the place of his fingers, and he kisses me like he is pouring out everything he wants to say, like he is trying to leave part of himself here with me. "I love you," he says. He says it again and again. "You're my life," he says, kissing my neck, my breasts, my face. "You and Gabe are all I've got. I can't lose you. Do you hear me?"

"Yes."

"Tell me it's going to be all right, then."

"No," I say. "I can't tell you that."

He gives a long, frustrated sigh. "Then tell me you love me, at least. Say it now so I can hear."

"I love you," I tell him. "I love you more than you know."

He grins at me through his tears. I can see it in the light that filters in from the street, from the headlights of passing cars. "Not as much as I love you." It is an old joke between us. "But I can deal with that."

"You're wrong."

"No," he says. "I'm not." And then he kisses me again, and he is making love to me there on the couch in the dark, both of us still crying. There is a desperate edge to the way we come together, each of us afraid that we are going to lose the other—him to the mountain, me to whatever mysterious forces drive couples apart. Remember this, I tell myself as he arches over me, as I rise to meet him. Remember.

TWO

Nicholas

I am somewhere. Where, I am not sure. It doesn't seem to matter. A big white room, maybe, or a dark tunnel. Sometimes there are flashes of light, explosions of bright color that I watch with interest. Then they go away again, and there is nothingness, like when you stare up at the ceiling of a room at night with the lights turned off. None of this bothers me. It is quiet where I am, for the most part, and peaceful.

I'm unaware that my body has been gone until it starts coming back, in sharp, alarming gusts of pain that fade as quickly as they come on. My legs, my chest, most especially my head. I try to figure out why this should be, but come up with nothing. Then there are voices, and a needle, and the pain retreats again. Back I go to the big white room.

I lie there, waiting to see what will happen next. It occurs to me that maybe I should panic, but what would be the point? Besides, I don't seem to have the energy, what with the flashes of light and the pain and everything. So I lie still, there inside my head in the big white room. And possibly, I fall asleep, assuming that I was awake to begin with.

The reason I think this is that I am suddenly cold, and instead of seeing the big white room or the dark tunnel around me, I see the side of a mountain, which I am climbing. I can feel my body again, and it doesn't hurt. In fact, it feels pretty damn good, and I am—happy.

I climb and climb and watch the sun rise. Even through my glacier glasses, it burns my retinas, but I refuse to look away. They are opposing elements, fire and ice, and I am caught in the middle. The light is pitiless, shining from the sun, reflecting off the snow. It washes me clean, lays me bare.

For a moment I am frozen. There is no *before*, there is no *after*. There is only me, strapped to this hunk of rock, something the earth coughed up when it was having an off day. I am reminded of a bumper sticker—*Be Here Now*—but instead of serenity, I am filled with dread. The mountain's staggering beauty seems sinister, a vindictive mistress. Apprehension washes over me, threaded through my muscles, coiling in the pit of my belly.

I need to keep moving, to put this misplaced unease behind me. Sinking my ice axe, I step up, onto a glacial expanse. I brace myself to slip, but that doesn't happen. Instead my boots hold steady and grip, metal squeaking in protest as it bites into the ice.

Looking for a place to anchor in, I take a few steps onto the glacier's surface. I am high enough that I can look down on the clouds. In the distance, I can see huge plumes of snow blow off the peak above in the growing light of the sun—a sight that gives me pause, no matter how many times I've taken it in. I breathe to center myself, though it's a futile effort up here, where the air is so thin. Still, alone on the uneven, snow-laden crust of the glacier, the ice wall looming jagged below me, I am filled with an incredible sense of connection and fulfillment. I feel like giving the finger to whatever caused my earlier sense of foreboding: *I am here*, so there.

"Slack," I yell down the mountain. It's been windy for most of the trip and we've had to communicate with rope signals, but today it's clear and my voice carries just fine. A couple of seconds later the rope loosens, and I pull on it once, then again.

That's when I hear it, an earth-rending roar that can only mean one thing. For an interminable second I look up, turning my face into the warmth of the sun—but it, too, is gone. In its place is a wall of white, hurtling down the mountain.

Avalanche.

When you look death in the face, your life is supposed to unspool before your eyes, but I see none of mine. If only I had, perhaps everything would have been different—a thin chalk tracing between here and there, connecting *before* to *after*. Instead I see flashes: a small, blond boy in the middle of a playground, tracing the dirt with a stick; a brown-haired woman with her head thrown back, laughing, her throat a sleek marble line; a dark-eyed, smiling man sitting cross-legged by a campfire, guitar in his lap and tattoos on his upper arms, leaning forward like he's listening to someone.

I have an instant to wonder if I am seeing a future that might have been.

The avalanche hits me, like nothing I have ever known. It takes me down, and I am flying. Somehow I still have my axe, and I twist, trying desperately to jam it into something, anything, even though I can't tell which way is up. For a moment there is air, and I take my chance: a deep breath, the most I have in me. Then everything stops. I slam into something, then again. Pain splinters through my legs, encircles my ribs like an overzealous lover. I cup my hands around my face, carving out an air pocket, just before the snow settles around me, immovable as concrete. Normally this gesture connotes surprise, horror, fear—but for me, in this instant, it represents something else, something I thought I left behind a long time ago. In my cupped hands, I hold the last of my hope.

In the minutes before the pain swallows me, before the lack of oxygen drags me under, my mind is strangely blank—like staring at a movie screen before the projector is turned on. Then I hear a buzzing sound, an echo. And on the blank screen a loop of images begin to appear: A small boy kneeling in the dust. A woman laughing. A man, cross-legged and attentive. I will the boy to raise his head and look at me, but he never does. His shoulder blades push against the thin cotton of his T-shirt, insistent. He is so young.

The echo is gone now. It is just me, trapped and trembling. And though the silence around me is absolute—I might as well be floating in the airless, high-pressure vacuum of outer space—I hear a fragment of poetry, as clearly as if the speaker is sitting beside me. It is a man's voice, low and husky, urgent. It is no one I know.

Thus, though we cannot make our sun
Stand still, yet we will make him run.

Andrew Marvell, I think, before the air in my hands is replaced with carbon dioxide and my throat closes. Grief floods me, and then everything narrows to a sharp point: another needle, sinking deep into my thigh. Down I go again.

Suspended, I float. Into the silence comes a worried female voice: "Nicholas, can you hear me?" Someone squeezes my hand, and I imagine they must be talking to me, though I have no immediate sense of recognition. I try to squeeze back, but my body is gone. This should bother me, but it doesn't. Oh well, I think, floating away.

The voice continues, directed toward someone else this time: "Shouldn't he have woken up by now? You said in a few hours . . ."

Footsteps cross the floor, pause beside wherever I am. "Be patient. We had to give him some extra sedatives, since he was thrashing around so much. He'll wake up soon. Why don't you go home and get some rest?" Fingers touch the inside of my wrist, then encircle my jaw, turning my head from left to right.

The hand tightens around mine, nails digging in. "No thank you," the voice says, polite but cool. "I think I'll just stay here."

"Suit yourself," says the other voice. It's also female, but the tone is less personal, somehow. I hear the footsteps retreat.

I am asleep, then, or unconscious. Am I in the hospital? What has happened to me? I try to figure it out, but come up blank until I remember my dream: the mountain, the falling, the lack of oxygen. Aha. No wonder I am hurt. In fact, it feels like a miracle I am alive at all. I remember the choking, suffocating feeling, my pointless fight for air, and shudder. It must be the brown-haired woman who is with me, then. I am happy that I get to see her again, assuming that I can indeed see. I try to open my eyes, prepared for my body to resist, but to my surprise they open easily. I see . . . nothing. The world is dark. Perhaps the lights are out in this room, wherever I am?

I turn to ask my companion, eager to see her face, even the outline of it in this darkness, but her hand is no longer tight around mine. Instead, I am gripping something—a handle? My back is weighted with a heavy pack and metal clinks around my waist. I raise my arm experimentally and whatever I am holding comes with it. There is a focused, localized light and in it I see that I am gripping some kind of axe. Without warning, my arm swings high, and the axe bites. I step up, expecting to slide, but my feet grip the ice and hold. Again I swing the axe and step. Other than the noises my efforts produce, all is silent. I swing and step, swing and step in the silence. Panic grips my heart.

I am on the mountain again.

With the eerie inevitability of déjà vu, the sun rises, a full round orb set against a backdrop of vivid oranges, reds, purples, and yellows, so true that they could be the standards against which all other colors are measured. The sun regards me like an accusing, omniscient eye as I place the ice screw, hoist myself up onto the glacier, pull up the slack in the rope. Above me the monster lets loose its ancient roar and down I go, down and down and down. My body tumbles, slams, jerks. I swing my axe, trying to arrest my descent, but it is as pointless as the first time. Something is having its way with me and it isn't going to stop until it's done. I feel my ribs crack, my legs twist in ways legs were never meant to bend. My head ricochets off a rock-hard surface and, despite my helmet, liquid courses down my face, warm and wet. Then the noise stops as abruptly as it's begun and my body is still, hands cupped around my face. I see her face and I long for home with all I have. There is air. Then there is not.

I lie still, reminding myself that I am dreaming. This is the past, I tell myself. I am not on the mountain anymore, I am somewhere else—in the hospital, most likely. I inhale and sure enough, my lungs fill obediently. My chest hurts, but I can breathe. Air has never seemed so miraculous. I breathe in and out several times, partly just because I can and partly to slow my racing heart. As my heartbeat slows I become aware of an irritating noise close by, a shrill repetitive beeping. It sounds like an alarm. Maybe this whole experience was a dream in its entirety—not just the mountain, but the needles and the voices, too.

I sample that idea for a moment until I hear her call my name over and over, worry plain in her tone: "Nicholas? Nicholas?" She has a pretty voice, lilting, but right now it is strained with concern. "What's wrong with him?" she demands, and someone answers, "It's just the heart monitor. He must be waking up."

So I am in the hospital. That figures. No more climbing for me, I decide. The annoying beeping stops and I try hard to hang on to semiconsciousness. I could do without reliving that whole avalanche experience. Bad enough to go through it twice. Besides, whoever it is that's here with me seems to really want me to wake up. Maybe I could give it a shot.

As clarity begins to return, it strikes me as odd that I don't know her name. I can see her face as plainly as if my eyes were open—large, sleepy-looking brown eyes fringed with thick dark lashes, wavy chestnut hair framing a pale heart-shaped face, mobile mouth with a lower lip that's fuller than the upper. I know how she looks when she laughs, that she throws her head back and gives it all she has, that her teeth are white and straight, except for a crooked one on the bottom that she always tries to hide when she smiles. I know the hollow where the sweep of her neck meets her shoulder, and the temperature of her skin. I know how she makes me feel, protective and cared for all at once, possessive, lucky, and what she looks like when I am inside her, eyes staring deep into mine. I even know her smell: homey and wild at the same time, like roasting marshmallows around a campfire on a cool late summer night.

But her name? I have no idea.

I try hard to think of it, casting my mind outward like a net, but when I haul the net back in, it is empty.

This can't be normal. For the first time in my half-awake state, I feel fear grip me. Sure, I was afraid on the mountain, but that was different. That is behind me. This is now, and it is not good. I should know her name. Surely that is not too much to ask.

I try again, picturing her face, then concentrating as hard as I can, but nothing comes. And gradually I become aware that that is not the only thing that is a blank.

For instance, I know that my first name is Nicholas, because I have heard her say it. But would I have known that otherwise? I can't say with certainty that I would. And my last name doesn't seem to be forthcoming. Nor do I know any other pertinent details about myself, other than the fact that I like to climb mountains, and apparently I took a nasty fall off one of them. I cannot think of where I live, or what I do other than climb, or if I have any brothers or sisters, or what football team I root for. It is as if I were born right at this moment. I try again to open my eyes, but nothing happens except that the alarm starts shrieking again.

Her hand is warm on my face, warmer than I remember. "Nick. Honey. Wake up, please. Please wake up, sweetheart."

I want to tell her that I am trying, but my mouth won't cooperate. Around me there are other voices now, doctors or nurses, I imagine, from the content of the conversation. "Look at his

BP," one says—male, and fairly young, judging by the sound of it. "It's really spiking. Do you think we ought to get Dr. Perry?"

"Give him a moment," says someone else, the female voice I heard earlier. "Let's see if it keeps up. I hate to give him any more morphine. He's had a lot already." There are footsteps, and then a hand on my arm, rougher than hers. "Nicholas, can you hear me? If you can hear me, wiggle your fingers."

I'm about to give this up as a lost cause when I land back in my body with what seems like ought to be an audible thud. No more floating, no more tunnel, no more big white room—I am in a bed, for sure, and I can feel a light sheet drawn over me, draping my chest and torso and my legs, which I am sure must be badly broken, given my memory of the fall. I can feel my limbs now, feel my chest rise and sink. This has to be a good thing.

I channel all of my energy into my right arm, the one she is touching. I can do this, I tell myself. And then I wiggle my fingers.

"Did you see that?" It is her voice, filled with excitement and hope. "They moved, didn't they?"

"They sure did," says the owner of the hand. "Good work, Nicholas. Now open your eyes."

I am not sure that I want to, but anything has to be better than where I am now, this weird little world of half knowledge, so I do my best to comply. And what do you know? My eyes open right up, and I blink to focus them.

I am in a hospital room, all right. Hovering over me is a youngish woman with light brown hair, tied back in a ponytail, and horn-rimmed glasses like you'd expect to see on an old-fashioned librarian. She's wearing blue scrubs patterned with roller-skating cats—a nurse, I imagine. "Welcome back," she says to me.

I clear my throat, cough, and manage to get a word out. "Thanks," I say. My voice is croaky and rusty from disuse, but at least it works.

Before I have a chance to formulate any questions—like where I am, or how I survived that horrific fall—a second woman's face appears in my line of vision. It's a very pretty face—angular, with high cheekbones and green eyes, set off by long, straight red hair—and at the moment it is wearing an expression that commingles worry and relief. "Nicholas, thank God," she says, and her voice is the same one that was begging me to wake up just a few minutes ago. Her green eyes are sparkling with tears.

Now I am really confused. Worse than not knowing her name, I don't recognize her at all. This is not the woman I saw when I was thinking about the mountain. This is a total stranger.

Panic shoots through my limbs, and the monitor goes crazy again.

THREE

Aidan

I am sitting in J.C. and Roma's tent, shivering. Wherever we are, it is cold as hell. The inside of the tent is covered with a layer of ice, the way it always is when the temperature drops low enough. It's condensation from our breath, which is pretty nasty when you think about it. I breathe in, feeling the familiar ache in my lungs, then out, expecting to add to the frozen scrim that coats the VerTex. And that's when things get weird—nothing happens. It's below freezing in here, but I can't see my breath in the air.

J.C. lies zipped into his sleeping bag, staring up at the ceiling. Next to him, Roma snores. He has a deviated septum and it's not his fault, but I'm sure J.C. wants to hit him. I know I would. Roma's a great guy, but sleeping at altitude's tough enough without a circular saw running next to your head.

"Hey, man," I say to J.C., but he doesn't answer, which is strange. I wave at him and he doesn't react. Instead he rolls to the left carefully, like he's trying to find a position that doesn't hurt, and flinches. I know why: Every time he moves, some of the ice on the ceiling of the tent falls down on him. It's not the best feeling in the world.

J.C. shakes his head from side to side, trying to dislodge the particles of ice, and winces again. He's got a tight look around his eyes, like he has a bad headache. I look closer and see that he's been crying. What the hell is going on here?

"Hey," I say again, and again he doesn't reply. Something is wrong, and I'm sure J.C. knows what it is. I am tempted to shake the answer out of him, headache be damned, but a growing sense of discomfort holds me still. I try to think about what mountain this is, what expedition, and come up with nothing. I don't know where I am. I don't know where I've been. There's a crucial fact I ought to remember, a puzzle whose answer is almost within my grasp. But every time I try to figure it out, I come up against a wall. I can't think around it, I can't go through it or over it. It blocks my way.

Maddie. Is something wrong with Maddie? I think of her and feel a sense of panic, like there's something I need to do, a promise I need to keep. I think of Gabriel, my small warrior boy, and sadness sweeps me. Something is wrong, but I can't put my finger on it. I feel . . . adrift, somehow, dislocated in space and time.

I look around the tent, searching for clues, but all I see is J.C., who rubs his temples, pulls his sleeping bag up to his chin. "I'm sorry," he says quietly, so he won't wake Roma. "I'm so fucking sorry." He closes his eyes then and falls into a fitful sleep.

He dreams a memory, and somehow I dream with him. We're in my backyard in Boulder. Maddie is very pregnant with Gabe, maybe seven months along. I see us from J.C.'s perspective: We are smiling, in love. But he is not smiling. In fact he's just broken up with his girlfriend, Elise. He is depressed, and the happier we look, the worse he feels.

"How did this happen?" he says in our general direction. "It's like some cruel joke."

Maddie looks surprised, like she has no idea what J.C.'s talking about. But I know. "This is ridiculous," he says, tossing a bottle cap from one hand to the other. "All I ever wanted was a relationship that worked out and a family."

This isn't the total truth. Yeah, he'd wanted those things, abstractly. But really, he wants them with Maddie. He wants what I have. Usually he's got better control than this; he wouldn't bring it up at all, much less in front of her. But he is drunk, and mad, and he just keeps going. Maybe he figures he has nothing to lose.

"You were never after any of that," he says, his eyes accusatory. "You told me enough times you just wanted to climb, travel, have good friends, good times. And now look at this shit. Here you are, with Maddie and a baby on the way, happy as can be. And here I am, doing this." He gestures at himself, sprawled in one of the deck chairs, at his beer. "What kind of fucked-up universe do we live in?"

I drop my arm from Maddie's shoulders and step away from her. It's the least I can do, with him so upset. "I don't know," I tell him. "Maybe I just got lucky."

"You sure did," he says. In the dream, I feel how torn up he is. She's pregnant, for Christ's sweet sake. We're married. What's wrong with him?

The dream fades and he surfaces again, blinking at the dull light. I'm forced outward, back into the frigid air of the tent. Whatever was wrong then, it's no better on this cold gray morning. He still loves her, that hasn't changed, but something else has. What?

"I miss you, buddy," he says. He's just mouthing the words, really, but I can hear him. "You were the closest thing I had to a partner in this crazy life of mine." He's quiet for a second. Then he says, "She's gonna hate me, and it will break my heart." He rubs his temples, trying to chase the headache away. When he speaks again, he sounds sad but determined. "You never gave up, A.J., and neither will I. I'm going to take care of your family. I swear I won't let you down."

He closes his eyes again. The dream scatters into air, and I go with it, seeded with doubt, riddled with certainty.

The next time I collect myself, I am in Gabe's room. He's awake, his soft blue blanket pulled up to his chin, his white teddy bear lying on his pillow. His surfer night-light, the one with the devil on it that I brought back from Tasmania, gives the room a dim glow. In it I move toward him, sit down on the bed.

Gabe's head turns toward me. His eyes go wide, and he shivers, like he's cold. "Daddy?" he says, like maybe he thinks I'm someone else. I try to answer him, but although I feel my mouth move, no sound comes out.

"Daddy!" he says again. "How come you're home from Alaska? Why do you still have your mountain clothes on? Are you all done climbing?"

Alaska, I think. The McKinley expedition. Of course.

I look down at myself and he's right. I'm wearing my black Marmot soft shell and my alpine pants. My gear's clipped around my waist, and when I look at my hands, I see my gloves. Snow coats the fabric. I look farther down and there are my mountain boots, complete with crampons. The bed is cold and wet where I'm sitting.

"The heat is broken, Daddy," Gabe says. "I was going to fix it if you didn't come home."

I think about that one for a second. It's June. It should be warm, no need for the heat. Gabe's right, though: It's not exactly cozy in here. Of course, that could be because I'm coated in ice and snow. Which brings me back to Gabe's question: Why am I sitting here on his bed, in full-on climbing regalia, in the middle of the night? How did I get here?

I have no answer for this question, which disturbs me mightily. Last thing I can remember, I was on McKinley, getting ready to lead that epic pitch. Then I was sitting in J.C.'s tent, listening to him talk to himself. But that was a dream, right? Surely it was a dream.

Maybe I am dreaming now. It's the only way to make sense of things. Unless—no. Oh, no. Surely not.

Here I am in Gabe's room, dressed like I was for the McKinley expedition.

J.C. couldn't see me, couldn't hear me. But I could hear him, apologizing, telling someone he'd miss them. He'd been crying. I've never seen him cry, not even when Ellis died.

I promised her I would come back. I swore it. I promised I'd never let her down.

I lied.

Gabe throws the covers off and crawls to the end of the

bed. His teeth chatter as he throws his arms around me, Teddy clasped in one small fist. I try to hug him back, but my arms close on nothing. I am gone, falling alone into the dark and the ice and the cold. I rail against the darkness, I scream, I pray. It makes no difference.

It is June, but I am freezing.

FOUR

Madeleine

Someone is shaking me, hard, their small fingers digging into my arms. "Mommy, wake up," I hear Gabe say. "Wake up."

I blink my eyes open, pushing my hair away from my face. "Gabe? What's wrong, honey? Are you okay?" I switch on the bedside lamp and see him standing there in his Batman PJs, hugging Teddy to his chest. His face is all screwed up, like he's trying not to cry.

Out of habit I glance over at Aidan's side of the bed, but it's empty; he's more than three thousand miles away, most likely leaving high camp right about now, if the itinerary he left for me and Gabe to follow has held true. With an expedition like this one, of course, you never know. So much depends on the wind, the visibility, the condition of the snow, on luck.

Or on whether the mountain will have you, I think, then

shiver into the warmth of the room. J.C.'s prone to talking about the big peaks as if they've got a will of their own, a notion that Aidan dismisses as New Age bullshit and I find alternately enchanting and ominous. He says a prayer to the spirits of the mountain every time he climbs, for clemency.

"What's the matter?" I ask Gabe again, rubbing my arms to chase the goose bumps away.

"Daddy," is all he says. His teeth chatter.

"Daddy what? Did you have a bad dream?" I open my arms and pull him onto the bed. "It's fine, I'm here. Don't worry." I pet his hair, and he curls against me. "You're freezing, buddy. And your feet are wet. Did you have an accident?"

"No," he says. "Daddy was here. In my room."

"Don't be silly. You know Daddy's on Mount McKinley. You had a dream, that's all. But he'll be home soon." I rub his arms to warm him up. Poor little guy. He's missing Aidan, I know he is. There's a Father's Day party next week at his preschool, right before they let out for the summer. I could tell he was disappointed that Aidan was going to miss it, even though he pretended that it was fine. "Just two more Tuesdays, right?" I tell him, since we've been counting the days on the calendar until his daddy will come home.

He snuggles against me, under the patchwork quilt my mother made for us after we got married. "Mommy, something happened to Daddy on the mountain," he says in his smallest voice. "He's not coming home."

The certainty in his voice gives me chills, and I don't say anything for a minute. I can't; it's too close to what I've been thinking since Aidan told me about the McKinley trip. I thought we'd done a good job of keeping our disagreement from Gabriel.

Obviously, I was wrong. "That's a terrible thing to say, buddy," I say. "Why would you say something like that?" Fear makes my voice tight, angry. But before I can apologize, Gabe starts to cry.

"I saw him in my room. He was all snowy. He left a puddle on the floor."

I feel like a terrible person, taking my fear out on a four-year-old. "You had a bad dream, that's all. I know it's scary when Daddy's away. Mama gets scared, too. But your daddy's a good climber. He'll be home in just a little bit and then he won't be going away again for a long time." I force myself to sound calm, like I know what I'm talking about. Madeleine the Oracle, that's me. Emotional Sherpa to the Discontented, as Aidan used to say.

He hides his face in my hair. "My room was cold," he says into my neck. "I stepped in the puddle."

I hold him away from me, looking into his face. He stares back at me, still and stubborn. "Gabriel, it was a dream. A nightmare. We'll call Daddy tomorrow and you'll see he's fine. You want to stay in here with me? You and Teddy can sleep right here, on Daddy's pillow."

He shakes his head back and forth. Now he is crying in earnest. "Something's wrong," he says. "Something bad happened to Daddy on the mountain."

I am going to kill Aidan when he gets back. I am going to kill him. "Stop it, Gabe," I say. "You can't know that. You had a dream, that's all. Sometimes they feel like they're real, but they're not. Daddy is fine. Nothing is going to happen to him. He told you that himself, before he left. Does Daddy lie?"

"He didn't lie," Gabe whispers. "He just didn't know." Tears drip down his chin and onto poor abused Teddy.

We regard each other in the light from the lamp. His eyes are wide. The house is quiet, save for his breathing, choky with tears, and mine, scared and quick. He shakes.

Then the phone rings, breaking the silence to bits, and everything goes wrong for real.

I move toward the phone with the eerie inevitability of sleepwalking. My feet stick to the floor with each step. Gabe has followed me, clutching his teddy, and he looks so tiny in the light from the hall. I want to protect him from this horrible phone call. But who will protect me?

"Hello?" I say, steadier than I feel. Maybe if I pretend this is a normal turn of events, that my phone regularly rings at two in the morning, everything will work out fine.

J.C. is on the other end. Even through the static of the satellite phone I can tell that his voice is laced with tears. "Maddie," he says, and in that one word I hear the weight of the world.

"No," I tell him. "No."

"I am so sorry," he says to me. Avalanche, he says. Unexpected. Missing. Search and rescue. Too long without air. Fast. I don't think he knew what hit him. Sorry sorry sorry so sorry. He says a lot more but I'm not listening. Instead I just see Aidan's face in front of me, feel his hands on mine. Come home, I say to him. Please come home. And then I say it aloud, into the receiver that I am clutching so hard my fingers hurt.

"You bring him home to me," I tell J.C., as if an authoritative approach is what's called for in this situation. "Find him and bring him home."

"I wish I could," he says. Static crackles and flares between us.

"Please," I say, switching tactics. "Please, J.C." I don't know what sense this makes. After all, it's not like J.C. has kidnapped

Aidan and is holding him hostage. But somehow I feel like if I ask nicely enough, if I beg, everything will be all right.

There is silence. Then through the static comes J.C.'s rough, ragged sobs. I have never heard him cry before, and it is that, more than anything else, that undoes me, makes me believe this is real. "He loved you, Maddie," he says. And then the line goes dead.

I stand there in my dark house, gripping the phone. I don't know what I am waiting for—maybe for J.C. to call me back and tell me that this was all a mistake, that they have found Aidan and everything is fine. But the phone doesn't ring again. It's silent in my hand, an innocent-looking instrument of destruction.

Aidan, where are you?

Gabe is standing in front of me now, his teddy dangling from one hand. "Mama?" he says, looking at me with those blue eyes that are so much like Aidan's, it makes my heart hurt. I put my hand to my chest. How will I tell him that his daddy is dead?

But then I remember: He already knows.

My knees buckle and I sink to the floor, dropping the receiver. Gabriel kneels next to me and very carefully, he hangs up the phone. Then he goes into my bedroom and comes back with the quilt. It's way too big for him to carry, so he drags it along the floor behind him, a determined set to his lips. He tucks it around me, then steps back. His eyes are grave in his small, pale face. "Daddy's not coming home, is he," he says, and it's not a question.

I shake my head.

Tears well up in his eyes, and I can see him fight them back. He is so much like his father, it frightens me. "What did Uncle J.C. say?"

I will my voice to come out steady. My heart feels as if it is frozen and broken all at once, splintered into small icy pieces in my chest. "Your daddy had an accident on the mountain," I say, and wince at how it sounds. Saying it out loud makes it real. "There was an avalanche." I pull the quilt tighter around me. "Do you know what that is?"

"When the snow all comes down at once. Daddy showed me on YouTube."

Of course he did. "There was an avalanche on the mountain and your daddy couldn't get out of the way in time. He got stuck under the snow and he couldn't get out." Goddamn it, Aidan, I think. Damn you for making me say this to our son.

Gabe's brows furrow. "Why couldn't Uncle J.C. find him?"

"I don't know, honey. Maybe there was too much . . . too much snow." My teeth start to chatter. I told him not to go. I told him over and over. And now look what's happened.

Now the tears do break loose. They cascade over Gabe's cheeks, and his lower lip trembles. "But Daddy will be cold," he cries. "He'll be cold under all the snow all alone."

I try to respond, but for a moment I can't. I have a horrible visual of Aidan buried under snow and ice, trying to claw his way out, struggling for air until he has to give up. Hold on, I tell myself. Don't fall apart. Aidan wouldn't want you to fall apart. He'd want you to be strong for Gabriel. One of the shards of ice twists in my chest, and I gasp; but the pain is somehow what I need. It distracts me enough so that I pull myself together. "Daddy can't feel anything anymore," I tell Gabe. "He can't feel the cold."

"But where is he?" Gabe wails, and I know just what he means. I start to tell Gabe that he is in heaven, but then I hold back. Maybe they'll find him, I think. Maybe he isn't dead after all, really just missing. I think about all the times he rescued other climbers when no one else was willing to take the risk or bivvied on ledges so narrow he didn't dare roll over in his sleep, the way J.C. and Roma always said he was like a cat with ninety-nine lives instead of nine. He was so confident about this climb. Maybe too confident.

I open the quilt and pull Gabe to me. We rock back and forth on the floor, Teddy pinned between us. I lower my face into his hair, those dirty-blond tangles that are so much like Aidan's. At least there is this, I tell myself. At least I have this.

"He was in my room," Gabe says through his tears. He's got a handful of my hair and he's tugging on it like he used to do when he was a baby. It hurts a little, but I don't care. I need to feel something, anything, other than the jagged, ragged twisting in my chest. It's like I'm outside myself, like everything I feel is an echo of the real thing.

"Mommy," Gabe says, pulling on my hair again. "He was in my room, for real. He sat on the bed. He had his mountain clothes on. The room was all cold, like it was winter. He left a puddle. If he's stuck under the avalanche, how did he get to be in my room?"

"You had a dream, Gabriel," I tell him. A prophetic dream, to be sure, but a dream nonetheless. What is the alternative, that Aidan visited Gabriel before he went . . . wherever it is that he is now? And if that's the case, why didn't he come to me? Again the pain ripples through me. I draw a deep, sharp breath. *Strong*, I tell myself.

"It wasn't a dream," Gabe says, stubborn as Aidan at his most insistent. "It wasn't. He was there."

I can't argue about this, not now. "Okay, honey," I say, stroking his tangled hair. "Okay."

"I want Daddy," Gabe says into my hair. He isn't whining. He's stating a fact.

"I do, too," I tell him, rocking us back and forth. "I do, too." It feels like a cold hand is gripping my heart and squeezing. I close my eyes and Aidan's face floats behind my lids, smiling his little half smile. I open them again and he is gone.

I know I should do something. I should call my mom, I should call my best friend, Jos. I have to call Aidan's mother and his sister, I realize with dawning horror. And what about his dad? I don't want to call anyone, I don't want to pass this news along. Right now it's contained within the four walls of our living room. I feel like the universe could still take it back.

The phone rings again. I wriggle my arm loose from the quilt and reach for it, hoping that it's J.C. calling to tell me he made a mistake, that everything is fine. But in my heart I know better. I reach for the phone, holding Gabe's small, soggy body against me with my other arm, and I hope against hope for a miracle.

FIVE

Nicholas

I lie still under the starched white sheets, concentrating on slowing my heartbeat. Adrenaline whips through me, settling in my stomach like a cornered animal biding its time. I breathe in and out, fixing my gaze on a bad reproduction of Monet's *Water Lilies* that some sadistic interior designer's hung on the wall facing my bed. Bit by bit, I force the panic to retreat.

"Nicholas," the nurse says. I make myself focus on her, on the name tag that's pinned to her uniform: Tanya, it reads. It is crooked.

"Yes?" I answer.

"Do you know where you are?"

"Hospital?" I hazard, glancing around. My voice is hoarse, but it betrays no anxiety. Point for me.

Her broad face creases with a smile. "Good guess. How do you feel?"

I take a moment to figure that out. Oddly enough, I feel nowhere as bad as I would expect to, given what happened. I try to wiggle my toes, and they comply. My legs aren't broken after all, then. How is that possible? I felt them bend the wrong way, felt them snap. I run my hands over the sheets covering my legs, and sure enough, they're not encased in casts. My ribs do ache, and my head . . . I raise one hand to my face and feel a bandage on my cheek, another one on my forehead. Yes, my head definitely hurts. But here I am, among the living.

"Not too bad," I tell Tanya, "considering."

"That was quite an accident you had," she says. "You're a little banged up, still."

Still? "How long was I out?" I ask.

"About twelve hours. Your girlfriend here was getting pretty worried about you." She gestures toward Ms. Red Hair and Green Eyes.

My girlfriend, huh? Something is not adding up. I shake my head a little bit, trying to clear it, which is a big mistake. Pain stabs behind my eyes. "Ow," I say.

Tanya laughs. "Maybe not the best idea," she says.

I do my best to ignore my alleged girlfriend, who has a tight grip on my hand—in fact, her nails are digging into my palm. "What else is wrong with me?" I say to Tanya.

"A couple of broken ribs, some bruising, a mildly sprained ankle, a few deep cuts on your face, and then of course you hit your head, which got the worst of it. Oh, and some serious road rash." She rolls her eyes.

Road rash? I try hard to figure out how road rash has anything to do with falling off a mountain and getting trapped under a ton of snow, and come up with nothing. "I don't get it," I say. "How did I get road rash, exactly?"

"From the accident. You were on your motorcycle, and the car wasn't going that fast, but it threw you quite a ways. You hit the asphalt before you rolled into the grass. You must have had your hands up to cover your face—your arms got scraped, but better that than the other, right?"

Steady, I tell myself. "I was hit by a car?"

"A red Nissan Altima, to be exact," the woman who's supposedly my girlfriend says. I swivel my head to look at her. "You don't remember, Nick?" she says, squeezing my already-battered hand.

I shake my head, more carefully this time. "I remember a mountain—and falling—and . . ." My voice trails off as I see the complete bewilderment on both of their faces, the lack of recognition. "I guess it was a dream," I conclude. It didn't feel like a dream to me, but right now I seem to have bigger problems than figuring out how I wound up in this hospital bed. I look from one of my attendants' faces to the other and see worry plastered all over their features, though Tanya is mostly managing to conceal it under layers of professionalism. "Never mind," I say to both of them.

"What's the last thing you remember?" Tanya asks me.

I think back, but come up against the same brick wall I encountered earlier. Actually, more than a brick wall: It resembles a void. When I try to picture anything before I swam to consciousness in the hospital, there's just—nothing.

I say as much to Tanya, who tells me, "That's not so much to worry about," in her best Reassuring Nurse tone. "A lot of times, after a trauma to the head, it's not unusual to forget the events leading up to it. Your body's way of protecting itself."

I grit my teeth, swallow hard. "No," I say. "When I say nothing, I mean—nothing. I don't remember the accident, I don't remember anything before the accident. I don't know who you are"—I gesture in the direction of the redhead—"or where I live or what I do for a living. Everything is—well, it's just blank."

Silence falls.

"That's not normal, is it?" I say to Tanya. "I mean, this doesn't usually happen, right?"

"Not usually, no," Tanya says, her good cheer lost.

"You don't remember me?" the redhead says. She sounds shocked, which I guess makes sense. I have a moment of irritation—isn't it more significant that I don't remember *myself*? Then again, maybe I've known her for a long time. I force myself to be polite.

"Sorry," I answer. The silence endures. She drops my hand.

After a bit I say, "This sounds like a weird request, but can I have a mirror?"

The redhead turns away and fishes in her purse. She hands me a compact and I flip it open, peer into it. There I am: tousled shock of jet-black hair with serious bedhead, startled blue eyes, truculent set to my jaw, which is covered in dark stubble. There's a gauze bandage on one of my cheeks, and another one on my forehead. It's creepy, but nothing resonates. This could be anyone's face. It doesn't feel like mine.

I close the compact and hand it back to the redhead. "What's your name?"

"Grace," she says. Nope. Nothing.

"Nicholas, do you know what year it is?" Tanya asks.

I flail about in the empty room that is my mind. A date appears and I grab at it, tell her. Apparently I am right, because she smiles.

"Very good. How about the date?"

I think hard, but only the month comes to me. "June something?"

"June eighth. What's your full name?"

Just like that, the small measure of self-confidence I've accumulated is gone. I try to think beyond "Nicholas" and come up blank, yet again. In the hoarse croak that is my voice for the moment, I say: "I don't know."

"Sullivan," Grace says. Her long hair brushes my arm as she leans over me. "Nicholas Sullivan."

"Nice name," I say, trying to hold the panic at bay with a small attempt at humor. "Am I Greek, or Irish, or what?"

"Both," says Grace.

"Ah." The silence stretches out for a bit, and I think of a thousand questions I want to ask. It's hard to tell which one is the most pressing. Finally, I settle on an immediate need. "Could I have a glass of water, please?"

"Sure," Grace says. "I'll get it." And off she goes.

I look down at my hands. One of them has a needle in the back of it—an IV, I assume, since I've been out of it and not eating, and for the pain meds, too. "Can this come out?" I ask Tanya.

"Let me just clear it with your doctor. But I don't see why not, now that you're awake."

"How long?" I ask, gesturing toward my head.

"I'm sure that Dr. Perry will request a psych consult. They'll be able to tell you more," she says. "Global amnesia like this isn't anything I have experience with. I wish there was more I could say. I know you must be very scared."

"I'm not," I say. "What I am is . . . confused."

"Of course you are." She pats the hand that doesn't have

the IV. "Let me page your doctor now, and we'll see what we can find out."

Dr. Perry arrives ten minutes later. She is a statuesque black woman, with skin the color of burnished mahogany, a complex braided hairdo, and a businesslike manner. "You're awake," she says in an accent that I identify as West Indian—Jamaican, maybe. Apparently my geographic knowledge hasn't taken a hike along with my sense of self, which is an interesting tidbit to consider. "How do you feel?"

"A little achy, but okay," I tell her. "The thing is, I can't remember anything. I don't remember the accident, for sure, or my name, or anything about me, or"—I gesture at Grace, who has just made her way back into the room with a bottle of Dasani—"her, either."

"Sometimes this happens, after a blow to the head. It's called post-traumatic amnesia, and it usually doesn't last that long." She smiles at me, in an attempt to be comforting. "Give yourself some time."

"How much time?" My voice cracks. "Am I supposed to wander around like Rip Van Winkle, just waiting to figure out who I am?"

"Rip Van Winkle, huh?" The smile is still pasted on. "I see you remember something."

"He knew the year," Tanya volunteers.

"Hmmm. Nicholas, Tanya may have asked you some of these questions before, but I'm going to do it again, in a more formal fashion. It's called the Galveston Orientation and Amnesia Test. Are you ready?"

"Sure," I say. "Shoot."

She asks me my name (which I only know because they told

me what it is), where I was born, where I live, where I am now, how I got to the hospital, the last thing I remember, and a whole bunch of other stuff. The only information I can come up with is nonpersonal in nature—the month and the year. "Everything else is just blank," I tell her. "Like it's been erased."

"All right," she says. "Don't worry. Give yourself some time."

"You said that already," I tell her.

She smiles. "I see your short-term memory is working just fine."

I shift my focus to a problem I can solve. "Could you please disconnect me from all of this stuff?" I point to the heart monitor, the IV, with my free hand. "I feel like the Bionic Man."

"I don't see why not," she says after a quick check of my vital signs. She gives the A-OK to Tanya, who sets about freeing me. "Would you like to get up and walk around?" she asks after I've been liberated.

"That would be great," I tell her. "Can I?"

"Sure. Just take it easy. You were out for a while, there." She stands next to the bed while I sit up gingerly and swing my legs over the side. "Sit there for a minute," she says. "Let your blood pressure adjust."

So I sit until she tells me I can get up. Grace hovers as I get to my feet. I want to tell her to leave me alone, but I catch myself: She is my girlfriend, after all. It's natural that she'd want to make sure I'm okay. It's not her fault I'm so irritable. I give her a smile as I boost myself to my feet, where I stand for a moment, take one step, then another. I'm shaky, and my head and ribs throb, but otherwise I'm fine. "How far can I go?" I ask Dr. Perry. "And when can I get out of here?"

"You can walk as far as you feel like. And as for when you

can leave the hospital, I'd like to keep you one more night, for observation. Tomorrow morning, if you feel fine physically, you can go home."

"What about this?" I gesture toward my head.

"I'm going to call in a psych consult to have a look at you, make sure there isn't anything else going on. If the consult doesn't turn anything up, then we'll just have to wait and see. Try not to worry too much."

"Easy for you to say," I mutter. But off I trot like a good boy, Grace tagging along.

"How do you feel?" she asks.

"Like a stranger in a strange land," I say. Now she's looking at me funny, so I elaborate: "You know, Robert Heinlein. Or maybe Iron Maiden, depending on your point of view."

She's staring at me like I just produced a rabbit from a hat. "How can you remember that stuff, but not your own name?"

"You're asking the wrong person," I tell her wearily.

We make a few circuits of the hospital floor before Nurse Tanya flags me down to let me know that the psych consult is ready for me. So off I go for more tests, which I fail with flying colors.

"God, I wish I had a cigarette," I say after the psychiatrist leaves, mostly to myself but partially to Grace, who is sitting in the chair next to my bed.

She gives me a perplexed look. "You don't smoke," she says. "You never have."

"Oh," I say. "Okay." I'm not sure what to make of this bit of information, so I blow it off. "Maybe I should start," I tell her, and she laughs.

"Probably not," she says.

"Tell me about me," I ask her.

"Hmmm. This is strange. Okay. Like you already know, your name is Nicholas Sullivan. You live here, in Wilmington, North Carolina, and you teach social studies at New Hanover High. But it's summer now, so you're on vacation."

"How old am I?"

"Thirty-three," she says.

"And how long have you and I been together?"

"Two years," she says. "Two years last month."

"Wow. Pretty serious, huh?"

I mean it as a joke, but she lowers her head, staring down at the floor as if I've hurt her feelings. Just when I'm about to apologize—it must feel shitty to have your significant other act completely clueless about what you mean to them—she lifts her head and looks me in the eyes. "We're planning to get married, actually," she says.

"Married?" My voice cracks in surprise. I look at her left hand, which is resting on the bed next to me. "You're not wearing a ring."

"We haven't gotten around to making it official. It was—well, it just happened, really."

"Wow," I say. "Okay. Can we take this slow? Start at the beginning. How did we meet?"

"I'm a violinist," she says. "I play in a rock band. You came to one of my concerts."

"Is that what you do for a living?"

"I wish. No, I'm a graphic designer. I work for a small company."

I file that away for future reference. "You said I teach social studies, right?"

"Yes."

"So my degree is in . . . what?"

"Political science, from Chapel Hill. And then you have a master's in education from UNC Wilmington."

"Where is my family?" I ask her. "Why are you the only one here?"

"Well, your parents are dead. And you're an only child."

"Whoa," I say. "Rough. How did they die?"

"In a car accident. It was before I met you."

"What about my friends, then?"

She smiles. "Oh, you have a lot of friends. Taylor and Jack are the ones you're closest to. I imagine they'll be here any minute, as soon as they get off work. I called them while you were talking to the psychiatrist."

"What do they look like?" I ask.

"Taylor is tall and skinny, with short brown hair. And Jack is kind of a burly guy, with a goatee."

No sooner does she finish her sentence than they burst into the room with identically huge grins on their faces. I hold a slim hope that I might recognize them, but no such luck. They stay until visiting hours are over, quizzing me, giving me bits of information about myself, chatting. It's late when all three of them leave, and I walk back to my room from the visitors' lounge and crawl into bed. I'm exhausted. Maybe when I wake up tomorrow, I will be myself again, my real self, with all the parts and pieces intact. In the meantime, I am incapable of processing any more information.

I watch TV for a while, an old episode of *The Twilight Zone*. But it cuts a little too close to the bone, and so I turn it off, along with the light, and lie there. After a while I drift in the direction of sleep. The world is comfortably, soporifically black, except for the sun that's beginning to rise in a brilliant display of color. The metal teeth are still attached to my boots—crampons, they're called; why did the name escape me before?—and they shriek as they bite into the ice. The cold air stings my lungs. Then comes the roar, the wall of white, the flight through the air, the pain. There is her face, well-known and well loved; there are his fragile bird's-wing shoulders. There is the fragment of poetry, delivered in that husky voice that is not mine.

That is the first night I wake on my hands and knees on the floor, slicked in sweat, my breath coming hard in my throat like it did on the mountain, like needles stabbing me. I cover my face with my hands, there on the linoleum floor of the hospital, and I cry like a child. I cry because I don't know who I am, sure, but I also cry because I am missing her, the woman with the long brown hair and the incredible laugh, the heart-shaped face and the pale skin, and him, the small boy who has his back to me. I miss the dark-eyed man, with his smile and his listening look. I cry because I know something is terribly wrong, that I am mis-placed, somehow, lost in space and time. I cry because I don't know what is happening to me, or what will happen next. And then, with sudden grim resolve, I splash water on my face, put on a shirt from the stash Grace showed me, and make my way out of the room to find myself a cigarette. Because for someone who doesn't smoke, I am having a hell of a nicotine fit.

SIX

Madeleine

The morning dawns cool and clear, typical for late June. I sit
at the kitchen table with my coffee, staring into the mug.
Gabe gave it to me for Mother's Day last year; he painted it at
one of those do-it-yourself pottery places, with his father. Aidan
made me a little plate to match, with caricatures of him and me
and Gabe. When you looked at the plate closely, you could see
that all the faces were in the shape of hearts. Hidden in all the
images, twined in our hair and our eyelashes, concealed in the
folds of our clothing, was the message "Gabe ♥s Mommy." Gabe
and I had made a game of finding all the words on the plate
while Aidan sat across from us with one eyebrow raised, refusing
to tell us how many we'd missed. "Where's the fun in that?"
he'd said. "You just keep looking. I'll let you know when you're

done." And then he'd crossed his legs and started humming, just to piss me off.

My cellphone rings, and I glance at it. It's Jill Sutherland, one of the guides for Aidan and J.C.'s company, Over the Top Ascents. I know I should talk to her—this is the third time she's called in the past two days—but I just can't bring myself to answer. She wants to know how she can help, which is kind. The thing is, how can I tell her what I need when I don't know myself?

Jill gives up, and I go back to staring into space. Then the phone beeps again, a text this time. I pick it up. It's from Lila, my editor at Boulder's *Women's Magazine*. I had a piece due yesterday, a personal essay on the challenges of motherhood when your husband is a professional climber. I'd planned to write about how I missed Aidan when he was gone, but how his absence also gave me a sense of freedom and independence. As glad as I had always been to have him home, as relieved as I was to feel his arms wrapped around me, to know he was safe, it always took me a while to adjust to having him in the house, making decisions about Gabriel, talking to me when all I wanted to do was think. And as soon as I'd made the adjustment, he'd be off again, disappearing into the office with maps and charts, on the phone with potential sponsors, giving speeches and slide shows to raise money, and then getting on a plane. When he was gone, I felt like a single mother, or a military wife.

I'd told Aidan about the piece when I'd pitched it, and he'd put his head in his hands. "You're going to ruin me," he'd said. "Feminists will attack me when I walk down the street. What are they gonna call it? 'Selfish Asshole Abandons Family for the Sake of Personal Gratification and Athletic Glory'? Or did you have something more flattering in mind?"

"Do you not want me to write it?" I'd asked him, and he'd laughed.

"Write what you want, honey," he'd said. "You put up with me, don't you? You're only telling the truth. Write whatever the hell your little heart desires."

Needless to say, I haven't submitted the piece. Not only is it impossible for me to concentrate for more than two minutes at a time, but the subject matter itself is ironic to the point of tragedy, given the circumstances. Ever the responsible person, and operating in a state of shock, I'd emailed Lila to let her know what had happened and that I wasn't going to make the deadline. She'd emailed me back, called twice, and now here she is, texting me. *Call me,* her text reads. *I am v. worried about you.*

I sigh and close my phone. Then I glance at the digital clock on the stove. With a start, I realize that the search and rescue team is due in any minute; Roma posted their flight information on Facebook yesterday, along with a bunch of photos. I tried to look at the pictures from the rescue effort, but every time I saw J.C., Jesse, and Roma standing together without Aidan, it broke me a little more inside.

The Facebook site is hard for me to handle. I'm overwhelmed by how many people knew Aidan, on how many people he'd left an impression. There are a ton of comments about his charisma, his determination, his talent as an alpinist and mountaineer, his excellence as a public speaker. People have written about what an excellent guide he was, what a good friend, how he was always up for a new adventure, how he'd try anything, how he was always the last guy to leave a party and the first one up in the morning. A couple of the filmmakers who worked with him, including Roma and his buddy Spy, have written about how he hammed it up for the camera, how he loved to be the center of attention and the more they focused on him, the wilder he got. Some of our close friends have posted comments about his talent as an artist, his patience as a father, his commitment to his family.

J.C.'s posting is one of the last, uploaded just before they left Alaska. He's written only, "Thanks for all of your support. It's been hard times out here. He will be missed. RIP A.J." I stare at these few short lines, reading them over and over. J.C. is the master of understatement, and this posting is no exception. I know how much he has left unsaid.

The comments hurt, but the pictures are worse, somehow. I don't know where all of them have come from, but there are hundreds, a photographic chronicle of Aidan's adult life and career. Everywhere I look, there he is, halfway up a mountain with his ice axes dug in; perched on the edge of a cliff, grinning; swinging from a rope with his arms flung out wide. There are pictures of him and J.C. and Roma drunk at the Walrus, their arms around one another's shoulders, the night Over the Top Ascents first turned a profit; pictures of him and Gabe at the Spot, with Gabe hooked into a harness, making his way up a wall with Aidan belaying him from below, looking as proud as if Gabe had just memorized and recited *War and Peace*. There are pictures of him cliff diving in Hawaii and pictures of him fording a river in Thailand, the sharp end of the rope tied to his waist. There are pictures of him I've never seen, high up on some godforsaken peak with snow coming down on his jacket and his gear and his hood, only his nose peeking out, smiling like he couldn't be happier. There he is, summiting Annapurna with an orange oxygen mask strapped to his face, and then without the mask the next time he went up—*Just to see if I can do it*, he told me. His North Face videos are on there, too, and all the times

Roma went along on expeditions to film him and J.C. There are pictures of the Shishapangma trip, with him and J.C. raising a glass to Alex Lowe, and pictures of him scaling Morocco's Taghia Gorge. And then there are recent pictures of him and me together, which I didn't expect to see, sitting on our back patio holding hands and looking happy, at a café in downtown Boulder. After I see those, I have to close the laptop and walk away.

The images have stayed with me, though, and the worst part about them is, they have set off some horrible kind of ricochet effect. I see him everywhere I turn—behind the wheel of his Jeep, having a beer with J.C. in the backyard, lying on the floor of Gabe's room, helping him build a Lego city. He's there, I swear it. Over and over I glimpse him in my peripheral vision, but when I turn to look at him, he's gone. When I close my eyes, pictures of him spool out, like a reel. It's like he's the only thing I can see, with my eyes and my imagination, too, like he's demanding my attention.

With Gabe around, I haven't allowed myself to sink into memories of Aidan; breaking down is an indulgence I can't afford. He isn't here now, though, and I relax into that thought like warm bathwater. I put my head on my hands and breathe deeply—in through my nose, out through my mouth, like we do in Vinyasa Flow. It's odd, but I can smell Aidan now, his earthy, woodsy scent, like leaves on the forest floor. If I concentrate, I can feel him standing behind me, his hands on my shoulders, bracing me. I lean back into the feel of his hands, the line of his body, and let myself remember.

SEVEN

Madeleine

The first time I saw Aidan James, he stopped my heart.

I mean this literally—not in a gushy, love-at-first-sight kind of a way. I was walking down a tree-lined trail at Wildacres Retreat in the mountains of North Carolina, obsessing about snakes, pondering the writing workshop I was about to lead, and wondering whether I should have worn different shoes, when I happened to look up and see a man dangling from a tree branch, about thirty feet in the air. All I could think was that he was going to fall to his death, and I'd be the only witness, haunted to the end of my days by his spectacular crash to earth. My heart stuttered in my chest. Staring up at the suspended figure swaying in the breeze, I screamed, a shrill, jagged sound that echoed off the trees, the ground, the not-so-distant mountains. And then I tripped over a log and landed on the damp, pine-needle-covered ground, scraping my palms and bruising my knees.

As I was collecting my breath and my dignity, I heard his husky voice for the first time. "You okay?" He sounded concerned, but I could tell he was stifling laughter nonetheless.

From my ignominious position on the forest floor, I glared at him. I couldn't make out his features very well from this far down. My first impressions were of his long legs, clad in beige cargo shorts, and his utter nonchalance. "Shouldn't I be asking you that question?"

He shifted his grip on the branch. "I'm absolutely fine. Why did you scream?"

Irritation loomed. "Why do you think?"

"Do you always answer one question with another?"

Great. He was psychoanalyzing me. "Are you always so impossible?" I snapped.

Now he did laugh, a full-throated sound that made me want to smile despite myself. "So they tell me."

"Well, they're right."

He did a chin-up. "Good to know."

I got to my feet, brushing the pine needles off my jeans and wiping the dirt from my hands. "What are you doing up there, exactly?"

"What did you think I was doing?" His voice was dry.

Two could play at this game. "Deciding how to end your miserable existence, maybe?"

"Thirty feet off the ground? I'd probably just wind up with a bunch of broken bones and a concussion."

I craned my neck up to judge the distance more clearly. "What are you made of, rubber?"

"Gumby is my alter ego," he replied.

He was mocking me. Fabulous. "If your life's not in any immediate danger, then I guess I'll be on my way." I gestured down the trail.

"Okay then. Nice meeting you. Thanks for stopping by." He took one hand off the branch to wave at me. How could his arms not be tired? Was he part monkey?

"My pleasure." I let a full measure of sarcasm flood my tone.

"Be careful," he called after me as I made my way deeper into the woods. "You want to watch out for those logs. They can come out of nowhere." He was laughing again.

As I wandered along, I contemplated the many ways in which I'd found him aggravating. First he'd frightened the hell out of me, then he'd somehow turned the tables so that I was the one who was taking her life in her hands, just by ambling down a quiet mountainside trail. (Although, when I thought about it, I had to admit that I'd taken a pretty spectacular wipeout right on terra firma, while he was safe and sound in midair, the bastard.) And then there was the laughing: You'd think that a grown man who decided to hang from trees like an orangutan would be a bit embarrassed about it, or at least feel the need to offer an explanation—but not this guy. No, he'd made me feel like the crazy one, even had a good laugh at my expense, and then sent me on my way without so much as an apology for scaring me half to death and ruining my jeans. Yet somehow, I couldn't stop thinking about him.

I told myself that this was because he was so rude. Who wouldn't rehash such a bizarre encounter? I pictured myself back in Chapel Hill, telling the story to Lucy and Jos over lattes at Caffé Driade. They wouldn't believe it, either. I could hear

Jos now: "You found him hanging from a *what*? And he had the nerve to laugh at *you*? The prick." And Lucy, ever the lawyer: "I bet if he'd given you a heart attack, you could have sued."

Bolstered by their support, however imaginary, I soldiered on until the trail looped around to where it had begun, depositing me in front of Wildacres Retreat's flagstone pavilion, with its spectacular view of western North Carolina's Blue Ridge Mountains, which today were shrouded in clouds. Shaking off the memory of my brief encounter with Monkey Man—God only knew what bizarre convention of human beings had brought him here—I made my way to my room to change my clothes. I had a writing workshop to lead in an hour. Teenagers are a difficult audience at best, and this group, ten smart, savvy girls from the projects in Durham, was especially challenging. I'd hoped that my stroll would clear my mind and help me prepare for the class ahead. Instead, I felt more muddied than when I'd begun. Pulling on a clean T-shirt, I took a deep, cleansing yoga breath, grabbed my bag, and headed out into the mountain air.

In the end, my class went well, although it was challenging enough to demand all of my attention. The girls filed out of the room for dinner, and as I gathered their journals into my shoulder bag, the only thing on my mind was how to wrap up the class the next day: Would they be willing to read their pieces aloud? Should I combine their writing and photographs into a chapbook and send them copies when the retreat was over, or would they think that was stupid? Deep in thought, I bent to put the rest of the journals into my bag. I was straightening up when I heard his voice.

"Hey," was all he said, but I'd been so far into my own little world that it startled me. I jumped about a foot, and the journals came cascading out of my bag. I hadn't expected to see anyone, much less a strange man who'd been hanging from a tree and giving me a hard time the first time we'd met. Maybe he was a lower primate and a stalker, all rolled into one alarming package. I glanced around for support and saw no one—my students were long gone, and everyone else had probably made their way to the dining hall by now. It was just me and Monkey Man, who looked like he was about to start laughing again.

"That's twice," he said in that low, amused tone I remembered, crossing the floor in two easy strides to help me pick them up. "At least you didn't scream." He joined me on the floor, where I was blushing a deep red and shoving the journals back into my bag as fast as I could. We started to stand up at the same time and nearly collided. He reached out to steady me, and that's when I got my first real look at Aidan James.

Then I was speechless, a rare occurrence. Close up, tree-boy looked to be in his late twenties, like me. Lean and muscled, he had wavy dirty-blond hair, long enough that he had to brush it out of his eyes, which were a deep, saturated cerulean. They were set far apart, which worked with his high cheekbones. It didn't look like he'd shaved in a couple of days; blond stubble covered his cheeks and chin, but on him it was sexy instead of sloppy. His nose was long and narrow, like he'd just gotten off the *Mayflower*. But what got me the most was the light in his eyes, like he was in on a big secret and couldn't wait to share it. Energy radiated off him in waves. Even standing still, he seemed incredibly *alive* somehow. It was like nothing I'd ever felt.

He grinned at me. "Aren't you going to say anything?"

I realized I was staring, and ducked my head. "Oh. Sorry. I just—you scared me."

"I know. Like I said, that's twice." He handed me the last of my journals. "I came to apologize, but now I guess I owe you double. Can I take you to dinner?"

I gaped at him. "I don't even know your name."

"Oh. How rude of me." He extended his hand. "I'm Aidan James."

"Madeleine Kimble," I replied, shifting my bag onto my shoulder so we could shake. "Maddie."

"Nice to meet you," he said, smiling away. His hand was warm. "So what about dinner? Care to join me?"

Everyone at Wildacres ate together in the main dining hall, and the meals were paid for in advance. I knitted my eyebrows. "Are you asking me if I want to sit with you tonight?"

"When you put it that way . . ." His smile faded to a little half grin, more of a smirk than anything else. "Yes, I guess that's what I'm asking, unless there's a little bistro around here that I don't know about."

I regained my equilibrium enough to glare at him. "Very magnanimous of you."

"It's the least I could do," he said. "I'll carry your bag if you want." He held out his hand for my shoulder bag. I pulled it away, and he chuckled. Just like last time, I had to fight a smile. What was it about this guy?

He took a step back and headed for the door without another word. At the doorway he turned, that smile lighting his face again. "We got off to a bad start, so I'm going to try again. Humor me." He took advantage of my renewed speechlessness to knock on the open door, gesturing at me to respond when I stood, frozen, bag in hand.

"Come in," I said, feeling like an idiot.

"Hey," he said once more. "Sorry about scaring you before. I'm Aidan James."

"Madeleine Kimble," I said, for want of a better reply.

"Nice to meet you."

I scrambled for something to say. "How did you know I was in here?"

"I was watching you teach."

"You—what? From where?" It was a stupid question. The room had a wall of windows that opened onto the flagstone patio. I'd been facing away from them when I was working with the kids, and on the rare occasion that I'd turned around, I'd been way too absorbed in what I was doing to notice him.

"Don't be self-conscious. You're good at it. The kids like you."

"You were spying on me," I said, indignation clear in my voice. "That's creepy."

"Sorry," he replied, not sounding particularly repentant. "I figured you'd probably notice me standing there, given the enormous transparent wall and everything. If espionage was what I was after, I would've chosen a slightly more secluded vantage point."

There was really nothing I could say to this without sounding like an idiot, so I didn't bother. He was right, it wasn't his fault I was so unobservant. Still, the thought of him on the patio, scrutinizing my rapport with my students and my teaching methods, wasn't exactly soothing. *Stalker*, I thought again, and wondered how I'd call for help if he decided to accost me. It would be just like me to escape to a quiet mountain retreat, far from the proverbial madding crowd, and come face-to-face with a crazy person who wouldn't leave me alone.

My discomfort must have shown on my face, because he hurried on, in a more conciliatory tone. "So anyhow, I didn't mean to freak you out earlier, and I was wondering if I might be able to make it up to you at dinner tonight."

"Well . . ." I began, and then trailed off. Did I want to go to dinner with this guy? On the one hand, he was superlatively gorgeous. On the other hand, he seemed to bring out my inner moron. Maybe I would just spend the evening making a fool of myself, and the subsequent hours kicking myself. I was a little too bruised for comfort already.

"How about if I say 'please'? Please will you go to dinner with me, Madeleine Kimble?" He'd turned the full force of his blue eyes on me, and it was unsettling. There was an intensity to the way he looked at me that made me feel like he had me half-undressed already. Worse than that, I felt like he could see right through my clothes into what lay beneath—thoughts, feelings, desires, and all. I squirmed.

"Pretty please? I promise to behave." He raised one eyebrow, a trick I had yet to master.

I opened my mouth to reply but with no good idea of what I was going to say. What came out was this: "What were you doing in that tree?"

"Is our dinner date conditional upon my response?"

I revised my original opinion. Maybe he was a monkey, a stalker, *and* a lawyer—a crazy, tree-hanging, flirtatious-as-hell litigator. That seemed unlikely; he didn't look like the type of guy who spent a lot of time behind a desk, but hey, anything was possible. "I thought I was the one who answered one question with another," I retorted. Banter was fine. Banter I could do.

"Fair enough. I'm a climber. I got bored. Also, it's good exercise."

This was not the answer I'd anticipated. "Climber, like rock walls?"

"Climber, like Everest." He was grinning at me again.

"Right."

"You don't believe me? Would you like to Google me?" He was making a beeline for my laptop, still on the table behind us.

"You climb mountains?" It just figured.

"Mountains, glaciers, ice, whatever's around."

"And trees," I reminded him. "Don't forget trees."

"Like I said, whatever's around."

"You go around hanging from trees whenever you get bored?"

"Upper-body strength," he said. "I'm not good at just sitting around."

I stared at him, my arms folded, until he went on. "I got in last night, and I woke up early to go running, but then I had to give a talk to a bunch of folks for Outdoor Adventure Weekend. You know, owl prowling, orienteering, and me, your friendly neighborhood climber. So after that, I decided to blow off some steam."

He'd just gotten here last night. That explained why I hadn't seen him around. I would've remembered, for sure. "Did you really climb Mount Everest?"

"If I say yes, does that mean you'll go to dinner with me?"

"Maybe."

"Fine. You want the truth?" He shifted from one foot to the other. "I got three hundred feet from the summit and had to turn around. Weather. I'm going back in a few months to try again."

He looked so sheepish, it was my turn to laugh. He looked puzzled, and the more puzzled he looked, the more I laughed. What kind of ridiculous day was this? It just kept getting better, too. No wonder he'd found my incident with the log so hilarious. I considered it an act of supreme balance if I walked the morning's first cup of coffee across the room without spilling it, and here he was, feeling embarrassed because he hadn't made it to the top of the tallest mountain in the world. If there was ever a sign that two people were mismatched, this was it.

The look of puzzlement on his face began to fade, morphing into something else. It took me a moment to realize that I'd hurt his feelings with my little laughing jag. I put real effort into trying to stop, and wound down into giggles. When I could speak I said, "I'm not laughing at you. I'm laughing at myself."

The eyebrow again.

"No, really. I have no sense of balance at all, like you might have noticed." I gestured at the journals in my bag, and then outside, in the vague direction of the trail where I'd run into him earlier. "I can barely walk uphill. If I tried to make it up one of the little mountains around here, I'd fall halfway down in about a second."

"No you wouldn't," he said. "I would never let you fall." He sounded offended.

"You haven't done a great job thus far," I snapped before I could help myself.

This time he lost it. He laughed with the same abandon he had before, wild and contagious, until I was laughing, too. "You're right," he said. "Our first expedition, and I totally suck as a guide. You don't owe me a thing."

I considered his fantastic laugh, twisted sense of humor, and good looks, and surrendered. "You win," I said to him.

"I win what?" he said, wiping his eyes.

"Dinner. I'll go to dinner with you."

That sobered him up. "You will?"

"Uh-huh."

"Okay," he said. "Great." He loaded my laptop into my bag, succeeded in taking it from me this time, and held out his arm. I stared at it. "What's that for?"

"You," he said, looking at me as if I were just a little bit dim. "There's a bunch of steps between here and the dining hall, not to mention some uneven terrain, and like you said, balance isn't your strong suit."

At a loss for words, I simply looked at him.

"I promise not to let you fall again," he said. "Scout's honor." And so I took his arm.

EIGHT

Madeleine

It couldn't have been more than a hundred yards to the dining hall, but that was more than far enough for me to feel ridiculous. More than anything, I wanted my arm back. For one thing, it seemed absurd to be making my way toward dinner with my arm threaded through his. He was a virtual stranger, and it's not like we were on our way to the opera or something. Furthermore, I wasn't so physically handicapped by my own clumsiness that I couldn't walk the length of a football field without falling over. I didn't need my own seeing-eye human to watch out for stray tree roots and crevices. Well, maybe I did, but I certainly didn't want the world to know it. And then there was the matter of his physical presence. I was hyperaware of all the places where his skin touched mine, which, given the warm weather and our attire, was plenty. Every time I stole a glance at him, my stomach lurched, and from the smirk that was playing around his lips, I had the feeling he wasn't immune to my discomfort.

Yes, I wanted my arm back all right. I also wanted to rescind my agreement to his dinner invitation, closet myself in my room, and snack on my considerable stash of granola bars for the remainder of my stay. But I couldn't figure out a graceful way to make any of this happen, so I kept on walking.

The more uncomfortable I get, the quieter I become. Aidan was the opposite—either that, or he was as comfy as he could possibly be. The whole way to the dining hall, he made an alarming amount of small talk, mostly about the flora and fauna we passed along the way. After he'd pointed out three kinds of edible mushrooms, one kind guaranteed to give you considerable intestinal distress, and mountain golden heather (on the federal endangered species list, planted here deliberately), I recovered enough to give him the eye.

"Are you a closet botanist?" I demanded, interrupting his latest observation about how beautiful the Devil's walking stick was in the fall.

He shook his head. "Nope. I just like nature."

I chuckled.

"You don't?"

"I'm not anti-nature, or anything. I just haven't seen enough of it to have an opinion. I was raised in the city."

"What city?" he inquired, guiding me around a large gray rock that protruded from the path.

"New York City. Brooklyn, to be exact."

"Brooklyn has nature," he said. "What about the Botanic Garden? What about Prospect Park?"

"Let me amend that. I haven't seen much—how should I phrase it?—uncontrolled nature. Which this definitely counts as, in my opinion."

"This is uncontrolled nature?" Again with the eyebrow.

"To me it is."

"Hmmm," he said, compressing his lips into a thin line. He seemed to be trying to hold back laughter.

"You say tomato," I muttered, staring at the ground in an attempt to wrest back some control over our progress. I was about to step onto a pile of moss when he stopped abruptly, then pulled me behind him. He kept a tight grip on my wrist.

"Hey," I complained, trying to twist free.

"Shhh," he said, his eyes fixed on the ground.

Annoyed, I complied nonetheless. He began backing away down the trail, pushing me with his body. I felt like a cow being herded, and opened my mouth to protest, then shut it again as he came to a halt about ten feet from where we'd started. "Whew," he said, tugging me again so I stood next to him.

I'd had it with being led around like a farm animal. "What the hell was that about?"

Wordlessly, he pointed down the trail. I looked but saw nothing out of the ordinary. "What?" I asked. Maybe he really was crazy, on top of everything else. That would be just my luck.

He still had hold of my wrist, and this time he pulled me so I stood in front of him. He put one hand on my shoulder to keep me steady and, lifting the hand that had hold of my wrist, he pointed again. "*Agkistrodon contortrix mokasen*," he said. "Northern copperhead, to the uninitiated."

I gulped. "Oh," I said. Peering closer, I saw the brown and gray body slithering across the path, almost indistinguishable from the twigs and leaves in its path. Its wide head lifted to look at us, and even from this distance I could see its forked tongue dart out, tasting the air.

Our bodies were only a few inches apart, and he had a good grip on me. His quiet laughter shook both of us. "Maybe you were right about the whole uncontrolled nature thing."

"I told you so," I said.

"They're usually nocturnal. Maybe this guy's lost," he mused as we watched the copperhead reach the other side of the path and disappear into the trees. He sounded concerned for the snake's safety, which made me smile.

"Thanks for rescuing me," I said, imbuing my tone with enough sarcasm so that he knew I wasn't the helpless-maiden type.

"You do need a guide. You would have stepped right on the freaking thing if I hadn't stopped you." I couldn't see his face, but I would have been willing to bet he was smirking again.

I dug deep and came up with something I'd seen on the Discovery Channel during a snowed-in weekend in the Adirondacks with my parents. "They're venomous, but their bite isn't fatal, right? So I would've suffered for a while, but everything would've turned out okay."

He spun me to face him like we were dancing. "You know more than you let on. Are you a closet herpetologist?"

I could give as good as I got. Tilting my head, I ran my free hand through my hair, letting it cascade over my back. "If you're asking me if I have a nasty venereal disease, the answer is no. Not that that's any of your business, on a first date. And speaking of which, would you mind letting go of my wrist? You're hurting me, and it's a little too early in our relationship for S&M."

He dropped my wrist like it was on fire and let his hand fall from my shoulder. "That's too bad," he said, his voice a few notes lower and his blue eyes locked on mine. "The second part, not the first. The first part is purely good news."

Jesus, how did he *do* that? The few inches between us suddenly seemed like way too much—or not nearly enough, if I wanted to hang on to any semblance of dignity. I stepped a full foot back. "Whoa, captain," I said.

"Sorry," he replied, not looking the least bit apologetic.

I don't know what I would have said in return if a full complement of my students hadn't appeared, making their way down the trail to dinner. "Hey, Ms. Maddie," they singsonged as they passed me, ogling Aidan as they went. One of them even went so far as to walk backward down the trail and give me a thumbs-up.

"Oh, that's just great," I said to myself. Aidan was laughing.

"Come on," I told him, sounding every inch the bossy schoolteacher.

"Yes, ma'am." He gave me a little salute and started walking again. This time he kept his hands to himself.

We made it to the dining hall without further incident, although we were somewhat late—most of the folks already had full plates of food, my students included, and were busy eating. Luckily, this meant that although plenty of people glanced up when we walked in, and a few waved to us, none of them felt compelled to offer us a seat.

I tried to serve myself, but Aidan was having none of it—"This is a date," he said, rolling his eyes—so instead I went to sit down, as far from my fellow faculty members as possible. Several of them turned their heads to follow my progress as I made my way to an empty table.

I amused myself by imagining what type of gossip would be circulating among the cabins tonight; then Aidan arrived, balancing two heaping plates like an experienced waiter. "Here you go," he said. "I didn't know what you liked, so I got everything." He set my plate in front of me with a flourish and settled down at a seat across the table.

"You are truly nuts," I said, staring down at my overfull plate, on which collard greens, ham, sweet potatoes, biscuits, macaroni and cheese, and something that looked suspiciously like Jell-O salad all jostled for their fair share of space.

"You're welcome," he said, spreading his napkin on his lap and handing me mine. He reached for the pitcher in the middle of the table and filled our water glasses, then lifted his in a toast. "Here's to not stepping on that copperhead. And to our first date," he said, grinning so widely that I couldn't help but smile back. I lifted my glass and touched it to his. We could have been anywhere, that was the crazy thing. While he was looking at me, I didn't hear the noise of the dining hall or notice any of the other people eating. It was just me and him, and it was freaking me out.

Aidan wasn't nearly as oblivious to our surroundings. "People are staring at you," he told me.

"Uh-huh."

"Why is that, exactly?"

"My incredible charisma, for one thing. And my amazing grace."

One side of his mouth twitched upward in a smile. "Oh. I see. Any other reasons, or is that it?"

I poked the Jell-O salad with my fork. "Those are the other people who teach in this program with me. I usually sit with them. They're probably taking bets on who you are and why I'm over here with you."

"Does that bother you?" he said, peppering his macaroni.

"Not really. I mean, I don't date—I haven't for a while—and they're not used to seeing me with a guy, so that's part of it. And then they're just gossipy, by nature, and they've been up on this mountain for a week with only each other and the kids for company, so they're getting pretty desperate."

He absorbed this. "Why don't you date?"

"I got out of a relationship about a year ago and I've been taking a break. It's not that I don't date," I said to clarify. "It's more like I've been on hiatus."

"I guess I should be honored then."

"Something like that." How the hell we'd found our way into this territory so soon after we'd sat down was beyond me. I stabbed morosely at a forkful of collard greens.

"They're still staring," he remarked.

"Big surprise," I said to my plate.

"Want me to give them something to stare about?" His voice was mischievous, and I looked up to discover that he'd turned the full force of his eyes on me. God, his eyelashes were long. I'd never seen eyes quite that color before, such a powerful, arresting blue.

He cleared his throat. "See something you like?"

Blood rushed to my cheeks, and I dropped my gaze—not much use, given that I wound up staring at his full lips instead. Figuring that I might as well resign myself to having a completely humiliating day, I forced myself to raise my head. "No to the first," I said. "And yes to the second, if you must know."

There was a full beat of silence, and then he laughed. "Good," he said. "I do, too."

"Glad we got that out of the way," I said.

"Yep. Now let's eat. I'm starving." He buttered a piece of bread from the communal basket and handed it to me.

When I'm nervous, eating is the last activity that appeals to me. I took a bite of bread and chewed it gamely. It sank to the pit of my stomach like a large pebble and sat there. Aidan, on the other hand, was spearing one forkful of food after another. I'd never seen someone eat so fast and not choke in the process.

He swallowed a giant mouthful of sweet potatoes and wiped his mouth with a napkin. "Tell me about yourself," he invited.

"Um. What do you want to know?"

"Whatever you want to tell me. Where did you grow up? What do you like to do? And do you hate everything I put on your plate? Because you're not eating."

"The food is fine. I'm just not very hungry."

"I could get you something else," he said, looking worried.

"I don't see how. I think you've put the entire contents of the kitchen on this plate. Besides, I'm not hungry. I'll eat later." I prayed that he'd drop the subject; I truly did not want to explain to him that he made me as jumpy as a cat. He'd dine out on that one for weeks.

"Okay," he said. "If you're sure."

"I'm sure. I'm fine. Really."

He gave me a skeptical look. "All right, then. So, since your mouth's not full, you've got no excuse not to talk. Give it up."

"I'm from Brooklyn. I think I already told you that."

"But now you live here?"

"I live in North Carolina, but not here in Little Switzerland. I live in Durham, which is in the middle part of the state, in the Triangle."

"What brought you down here, then?"

"I went to school at Carolina, for journalism and creative writing. And I liked it, so I stayed."

"And now you teach."

"Well, yeah. That, and I write."

"Novels? Articles? What?"

"Articles, mainly. Some newsletters and brochures, and things like that, for nonprofits. I'd like to write a book one day, but I guess I just haven't been inspired by the right subject yet." I swallowed a mouthful of water and wiped my face with a napkin, feeling a little bit more at ease now that we were in familiar territory. Plus, I was beginning to get used to his good looks, and the focused way he regarded me whenever we were talking; it was still unnerving, a little bit, but not so much so that I was afraid I was going to drop my water glass right into my lap. "How about you? Where did you grow up?"

"Me? Oh, everywhere. My dad was in the military, so we traveled—Germany, Alaska, Florida, you name it. We were all over the place. Some good spots, and some that I wouldn't much care to revisit. At least it was interesting."

"Did you have a favorite place?"

He mulled that one for a minute. "Alaska, I think. It's where I learned to climb, anyhow."

"I've never been there. What's it like?"

"It's beautiful."

"So where do your parents live now?"

It was the wrong question; I could tell that from the way his lips compressed into an even line before he answered me. "My mom lives in Florida. And my dad, I have no idea." On the surface, his tone was light, but I could see I'd ventured into dangerous waters.

"That must be hard," I said for want of a better response.

"No, not really. He was an asshole." Aidan's voice was flat. When I chanced a look at his face, his lips were pressed into that thin line again, and his eyes were darker than they'd been before. He saw me looking at him and forced a smile.

"Enough about my dad," he said. "Anything else you want to know?"

I cast around for a safe subject. "Did you go to college?"

"Yeah, CU Boulder. I was an environmental studies major. It let me spend the most amount of time outside."

Aha. Perhaps that explained his extensive interest in wildlife. "I've never met a climber before."

"I'm your first, then." He gave me his flirtatious half smile again.

I ignored it. "Where have you climbed?"

"Like I said, wherever I can. I do rock climbing and ice climbing, and big mountain routes. I live in Colorado, so I do a lot of climbing there. But I also travel around, to Utah, New Mexico, California, Wyoming, Alaska, and a ton of other places, which is fun. And then sometimes I do expeditions out of the country, which I love. A lot of times I'll go along as a guide, so I get to make money, but sometimes I raise funds and go with my own team, just for the experience. That's what I'm doing right now."

"Raising money for your own expedition?"

"Yeah, to Switzerland, the North Face of the Eiger. Like I told you, I came here to give a talk, a kind of motivational speaking thing. You know, the power of positive thinking, determination gets you everywhere, blah blah blah. It's decent money, plus I'd never been to North Carolina before and I heard there were a few good crags. So, here I am."

"What else do you do?"

He thought about that one, cracking his knuckles. "Let's see. I work at a climbing gym, setting routes and giving lessons. I like to draw, and I read poetry. I don't have the longest attention span in the world, so that's easier for me than novels, although I do read some nonfiction, if I'm interested enough. I travel around giving talks, like I said. Sometimes I work construction, if I'm running low on funds. Oh, and I'm starting my own guiding company, with my buddy J.C."

An entrepreneur. Hmmm. "What's it called?"

"Over the Top Ascents. It's just in the beginning stages, though." He looked embarrassed again, like he had when he told me he'd had to turn back three hundred feet from the summit of Everest. I had the feeling that beneath his laid-back exterior lurked a true perfectionist.

"You're a busy guy," I told him.

"I'm just not good at sitting still. Speaking of which, are you going to eat anything?"

I looked down at my untouched plate. "I don't think so."

"You want to go for a walk, then? Because I'm done, and people are still staring at us."

"Surely not."

"They are, I swear. Here, give me that." He took my plate and his own, brought them to the bins by the kitchen, and then came back to the table. "You ready to go?"

"Sure," I said. I got to my feet and followed him out of the dining hall, back onto the path, where he pulled a crumpled pack of American Spirits out of his pocket.

"You smoke?" I asked him.

"Is that a problem?"

"Not hugely. I just thought, since you're a climber and all, it wouldn't be compatible."

"It's not," he said. "I'm trying to quit. With limited success. I take it you don't?"

I shook my head. "But go ahead. It won't bother me."

He lit his cigarette, and we kept walking. "So," he said. "Tell me about the guy."

"What guy?"

"The one that put you on hiatus."

"Oh, Andrew. There's nothing to tell. We were together for a while, and it isn't like anything spectacular went wrong. We just . . . got tired of each other, I guess. Or maybe we wanted different things. We'd been dating for a couple of years, and we were at that point where you have to make a decision—move in together, or break up." I was proud of how unemotional I sounded. In reality, the experience had been devastating, more because it made me doubt my own judgment than for any other reason. I'd sworn off men for a good long while, in the wake of it. Until now, in fact.

"So you broke up," he said.

"Yeah, we did. And then he moved away, to go to med school." I glanced sideways at him. "How about you?"

"How about me what?"

"Do you have a girlfriend?"

"Nope," he said. He didn't elaborate, either.

We walked for a while without talking. I felt comfortable with him, so much so that when he reached out and took my hand, it didn't take me by surprise. We fell into step beside each other. His hand was warm, the fingers calloused.

"It's going to rain," he remarked, crushing his cigarette under his foot and then putting the butt in his pocket. He didn't litter. I liked that.

"How can you tell?"

"I can tell. We should start back, if we don't want to get caught in it."

So we turned around and walked back, winding up on the flagstone patio that overlooked the mountains. The patio was empty, and we sat and talked for a while. As the sun retreated below the horizon, Aidan pulled a pad of paper and a pen out of the pocket of his cargo shorts. He propped the pad on the arm of his chair and started sketching something, as if that were a perfectly normal thing to be doing in the middle of a conversation.

"What are you doing now?"

"Just drawing, while we still have some light. Maybe we should move over here, where I can see better." He got up and resettled himself in another chair, under the glow from a lantern mounted on the side of the building.

"What are you drawing?"

"Be patient. You'll find out."

I sat back and watched him. There was a look of total concentration on his face, and from time to time he bit his lower lip. Occasionally he glanced up at me, as if he was trying to get something right. Then he looked back down and kept on sketching.

"Can we talk?" I said. "Or would that distract you?"

"No, talk away. I like the sound of your voice. It's very soothing."

This from the man who had the most erotic voice I'd ever heard. "Okay," I said. "I was just wondering . . . why you wanted to go to dinner with me."

"What do you mean?" He raised his head from his mysterious piece of artwork. His eyebrows drew down.

"The first time we met, I tripped over a log and fell on my face. Then I spilled my books all over the floor. I'm not the most

athletic person in the world, or the most graceful. And here you
are, Mr. Mountain Climber Extraordinaire."

"I don't care about any of that," he said. "I think you're
smart, and funny, and beautiful. There's lots of stuff I bet you
can do that I can't. Like write, for one. I don't know how to explain it, really. There's just something about you. Why did you
go to dinner with me, for that matter?"

"You wouldn't take no for an answer," I said, which was the
truth—as far as that went.

"Oh, yeah. True enough. Well, here you go." He stood up
then, and handed me the picture. And then he walked away,
toward the railing, and stood with his back to me. The wind
had picked up, and it blew through his dirty-blond hair, rippled
his clothes. I had to use both hands to hold the picture steady.
I spread it out on my knees. He thinks I'm beautiful, I thought,
and a warm feeling spread through my midsection as I looked at
what he'd drawn.

At first glance, it was a picture of a tree. Not just any tree, I
realized, but the one he'd been suspended from when we met.
I saw the log at the bottom, lying at an angle across the trail. I
was struck by his attention to detail—the gnarled and twisted
roots, the leaf-laden branches. He had some artistic talent, a fact
that I stored away for later analysis. I was about to call after him
when I looked closer. Like Al Hirschfeld's New York Times Nina
cartoons, which I'd loved when I was a little girl, the first impression of this picture was just the beginning. Everywhere I looked,
Aidan and I were hiding. Our nude bodies were intertwined to
form the trunk; our feet melted into the roots; our hands reached
into the branches; our faces were duplicated within each leaf. In
some of the leaves we were smiling; in others we were kissing,

eyes closed. I could see each line of our faces, each shade of our expressions.

At the bottom of the picture, he'd printed in neat, angular writing:

Thus, though we cannot make our sun
Stand still, yet we will make him run.

Below this was his full name—Aidan Sebastian James—and his phone number.

I examined the picture for a long time, the lines of poetry beneath. They were excerpted from Andrew Marvell's classic "To His Coy Mistress," which begins famously, *Had we but world enough, and time.* The hell with Anaïs Nin; this has always been one of my favorite erotic texts. These are the last two lines.

I had never believed in fate, but standing on the deck at Wildacres, the wind whipping through my hair, Aidan's drawing in my hand, I began to change my mind.

The picture in my hand, I stood up. He had turned around and was standing there, looking at me, three feet away. His gaze was steady.

Sure enough, a light rain began to fall. I folded the picture and put it in the pocket of my jeans. When I looked up he was still staring at me, as if the rain were immaterial. In the light mounted on the side of the building, I could see the drops falling in his dirty blond hair, darkening it.

I found my voice. "I've never been propositioned by picture before."

This made him smile, though the expression in his eyes never changed. "Is that what you think this is? A proposition?"

"Isn't it?"

For the first time, uncertainty crept across his face. "Maybe. Maybe it's something more."

I took a step closer to him. "What else could it be?"

"I'm not sure. I only know what I want."

"And what's that?" My voice trembled.

He closed the distance between us and took my hand. The rain came heavier now, pelting us. I blinked the water from my eyes and shivered. He, on the other hand, seemed oblivious to the fact that it was pouring. We could have been having this conversation on a sunny beach in Baja. He twined my fingers with his. We fit.

We stood, hand in hand, waiting for his reply. I thought about what I wanted: to stop feeling restless, to find a place to call home, to meet a person who saw me for myself and loved every part, even the quirky ones. To get out of the rain and to kiss Aidan James, not necessarily in that order.

Even then, though, I recognized his stubborn streak, which mirrored my own. He would answer when he was ready and not before, so there we stood, getting soggier by the second. As I looked down at our hands, feeling the rain hit the back of my neck and soak my hair, I was suffused with a strange sense of momentum, as if I'd been propelled to the edge of a cliff and had paused for an instant before jumping.

Raising my head, I met Aidan's gaze. He was smiling, a funny little half grin. "What?" I whispered.

In response, he tugged me out of the light, into the shadows. Against the railing, he took my other hand and turned me to face him, pulling my body full against his. Through the wet fabric of our clothes, I could feel him as clearly as if we were naked—the long, lean muscles, the coiled strength. He bent his head and rubbed his face against mine, inhaling; the stubble scratched my cheeks, but I didn't push him away, not then and not when he trailed his lips down my neck, licked along the path he'd left, and then followed his tongue with his teeth—not biting, but grazing the surface of my skin hard enough to let me know he could. He slid his hand under my fleece and my T-shirt, cupping my left breast, and left it there, spreading his fingers wide. It took me a moment to realize that he was feeling my heart beat.

I shivered again, this time not from the rain or the cold. In response, he pulled me closer and unbuttoned my jeans, pushing my underwear aside and entering me with his fingers. His hands were wet and so was I. He kept his eyes on mine as he bent his head again. Against my lips he whispered, "You," answering both of my questions with a single syllable and then kissing me so thoroughly that I couldn't have replied even if I'd wanted to. He was everywhere: running his fingertips over my nipples, tracing my mouth with his tongue, filling me. I didn't care where we were, that we'd just met, that my students could come outside and discover us at any moment. I didn't care that he was fully dressed, whereas I . . . wasn't. There was only Aidan, and what he was doing to me. He lifted me onto the railing, high above the ground, and I forgot to be afraid.

"Be with me?" he asked. His fingers traced my lashes, and I opened my eyes. There he was, an inch away. His face was open and sincere, his blue eyes wide.

At the edge of the cliff, I took a deep breath and jumped. "Yes," I said to him, and felt myself let go of the way everything had been. "Now please."

There on the railing, in the dark wet night, he did as I'd asked. I never worried about falling. I knew he would catch me.

We made love for hours, in the shadows at 3,300 feet, then

in his small wooden room, both of us undone by the force of it. He licked first water and then sweat from my skin, drinking us in, and I felt my clenched heart reveal itself like a moonflower, that pale mysterious bloom that opens only at night.

As dawn broke over the mountaintop, I woke to find the sheets pushed to the side, my body bare. Aidan lay next to me, tracing the contours of my breasts, my belly, my hips. Self-conscious, I tried to cover myself, but he pinned my hands.

"You are so beautiful," he said in that husky voice that sent shivers rushing through me. In the faint light that streamed through the window, I watched him move over me, into me, with a focused, seamless grace. As he lowered his face to my breasts, I closed my eyes.

He chanted my name like a mantra, like a prayer. Outside, the rain came down and down.

NINE

Nicholas

"Take it from me," I say to Taylor. "Becoming reacquainted with your own life is not a process for the faint of heart."

He makes an unintelligible noise around a mouthful of food. We're sitting outside on the patio of this pizza place called the Mellow Mushroom, which is sort of a foodie version of Alice in Wonderland meets Woodstock, complete with a giant fourteen-foot-tall mushroom that's visible from Oleander Drive. The pizzas here have funky names, like the Philosopher's Pie and the Magical Mystery Tour. Despite the kitschy menu, the food's pretty good, and they've got an impressive selection of microbrews. Also, Grace's band—Beacon Rubber Philharmonic—is performing tonight, and so Taylor and I are playing groupie. We get to hoot and holler and cheer. It's kind of fun.

He finally swallows his giant bite of Kosmic Karma and

washes it down with a mouthful of beer. "I'm sure," he says. "I can't even imagine, dude."

Taylor cracks me up. He's a surfing real estate lawyer who regularly peppers his conversation with words like *awesome* and *rad*. And *dude*, of course. He's also a dyed-in-the-wool Southern boy whose family has lived in Wilmington for generations—they own a huge revivalist mansion downtown that Taylor's told me is on the Historic Wilmington home tour every year. Consequently, he opens doors for women, says "y'all" without a trace of irony, and uses creative expressions like "in the short rows" to describe when he's almost done with a particularly onerous task. His good-old-boy exterior conceals an astute intelligence and a wicked sense of humor. I like him very much.

"It's exhausting," I say, watching him cram another piece of pizza into his mouth.

"I bet," he says, or at least that's what it sounds like.

"Especially on a practical level. Take my kitchen, for instance. Nothing's where I think it ought to be. Not the microwave, not the glasses, not the silverware. It took me forty minutes to make a grilled cheese sandwich yesterday, and then I burned it anyway, because apparently I don't know how to cook. It would have been nice to have known that before I almost set the house on fire, but oh well."

He gives me a peculiar look. "You can cook just fine. You were always making these crazy meals for Grace. Like, gourmet and shit."

"Well," I say, perplexed, "I can't cook now."

"That's weird."

"Tell me about it." I look up, in the direction of the small stage. Beacon Rubber Philharmonic has only three members—a guitarist, who's also the vocalist, a cellist, and Grace. She's radiant in a loose white dress, really into the music. I watch her draw her bow across the strings of her violin, watch her body sway. The song is "Satellite," by Dave Matthews, and she's tearing it up. Her red hair isn't tied back, and it flies everywhere. She tosses her head back, so it doesn't cover the strings.

Grace is another puzzle. In the weeks that I've been home from the hospital, I can't shake that initial sense that she and I don't belong together, that something's amiss. I think she's beautiful, sure. I've gone to see Beacon Rubber play a bunch of times, and even I can tell that she is exquisitely talented. She's gorgeous when she plays, passionate. And she loves me. Despite this happy confluence of circumstances, my heart remains unmoved. This is a problem, especially since she is my fiancée.

Taylor follows my line of sight. "Everything copacetic with Grace?"

I haven't talked to anyone about my feelings for Grace, or rather the lack thereof. Taylor's question catches me off guard, though, and so I answer it honestly. "I don't know, man. I mean, she tells me things were going great. Hell, she said I proposed to her, and she said yes. But something just doesn't feel right."

He looks confused. "You two've been together a couple of years, right? And you never mentioned any major problems to me. Granted, you never told me you were gonna pop the question. Then again," he says, grinning, "maybe you've got a rich inner life you're afraid to share with Uncle Taylor, for fear he will mock you mercilessly."

"Yeah, I'm sure that's it." I take a generous gulp of beer. "Anyhow, that's not the point. The point is that here's this woman who knows me really well, right? And I don't know the first thing about her, other than what she's told me. How can I marry someone that I don't even know?"

"Ever hear of arranged marriages? People in the Third World do it all the time."

"Don't be a dick, Taylor. It's a problem. She still wants to be with me. And I just feel crappy about it. Like I'm taking advantage of her."

Now he's staring at me. "You've got to be kidding, Sullivan. She's hot as hell. She's into you, despite the fact that you're a walking freak show. Go ahead and get lucky."

"It's not that simple," I say, staring down into the remains of my pale ale. It's not that I'm not attracted to Grace. I am. When she kisses me, my body responds like it should, all systems go. But when I think about kissing her back, about taking it further, the laughing woman's face fills my field of vision, like she's standing in front of me. I end up backing away from Grace, telling her that I don't think being with her is a good idea, like a freaking virgin on prom night. Needless to say, this doesn't go over well. She's running out of patience with me, and I don't blame her. We've gone from seeing each other every day to going out a couple of nights a week, and I've managed to make at least one of those a group affair, like tonight.

While I tell myself that I'm taking the moral high ground by opting out of having sex with a woman I don't love—and who claims to be in love with me—I still feel like a complete ass. She looks so disappointed every time I turn her down, so sad. I have succeeded in hurting her feelings, as well as in making her cry, and, most recently, telling me that if I'm going to be so mean to her, she's not going to speak to me anymore. This may be for the best.

Problem is, not only am I supremely horny, but I'm also lonely. I spend a lot of time walking my dog—Nevada, a beautiful golden retriever who has been staying with Taylor and is thrilled beyond belief to see me. I think Taylor has been spoiling him, because every time I eat anything, Nevada sits down next to me, his heavy head in my lap, and stares up at me with these big, expectant eyes. Then again, maybe I've always fed him table scraps. Who knows? Not me, of course. I suppose I could ask Grace, but that just seems pathetic.

"I'll be right back," I say to Taylor now, pushing my chair back from the table. "Smoke break."

"I can't get over that." He shakes his head. "You were always so anti. Used to show your students those damn PSAs where everyone was lying on the ground in body bags. Now it's like Philip Morris has you by the balls."

Since I don't have a good response to this, I ignore him and make my way to the parking lot, where I dig my pack of death sticks out of my pocket and light one. Fucking filthy habit. Couldn't I have woken up with a more useful add-on, like a superpower or even an affinity for tofu? Instead I crave charred meat and am hell-bent on polluting my lungs. Fantastic.

I stand in the parking lot, blowing smoke rings so perfect you could shoot an arrow through them and trying to think about something normal, like the spackle and sandpaper I bought today to fix the holes in my living room wall. I live in a neighborhood called Carolina Place, not too far from downtown Wilmington. It's got sidewalks and a park and narrow streets lined with turn-of-the-century bungalows, one of which is mine—a yellow one-story with green trim. There's a porch, complete with the obligatory swing, and a deck out back. Grace tells me that I renovated my house from the bottom up, that I did most of the work myself. "So I'm handy," I say, adding that to the growing arsenal of information I have about my life. Fake it till I make it, that's my motto.

Faking it is something I do a lot, especially when it comes to pretending that my life is all business as usual. School isn't back in session until August, which doesn't help. The days stretch out, long and empty, and I try to fill them with productive distractions. I go to the grocery store, take walks with Nevada, surf with Taylor and Jack, spend time with Grace. I helped Taylor build a fence for a Work on Wilmington volunteer project, stained Jack's new deck, took my mangled Harley into the shop to have it fixed. Right now I'm driving a crappy old blue Honda Accord, which I guess is all I can afford on a teacher's salary. I wish I had my motorcycle back already. It would be more fun, especially in the summer.

I try to keep busy, and to stay awake as long as possible, because every time I fall asleep, there's the dream. It doesn't matter if I sleep on the couch, the bed, the carpet. Every time, I wake up on my hands and knees, sweating like I've run a marathon, struggling for breath. It's gotten so that I'm afraid to close my eyes. As soon as I do, the mountain looms in front of me, massive, covered in ice and snow. No matter how hard I try to wake up, no matter how hard I try to tell myself I am dreaming, the scenario plays out: the climb, the fall, the lack of air, the images rolling one after the other, the lines of poetry—which I've looked up online. Marvell, like I thought. The weird thing is, I don't know any of the other lines of the poem, and I don't know anything about Andrew Marvell. And given that my knowledge of popular culture, of books and politics—of anything that doesn't have to do with my personal life—has survived the accident intact, this strikes me as peculiar.

As if all of this weren't bad enough, whatever personality I've managed to maintain is, at least according to Grace and my friends, a little bit off. It started with the cigarettes—American

Spirits are my brand, there was never any doubt in my mind—and has spread to other things, like the type of music I listen to, what I'm good at, and even what I like to eat. Dr. Perry has told me that this can happen after traumatic head injuries, that it will fade with time. Which is all well and good, but it doesn't change the way Grace looks at me when I pull a bottle of Gatorade from the refrigerator or tell her I can't stand tuna fish, or the way Taylor scrutinized me when I sketched an impromptu, accurate rendering of Nevada catching a ball in midair—like I'm a pod person from the planet Amnesia.

I've started to feel like maybe there's another person inside of me, dreaming that awful dream and missing the woman and the little boy. It's crazy, I know. I have the oddest feeling that on top of losing my sense of self, I've become a stranger who smokes American Spirits and climbs mountains and draws pictures and knows Marvell. Which is impossible, of course. And delusional. And just plain creepy.

The end result of all of this is that my self-confidence is shot to hell. I still can't remember anything, which is, of course, disastrous in and of itself. Then the things that I do remember aren't real, and half the time I eat something, drink something, do something, or say something, I get the pod person treatment. Obviously, I'm not sleeping well. This can't go on, I'm sure of it. Something's got to give.

I've tried to convey some of this to the psychiatrist Dr. Perry recommended, with dubious results. I don't dislike Dr. Green. He isn't a bad guy, but he doesn't really seem to know what to do with me, which makes two of us. We've spent a lot of time talking, and he's tried everything in his little bag of tricks, from talk therapy to Ambien to hypnosis. I was hopeful that the latter would produce some kind of miraculous results, but no such luck. The whole time he was instructing me to envision myself relaxing on a sandy beach, I was half-tempted to break into the chorus of "Hypnotize," by The Notorious B.I.G.—after all, I might as well make use of the one aspect of my memory that seems to be in great working order. I stopped myself just in time. He's doing his best. It's not his fault I'm such a crappy patient.

Instead, I told him about the dream, and he said that made sense, it's me externalizing my anxiety or some such bullshit. I told him about my new habits, the smoking and the drawing, and he said sometimes when you're in an accident like mine, other parts of your brain compensate for the ones that have been damaged. *Don't worry,* he said. *Everything will be back to normal soon enough, and if not—well, artistic talent isn't such a bad thing, is it, and I'll just write you a prescription for Wellbutrin.* And then he laughed, which I did not appreciate.

The next session we had, I told him about the sense that my life's on hold, that it seems like there's nothing to it. He said that was logical, that until my memories came back, it was natural that I'd be "a bit at sea." This was not what I meant, exactly. It's not that I don't have things to do from one day to the next, or people to do them with. It's that all of this stuff seems to add up to nothing. The sense of happiness I had when I was climbing, the rush of love for the dark-haired woman and the little boy, those things have weight. Compared with them, my day-to-day life seems meaningless, just a bunch of hours strung together.

When I related all this to Dr. Green, he nodded his head. "Hmmm," he said. "You're not working right now, are you?" I told him that I wasn't, that I won't be teaching again until the fall. His brilliant conclusion was that my life lacks structure—that if I were in a classroom, I'd feel a lot more inspired. He recommended that I give myself some time.

For all I know, he could be right. But when I think about getting up in front of a classroom full of high school students and talking to them about the American political system, I don't feel a thrill of excitement. What I feel, instead, is dread. I don't know if this is because I have no actual memories of teaching or planning a curriculum. I guess it could be plain old stage fright. The thing is, it's not working with kids that turns me off, it's the setting—the confines of a classroom, standing up in front of a group of students day after endless day, year after year. When I think about it too hard, I want to flee for the nearest exit as fast as my legs will take me.

I've done my best to make sense out of this, poking around my life to see if I was planning to switch careers anytime soon. I asked Grace, and she said I was good at my job, that I had no plans to do anything else. I asked Taylor, and he said no, man, you liked it because you got the summers off and you could hang out at the beach. Then I asked Jack, and he gave me a blank stare. It's a living, he said. You're not supposed to love it. You do what you gotta do. The latter seemed like such a grim assessment, I resolved to never bring up the subject again. Maybe I've had a personality reassignment or something.

I could handle all of this, I think, if it weren't for the dreams. Last week, in an effort to get a grip, I drove out to Climb On!, an indoor rock climbing gym located in Wilmington's outer reaches. I thought that maybe something there would resonate with me, that perhaps I had a secret life as a mountain climber and that's why teaching social studies seemed tame in comparison—but that didn't happen. I looked at the walls covered in multicolored holds, the dudes climbing upside down in what the front desk person told me was called the Cave, and shuddered. Not only was none of it familiar, but when I stepped into a harness and started making my way up one of the routes, I got vertiginously dizzy. By the end of my sojourn to Climb On!, I learned yet another new thing about myself: I do not care for heights. Not at all.

So much for my secret-identity theory. I'm back to pissing Grace off, drinking too much, and wandering around like one of Oliver Sacks's prime case studies. In my spare time, I sit and picture the dark-haired woman, trying to figure out why her face calls up such strong feelings—way stronger than anything I feel for Grace. When I think about the dream woman, the sense of ennui that pervades my daily life is gone. I feel . . . open, like anything is possible, and happy. But I also feel sad, because I miss her—which is impossible, given that she's a figment of my imagination. I close my eyes, and I can feel her shape under my hands, smell her scent. I can hear her voice. When I touch myself, hers is the face I see. I don't fight this as hard as I should, because it's nice to feel something for once, other than confusion. If this is the worst delusion life can throw at me, I'll take it . . . even if that crazy dream is the price.

Watching cars jockey for space in the crowded parking lot of the Mushroom, I decide that I'm going to quit seeing Dr. Green. For one thing, he's not helping. It's pretty poor if you walk into your shrink's office and, instead of confessing your innermost feelings, your first urge is to bust out a cheesy rap song. For another, I'm not certain what it is that I want him to do. I'm willing to buy that this whole experience is just some funky coping mechanism dredged up by my frazzled subconscious . . . but if he could prescribe some magic drug that would eliminate the dreams tomorrow, I'm not so sure I'd stop by the pharmacy. I want to hang on to the feelings that I get when I see the woman and the little boy, and the man who has something to say. I want to feel energized, fulfilled, like I did on the mountain before the avalanche hit. If I could just figure out how to accomplish this without falling to my death over and over and waking up like an advertisement for Right Guard, well, then I'd be getting somewhere.

I am Ambivalent with a capital A.

Sighing, I crush my cigarette under my foot, toss it into the trash, and walk back to the table. Grace is sitting next to Taylor, waving her hands around like she always does when she talks. It's a wonder she hasn't knocked over my beer. For someone named Grace, she is remarkably without any. Sad, but true.

"Nicholas!" she says when she sees me. Her face lights up. "What did you think?"

"It was great. Sorry I missed the last few songs."

"I keep trying to get Grace to play 'The Devil Went Down to Georgia,' but she won't," Taylor says, looking as pouty as it's possible for a six-foot-three adult male to look. "You should try to persuade her, Sullivan. I bet she'd rip that song a new one."

I sit down, smile at Grace. "You ought to do it. Otherwise he's liable to start yelling 'Freebird.'"

"In which case, I shall evict him," she says, taking a sip of my beer and waving goodbye to her bandmates, who are loading out. The set was acoustic, so there isn't that much to break down. Taylor, being the opportunistic male that he is, jumps out of his chair and runs over to see if he can help the cellist carry her instrument ten feet to her car. She is pretty, and he has a buzz on. Hope springs eternal.

"So," Grace says. "It's early. Feel like going downtown?"

"I'm kind of tired," I say, which is the truth. "Taylor and I got up early to go surfing, and then I went for a run with the dog. I'm beat."

"Why don't we just hang out at your place, then? I got *Taken* on Netflix. We can make popcorn, have a lazy night."

"Maybe some other time."

Her face falls. "I don't get it, Nicholas. Why are you acting like this?"

"Can we just take it slow? I've got a lot on my mind. I need some time," I say, parroting Dr. Green. I wish I had something more satisfying to say to her, but this is the best I can do. The more specific I get, the worse I will make her feel. I'd rather protect her from collateral damage while I figure out what's going on in my addled little brain.

Regardless of the purity of my intentions, I don't expect my request to go over well with Grace, and it doesn't. "I've given you time," she says, looking disgusted. "I've given you two years of my life."

"I know you have. I'm sorry. I just—I don't know that this is what I want right now." My voice comes out so low, I'm basically mumbling, but she hears me anyhow.

"You don't know that this is what you *want*? Are you kidding me?"

The latter seems like a rhetorical question, so I don't answer it. This does not please Grace. "Are you breaking up with me?" she says, clutching my pint glass so tightly that I'm afraid it'll splinter in her hand.

"No. At least, I don't think so. I'm just asking for some space. You can understand that, right?"

One look at Grace's face tells me that indeed she cannot. "What I understand is that when I went to sleep three weeks ago, I had a fiancé who loved me. I was happy. I was starting to plan a wedding, for God's sake." She looks away, and I pray that she isn't going to start crying. "I was willing to accept that things would be different after the accident. But this isn't fair, Nicholas. It's not fair."

Of all the tactics she could have taken, this is perhaps the most incendiary—not least because I have been holding back in large part out of a desire to treat her with some kindness and dignity. It pisses me off, and I retaliate without thinking. "Oh, I'm sorry, Grace," I say. "Do you think having my memory wiped like a messed-up hard drive is a stellar example of fairness at work? Do you believe this has primarily happened to *you*? I'm sorry that my accident and my amnesia have proved to be such an inconvenience. I'd hate to trouble you any further."

The moment the words are out, I want to take them back. I look at her, at the spots of red burning high on her cheeks, the angry set of her jaw, and know that it's too late. If glares could kill, I'd be six feet under. She is furious, and I deserve every bit of it.

"I'm sorry," I say, sincerely this time.

"And I'm leaving." She gets to her feet, shoulders her violin, and pushes past Taylor, who has failed in his mission and is returning to our table. We watch her hightail it for the parking lot, back ramrod straight under her white dress. I have plenty of time to stop her, but I don't. Instead I sit and finish my beer. I let her walk away.

TEN

Madeleine

It's been a while since I thought about that rainy night at Wild-acres. It didn't hurt as much as I thought, remembering. Maybe I'm just numb.

I take a fortifying gulp of my coffee and pull the computer toward me again, intending to see if any members of the expedition have updated the Facebook page. But before I can log in, the doorbell rings. I figure it's my mom, maybe bringing Gabe back early from his night at her hotel—she and my dad have flown in to be with me, but for some reason they've elected to stay at the Boulderado, rather than at our house—and I struggle to put on what Aidan would call my game face. I've got a smile all ready to go when I open the door.

It isn't my mom, though. Standing on the front porch like I've somehow summoned him via Facebook is J.C., looking rumpled and worn-out, as if he hasn't slept in days. Maybe he hasn't. There are circles under his eyes, his black T-shirt is wrinkled, and he needs a shave. I stare at him, and the smile fades right off my face. I open my mouth, but nothing comes out.

"Hi," he says, and he holds out his arms.

For a few seconds I stand there, frozen. J.C. is home. He hasn't found Aidan, he hasn't found Aidan's body. He will most likely tell me a bunch of things I don't want to hear, and life will go on, one plodding moment after the next. As much as I want to shut the door and run away, to crawl into my bed and pull the covers over my head and pretend that Aidan will be home next Tuesday just like he promised, I know I can't do that. J.C. and Jesse and Roma have risked their own lives to search for Aidan in bad weather and avalanche conditions. J.C. was the last person to speak to Aidan, the last person to see him. He loved Aidan, too. He is hurting, just like me.

I step over the doorsill and into J.C.'s arms. They close tight around me, and he holds me like he doesn't want to let go. I remember when Ellis died, when I came home and found Aidan in my living room, how sorry I felt for Patty, how angry I was. Now it is my turn.

J.C. maneuvers us inside and shuts the door behind us. He lowers his face into my hair. "I am so sorry, Maddie," he says. "I'm sorry I couldn't bring him back. I tried as hard as I could. The whole team did."

"I know."

"We'll go back, I promise. We'll go back in the spring."

I nod.

He takes me by my upper arms and holds me away from him, looking into my face. "How are you?" he says, like he really wants to know.

I start to tell him that I'm okay, which is the standard line I've been giving everyone, but he's regarding me with such concern that I can't bring myself to lie. Somewhere inside me I feel it rising, the tidal wave of grief I've been holding at bay. "J.C.," I say, and then the tears come. My face crumples, and I start to sob so hard I can't catch my breath. I gasp and choke for air, and when I have it, I'm ashamed of what I do next: I make my hands into fists and start hitting every inch of J.C. I can reach—his chest, his arms, his face. He doesn't defend himself. He just stands there.

"Why?" I scream at him. "What is the point of this stupid shit you do? Why are you all so crazy? There was no reason this had to happen! What the hell is wrong with you? If you had just stayed here, if you had just listened to me, none of this would have happened! Why didn't you listen to me?" My fists pound J.C.'s chest until he takes them in his big hands and holds them still. And I realize I am not yelling at him, not really. It's Aidan I want to say these things to, even though they might apply equally well to J.C. But Aidan isn't here.

"I'm so sorry," he says again, and he sounds abject. "I miss him, too."

He'd be within his rights to get pissed off; after all, no matter what I'm going through, I've just beaten the crap out of him, and all he's done is try to bring Aidan's body back to me, at considerable personal risk. On his face I don't see any anger, though; just exhaustion, and sadness, and worry. His concern undoes me and I start sobbing again, inelegant, gasping sobs. He pulls me against his chest, trying to hold me still. I am ruining his shirt, but I can't bring myself to care.

"Where is Gabe?" he asks when it's clear I'm not capable of pulling myself together.

"At my mom's hotel," I manage to say.

"Okay," he says. "Okay." He picks me up then and carries me to the couch in the living room, which reminds me of Aidan and makes me cry harder.

"I'm sorry," I have the presence of mind to say through my sobs. "I was trying . . . to be strong . . . like he would have wanted . . . I was doing really well until you . . ."

He sits beside me on the couch. "You haven't cried for him at all, before now," he says, and it's not a question.

I shake my head, feeling like Gabe when he's too upset to use his words.

His arms close around me again. He is not Aidan, but he is warm and comforting. I feel safe with him, and I bury my head in his chest.

"I'm here," he says, rubbing my back. "You go ahead and cry, Maddie. Cry all you want."

And so I do. He holds me and I cry for all I've lost, all I might yet lose.

It is a long time before I calm down. Every time I think I've gotten myself under control, something sets me off and the tears come again. I'm pretty sure that I've destroyed J.C.'s shirt, but it doesn't seem to bother him. He kisses the top of my head and rocks me back and forth, his arms tight around me. "Let it come out," he says in my ear. "Let it go." He rubs my back in circles like I'm a baby he's trying to put to sleep for the night.

Eventually my sobs subside, replaced by embarrassment. I pull back to look at him. His dark eyes are dry and narrowed with concern. "I'm sorry," I say in a voice made hoarse from all the crying.

"You've got nothing to apologize for," he says, using the bottom of his shirt to wipe my face. He settles his arm around my shoulders.

"I didn't mean to dump all over you like that. I don't know what happened."

"I don't mind. I wish I could cry like that, myself. Maybe I'd feel better."

"Your shirt's a mess," I say after closer inspection. "You want a new one? I could give you one of Aidan's."

He looks down at himself and makes a face, as if he's only just realized that his T-shirt is soaked through with tears and snot. "Sure," he says. "If it's not too much trouble."

"Not a problem," I say. But I don't get up. I'm imagining going into Aidan's dresser and rummaging through his shirts until I find one to give J.C. I know this is the least I can do for him, but the thought of it horrifies me. I'm pretty sure it would be the end of my hard-won composure.

As if he can read my mind, J.C. stands up. "Why don't I go get it? I know what'll fit me. I've borrowed plenty of A.J.'s stuff before." And before I can say anything, he goes off down the hallway. I hear my bedroom door open, and then the sound of a drawer sliding out. In a minute J.C. strides back down the hall wearing Aidan's white Chamonix T-shirt.

He gives me a quick once-over. "Maddie, when's the last time you ate?"

I think back. "I don't remember," I admit. "I had coffee this morning."

"That doesn't count."

"People keep bringing food. All these casseroles and things. But I can't eat them. They're all . . . glutinous. And then some of them have probably gone bad."

He wipes his hands on the front of Aidan's shirt. "Why don't you let me make you something? You go take a hot shower and relax, and I'll make you something you like, how does that sound?"

Tears fill my eyes again. I feel like a leaky faucet. "Why are you being so nice to me?" I weep, like an idiot. I could kick myself, but J.C. just puts his arms around me and holds me again.

"It's okay, sweetie. It's okay," he says. And of course it's not okay, I don't feel like anything will ever be okay again. But I appreciate the sentiment.

"There goes shirt number two," I say when I stop crying.

"It's all right. You've got more. I don't think A.J. would mind." He gives me a sad little smile, shakes me lightly. "Now go wash up. Scoot, go on. I've got cooking to do." He sounds so definitive, and I am so relieved to be presented with a concrete task that doesn't require thought or responsibility, that I comply. He wanders into the kitchen, and I hear the refrigerator door open as I walk down the hallway to the bathroom.

Under the spray of the shower, I rinse the tears from my face, shampoo and condition my hair, and then just stand there, letting the water wash over me, and my thoughts roam. For some reason—maybe because I've already spent most of the morning reminiscing—I wind up thinking about the first time I came to visit Aidan in Colorado. He had a ridiculous number of frequent flyer miles, and I had a flexible schedule, so in the six weeks between when we met at Wildacres and his trip to Switzerland, we saw each other a lot. I came to Boulder for two long weekends, and he flew back to North Carolina twice.

I remember that first time so clearly, because I was nervous. What if I'd imagined that connection between us? What if it had just been lust, and he turned out to be a total ass? Then again, what if it hadn't, and he didn't? He was leaving in a month and a half for the Eiger. He'd be gone for another two. Then he'd come back, sure, but we lived more than fifteen hundred miles apart. (One thousand, six hundred and eighty-nine, to be precise. I'd Googled it one day when I was feeling particularly fatalistic.) I didn't want to have a long-distance relationship, not on a permanent basis, anyway. Yet there I was, getting on a plane to go see Aidan James.

It was a Friday morning when I flew into Denver. I remember that, too, because he'd taken off from the climbing gym where he worked to pick me up. Lack of sleep had made me woozy—I'd taken the first flight out of Raleigh I could get—and it took me a while to navigate the airport. Once I got outside, it took me even longer to locate Aidan.

I found him after a protracted search, leaning against his Jeep, which sported an impressive collection of bumper stickers: *Will Belay for Food, Leave No Trace, I Do My Own Stunts, Got Cams?* He had his wraparound sunglasses in place, baseball cap pulled down low over his eyes, headphones in. He looked like a movie star in disguise.

I sneaked up beside him and pulled out one of the earbuds. "Hey, Culligan Man," I whispered in his ear.

He jumped about a foot. "Maddie. You scared the crap out of me."

"Hello to you, too. Are you going incognito?" I tugged at the brim of his baseball cap.

"Oh, sure. Can't let them see me here." He pulled off the sunglasses then and kissed me. I kissed him back. And then I yawned.

"That good, huh? Should I be insulted?"

"It's not you," I said, yawning again and covering my mouth with my hand. "I'm just exhausted. Could we possibly go get some coffee?"

"Sure. Why don't we pick up some for J.C., too? He's at work, but his boss is a friend of ours, this guy Ellis. He won't mind if we drop by, and that way you'll get to meet J.C. I've told him a lot about you."

So off we went to get coffee, and then Aidan drove to the construction site where J.C. was working, in a little town called Golden. It was a half-built house, carved into a mountainside. A couple of guys were on the roof, shirtless, nailing down shingles. Aidan put two fingers in his mouth and whistled, and they both looked up. They waved. Then one of them said something to the other, walked across the slope of the roof like he was on flat ground, and started climbing down a ladder that was leaning against the side of the house. He reached the bottom and headed our way.

This had to be the infamous J.C., I thought as I watched him approach. He was about six-two, taller than Aidan's six feet and broader, too, with olive skin, dark eyes, a square jaw, and short brown hair that was tousled with sweat. His upper torso and his arms were tightly muscled, and when he smiled in greeting, his eyes crinkled up at the corners. They were kind.

His good looks weren't flashy or overwhelming, like Aidan's; they had as much to do with the warmth of his grin as they did with the shape of his face. Still, the two of them together were a force to be reckoned with. Had there been something special in the Pensacola water? Or did they come in a two-pack, like Twinkies or something?

As J.C. got closer, I could hear that he was whistling; it took me a few moments to recognize the melody line to *Something Wicked This Way Comes*. "Hey," he said when he came to a stop in front of us. "To what do I owe the honor?"

"We brought you iced coffee," Aidan said, handing him the cup. "And I wanted you to meet Maddie. Maddie, meet J.C. He's the guy who keeps me on an even keel."

"That's me," J.C. said, taking a sip. "I follow him everywhere he goes, chanting, 'Serenity now. Serenity now.'"

"Om shanti shanti om," Aidan intoned, and J.C. grinned.

"Nice to meet you," he said, taking my hand. There was a small black tattoo on his left bicep, and another on his right; they looked like Asian characters, and when I asked Aidan later, he told me they were the Kanji symbols for truth and harmony. The one on his right arm rippled as he shook my hand. "Sorry about the sweat factor. I'm usually cleaner than this."

"Don't believe a word he says," Aidan warned me. "He's a climbing bum. They're all nasty, present company excluded." J.C. released my fingers and tried to cuff him across the head, and Aidan danced backward, out of his reach.

"I gotta get back to work," J.C. said, one corner of his mouth quirking up. "Thanks for the coffee." He lifted it in a salute. "It was great to meet you, Maddie. See you slackers later." And back up the ladder he went.

The three of us ate dinner together that night, outside on the patio of the funky house J.C. and Aidan shared. That house was an experience. It was near downtown, within walking distance of Pearl Street Mall. A previous homeowner had painted the wood siding a vibrant purple, and inside, each room was a different color; the kitchen was canary yellow, the dining room burnt orange, the living room midnight blue. Aidan's bedroom was sage green, with a four-poster bed he'd inherited from the previous tenants ("They were too lazy to move it," he said, "but think of the possibilities") and hardwood floors. The living room opened into the backyard, which had a flagstone patio, complete with picnic table, grill, and a mismatched smattering of chairs.

"We eat out here a lot," Aidan said as we stood in the backyard, the last stop on his impromptu house tour. "Even I can handle grilling a burger without mangling it too badly. J.C.'s the grillmeister, though. He makes some sick marinades. Spicy as hell, and he never warns you, either. Just lets you dig in, and then laughs his ass off when your mouth's on fire."

Understandably, this assessment of J.C.'s culinary character made me a little nervous when he offered to make dinner that night. As it turned out, though, I had nothing to worry about. He made a simple meal, but a good one—grilled chicken, Caesar salad, roasted potatoes—and while we ate, we talked. Aidan had already told me they'd known each other since their freshman year of high school in Pensacola, where both their dads were in the Marines. After they graduated, he'd taken off for Colorado, but J.C. had stuck around at University of Florida in Gainesville, where he'd majored in architecture.

"He tried to get me to come with him, but I told him no way," J.C. said. I hadn't noticed it at first, but he had a slight Southern accent that surfaced from time to time. When I asked, he told me his dad had been stationed in Georgia before they'd moved to Pensacola, which explained the drawl—and maybe the good manners, too. "I'm a Southern boy at heart," he said. "The cold's not really my thing."

"So how'd you wind up here?" I asked.

"Oh, I came out to visit him on spring breaks and stuff, and he got me into climbing. Just small stuff at first, but then somehow he roped me into doing El Cap, no pun intended. I nearly killed both of us about eight times on that one, remember, A.J.?"

"Not likely to forget," Aidan said. "Or forgive."

J.C. shot him the bird. "Anyway, the summer after we graduated, A.J. moved out to Carbondale, which is about three hours from here. He went on and on about how great it was. I finally moved here just to shut him up. He tricked me, getting me to come up here when it was warm. I've been freezing my ass off every winter since."

"Oh, you love it," Aidan said. "Don't lie."

"You call him A.J.?" I said to J.C. with surprise.

"Most people do. It's his initials, you know, like J.C. for me. I don't know, I've always called him that, since high school. Maybe I started a fad." He took a bite of his salad. "Long story short, I thought I was just hanging out with this crazy dude for the summer. Then he got me hooked on the crags, and the rest is history."

"How come you never told me that?" I asked Aidan.

"What? That I'm responsible for J.C.'s dirty little habit?"

"Damn enabler," J.C. said, leaning back in his chair.

"Not that," I said to Aidan. "That you usually go by a nick-name."

"Don't take it personally." J.C. poured himself some water from the pitcher on the table and refilled my cup. "He's the original chameleon. Knowing A.J., he's probably got a third identity squirreled away somewhere. You know, in case of emergency, break glass."

I started laughing, and Aidan rolled his eyes. "That's me, special ops all the way." He speared a mammoth forkful of potatoes. "I knew you two would get along. You have the same messed-up sense of humor."

"Great," J.C. said. "You're dating a female version of me, except shorter and Jewish, instead of Italian. She even has brown hair and brown eyes. What do you know. You and I could've gotten together a long time ago, and saved ourselves a lot of trouble."

Aidan crumpled his napkin and threw it at him. "Fuck you," he said.

"Apparently, you wish you could," J.C. said as he ducked out of the way. "Sorry, buddy. This ship has sailed, and it ain't going in your direction."

The funny thing was, Aidan was right. J.C. and I got along well, from the start. He wanted to know all about me—where I'd gone to school, what I did, where I lived. And when I answered his questions, he listened and then asked some more. He figured out the way I liked my coffee and prepared it for me, unasked, with the attention to detail of a fellow caffeine addict. When Aidan had to go into the climbing gym on Saturday, J.C. took me to the farmers' market, laughing at the way my eyes widened—"They're bigger than your stomach, that's for sure," he said after I loaded up on mango sticky rice, summer rolls, and chocolate croissants—and ate with me in the park, finishing my leftovers with gusto and regaling me with stories of some of his more insane exploits.

"I mean," he said, stabbing a slice of mango with enthusiasm, "there I am, trying to ford this thing that's supposed to be a stream, but I've picked the exact wrong place, because it's just crazy rushing rapids. I'm tied into the rope, and I can see the other side, but I don't know how I'm going to make it across. My friend Nathan is on the bank, anchored to a tree, and I can hear him laughing his damn fool head off. I'm soaking wet, I'm freezing my ass off, and just when I think it can't get any worse,

I hear a noise and I look up and there is an honest-to-God grizzly bear on the other bank, standing just where I'm going. She doesn't look happy about it, either. I look down, and I realize that I am standing right in the middle of this giant school of salmon, which is of course the bear's dinner. And I think, I am toast. I'm going to be the main course, and the salmon is going to be dessert."

"What did you do?"

"What could I do? I had three choices: stand there and wait for the bear to charge me, or try to get across, toward the bear—which seemed like a really bad idea—or beat a hasty retreat. I chose option C."

"And the bear?"

"I didn't wait around to find out. I grabbed that rope and hauled myself out of the water as fast as I could, and Nathan and I took off running. The bear didn't follow us. Too busy eating the salmon, I guess." He smiled at me.

"You're nuts," I said.

"I prefer to think of it as open to experience." He lay back in the grass, his hands knotted behind his head, letting the sun warm his face. I sat next to him, thinking about how lucky I was to be there, sitting in the grass of this beautiful park with a full belly and good company, waiting for the guy I was dating to get off work so we could spend the afternoon together. I felt more complete than I had in a long time. It was a satisfying feeling. It was the beginning.

I'm jolted back to the present by the feel of icy water on my skin. I guess I've been in the shower longer than I thought. That's been happening a lot—I keep losing track of time, staring at the wall and discovering that hours have passed. Shivering, I turn the water off and wrap a towel around myself. Then I head into the bedroom to pull on jeans and a T-shirt. I even braid my hair.

When I walk back into the kitchen, feeling marginally more like a human being, J.C. is setting the table. "Feel better?" he says, folding a napkin in half.

"A little bit. Less salty, anyhow."

"Sit." He pulls a chair out for me, the same one I was using this morning, and I slide into it. "I moved your laptop to the counter so it wouldn't get messed up," he says as he pours fresh coffee into a mug.

"Thanks. I was looking at the Facebook site, before you came."

He's opened the refrigerator to search for creamer, so his back is to me. "And?" he says, his voice as neutral as he can make it. I wish I could see his face.

"It was pretty overwhelming," I tell him. "Don't get me wrong, I'm glad so many people cared about him. I just don't know how I'm supposed to respond. There's so much . . . all the photos, and the videos, and the things people wrote. It's a lot to take in."

He sets the coffee in front of me and pours a cup of his own. "I know what you mean. I could barely stand to look at it, myself. It was Roma's idea."

"I could see that."

"Here," he says, bringing a series of small plates to the table: avocado, zucchini, red cabbage, shredded cheddar, limes, sour cream, chopped fresh cilantro. I had no idea this stuff was even in the refrigerator; my mom must have gone crazy at Whole Foods, in hopes that the magic combination would lure me into eating. J.C. extracts a stack of tortillas from the oven and sets them in the warmer with a subdued flourish. "Build your own burrito," he says. "What do you think?"

I look at the array of items. Somehow, separated like this, they are less threatening, more appealing. "I think this is the only thing I could possibly consider eating right now," I say, which is the truth. "Thank you."

"No problem. I should probably eat, too. Alaska Airlines isn't known for its stellar cuisine." He settles opposite me, coffee mug cradled in one hand.

"You've lost weight," I observe.

"You know how altitude is. And that climb is one hard slog. Plus, after it happened . . . well, eating was the last thing on my mind."

I don't say anything, just pull the plate of tortillas toward me. J.C. watches me without blinking. The circles under his eyes are dark purple, and I wonder again about the last time he slept. "Can I ask you something?" he says as I squeeze a lime over the avocados.

"Of course."

"How did you know?" he says. He leans across the table, his chin propped in his hands.

There is no use pretending I don't know what he means. "I have no idea. It was just a feeling. I had it from the moment he mentioned going, and it just got worse and worse. But no matter what I said, he wouldn't listen. So here we are."

"Huh," he says. "Freaky."

"Tell me about it." I stab a slice of avocado with my fork, although my appetite has diminished as quickly as it revived. "And I've got more where that came from."

"What do you mean?" He eyes me curiously.

"The night you called me, I was already awake. Gabe had a bad dream. He told me his dad was in his room, all snowy, is what he said, and when he left, there was a puddle on the floor. And the weirdest thing was, Gabe's clothes were all wet and cold, and not from pee, either. He was crying, and he told me that he thought something had happened to his daddy on the mountain, that he didn't think Aidan was coming home. I was trying to tell him it was just a dream, not to worry . . . but then the phone rang, and it was you."

"No shit," J.C. says.

"What do you make of that?"

He piles ingredients on his tortilla with studied nonchalance. "I don't know, Maddie. He probably heard you and A.J. fighting, and it morphed into some crazy subconscious deal that came out as a nightmare. The timing was bizarre, sure, but that's about it."

"I guess," I say, heaping sour cream on top of the zucchini.

"What's the alternative? That A.J. paid him some kind of goodbye visit on his way from this world to the next?" His voice is harsh.

I don't believe that myself. In fact, I've spent a fair amount of time arguing J.C.'s very point of view during the last two weeks' late-night sleepless sessions. But for some reason, I feel compelled to play devil's advocate. "Is that any weirder than my premonition, or whatever you'd call it?" I say, looking him right in the eye.

He shifts in his chair. "I guess not," he says. "I don't know what to think. My brain is fried. Sorry if I offended you."

"You didn't offend me," I say, and my voice is as weary as his own. "I don't really believe Aidan was in Gabe's room, myself. I don't know what's wrong with me. Sorry I snapped at you."

"No apology necessary," he says, pushing the plate of cilantro my way. We eat our burritos in silence until Gabe and my parents come home.

ELEVEN

Madeleine

After J.C. leaves, Gabe and I stumble through the rest of the day. My mom gives him a bath and reads him a story, while my dad stands around looking as if he'd rather be anywhere else. When they go back to the hotel, though, he hugs me hard. "I love you, Maddie-berry," he says. It's an old nickname, one he hasn't used in years, and it makes me tear up. I tell him I love him, too. Then I go to bed. Almost immediately, I dream.

I'm at my old house, in North Carolina, standing on the porch, my key in my hand. It's about three months since my first visit to Boulder, and I've just gotten back from teaching a writing workshop for Duke's continuing education program. There were about eight people there, ranging in age from their twenties to their sixties, and all of them asked interesting questions.

I'm feeling happy with myself as I get out of the car and walk toward my house, and it's a welcome feeling.

I haven't felt truly happy in a while, not since I went to see Aidan right before he left for Switzerland and caught him kissing someone else at the expedition's goodbye party. We haven't spoken since. He took off for the Eiger with J.C. and Ellis after that, and I came home to lick my wounds. I spent about a week closeted in my house, eating Oreos and cursing Aidan James. I interviewed people, I wrote articles, I met my deadlines, but as soon as I'd completed a task, I ran down like a windup toy whose key had completed its final revolution. At least I didn't tell him I loved him, I thought. That would have been really humiliating.

My closest friends, Jos and Lucy, made it their personal mission to dislodge me from the worst of my funk. After I unloaded the whole ugly story on them, they responded with appropriate best-friend gestures of sympathy. But neither of them is the type to wallow for long, and they weren't about to let me wallow, either. Over the course of the last eight weeks they've come up with a variety of alliterative names for what happened, including the Denver Debacle, the Boulder Blitzkrieg, and the Creepy Colorado Climber Cataclysm. Thanks to them, I've almost succeeded in having a sense of humor about the whole situation.

As I come up the steps, for once I am not thinking about Aidan. I'm thinking about my workshop, hoping I did a good job. Teaching absorbs a lot of my energy, no matter how much I love it, and I'm looking forward to kicking off my shoes and watching an old movie. I put my hand on the doorknob, about to insert the key. And then I freeze.

I've forgotten to lock the door, something that surprises me. Usually I'm pretty obsessive about it. I'm turning the knob from left to right, wondering if a serial killer is closeted in my bed-room, when the door opens. On the other side is Aidan James, and he looks terrible—skinny, unshaven, and like he's gone nine rounds in the ring. There are shadows under his eyes, and his lips are cracked.

Relief washes over me like a tidal wave, followed by fury that he'd have the nerve to show up like this after what he did, complete with an invasion of my personal space. I'm torn between wanting to kiss him, cracked lips and all, and wanting to punch him. Paralyzed, I do neither. We stare at each other in silence until he says, in a hoarse voice, "Sorry if I scared you. I had a key."

When I don't reply, he has the good grace to look abashed. "And, um, I was afraid if I didn't use it, you wouldn't let me in."

"That was a fair assumption."

He moves aside so I can pass, and shuts the door behind him. Then he just stands there, wearing khakis and a blue T-shirt, looking more exhausted than I've ever seen a person look. There's a healing gash across his left cheekbone and another one on his forehead. More than that, the light has gone out of his eyes. They look glazed. I've seen Aidan a lot of ways—confident verging on arrogant, angry as hell, filled with enthusiasm about a new route or a great day. I've seen him focused and I've seen him when his mind is thousands of miles away, in the Himalayas or Aconcagua or some other godforsaken place that I can only imagine. But I've never seen him like this, wrecked and stricken, lost. I can't help it: I step closer and hug him. He feels insubstantial somehow, like he might vanish at any moment.

For a moment he doesn't move. Then his arms go around me, holding me so tight I can't breathe. He buries his face in my neck, takes two hitching breaths, and then he's sobbing. His knees give and together we sink to the floor. Through his tears I can hear him saying something over and over. It takes me a long time to realize he is repeating the same three syllables: "I'm sorry."

There on the floor, I hold him, rock him like a child, stroke his tangled hair. I wait, a feeling of dread spreading throughout my body. For Aidan to disintegrate like this can only mean that something horrible has happened, something far worse than his little fling with the blond bimbo. I open my mouth several times to press him for details, but then close it again. I'm not sure I want to know.

After a while his sobs taper off and he pulls back. He won't look at me. Finally I put one hand on either side of his face and turn his face toward mine. Tears streak his cheeks, and without thinking I wipe them away. Before I can finish, he reaches out and grabs my hand. He holds it to his face and closes his eyes.

"Ellis died."

"Oh no." I picture Jim Ellis in my head as I last saw him, downing a Corona in Aidan's living room, playing air guitar like the world's oldest frat boy. Then I think about his wife, the way she'd compressed her lips whenever the conversation turned to the Eiger. "Poor Patty," I say aloud.

"It was my fault." Tears make their way out from under his closed lids, tracking down his face and dripping onto his T-shirt. He makes no move to wipe them away.

"What happened?" It's all I can think to say.

Aidan says nothing for a long time. His sentences, when they come, are jagged, as if he has to force each of them out one syllable at a time. "Ellis got sick—cerebral edema. It was bad. The weather turned on us, and we couldn't get a copter up there. No visibility. So I started lowering him and J.C. both down, together.

Then the cornice I'd tossed our slings over came apart, and all hell broke loose. J.C. got knocked out and the two of them went right over the lip of a crevasse. My axe finally bit about ten feet from the edge. When J.C. got it together, he hauled his end of the rope up. It was totally shredded, like someone cut it with a knife. He climbed out, beat to shit—how he didn't break a limb is beyond me—and I rappelled down to look for Ellis, but he was just . . . nowhere." He draws his knees up to his chest and puts his head down on his folded arms, as if telling me this has absorbed the last bit of energy he has.

It's a terrible story, and for a moment I can't think of how to respond. "I'm so sorry," I say. "But it wasn't your fault, Aidan. How can you say that?"

"Ellis trusted me. His face, before I lowered him down—it was so scared." His shoulders heave. "I should have been able to stop our fall earlier, before the rope got sliced. I tried. I swear I did." He takes a shuddering breath. "Maybe I should've anchored into the rock instead of using the slings, to begin with. Or maybe the rope was just frayed when they went in, Maddie. Maybe if I'd anchored my axe and my blades in faster after we fell, gotten to the edge sooner, I would've been in time. I had a shitty time getting solid purchase, plus I'd lost half my gear when we went down and I had to improvise. I didn't want to fuck up twice. I wanted to be sure I had a bomber anchor going, or as much as I could, under the circumstances. But what if the anchor was fine to begin with, and the time I spent fucking with it cost Ellis his life?"

I scoot over to him and try to lift his head. No dice. "Aidan," I say, trying to sound soothing, rather than how I really feel—enraged that this stupid mountain has robbed Patty Ellis of her loving, if obsessive husband; terrified that Aidan almost died, and that he might well be next; relieved beyond measure to have him safely home; furious for what he'd put me through. "I'm sure you did everything you could. Patty will know that. You're not Superman."

"We called her when we got down," he says into his arm. "I had to tell her. It was . . . the worst phone call of my life."

There is nothing I can say to that, so we are quiet for a while. I rub his back through the thin T-shirt, trying not to let my mind wander. Still, I can't help but wonder how Patty felt when she got that call. No matter how Aidan had behaved, losing him that way would've destroyed me in more ways than I cared to admit—and I'd come pretty damn close, I realize now. I hold my hand still on his back, feeling the heat of his body through his shirt, and trying to reassure myself that he is here.

After a few long minutes, Aidan says, "We fell at least six hundred feet before I got my axe to stick. I thought I had it a couple of times, but it broke loose and there we went again. I could see the crevasse and I thought we were dead for sure. They were going to pull all of us down before I could stop it. I was going to die in a fucking crevasse on that goddamn mountain and you would never know what happened to me." He pauses then and grips his knees tighter. His knuckles are white, and when his voice comes, it is quieter than before. "I wouldn't have ever had a chance to tell you how I feel or why I was so stupid. I hated that more than the dying, I think."

He has my attention. My hand stills on his shoulder blades.

"There's no reason why that happened to Ellis. He's never had a problem like that at altitude before. But it happens, Maddie. It can happen to any of us. And Ellis, he was a family man. He was careful. Patty and the kids, they always came first. I have to be honest with you, I've never been like that. It's been me and the mountain and I've always pushed the envelope. I didn't have anything to lose. But now I have you."

He lifts his head and twists to face me. "I know I fucked up, okay? I ran away before I even left. But I don't know how to be a good . . . boyfriend . . . and a climber. I don't know if the two are compatible. I don't know how to balance them." He is still gripping his knees with one hand; the fingers of his other hand drum on his upper arm, faster and faster.

"Isn't that ironic," I say. "You're right, you never promised me anything."

"No. But I wanted to, and it scared the shit out of me." His voice is level, but I can feel the effort it takes for him to keep it that way. I'm willing to bet that it takes a lot more courage for him to show me the real, unadorned Aidan James than it does for him to negotiate a tricky ice fall at seventeen thousand feet. Still, he keeps his eyes on mine and doesn't look away.

"Please say something," he says.

"What did you want to promise me?"

He doesn't answer right away. He goes still, and his gaze turns inward, as if he has to steel himself for what he is going to say. I wait.

Finally he comes back to himself and takes my hands in his, like he did that first night at Wildacres. "Everything," he answers.

I swallow hard.

Aidan traces his calloused fingers along my palms, following my lifeline to the place where it meets my wrist. He is looking at our hands when he goes on. "I've been with a lot of women, Maddie. I never tried to hide that from you. But us . . . it was different. It was something special. For the first time there was someone who I wanted to be with just as much as I wanted to put up a new route or stand on the summit. More, even. And the way you looked at me, I thought you might feel the same way. It scared me to death." He circles my wrists with his fingers, then releases me and braces his hands on his knees. "So I ran. I fucked it up so I wouldn't have to figure out what came next, and I told myself I didn't care. Then I went up on the mountain and all hell broke loose. And then I couldn't lie to myself anymore."

Happiness courses through me. Aidan hadn't cheated on me because he didn't care about me. He'd cheated on me because he cared too much. Then the ludicrousness of that concept dawns on me, and I become abruptly, completely furious. "What are you saying? You messed around with that slut to . . . what? Make me so mad I'd have nothing to do with you? You let me catch you on purpose?"

Aidan feigns sudden interest in the seam of his khakis. "It was a dick move. Obviously. I don't expect you to forgive me."

Rage is winning out over sympathy as my dominant emotion. "No pun intended. If you're not after absolution, then why the hell are you here?"

He lifts his head. His eyes are a dark, deep blue, and the look they hold pierces my heart. "I love you, Maddie," he says, his husky voice just above a whisper. "I just wanted to tell you that, in case it makes a difference."

I sit, stunned. He might as well have hit me over the head with a crab mallet. "You what?"

"You heard me."

I lower my head into my hands. "You are *so* fucked-up."

"I know."

At a loss, I leave my head buried in my hands rather than face him. What a mess.

"Please say something," he begs.

"That's getting to be a familiar refrain," I say to the inside of my palms. "Besides, I already did."

"Tell me something I don't know then." An edge of desperation creeps into his voice.

"You are emotionally retarded," I mumble.

"Perhaps you missed my earlier request." He tugs at my hands, trying to get me to drop them so he can see my face. "Maddie, please say something. If you don't love me, just tell me so I can stop humiliating myself and get the hell out of here. I'll go bury myself in a big dark hole and you'll never hear from me again."

"And melodramatic," I add, resisting his attempts to lower my hands. "Did I leave that one out?"

"For Christ's sake," he says. He's starting to sound mad.

I drop my hands. "Say it again."

"For Christ's sake," he repeats, sounding madder than before.

"No, not that. The other thing. Say it again."

This time his eyes meet mine without reservation. I can see into their depths. I can lose myself there. Despite what he's done, he is still mine. He's all I want, and I curse myself for it. Look what happened to Patty Ellis.

"I love you," he says, low and clear and sure.

"I forgive you," is what I say. "Because I love you. Against my better judgment."

A wave of emotions rolls across Aidan's face: fear, disbelief, joy. He leans forward and kisses me, deeper than he ever has. I taste salt on his lips. Before, his kisses always had an edge—hunger, lust, something that drove us forward toward an inevitable end. This is different. This is . . . tender. Every time his lips meet mine, I learn something new about Aidan James. He is letting me inside, and my heart leaps.

We kiss for a long time before he pulls back and frames my face with his hands. "You love me," he says. He is smiling.

"I do," I say.

"I could get used to hearing that."

"If you act like a human being rather than an ass, you'll get your chance."

"I'll do my best," he says, and draws my face to his.

"I missed you," I say against his lips.

"Yeah? What did you miss?"

"Oh, a lot of things. Your smile. Talking to you on the phone late at night. The way you raise one eyebrow when you think someone's full of it. I even missed watching you pore over those damn maps, trying to figure out what stupid thing you're going to do next. Just . . . you."

His hand makes its way under my skirt, tracing the contours of my thigh. He trails his fingers over the thin fabric of my underwear, and I have a moment of relief that I'm wearing a decent pair. Desire curls in my belly, stretches like a sunning cat.

"Did you miss this?" he whispers, moving his hand in small, slow circles.

I don't answer. In response, he picks up the pace. I rise to meet his hand and he pulls it away. He lifts my shirt and kisses my breasts through the thin fabric of my bra, running one finger along the scalloped edge of the lace where it meets my skin.

"Aidan," I say. I barely recognize my voice.

"What?" he replies, unhooking my bra with the dexterity born of long practice and letting it fall to the floor.

I know I should tell him to stop. For one thing, we haven't

talked things through at all. For another, what kind of message does it send that I am willing to do . . . this . . . after what happened the last time we'd seen each other? I gather my resolve. "Wait," I say to him.

"Why?" He lowers his head to my breasts again, catching the nipples with his teeth, flicking them with his tongue. His hands roam over me, tracing my back under my shirt, gripping my hips. "It's been a long time," he says, his face against my skin.

I'd been celibate for a year after Andrew, a deliberate decision. Compared to that, two months is nothing. As my oh-so-Jewish mother would say, Aidan James doesn't know from long times. Still, the sound of his voice, the feel of his hands on my body, melts my willpower and brings back a rush of memories that I've been doing my best to forget. I want him to fill me, so strongly it scares me. Where is my backbone?

Ignoring the heat of his breath on my skin, I struggle to remember the way he'd acted, all the reasons why I'd been so angry. "What, you couldn't find a pretty girl to share your tent?"

He rises over me, putting one hand on either side of my head. "I don't want anyone else," he says. "I've found what I'm after."

I look up at him. His hair has gotten long, past his chin. The ends brush my cheekbones. He holds himself away from me, his weight on his arms. I slip my hands under his T-shirt, running my fingers over the smooth skin of his back. His eyes are fixed on mine. "Have faith," he says, and bends to kiss me again.

TWELVE

Aidan

It's the strangest thing. I come to myself again in our bedroom, but where have I been? I remember falling into the darkness and the cold, fighting it with everything I had: *I will come back. I will find you.* I could swear I heard a voice speaking in Latin, in the cadence of the Catholic mass that marked my childhood. Then there was warmth, and a sense of emptiness, of space waiting to be filled. Welcoming me.

Nicholas, I think, and wonder why.

Maddie is asleep, her head pillowed on her hair. For a long moment I just look at her, take in every detail of her face. Then I lie down on the bed, curving myself around her body. I breathe in her familiar smell, bonfires and chocolate and *home*. I say her name once, then again. She doesn't stir, not even when I put my hand on her arm through the blanket.

I don't understand this. Gabe saw me, I know he did. Why not Maddie? Why can't I tell her I'm sorry? Why can't I say goodbye?

I put my hand against her face, feeling the heat of her skin. And then, just like what happened with J.C. on the mountain, I'm inside her dream somehow. We're together again on the living room rug of her house in Durham, six years ago. Maddie kisses me, and for one glorious moment my mind goes blank. I'm not worrying about how I'm going to get her to listen to me, or obsessing over the choices I could've made that would've saved Ellis's life. I'm not thinking at all, really, and it feels great. My body's on a mission. It wants what it wants, and that's just fine with me.

Then Maddie gets both of her hands against my chest and shoves me, hard. "Seriously, Aidan. Stop," she says.

I raise up on my hands so I can get a good look at her face. "What's the matter?"

"Oh, I don't know," she says, sarcastic as hell. "What could be the matter? You cheated on me. You nearly broke my heart. You almost died. One of your best friends did die. I didn't know if I'd ever see you again. Now here you are. You say you love me. Which is fantastic, because I love you too, goddamn it. But I just went from thinking you were the world's biggest ass to making out with you on my living room floor. Can you honestly tell me that you don't think I should be somewhat unsettled?"

I knew this was too good to be true. Somehow or other, I am going to pay for being such an asshole. It's only fair, I know that, but does this have to be the moment? "Now who's being melodramatic?" I say, trying to make light of things.

"I am not being melodramatic, Aidan. I am being serious." She rolls away from me, onto her side, and props herself up on an elbow. "Do you have any idea what the past two months have been like for me? First there was that stupid blond slut. You had your hands all over her. It made me sick. It made me want to kill you."

Guilt shoots through me, which is new. Usually by the time I fuck up one of my relationships—if you could even call them that—I am so over it, I could give less of a shit how the girl feels. In fact, the madder she is, the better, since that'll expedite my trip through Splitsville. Hearing Maddie talk about this, though, I feel awful. I don't deserve her, that's for sure. I do my best to arrange my features in a listening mode so that she won't be able to tell what I'm thinking, which is that I could have that skirt off in about three seconds and be inside her in another two. Luckily she's so invested in what she's saying, she isn't even looking at me.

"I am not a jealous person," she goes on, "but I'd have to have been *dead* not to react that way. It felt like you'd pulled the ground out from under me and stuck a knife in my back, all at the same time. How could you, Aidan? How could you do that to me?"

I hang my head. "I'm sorry," I say.

"You sure are," she says, yanking her shirt back down, which is too bad. I was enjoying the view. "So who was she?"

I am on my feet before I realize it, and I start glancing around the room for the nearest escape route. It's instinct, okay? But this is Maddie, and if she wants to put me through the grand inquisition, I pretty much have to deal. I make myself walk over to the couch like that was my plan all along, and I sit down. "She was just . . . some girl. I don't even know. Some random girl."

"Did you know her before that night at the party?"

"I guess, sure. She hangs around with Patty and Beth. But

we weren't friends, if that's what you're asking. We didn't have anything going on. Kate was there. She was interested. End of story." I can feel my jaw tighten up, and that stupid muscle starts jumping the way it always does when I get upset. J.C. calls me the Meteorologist of Fuckupsville, because whenever anything bothers me, it's all over my face like a weather forecast. Not him. The world could be ending and he'd be on his second cup of coffee, debating whether hellfire would precede or follow brimstone.

"All right," Maddie says. "I just wanted to make sure you weren't going to run off with her or anything."

Christ on a crutch. Run off with her? I'm lucky I remember her name. "Maddie. I love *you*. She was like a . . . I don't know, a convenience."

She grimaces, and I realize too late that maybe my phraseology left something to be desired, from a feminist standpoint. "Sorry," I say, shrugging, "but it's true."

She waves her hand, like she's dismissing this whole train of thought. I have a moment of relief, until she continues: "The thing is . . . I just keep thinking about Patty. Like you said, Ellis was experienced. He's been climbing for as long as you have, longer maybe. And I just . . . it could have been you who didn't come home, just as easy. I think of you as . . . invincible, almost. Like a force of nature. But the truth is, next time you might not come back."

"What are you getting at?" I fold my arms over my chest.

Maddie looks me right in the eye. "I won't ask you to stop climbing, Aidan. I would never do that. It would be horribly selfish of me, like you telling me that you didn't want me to write. I just want to get that out there."

I stare at her.

"I guess I just—I need to understand why you do it, better than I do now. Because climbing like you do—it's selfish, too. You know what you're doing puts your life in danger, you spend months away from home, and half the time you're here, you're gearing up for one expedition or recovering from another. Then you take off with a bunch of other people who are risking their lives just like you, just because they feel like it. It's like you're in the army or something, except the higher cause is yourself."

Oh, not this discussion. I have had it before, and I hate it. I open my mouth to interrupt, but she holds up a hand to stop me. "I'm not done. Climbing is such a big part of you, if you didn't do it, maybe you wouldn't be the same person I fell in love with. I get that. I just need you to tell me why, so I can try to understand. Is it some kind of ego thing? What makes it worth the risk?"

I don't say anything at first, because I want to give her a real answer. I've dated some girls who think that being with a mountain climber is fucking sweet, and some who get all pissy because I disappear for months at a time—which, of course, has served as my ideal exit route. When the former type of chick asks me why I climb, I generally feed her some bullshit about reaching the top of the world, going where no man has gone before, yadda yadda yadda. Then I watch her eyes get all moony, and the rest is history. As for the latter type, the second they start whining, I lose patience for being in their immediate vicinity. I've never tried to answer this question honestly, not in this context, and it takes me a little while to figure out what I want to say. "That's a tough question," I say, joining her on the floor.

She doesn't look up.

"I guess there's a number of answers I could give you, Maddie. And I don't know if any of them will make sense."

"Try me."

"I've told you some of this before . . . but when you're up there, you just feel so . . . alive, I guess. You're pushing yourself to the limits of your abilities and that's all there is. There's no worrying about the stupid stuff, bills, taxes, messed-up car, whatever. There's no place for that. You're just doing what you're doing for as long as it takes you to do it. It's . . . I guess what I'm trying to say is, it's pure. It's the purest thing I know."

She mulls that over. "Okay, I get that. Go on."

"Answer number two . . . I'm a restless person. You know how hard it is for me to stay still. And in normal life, there's no way for me to channel that, you know? But when I'm planning a climb, and then when I'm doing it . . . it focuses me. My mind is calm. And that's . . . I don't know, addictive, even." I bite the side of my index finger, trying to sort out what I want to say next. "When I'm putting together a team, giving talks, raising money, planning a route, the whole deal, it's like I have a purpose. And when we get there and start going up the mountain, everything comes together. All of my energy gets channeled into a point somehow, instead of being scattered all over the place. It fills me and I can do something good with it. And everything makes sense." She isn't saying anything, and I worry that maybe I'm coming off like a complete idiot. "Do I sound totally insane?" I ask.

"Not totally. Go on, please."

"Okay. Number three. This is the simplest one. I love it. I feel the most like myself when I'm climbing. I get to travel all over the world. I meet incredible people and I see places that most folks will never see. It's impossible to me that I should be so lucky. And to get to do it with my friends, to go places like that and then come back and do it all over again . . . I feel like it's what I was put on this earth to do. Cheesy, huh?"

"No . . . not cheesy. Kind of moving, actually," she says.

Huh. This honesty thing is going pretty well so far. Who knew? I pull her toward me so she sits between my legs, her back against my chest, and breathe in the bonfire smell of her hair. "A couple of years ago, I was reading some magazine in a doctor's office. There was this interview with Beck Weathers, the doctor that Jon Krakauer's team left for dead up on Everest in '96. He talked about how in a disaster like that, you find out what people are made of. It's impossible to pretend. And I think climbing's the same way, even when things are going well. You put your life in your partner's hands, or the hands of your team. You have to trust them completely, and they have to trust you. It cuts through all the bullshit, and you get to see who people really are."

"That makes sense. Like a personality litmus test, or something."

This makes me smile. "Sure, something like that." I take my thought process one step further, and then I don't feel like smiling anymore. "That's part of why I feel so awful about Ellis. He trusted me to do the right thing, to come through, and instead I let him die. Him and J.C. both, almost."

"Aidan, you can't control the universe," she says. "How could you know that cornice would collapse? If you hadn't gotten your axe to hold, all three of you would be at the bottom of that crevasse right now. When it counted, you did come through. You saved J.C.'s life."

Maybe. But I sure as hell ended Ellis's. "If I'd made a better decision about where I anchored the belay, his life wouldn't have needed saving," I say. The creepy thing is, I can hear my dad's voice behind each and every word that's coming out of my mouth right now. If this had happened on his watch, with one of his men, he would've nailed their ass to the wall. No matter what Maddie—or anyone else—says, I can't shake the feeling that I could've changed what happened on the mountain that day, rockfall or no rockfall. He was my responsibility, I think, biting my lip. It was my fault.

Maddie is staring at me with big, concerned eyes, and I try to do what I do best when things get heavy—laugh it off. "I'm sorry to dump all of this on you," I say. "It's like you're my emotional Sherpa, or something. Maybe I'll start calling you E.S., for short."

She knows me well enough to recognize the attempt for what it is, and ignores it completely. "Why are you so hard on yourself?"

"That's a long story, and I don't much feel like getting into it now. I've got other stuff on my mind." I slide my hands around to her breasts, trying to change the subject.

She's not having any. "Stop, Aidan. I'm not finished talking."

"So talk. I'm a good multitasker." I pull her tighter against me.

"I can't concentrate when you're doing . . . whatever it is you're doing."

I undo her shirt buttons for the second time tonight. "Is it that big of a mystery? Besides, I can concentrate just fine. Go on, please. I'm listening. It's only my mouth that's occupied." To demonstrate, I take her fingers and suck on them one by one. She draws in breath, sharp, and I turn her so she's facing me. I lift her onto my lap, her legs on either side of my hips.

"You are unbelievable," she says, but she doesn't sound mad anymore. She sounds into it, and I entertain the hope that we can pick up where we left off earlier, without further interruptions.

"Unbelievable good, or unbelievable bad?" I say against her neck, and she shivers. I have her shirt off now and am working on her skirt. She refuses to move to make it easier for me, so I settle for tugging her underwear off instead. Removing her skirt would be a bonus, but it doesn't have to happen. I'll take what I can get.

"That remains to be seen," she tells me, playing coy.

Not a problem. Coy I can handle. At last we are in territory that I know how to navigate, and I intend to take full advantage of that fact. I pull off my own shirt, evening the score. Then I stand up with her wrapped around me, unfasten the button on my khakis with one hand, and kick them and my boxers off. Leaning against the wall, I slide into her. "To answer your earlier question," I say, "my ego is gigantic. And talking about climbing turns me on."

Her body tightens around mine, but she doesn't say anything, which makes me laugh. Now that I have what I want, I can take my time. "I thought you wanted to talk," I say. "So here I am, talking. Did you change your mind? Would you rather just listen?"

"I give up," she says. "We can take a rain check."

I am on a roll. Why not push my luck a few shaky steps further, and see if it holds? "Can I just say one more thing?" I ask her, holding myself still.

She sighs. "Sure."

"It's a question, actually."

"Go ahead."

I put my hands on her hips, move her just a little, hide my face in her hair. My heart's drumming out a fusillade of beats, but I haven't come this far to back out now. It takes everything I have to raise my face, put my mouth against her ear, and speak. It's the scariest thing I've ever done, but I know it is right. She looks so beautiful. She feels so good. I can't see myself wanting anyone else, and I might as well go for broke.

"Will you marry me?" I whisper, feeling my pulse speed up like it does when I'm training hard. I remember lying on my axe in the snow with my heart crashing against my ribs, as much from anxiety as from adrenaline. Now, like then, I wait.

She says nothing.

My heart my heart my heart.

THIRTEEN

Nicholas

On Saturday afternoon, as I am contemplating whether to immerse myself in a giant vat of bourbon, there is a knock on my door. Nevada barks once in acknowledgment, then settles for sniffing the bottom of the door vigorously. He sounds like a hog hunting for truffles.

I open the door and there is Grace, resplendent in knee-high black boots and a flowing green dress that stops mid-thigh. With her red hair streaming over it, she looks like Christmas. I say this and she smiles.

"I guess that would make you the Grinch," she says.

Nevada is beside himself, whimpering with joy, trying to stick his nose up her skirt. I pull him back. "Quit it," I say. She kneels down and pets his head; he closes his eyes and licks her face in doggy ecstasy.

I observe this tableau until a semblance of social niceties comes back to me. "You want to come in?"

"I thought you'd never ask."

I stand aside and she gets up, squeezes past me. Her now-familiar lavender and vanilla scent fills the air. We stand in my living room, staring at each other, until I find my voice. "What are you doing here, Grace? I didn't think you were speaking to me."

"I'm not," she says, like the Sphinx.

I give up. "I was just going to have a drink," I say. "Want one?"

"What are you drinking?" She edges past me into the kitchen, Nevada in her wake. As always, her comfort in my house takes me by surprise. She knows it better than I do.

"Gentleman Jack," I say, trailing behind the two of them. "If I can find some."

"Bourbon?" Her sculpted eyebrows rise.

"Let me guess. I don't drink hard liquor."

She shrugs.

"Do you?"

She shakes her head.

I check the wine rack. "Shiraz, then? There seems to be an impressive collection."

She nods.

I cast around for a corkscrew, pulling drawers open at random, and she beats me to it, finding it in the first place she looks. I open the wine bottle—at least I remember how to do that—locate the glasses, and hand her one. "Okay, I'll bite," I say as I fill my own glass. "What are you after, Sphinx-lady?"

"I thought you might like to go dancing," she says.

It's my turn to raise my eyebrows. "Do I like to dance?"

She nods again.

"Am I any good?"

"You're not too terrible."

"You're not just saying that, so I'll get out on the floor and make a total fool of myself?"

Her mouth twitches, but she shakes her head. "I'd offer to sweeten the deal," she says, "but I'm guessing that would just freak you out."

I hazard a glance at her, alarmed. "What kind of music are you talking about?"

"Does it matter?"

"Only inasmuch as I am not going to a country-western bar, or a place where I have to do the shag," I warn her. "No beach music."

"You'll go?"

What the hell. It's superior entertainment to what I had planned for the rest of the evening—drinking my way to the bottom of a bottle, wallowing in my plight, then passing out on the couch. "Sure," I say.

She looks like she wants to throw her arms around me. "No line dancing, no shagging," she says. "I promise."

"Then let me go take a shower."

I let the hot water run over me, loosening my muscles. As a courtesy to Grace, I even wash my hair. Out of the shower, I throw on a black Pixies T-shirt, beige shorts, and my Pumas. Eyeing myself in the mirror, I decide I look almost human.

I run a comb through my hair and present myself to Grace, who has put on my Vanessa Mae remix of the *Four Seasons* and is sitting demurely on the couch, like she's waiting to be interviewed for a job. Nevada is curled up next to her, his nose tucked under his feathery tail.

"All right?"

For no reason I can tell, her eyes fill with tears. She looks into her lap, away from me.

Now what? I sit next to her on the side Nevada hasn't claimed, put my arm around her shoulders. "Did I do something, Grace? I mean, something else?"

Her voice is muffled. "Just ignore me, please. I promised myself I wasn't going to do this."

"Really ignore you, like go do something else and come back in five minutes? Or kind of ignore you, like talk to you about something stupid until you stop crying?"

The smile is back in her voice. "The former."

"No problem. I'll just . . . clean up the kitchen." God knows it could use it. "Come find me when you're done, um, not doing whatever you're not supposed to be doing."

She snorts, half laughter, half tears, and I make my escape.

It takes her longer than five minutes to pull herself together. I am loading the last of the impressive stack of plates into the dishwasher when I hear her come into the kitchen behind me. She clears her throat.

"Sorry," she says.

I don't turn. "No need to apologize."

"You still want to go?" She sounds like a little girl.

"Sure I do."

"It's early. We could take a walk on the beach with Nevada, then get some dinner, if you want."

"Fine," I say. I dump the detergent in and turn the dishwasher on, then collect my courage and look at her.

She is sitting on one of the kitchen stools. Her eyes are red around the edges, but the tears are gone. She has washed her face. "Why are you being so agreeable?" she says.

"Why are you still speaking to me?" I counter.

"Fair enough."

I attempt lightness. "Seriously, Grace, you're saving me from myself. My sole plan tonight was drunken oblivion. My liver should be thanking you."

"I'm a hero, then."

"Of sorts." I salute her with a little bow.

"Awesome," she says, pure Valley Girl. "Do I get a costume? I always wanted one, like Wonder Woman or something."

"No way. Seeing you in that star-spangled miniskirt might kill me." It just slips out, and in the silence that follows I wish I could crawl under the sink like the little kid from A *Christmas Story*.

Grace recovers first. "Aha. The monk reveals his true colors," she says.

"I'm sorry," I mutter, staring at my sneakers. What the hell is my problem?

"Don't be. It means you're still human after all."

I go to where she sits on the stool, place a hand on the wall on either side of her. "Hey, Grace," I say, an inch from her face.

"What?" she answers, looking up at me. Despite her bravado, she looks fragile to me, all high cheekbones and big eyes.

I don't have an answer, at least not one I'm willing to share with her. Silence descends again, and in it I can hear Johnny Cash coming from the living room; she must have put my iPod on shuffle. *Because you're mine . . . I walk the line.*

A shudder runs through me, part lust, part cowardice. I hold her gaze as long as I can stand it. "Let's go dancing," I say.

She slips from the stool, out of the cage my arms have made. "Whatever you say, big boy." Whistling for Nevada, she heads to the front door to get his leash, and I am off the hook.

We take my Honda. Nevada rides in the back, his tongue lolling out of his mouth. "Don't fall out now, buddy," I tell him. "It'd be a shame if you had to go to the emergency vet clinic, what with this fabulous night of line dancing we have lined up."

"No line dancing," Grace says. "I promised."

"You sure did. But how do I know I can trust you?"

"You don't," she says. "I guess you'll just have to take it on faith."

I laugh. "Well, *that'll* be a change."

We head down to the north end of Wrightsville Beach, where Grace says there's better parking. In the middle of beach season, I doubt there will be any parking. But I am trying hard to be agreeable, so I don't argue. Lucky enough, we do find a spot and it's late enough that we don't even have to pay for it, something that's fast becoming one of my pet peeves.

The wind is blowing off the Atlantic as we make our way up the narrow boardwalk and through the dunes, which serves to break up the hot, humid air to some degree. It still feels as if we're breathing through a wet sock, as far as I'm concerned. Nevada, on the other hand, is beside himself with excitement. He prances at the end of his leash, sniffing the air.

"You're not supposed to have dogs on the beach this late in the season," Grace says, apropos of nothing.

"Then why did you tell me to bring him?"

"I forgot," she says.

I start to get mad, then give it up as a bad job. "I guess I can't hold that one against you."

She gives me a startled look, realizes I'm joking, and smiles at me. "I guess not."

So we walk on the beach, Nevada gamboling ahead of us, dashing in and out of the surf, barking. Grace's long red hair blows in the wind, and after a while she secures it in a knot at the back of her head. She keeps glancing at me happily when she thinks I can't see, and I fight the urge to shake her. I wish there was some way for me to clarify that this is not intended as a Romantic Walk on the Beach, which is how she seems to be taking it. Maybe we used to do this all the time, before? Hell, for all I know, we've had sex in the dunes, or out there in the water. I don't have the heart to ask. Instead, I concentrate on putting one foot in front of the other.

When it comes right down to it, I feel like I owe Grace a good time. My dealings with her may be awkward and confusing, Alice-down-the-rabbit-hole-ish as hell, but they don't mess with my heart. Grace, on the other hand, has come out of a couple sessions with me, especially that last one at the Mushroom, looking like she's been immolated. She's right—she had a perfectly good life, with a guy who loved her. Now she's got me, moody as a cat and just as reluctant to be petted. I've lost myself; she's lost us. It's fair to say I got the shittier end of the deal, but still, her piece is no picnic. Staring over the breaking waves, I remind myself of that fact and resolve to be a better version of my current self for the remainder of the evening.

By the time we've strolled all the way down to the north end of the beach, onto the sandbar across from Figure Eight Island and back, we've worked up a decent appetite, and Grace asks me where I want to have dinner.

"Anywhere. You pick."

"How about Circa?" she says. "You always liked that."

"What kind of food is it?"

"Tapas. Small plates. It's downtown."

"Sounds fine," I say, even though I'm more in the mood for something simpler—pizza, maybe, or a burger. Saying this to

Grace, though, may be more trouble than it's worth. After all, what if I am not, traditionally speaking, a pizza-and-burger kind of guy?

We load Nevada back into the car, take him home, and dry him off. He looks after us mournfully as we lock the door and leave him behind. Truth be told, I envy him. The idea of going to dinner with Grace makes me nervous. It seems like a Date with a capital *D*, something that I have been assiduously trying to avoid. Yet here I am.

I park the car where Grace directs me and we go in. The restaurant is candlelit, with piano music and sophisticated décor. It is definitely a Date restaurant, I conclude as we settle into one of the dark wood booths opposite each other. The wine list alone would take me ten minutes to read, if I went through the whole thing. I peruse it dutifully, then give up. I have no idea what any of these wines are, or whether I enjoy them. And I am tired of asking Grace what I like. I order whisky, neat, which is what I was after this afternoon in the first place. She orders a glass of Wolf Blass Shiraz.

"To what?" she says, raising her glass.

I think for a moment. "To a good night," I say. "And to continuity."

She gives me her Sphinx-smile. "If you say so." And we drink. Then we eat: four kinds of cheese, filet mignon wrapped in puff pastry for me, duck for Grace. And then we drink some more. I pay, which puts the finishing touch on the Datelike vibe. Then we go dancing.

FOURTEEN

Aidan

Time has passed, though I can't tell how much. Maybe it doesn't matter. Nicholas won't let me through when he's awake, and his dreams aren't date-stamped. Sometimes when he's awake I can leave, and I always seem to go home, to our house in Boulder.

Tonight I'm in my now-habitual place by our bed, watching Madeleine sleep. She hogs the covers, but I've never minded. My body temperature runs hot. I sleep naked, and Maddie used to roll over and press herself against my back, to steal my heat. I complained, but only on the surface. Really I loved it, that we knew each other that well, that we fit. Plus, it cooled me off, which was an added plus. Tonight she sleeps restless, with the covers kicked off, and I stand next to her, snow on my pants, ice crystals on my gloves. It's nicely ironic.

I will her to open her eyes, to see me like Gabe did, but nothing happens. Instead she makes a sound in her sleep, like a small frightened animal. She pushes the pillows away from her face like they're suffocating her, and whimpers. She's dreaming, and not about anything good.

Before I really think it through, I'm on my knees next to the bed. I wind my hand into the thick fall of her hair and press my lips against her cheek. *Sweet dreams*, I think. I rummage through my memories until I think about a night I want to give her, if I can—the night she finally said she'd marry me, the night Gabriel was conceived. Something I want her to dream about, something we share.

But memory is a flighty temptress. It's hard to think about making love to her by the river, about the moment she said yes to me, without remembering the rest—what happened with J.C., how I told her about my dad. I kneel next to her and remember. She dreams for me, my lips cold against her skin.

FIFTEEN

Madeleine

I don't have a problem falling asleep these days, but I sure wish I did. It's not like I know what it was like for Aidan, being buried by the avalanche, but I have a good imagination and what I lack in knowledge, I've made up in creativity. I do everything I can to direct my thoughts elsewhere—take a long bath after Gabe's gone to bed, drink a glass of wine, attempt to stumble through a short story, since my attention span seems to have gone the way of all flesh—but almost every night, after I close my eyes, I see him fall, watch the snow bury him. I try to dig him out, but I am alone on the mountain. There is no one to help me.

My only consolation is that I've also been dreaming about us, how we used to be. It's like my dreams have a better memory than I do—they hold all kinds of details I've forgotten, like the way my green velvet couch had a stain from the Malibu Bay Breeze that Jos spilled on the arm, or how I used to have these gorgeous blue glass plates, broken in the move to Boulder, or how Aidan's eyes held all the light in the room when he told me to have faith. Those good dreams almost make the bad ones worthwhile. Almost.

Tonight, I stand at the foot of the mountain, watching Aidan fall. I know this isn't how it really happened, but in my dreams the avalanche is like a monster, chasing him. It is hungry, and he is what it wants. I call his name, over and over, but he can't hear me. There is nothing left for me to do but to watch him die. I listen to my voice echoing in the clear cold air, drowned out by the roar the mountain makes as it cracks apart, as it comes for him. The cold caresses my cheek, animate and intimate, like fingers stroking me.

Then the mountain is gone. I'm standing in the kitchen of Aidan and J.C.'s old house, the one Aidan and I lived in when we were first married, making coffee in the Cuisinart that looks like it could benefit from having its own remote control. Yawning, I open the refrigerator to look for milk. I find it, but it's expired two days ago. I open it anyway and am bracing myself to take a whiff when I hear the front door open and close.

"Hello?" I call, setting the milk down on the counter. With that now-familiar sense of déjà vu, I turn around. I know what will happen next, because I've lived it before. This is the day I came to see Aidan in Boulder, after he asked me to marry him and I told him I needed some time.

Sure enough, J.C. appears in the kitchen doorway, raindrops glistening in his short dark hair. He's wearing his work clothes—jeans, boots, and a black T-shirt that reads AD HD, with a lightning bolt in the middle. It's Aidan's shirt. His hands are dirty, and he has a fair amount of sawdust on his face. The olive skin of his arms is coated with it.

"Hi, honey, I'm home," he says. He looks me up and down, and I realize I'm wearing only a tank top and drawstring pajama pants—no bra, and no underwear, either, for that matter. "You just wake up?"

"Yep," I say, fighting the urge to cross my arms over my chest. "I got in pretty late last night, and then we didn't go to sleep right away."

"I know. I was here." His voice is neutral, but I can tell he isn't happy. The last time I saw J.C.—at the goodbye party for their Switzerland expedition in July, when I'd caught Aidan with someone else—he'd made it pretty clear that his interest in me was more than friendly. *I don't like drama*, he'd said, brushing my hair out of my face. *But I like you just fine.* Then he'd driven me to the airport without pressing the issue. They'd left for the Eiger a couple of days later, and I haven't spoken to J.C. since. Now here I am, debating whether to marry his best friend. It's a little awkward, on a number of levels.

"You were awake?" I say, making myself meet his eyes. "You should've come out and said hello."

"I didn't want to intrude," he says, and leaves it at that.

"You wouldn't have been intruding. I would have been glad to see you."

"That would've been one of you. I think A.J. was counting on having you all to himself."

"Aidan doesn't own me," I say, hoping J.C. was asleep when Aidan and I went into his room and shut the door. The alternative is too embarrassing to contemplate.

J.C. looks like he has several choice responses to that, but he settles for changing the subject. "Is that coffee fresh?"

"Just made it. And I was trying to figure out if this milk is still good. Do you have any ideas?"

He crosses the counter to me and sniffs it. "Ugh. Definitely not. You want me to pick up some more?"

"Would you? I'd really appreciate it."

"No big deal. You like milk, or half-and-half, or some of that fancy flavored creamer stuff?"

"Just milk would be fine. Thank you." This is one of the reasons I like J.C. so much—he's just naturally considerate. And he thinks of the details, which so many guys—okay, people in general—don't. How many guys would have offered to go back out right after they'd gotten off work, to pick up milk for their best friend's girlfriend's coffee—and then improved on that offer with a set of additional options?

A guy who had designs on said best friend's girlfriend, that's who.

Oh well, you can't have everything. And I really, really don't like black coffee, even with lots of sugar.

"I'll be right back," J.C. says, and lopes out of the kitchen like he's glad to do it. I hear the front door open and close again, and then the hum of an engine as his Forester starts up outside.

That's my cue to make myself more presentable. I go back into Aidan's room and dig through my suitcase for clean clothes. Then I grab my toiletry bag and make my way into the bathroom to brush my teeth and take a shower.

Under the hot water, I ponder whether being alone in the house with J.C. is a bad idea. Maybe he's forgotten about his momentary interest in me, that stuff he'd said when we'd hung out after Aidan was such an ass. It had to have disappeared in the wake of Ellis's death, buried under the weight of more serious considerations—so to speak. Maybe he'd been drunk, for that matter. Maybe he'd just been trying to cheer me up.

As for me, I have to do my best to squelch whatever curiosity I've had about him. It's inappropriate. I love Aidan, and I'm making up my mind whether to spend the rest of my life with him. It's completely wrong for me to wonder whether J.C. is as considerate in bed as he is in the other areas of his life. I'm just happy to see him again, and relieved he didn't end up at the bottom of that crevasse like Ellis. Who wouldn't be pleased to see someone, after they'd almost died? I need to pull myself up by my moral bootstraps and start acting like a decent person. After all, I'd given Aidan such a hard time about Kate, whom he hardly knew, and here I am, imagining making out with his best friend. What a hypocrite I am.

"Knock it off," I tell myself. I shampoo my hair, then condition it, trying to think of nothing beyond my first cup of coffee. That will fix everything.

When I step out of the bathroom, fully dressed, J.C. is standing there with a steaming mug. "I heard the water go off," he says.

"Just a second." I duck into Aidan's room and dump my dirty laundry and toiletry bag back into my suitcase. Then I go back into the hallway and hold out my hands for the coffee.

"I hope I got it right," J.C. says as I tilt the mug back to take a sip. "I tried to remember how you liked it."

I take a deep gulp, closing my eyes in appreciation. "It's perfect," I say, with complete sincerity.

"Good. Now let me get mine." He heads back to the kitchen,

and I follow him. He's changed clothes, into navy longboard shorts and a clean, sky-blue T-shirt. I try not to notice how the muscles in his shoulders shift under the shirt.

"So how's it going?" he says, his back to me as he doctors his coffee.

I consider what to say, whether to ask him about what happened on the mountain. In the end I decide discretion is the better part of valor. If he wants to talk about it, he'll bring it up himself. "Not too bad. Work is okay. I have a fair amount of freelance stuff to do, so that's good. Gives me the freedom to do things like this—take trips on the spur of the moment—as long as I have my laptop with me. You?"

"I've been better," he says, turning around to face me with his coffee mug in his hand. This close, I can see how tired he is. Small surprise he'd heard us come in; he looks like he hasn't slept in a week. "I've lost friends before. You come to accept it, when this is what you do. I mean, we've all got to be a little crazy, right? And this is the way it works out sometimes, the cost, or whatever. But Ellis—it hit me hard. His two little girls. Their eyes." He sighs. "Whenever I go over there, they look at me like I killed their dad myself. And Patty, she tries to act like she doesn't blame me, or A.J., either, but I see how she looks at me when she doesn't think I can see her. She can't stand me now. I promised Ellis that if anything ever happened to him, I would look after all three of them. But they don't want to have anything to do with me, so that's a problem."

There is silence, as I try to figure out what to say that will be helpful, or at least not trite. Finally I say, "He asked you, not Aidan?"

"A.J. is flighty. You want him to have your back in a crisis, for sure, but for the long haul? Come on. You know how he is."

Do I? I'm not so sure. The many faces of Aidan James, that's him.

"Doesn't matter anyhow," J.C. says. "She doesn't want anything to do with A.J., either. After all, he made the decision to toss those slings over the cornice, instead of taking the time to anchor in. Not that that would've mattered, necessarily, given that the whole thing ripped loose, but we'll never know. She doesn't say it, but I know she blames him for not short-roping Ellis down, or not arresting earlier, before we fell all that way."

That gets my back up, no matter how much sympathy I have for Patty and her children. "How was he supposed to do that? He was falling, too, and Ellis had to weigh at least two hundred pounds. And you were passed out, pulling you and Aidan down. He couldn't do everything."

"Yeah," he says, staring into the depths of his coffee mug. "Fat lot of good I was. If it wasn't for A.J. finding some decent ice, we'd all be dead."

"Do *you* think he made a bad decision?"

He tips his mug left, then right, watching the contents swirl. "I think he did the best he could. Should he have anchored in? Maybe, but there's no way we could've known the cornice was going to come down, and no guarantee that the spot we anchored to would've held. Plus, when you're up there, you've gotta be confident, you know? When the shit hits the fan, you don't have time to take a consensus poll. It's afterward that the doubts set in—should I have done this? What if I'd done that? Especially when you have family members to deal with. And I can't say a goddamn thing. I didn't object when he decided to use the slings, and I sure as hell wasn't any help once I got knocked out. I was deadweight on the rope. If he hadn't arrested like he did, we'd all be at the bottom of that crevasse with Ellis. A.J. saved our lives."

"How did you pass out, anyway?" Aidan has never been too clear on that part.

"I hit my head," J.C. says. "There was rockfall everywhere, and I'm not sure whether that's what got me, or whether I just banged into the face somewhere. Either way, I was out for the count." An expression I can't define crosses his face—maybe regret. "Ellis was in bad shape. He had HACE—cerebral edema. A.J. told you this, right? We gave him oxygen, and a shot of Dex, but it didn't make shit difference. He came to enough to know what was happening to him. After, I thought maybe A.J. should've never given him that shot. Maybe it would've been kinder." He shivers. "That crevasse—I just remember coming to, and hanging there in the dark, trying to figure out where I was. I could see a thin line of light, and then I heard A.J. screaming. I'd never heard him sound like that before. He'd been at it for a while. His voice was hoarse. And I knew there was no one below me on the rope. I could feel it. I hauled it up, and the end was just frayed. Cut through. When I saw that, my heart sank."

"What happened, do you think?"

"No telling. But I'd guess the rope caught on something and got sliced, either right before we hit the crevasse or right after. A.J. says he could swear Ellis was still on it all the way down. He told me he could hear him hollering, and the rope jerked hard when we went in, like there was weight on it below me . . . and then it didn't seem so heavy to him, anymore." I wouldn't have believed J.C. could look pale, but he manages. "After A.J. got me out, he went down to look for Ellis, as far as he could. He called and called, but Ellis never answered. I didn't know how

I was going to get him out of there. He just wouldn't give up. And my head hurt so badly I could barely see." He stops talking then, and looks grim. "Too many things just went wrong," he says when he starts up again. "It was bad. A.J. and I hardly spoke to each other the whole way home." He shakes his head, and I can tell he's trying to shake the memory out of it. "I always say too much when I'm around you," he says, looking at me as if I somehow am coercing the information out of him.

"You want to talk about something else?" I offer.

"Sure. You pick." He turns and starts rifling through yesterday's mail, piled on the counter. My guess is that he wants to hide his face.

"How come you're home so early?" It's the most innocuous topic that comes to mind.

He slits open an envelope, swivels back to face me, and then examines the contents with disgust. "It started raining, so they let us go. We were at a good stopping point, anyhow. We'd gotten a whole floor down, and everything else we had to do was outside."

"You're working on a house?"

"A pretty damn fancy one. We're putting on an addition." He's still scrutinizing the paper he pulled out of the envelope, but now he looks more exasperated than anything else.

"What's the problem?" I ask, pouring the milk into the sink, which he hasn't gotten around to doing yet. I wrinkle my nose as it swirls down the drain. Crossing the kitchen, I lean against the counter next to J.C., who has stuffed the paper back into the envelope and is fanning himself with it. Come to think of it, it's pretty warm in here, especially for October. Colorado is having a heat wave.

"Oh, just A.J. He's supposed to pay the power bill, but he forgets. So now we're two months behind, and we owe about two hundred and fifty dollars. Fun stuff."

"He's not so good with that kind of thing," I agree.

"Nope." J.C. puts the envelope down on the top of the pile. "But he has other redeeming qualities, I guess." It comes out sounding like a question.

I'm not up to dealing with doublespeak. "Sure," I say. "Who doesn't?"

"Enough redeeming qualities for you to consider marrying him."

Crap. "He told you, huh?"

"Of course. He also told me you're taking your time, making up your mind. That's a good thing, in my book."

So he hasn't forgotten all that stuff he said. My heart starts pounding, which irritates me to no end. I feel like turning and walking out of the room. But this is J.C., who'd been so sweet to me when Aidan was outright cruel. Sure, if he's still interested in me, it's bound to be awkward . . . but I feel like I owe it to him to listen. I make myself stand still and look him in the eye.

"He's . . . not stable, Maddie. He doesn't settle down. I don't think he's good for you."

I take a swig of my coffee, wishing it were something stronger. Like tequila, for instance. "What do you mean?" I ask, even though I'm pretty sure I know. I'd gotten the same talk from Lucy, after I'd told her that Aidan had proposed. "He'll go off gallivanting halfway around the world, and what will you do?" she'd said. "Sit at home and take care of the kiddies? Worry yourself sick over whether he'll make it back? You'll spend half your time away from each other. What kind of marriage is that? Does he have some kind of Odysseus complex?" She'd given me her patented Glare of Death. "Marrying a crazy mountain man who wouldn't know the truth if it bit him on the ass, just because you're sick of living and dying by your Day-Timer? It seems a bit extreme."

I'd protested that I loved him, that I loved the way he made me feel. I'd told her that when Aidan touched me, when he turned the full weight of his eyes on me, when he told me about the places he'd gone and the things he'd done, I felt different, new. I felt like I'd been living in a box, and he'd broken it down, shown me the world outside. It was exhilarating, I told her.

Lucy had looked at me like I'd confessed a predilection for bestiality, and then stuffed her mouth full of Brie so she wouldn't say anything she'd regret. She'd still glared at me, though, kind of the way J.C. is glaring at me now. Maybe she is in league with him, for real. Maybe they have a little club.

"We've been friends for a long time, and we've been through some bad shit," J.C. says. "I'd trust him with my life, and I have, many times over. But there's a difference between that . . . and being a good husband." His dark eyes focus on mine. "Don't marry him, Maddie. He will break your heart."

The words are so dramatic—even if the tone is matter-of-fact—that I can't help but laugh. The look on J.C.'s face puts an end to that pretty quickly, though. He is dead serious.

Discomfort, combined with a sense of guilt, gets the best of me. "Well, if you don't want me to . . ." I let my voice trail off. "Of course I won't, then. Good thing you got to me in time."

My sarcasm has no effect on J.C. "It's not funny. He goes through women like they're going out of style. You could do so much better."

"How? By dating you?"

"For instance," he says, inflectionless.

Oh, boy. Now what? I try to hang on to my sense of irritation—directed more toward myself than toward him—so I won't wonder what it would be like to kiss him, to feel those big hands on me. I look away from him so I won't be tempted to imagine anything more specific than that.

"Just think about it," he says, so quietly I can hardly hear him.

I turn my head to tell him I don't need to think about it, that I have no intention of leaving Aidan for his best friend, re-gardless of whether I decide to marry him—how Jerry Springer can you get?—and our lips meet. The kiss is inquiring, like he is asking me a question—which I guess he is—but confident, too. He doesn't touch me, otherwise. He kisses like he talks, like we are carrying on a conversation. We're standing several inches apart and he doesn't make any effort to step closer. He keeps his hands in his pockets. Still, the heat builds between us in a way I didn't anticipate. I know I ought to break the kiss, to step back from him and let him have it, and I'm gathering the wherewithal to do just that when someone clears their throat a few feet away. It's not a happy sound.

"Well, well, well," says Aidan. "Having fun?"

SIXTEEN

Aidan

When she hears my voice, Maddie jumps back from J.C. like she's been electrocuted. Her eyes are wide, and spots of color are burning high up on her cheeks. Some of it's shock, sure, but not all. I've seen that look before. I've seen it when I kiss her, when I'm inside her. I hate him for putting that look on her face. And for just a second, I hate her for wanting him. Goddamn it. This is what happens when you let your guard down. Maybe they've been fucking the whole time, and I'm just now finding out.

Half of me wants to jump him. The other half wants to turn around and get on down the road. The two cancel each other out, and I just stand there, leaning against the doorway. They stare back at me, and I feel the rage drain out of my body. In its place, clarity floods in. I am focused. I feel nothing. There's only one other time that this has happened to me, and I don't care to be reminded of it. I breathe in, out. "What the fuck?" I say, level and cold.

"Hi," J.C. says. "We weren't expecting you quite so soon." We've known each other a long time, and I know he remembers the last time I sounded like this. From the way his body shifts in response, I can see he's gathering himself to fight.

"I don't know what the hell you think you're doing, but if you ever put so much as a finger on her again, I will kick your ass so hard you'll wish you were dead," I say. There is nothing in my voice but warning. He hears it, and so does she. Her eyes widen, and he steps in front of her, shielding her with his body. This little act of heroism pisses me off even more; I'm not going to hurt her, and he should know that. Better than anyone else, he knows I'd never hit a woman.

"Jealous, A.J.?" he says. "How does it feel?"

"What's your deal? Can't get a girlfriend of your own, so you have to borrow mine?" I ask. It comes out conversational, like I really want to know.

"I'm standing right here. And I'm not a library book," Maddie says from behind him. We both ignore her. Right now, this is between me and him.

"That would be a change," J.C. says. "Given how you've got a little tendency to borrow *mine*, and all."

"Borrow, hell. It's not my fault you don't have what it takes to keep a chick's interest for more than five minutes."

"How would you know? The moment someone showed the slightest bit of interest in me, you were all over them. Can't take a little competition, can you?"

So that's what this is about. He's using her to get back at

me. "Maybe I ought to ask you the same question," I say, and I let my contempt show in my eyes.

"Maybe if you treated Madeleine with a little common decency, competition would be out of the question," he says right back.

Great comeback from the guy who had his tongue in my girlfriend's mouth five minutes ago. "How I treat her is none of your business."

"You made it my business when you fucked around with Kate and I had to clean up your mess. As usual. The difference is, this time you screwed up a good thing. This whole situation is your fault. If you'd kept your dick in your pants for once, none of this would be happening. I guess I should thank you." He sounds calm, like we're discussing the best way to free a big wall instead of his plan to move in on the woman I intend to marry.

"Thank me for what?" I say, each syllable its own isolated continent.

"For giving me a chance to get to know Maddie, here." He smiles at her, and I don't like that smile. I don't like it at all. It's . . . proprietary, and anticipatory, and a bunch of other things that make me very uncomfortable.

"Don't you look at her like that," I say, and even I can hear the menace that laces my tone. My hands clench into fists at my sides. His eyes flick to them, then away.

"I don't think you get to pick and choose how I look at people, A.J. And last time I checked, Maddie was a free agent. After all, she hasn't said yes to you yet, has she? Ever wonder why that is?"

"Stop it, J.C.," Maddie says. "You're making it worse."

"I'm not the one who made things worse. That's all on your

boy here. And now he's got to deal with the consequences." He gestures at himself, then at her.

"There are no consequences. This was a *mistake*. J.C., I'm not mad at you or anything, but you know as well as I do that this shouldn't have happened."

Truth, or a desperate attempt to restore equilibrium before It All Goes to Hell? I look from one of them to the other, wondering if he's making this shit up, or if she's really trying to figure out which one of us she wants to be with. That would be seriously messed up. I've never pegged her for a liar. She isn't the type, and I'm usually a pretty good judge of character. But she did kiss him back, and who the hell knows what else would've happened if I hadn't come in when I did? If I'd gotten here five minutes later, would he have been fucking her on the countertop? I visualize it for a second, and a red haze clouds my vision. Blood roars in my ears.

"Maybe it shouldn't have happened right at this moment. I'll give you that," J.C. says. "But that doesn't mean it shouldn't have happened at all."

Maddie doesn't respond, either because she agrees with him or because she has no idea how to reply. As for me, I'm done with his bullshit. He's baiting me, and I'm sick of it. "What are you trying to say?" I ask him, stepping through the doorway and into the kitchen.

"I just don't get why you think you deserve Maddie. You lead her on. You have the emotional availability of a hermit crab. Then you cheat on her, to her face, and don't even have the good manners to come out and apologize. Next you take off for two months and never call, email, or anything. Then you show back up after Ellis dies and dump your guts all over her. Why she hasn't told you to take a hike is beyond me."

"Again, standing right here," she says. "Capable of having my own opinions."

"Stay out of this, Maddie," I say. I know what he's trying to do. He's trying to provoke me, so he can control when I come at him. Well, two can play that game. "Step back," I say to her. I don't expect her to listen, but to my surprise she does, backing up against the dishwasher. "And you, motherfucker," I say to J.C. "You keep your hands off her and your opinions to yourself."

"I don't blame you completely, A.J. It's not like you had a great role model or anything."

A spark of rage flares through the coldness that's penetrated my limbs. "That's low," I say. My lips feel numb.

"It's the truth," he says, each word like a javelin. "After everything, you've turned out just like your old man, haven't you? I guess the apple doesn't fall far from the tree."

I stare at him, dumbfounded. Of all the things he could have said to me, this is probably the worst, and he knows it. We're in suspended animation for a moment, a fucked-up little triumvirate. Then I launch myself at him and take him down. We roll over and over on the dirty floor, knocking over the kitchen chairs and winding up against one of the cabinets. I'm on top, beating the crap out of him. He knees me in the stomach, then he punches me in the face. Can't have that. I get to my knees and pin his shoulders to the ground. "Take it back," I say.

"Fuck you," he says, and then he turns his head and bites me on the arm. It breaks the skin, and I watch a thin red line trickle down my forearm, onto my hand.

"I'm bleeding, you bastard," I say, grabbing him by the hair.

"Serves you right."

"Take it back. Take it back or I swear to God I'll smash your head right into the floor."

"Go ahead," he says, and he spits in my face. I keep my promise, pounding his head into the linoleum.

"Ow, goddamn it. Get off me, you nutcase!" He twists to get out of my grip, and when that doesn't work, the next time I lift his head off the floor, he uses the momentum to head-butt me in the face. My nose starts spurting blood. I can feel it trickling into my mouth, but the pain seems miles away.

"Take it back," I say again.

"What in particular would you like me to take back? The part about how you don't deserve Maddie? Or the part about how you screw everything that moves?"

"You know what part," I say. "Take it back and I'll let you up."

"And if I don't?"

"I guess we'll just have to find out," I say, and I smile at him through the blood. It can't be pretty, but he doesn't flinch.

"Come on, A.J. I don't feel like getting any more messed up than I already am. I'm going to have a hell of a headache. And I may have broken your nose."

Mr. Reasonable. "It's not broken."

"Whatever."

I shake him so hard I can hear his teeth rattle. "Quit it," he says.

"I'm nothing like him," I say, but there's a part of me that wonders if that's really the truth. I've managed to silence that little voice for a very long time, and I'm not happy that it's speaking up again. It took me a bunch of years and a lot of distance to put it to sleep.

"Whatever you say." He says it like he knows better.

"I'm not."

"Fine." He raises his legs from behind me, gets them around my throat, and pulls. I fall backward, hitting the floor, and he climbs on top of me and starts trying to mangle my face. I return the favor by attempting to choke him.

Unfortunately, Maddie picks this moment to intervene. "Stop it," she says. "This is ridiculous." She comes over to us and crouches down. "Stop it," she says, louder. She grabs his shoulder and he shakes her off. He's distracted, and I take the opportunity to deck him. The problem is, she gets in the way. I end up punching her in the ribs instead. She falls backward, slamming into the refrigerator with a spectacular crash.

That ends the fight. J.C. rolls off me, and we both stare at her. I turn my head sideways and spit blood onto the floor. "Are you okay?" I ask her.

"Yeah, I think so." She rubs her side. "It was more the surprise than anything else."

"Nice going," J.C. says.

"I'm really sorry," I tell her, and I am. I promised myself I would never hit a woman. Of all the shitty stuff I've done—lying, cheating, blah blah blah—that's never been among my faults. Nice to know I can add another one to the list, even if it was an accident.

"I know you didn't mean to do it," she says.

I get up and extend a hand to her, pulling her to her feet. Now J.C. is the only one on the floor, so he stands up, too. For a second he looks like he's going to make another smart-ass comment, but he manages to restrain himself. "Excuse me," he says in the polite voice he uses to hide what he's really feeling. That's just fine with me. I have no interest in knowing what's on his mind. I've heard quite enough for today.

We move, and he opens the freezer door, pulling out two bags of peas. He tosses one to me and presses the other one up against his eye.

"I'm going outside," he says in that same empty voice. "It's too crowded in here by half." He walks to the patio door, yanks it open, and stalks out. He's getting wet, but it's clear he doesn't give a shit. I watch him as he collapses into a chair, turns his face up to the rain. He closes his eyes and lets the water stream down his cheeks, washing away the blood, and I turn to Maddie.

SEVENTEEN

Nicholas

I am officially drunk by the time we walk into the club, which is jumping. Citizen Cope comes over the speakers and Grace pulls me onto the crowded dance floor.

"I've always wondered what the lyrics to this song are," she says into my ear. "'Let the drama kid die'? 'Let the drunk kid drive'?"

I smile. "I remember song lyrics, Grace. Would you like me to enlighten you?"

"How is that possible?" she asks me.

"I told you this before. If you need a pop culture reference, I'm your man. It's only my personal history that eludes me."

"Awesome," she says, total Valley Girl again.

"You want to know the lyrics, or not?"

"Please."

"'Let the drummer kick that,'" I tell her. "It's the name of the song. Well, the name of the song is 'Let the Drummer Kick,' but you get the idea."

"Aren't you useful," she says. "Let's see if you move as well as you talk." Then we are dancing, her arms around my neck. I spin her and she comes back to me laughing. She turns her back and presses against me; I put my arms around her from behind and we move to the music. Citizen Cope segues into Coldplay into old-school Kimball Collins. I shake my head and sweat flies everywhere, onto her arms, her face. Her hair is down now and it has a life of its own. It streams out behind her, it covers me.

I go to the bar for more whisky and when I come back, she is dancing by herself in the middle of the floor, eyes closed. All of the men and some of the women are staring. I thread my way to her and take her in my arms, dip her low to the ground. She doesn't open her eyes; she recognizes me, she trusts me, which is more than I can say for myself. My own eyes sting with sweat. We dance until the club closes for the night.

Grace drives us home afterward, lets us inside. Nevada is waiting by the door. He greets us with abandon and receives the pats that are his due. I let him out to pee and he obliges, then gallops off to get a bone from the stash in his basket. Back in the living room, I lean against the wall, willing the furniture to stop spinning.

Grace is taking off her boots. I look at her through half-lidded eyes. "Were those comfortable to dance in?"

"Kind of," she says. "More or less." Then she smiles. "No."

"Well, I couldn't tell. You were like a superstar tonight. Like Wonder Woman, for real. All you needed was the Lasso of

Truth, the indestructible bracelets, and the plane, and the illusion would have been complete." I grin at her from where I'm holding up the wall.

"Maybe next time we go dancing, I'll wear the costume."

"Is that a promise?"

She comes closer, so close I could reach out and touch her if I were so inclined—which, I reprimand myself, I am not. The dance floor was one thing. My living room at 3 A.M. is another situation entirely. "Admit it. You think I'd be hot in a Wonder Woman suit," she whispers into my ear.

"I think you're hot no matter what you wear," I admit. Whew. No more whisky for me.

She steps back, giggles. "Really?"

"Really." I hold her gaze. The tension from this afternoon is back. It fills the air between us. So much for needing the Lasso of Truth; in my case, all that's required is a substantial amount of alcohol, and I will say just about anything.

"Then why won't you make love to me?" Her eyes lock on mine now, uncompromising, and I know I need to tell her the truth—at least enough of it. She deserves that much.

I dig for the words. "Grace, I would be using you. Because you . . . you love me, or at least the version of me you remember. And I . . ." My voice trails off. What can I say? There is the obvious, the part she knows—that our time together is a blank, that as far as my memory goes, we met for the first time a month ago. And then there is the rest of it, the part she does not need to hear—that there is someone else, someone I have never met. Someone whose name I do not even know. Yeah, that would really brighten her day. Not to mention how crazy she'd think I am. "I'm not worth it," is what I come up with. I look down at my Pumas, which is fast becoming my signature move.

She takes my hand, steps closer. "Why don't you let me decide that?"

Burying my face in her neck, I try to hold this moment still in my mind and see Grace, just her. No mountain, no small boy, no laughing sunlit woman. Just Grace.

She turns, twines her arms around my neck, and presses her lips to mine. For a moment I respond. Then, as clearly as if he is standing next to me, I hear his voice. *No*, he says. *You don't want to do this.*

In that moment I don't know whether I do or whether I don't. What I do know is that I *can't*. I feel like I've been doused in ice water—shocked, and freezing. I've never heard that voice outside of my dreams before, but it is unmistakably his: low, musical, insistent. Maybe I am losing it now, for real—the last remnants of my life, absorbed into his. Either way, I don't feel like having Grace stick around to watch me fall apart.

"I *can't*, Grace." I unwind her fingers from around my neck, step away. I am shaking.

Hurt flashes across her face, like I have slapped her. "You don't want me," she says.

"That's not it. You must know that."

"Then what?"

"I can't do this with you. It isn't right."

She steps close again, touches my face. I can feel the hot imprint of each of her fingers on my cheekbone, a brand. Looking into the clear green of her eyes, I have a moment of doubt: Who would it hurt? I run my hands down her neck, over her breasts, daring him to interfere. She stands still for me, a statue under my fingers. I am so tired of being good. She is here. For some inexplicable reason, she wants to be with me. Where is the harm?

You know better. I can hear his familiar voice now, not angry but patient, like a teacher addressing a student. It infuriates me. Who is he to tell me what to do? Who the hell is he anyway? I have been so fucking lonely.

I braid my hands into Grace's hair, press her into the wall, cover her mouth with mine. It would be so easy to be inside her, so simple. And it has been so long.

This is a mistake. Not his voice but my own, more confident than I have heard it in a long time. It takes me a moment to realize I have spoken aloud; she freezes against me. Her eyes go wide.

"You need to go, Grace. I'm sorry." I step back from her, sit down on the edge of the couch. Desire fills my body like an ache, twined with regret. I must be crazy. I am a goddamn lunatic.

She runs a hand through her hair, straightens her dress, before she speaks. "Fuck you, Nicholas," is all she says.

I stare at the floor.

"Are you even going to look at me? Could you do me that courtesy?" Pure ice.

I look up. Her eyes are red-rimmed now, glassy with tears, but she glares at me as if she would like to bite. There is probably something I could say to make this better, but I have no idea what it is, and right now I am too tired to care.

I am prepared for her to do anything—throw something, swear at me some more, leave like I asked her to—except for what she does next, which is get on her knees, right there on my dirty hardwood floor. "What do you need me to do? Do you want me to beg?" Her hair falls all around her, cascades over the dress. It covers her breasts. She looks like a mermaid.

"Get up, Grace." I am horrified.

"I don't care that you don't remember." Now she has my hands in hers. She is pleading. "We can start over. Whatever you want. Just don't do this."

"Grace, please get up."

She doesn't move. She kneels there, between my legs, holding my hands in hers. She looks into my face like she can make my memory come back by sheer force of will. She is looking at me like she loves me.

But I am looking through her, to the other side. Whatever is waiting for me, it isn't here.

"Grace," I say. She gazes up expectantly. In her face I can see her faith in me. It hits me like a sucker punch. A wave of envy breaks over me, for the man I was before all of this happened—a man with an unbroken chain of memories. *This*, and then *this*, and *this*. A past with Grace, and a future. A life like a line.

But then I think back to my dream, the feeling of surprise as I cupped air to my face under the crushing weight of the snow, and I wonder whether that man was so lucky after all. For the first time, I wonder if I have been given a gift.

Grace pulls one hand free, rests it on my thigh. She trails her nails along my skin and I shiver. Desire sparks deep in my body, spreads through my limbs, but I don't move. Instead, I study her face like a map: where I have been, where I am going. I close my eyes and imagine sliding the dress to the floor, disappearing into her heat. She wouldn't fight me.

It is the mountain all over again, that moment where I am suspended between *before* and *after*. I shake my head, the tiniest of movements. My eyes burn.

"Nick." There is wonder in her tone. "Are you crying?"

I open my eyes, look at her. Sure enough, she is blurry, obscured by a thin veil of water. I take my hand out of hers, swipe the back of it across my face. It comes away wet.

"I'm sorry." It is a plea, a prayer. "Grace, I am so sorry. Believe me. Please."

"I've never seen you cry before," she says.

This is proof, as if I needed any more. "I'm not the guy you want, Grace. I'm not him."

With her free hand, she reaches up and traces my face, a pattern. It takes me a moment to realize she is following the trail of my tears. Her eyes on mine, she puts her fingers into her mouth, circles them with her tongue.

"This isn't a good idea," I say to her—a reminder and a warning.

"St. Nicholas," she spits at me. "When did you get so goddamn pious?"

But I am no saint.

In her eyes I see more than she means me to: her anger, sure, but beneath it the wreckage of broken promises and dreams destroyed. I see her pride and her stubbornness, her creeping sorrow. Beneath all of this runs a thin but steady stream of hope.

The hell with him. Let him try to stop me.

I lower myself off the couch, so I am kneeling with her, and place my hand on her face, feeling her pale skin heat beneath my palm. With my other hand, I lift the silken weight of her hair off her neck. I bring my mouth to the nape of her neck and graze it with my teeth, then bite, hard enough to break the skin. A thin line of blood wells up when I move my mouth away.

She inhales sharply but doesn't move, even when I look in her eyes, a dare. I pull her to her feet, unzip her dress with my teeth, peel it to her waist. She stands like a child while I push it to the ground. I realize with a start that she is naked beneath the dress. In the moonlight, she shines like a goddess.

She steps out of the dress and I kneel on it, run my lips down her belly. I probe her with my tongue, searching, until she gasps and grips my hair. "I love you, Nicholas," she whispers.

"Grace," I answer, just that. And I take off my shirt, unbutton my shorts, toss them and my boxers on the floor next to me. I stand with her, press my body against hers, bend my head to take her nipples in my mouth. I flick them with my tongue, I bite them lightly. She calls my name, and I pick her up, wrap her legs around me, slip inside as if I have done it many times before—which, of course, I have. My body knows her, even if I do not.

Against the wall I drive into her, again and again. The static in my mind recedes, and there is just Grace. Her hair is all over me, in my mouth, in my eyes. Her legs tighten against my back, she cries out. Now she is the one who is shaking. Good.

"Did he touch you like this?" I say to her. "Did he make you feel this way?"

We fall to the floor. Her heat is everywhere, enclosing me, gripping me. I find the arm of the dress, make a blindfold. I cover her eyes, pull out of her, rake her body with my tongue. "Who?" she says. She reaches down, grips me, slides her hand through the wetness that is hers. It is almost too much; I arch over her, into her. We move like we were made for it until I rip the blindfold free.

"Look at me, Gracie," I say, and she obeys.

"Who am I?" I say to her.

But she has no answer.

"Be free," I whisper against her neck, my voice too low for her to hear.

My eyes on hers, I finish what I started. We come together, but even as she calls my name and cries out, digging her nails into my back, I am already gone.

EIGHTEEN

Madeleine

The sliding glass door to the patio clicks shut after J.C. gives it a good yank—I'd forgotten how stubborn it used to be—and Aidan and I are on our own. "I'm sorry I hit you," he says again. He holds the bag of peas to his jaw, and winces.

"It was an accident," I say. "I'm sorry that happened with J.C."

"The fight? Or that you kissed him?"

"Both. And it may not be a distinction worth making, but he actually kissed me."

Aidan shifts the peas to his temple. He is silent, which makes me nervous. After a moment he says, "I can't talk about this now. I can't think right."

"Okay," I say, in the absence of a better response.

"I need a drink," he says. "And some space. I need to calm down."

"Okay," I say again. Swept with regret, I reach out to touch him, but he steps backward, out of my reach. His face is a careful blank.

"I have to get out of here," he says.

And he walks out the door.

That just figures. It fits Aidan's MO: When in doubt, run away. Which leaves me . . . where? Standing in his kitchen, still on my first cup of coffee, alone with J.C. once again. Fabulous.

Speaking of the devil, I have some choice words for him. I right the two chairs that are lying on their side, just to give myself some time to think, and then walk out to the patio. It is still drizzling, but J.C. is sitting in a blue lawn chair as if he doesn't notice, the bag of frozen peas pressed up against his cheek. His long legs are stretched out in front of him, crossed at the ankles. His feet are bare. It doesn't look like he's planning on going anywhere anytime soon.

He doesn't say anything when I come out. In fact, he's humming, a tune that I eventually identify as the Beatles' "Hard Day's Night." After a while he says, "A.J. leave?" without looking at me.

"Yes," I say, and he inclines his head.

"Figures," he says.

"Anything broken?" I ask him, purely to be polite.

"Uh-uh. Just my pride, maybe."

"Too bad."

"You don't mean that," he says.

"Try me." Maybe we're just going to speak in monosyllables for the rest of the afternoon. That'll be fun.

"I didn't mean to cause that much drama. But it would've happened sooner or later. I wasn't just going to . . . not say anything."

"Why the hell not? Or if you had to say something, fine. You didn't have to kiss me."

"I'm sorry," he says, and some of the bravado runs out of his tone. "I don't know what got into me."

I don't, either. I hadn't pegged J.C. as the type of guy who would start a fight with anyone, much less the guy who'd been his closest friend since high school. "You're getting wet," I tell him, to avoid saying anything with more import. It is only drizzling, but that's enough to mat his short brown hair and streak the blood on his cheeks—which, come to think of it, is probably Aidan's, not his. He looks bedraggled, and tired.

"So are you. At least, I assume." Taking the bag of peas off his cheek, he turns around to give me the full benefit of his face. "But it kind of feels nice, all things considered."

I gasp; I can't help myself. He looks awful. His jaw is bruised, and one of his eyes is turning black. As for his lip, it has stopped bleeding and started to swell.

"That good, huh?"

"You look terrible. I hope it was worth it."

He uncrosses his ankles. "I'll let you know in a couple of years."

"Can I ask you something?" Ignoring the rain—not to mention his comment—I pull up the chair next to his.

"Go ahead," he says, putting the peas back, this time on his eye. He doesn't sound curious, just exhausted.

"What you said about Aidan and his dad—what did it mean?"

He shoots me a sharp look with the eye I can see. "He hasn't told you?"

I shake my head. "I mean, I knew there was—something. But he'd never get specific, so I just left it alone. I figured he'd say something when he felt like it."

"Which will be never," J.C. says.

"He told *you*," I say, feeling just a tad bit whiny.

"Babe, I was there. He had no choice."

Babe? "It must be bad, then."

J.C. doesn't say anything for a minute. He shifts the peas to his jaw, stares into the rain. Finally he says, "It's not pretty. And to be fair, it does explain a fair amount of why he's the way he is. But I shouldn't have said what I did. That was shitty of me." He winds down then, looking uncomfortable. Talking so much, with his mouth the way it is, can't feel good.

"What happened?" I ask. I know it isn't right; I know I should wait for Aidan to tell me. But I've had enough of secret-keeping.

He gives me the eye again. "Nuh-uh. No way. I'm not getting in any more trouble. If A.J. wants you to know, he can tell you his damn self."

"But—"

"But me no *buts*, little girl. My lips are sealed. Or they would be, if my jaw didn't hurt so much."

"Fine," I say after a moment. "I'll just go look for Aidan, then."

"Be my guest," he says, leaning back in the chair again.

With a sigh of annoyance, I get to my feet and walk back inside. I grab my purse from Aidan's room and head for the front door, with no good idea of where I'm going. As it turns out, I don't have to go very far. He is sitting on the front steps, smoking a cigarette. Between the fighting, the climbing, and Aidan's smoking, it will be a miracle if he and J.C. live to see thirty. "Hey," he says when I open the front door. He doesn't turn.

"Hey," I say in response, and sit down on the step next to him. All I can see is his profile, and it looks battered. He has a darkening bruise just below his left eye and another one high on his cheekbone. He's gotten most of the blood off his face, and miraculously, his nose doesn't seem to be broken; it looks just like normal. His arm, however, is another story. It bears a perfect set of J.C.'s teethmarks.

"Nice, right?" he says, swiveling to face me.

"You've looked better," I say, shifting my weight in an effort to get comfortable. The rain has stopped, but the step is still damp.

"Thanks a lot," he says. "I've felt better, too."

Silence falls between us for a moment, while I try to figure out where to go from here. On the plus side of things, he isn't yelling. Then again, he doesn't look happy, either.

"I didn't expect—" I begin, just as he says, "The thing is—" We pause, stymied. He says, "Go ahead."

"I was just going to say that I didn't expect you to be out here."

"I didn't expect myself to stick around, either. But I'm sick of running. It gets old."

"So you're not mad?" I find that one pretty hard to swallow.

"I didn't say that. But I think maybe I overreacted, getting into that fight with J.C. I wouldn't have hit him if he hadn't started saying that shit about my father. Maybe I should have given you a chance to explain yourself before I went crazy, but I just snapped and that was the end of it."

"Aidan," I say. "You just walked in on me kissing your best

friend. Well, he kissed me, but that's beside the point. I think you had a right to be angry."

He smiles at me, that crooked smile that always tugs at my heart. "Honey, I'm the last one to be throwing a fit because someone I'm with kissed another person. And I'm the first one to know that things aren't always the way they seem."

I gape at him. "Have you had a personality transplant?"

Still smiling, he shakes his head. "I'm trying to do better, Maddie. I want to be someone you're proud to be with, not someone you need to make excuses for." He takes my hand, twining his fingers through mine. We watch people pass by: a mother and her daughter, clad in identical yoga outfits; a small boy learning to ride his bike without training wheels, followed by his father; an older couple, arm in arm, strolling on the sidewalk. After a bit he says, "So, you want to tell me what happened?"

"It was like I said, Aidan. We were just standing there, talking, and then he kissed me. I guess I should've stopped him right away, but he took me by surprise. And then you walked in, with spectacularly bad timing."

"Or spectacularly good timing," he says, staring straight ahead.

"How do you mean?"

"If I hadn't come in when I did, who knows what might have happened?"

"*I* know," I say. "Nothing. I would've stepped away from him and told him to quit it."

"And would you have told me what he did?"

That is a harder one. "Probably, just because I would've felt too guilty otherwise."

"Hmmm," he says, stroking my palm with his thumb. "Interesting. So he just kissed you, right out of nowhere?"

"Not out of nowhere," I admit. Here comes the part I've been trying to avoid.

"Go on."

"We were talking . . . about how he thought that you weren't good enough for me, basically. He said he would trust you with his life, that you were a great person to have in a crisis, but that you were . . . what did he call it? Flaky, over the long haul, and not husband material." That about sums it up.

Aidan doesn't say anything, and I hazard a glance at his face to see how he is taking this. He looks thoughtful. "Was this the first time he'd said something like this to you?"

"After you . . . after Kate, he kind of hinted that if we weren't together, he'd be interested, but he never tried to kiss me or anything. I thought he was just being nice to me, to cheer me up, since I was so upset. I didn't realize that he was still thinking about it, until today. Maybe it was the whole marriage proposal thing that got him going."

He says nothing.

"Are we okay, Aidan?"

"I think so." His voice is calm. "I've been out here for a while, trying not to lose my shit. And what I came up with . . . well, I did mess around on you, Maddie. I'm not going to do it again, and it's not like the kind of thing you can make even, I know that. But it makes me feel better, somehow, that you're not . . . how can I say this? Perfect, pure as the driven snow, whereas I have this mammoth strike against me. Does that make sense? It makes us feel more equal, to me anyway."

"So the fact that J.C. and I kissed makes you feel better about our relationship?" That is some twisted logic, right there.

"In a weird way, yes. Am I still mad? Yeah, at J.C. mostly. Do I wish it hadn't happened? Sure. Do I have some serious issues with him over it? You can put money on that, although he's right, I've done some shitty things to him over the years and this has been a long time coming. He and I will be okay, though. We understand each other."

"I don't get it. If you kissed Jos or Lucy, I'd be furious with both of you."

"Don't get me wrong. I'm not happy about it. But shit happens, honey. No one knows that better than I do. What kind of hypocrite would I be if I asked you to forgive me for having sex with Kate, but I couldn't handle you kissing someone else, even if it was J.C.?"

"You're being way too understanding about this," I say warily.

"The shoe's usually on the other foot. I'm kind of enjoying being the wronged party for once." He runs his hand through his hair. "Can I ask you something?"

"Me? Sure. What do you want to know?"

"What J.C. said before," he begins, his tone guarded.

"Which thing he said?" But I am pretty sure I know what Aidan means.

"About how you haven't said yes to me because of . . ." He trails off, swallows hard. "Because of feelings you have for him. Is it true?"

"Aidan. You think I'd be dating you if I was in love with your best friend? That's kind of tacky, to say the least."

"I didn't say you were in love with him," he says. "Just that maybe you had some feelings for him that went beyond friendship. You kissed him back, Maddie. I was standing right there. I can tell the difference."

I choose my words carefully. "I like J.C. very much. He's smart, he's kind, and he's interesting in some of the same ways that you are . . . the climbing, the traveling, all the experiences I haven't had. I enjoy talking with him. He's a good conversationalist, and he really came through for me that time when you got together with Kate. He's a great guy. I can see why you're such good friends. But you're the one I want to be with, not him."

"Okay. I can buy that. And believe it or not, I'm not asking because I'm jealous—or not totally, anyway."

Confused, I peer at him. "Why are you asking, then?"

He rubs his jaw. "Now it's my turn to ask you not to get mad at me."

"Why would I get mad?" Truth be told, I am already more than a little on edge. For one thing, talking about J.C. wasn't all that comfortable for me. And for another, anytime someone tells you not to get mad, you can be pretty sure that something you don't want to hear is coming next.

"This is a strange thing to say, I guess. But I just . . . how can I put this? If something happens to me, I want you to know . . . You could do worse than J.C., is what I'm saying. He would be good to you."

For a second I say nothing, as the implications of what he said settle in. Then I say, "Have you gone *crazy*?" so emphatically my voice squeaks on the last two syllables.

"Don't get all freaked out, Maddie. I'm just trying to be realistic."

"Realistic? By passing me on to your best friend? Chauvinistic, more likely!" My voice rises in pitch and decibel level with each successive sentence.

"Maddie. Calm down. I'm not passing you on to anyone. I've just lost too many friends. I want to know you're . . . that there's someone who loves you, if something happens to me." He sounds absolutely composed, and absolutely serious.

"Are you planning on having something happen to you?"

"Of course not. Don't be ridiculous."

"So when were you planning to tell J.C. about this plan of yours? Or have you already told him, and he thought he'd make good on it a little early?"

"It's not a plan. And I don't . . . I wouldn't tell J.C.," he says, ignoring my accusation. "I just want you to know. I wouldn't want you to do something and then . . . feel bad."

I slide away from him on the step. "Let me get this straight. We're not even engaged, but you already have yourself dead and buried, and me carrying on a torrid affair with J.C., who by that point could be married with five kids. You must think I'm pretty enterprising."

"It's not you," he says, and he sounds as if he wishes he could sink through the step himself, to the house's foundation and beyond. "Forget it. I wish I'd never said anything."

"That makes two of us."

"Forget it. Really," he says.

"You say that like it's a possibility. Honestly, Aidan. You can't just put something like that out there and expect me not to react."

"I'm sorry, Maddie. It was stupid. Change of subject. I'm guessing you want to know why I got so pissed off when J.C. said that thing about my dad, huh?"

"That would be nice."

His eyes scan my features like he is trying to make up his mind about something. Then he says, "Okay," and gets to his feet, holding out his hand to help me up.

"Let's go somewhere," he says.

. . .

We drive for about twenty minutes. Aidan leaves his hand on my knee, only removing it to change gears. Just as I'm about to accuse him of kidnapping me, he pulls off the highway and into a small town, dotted with coffee shops and places to purchase outdoor gear. He edges the Jeep down a narrow side street, whips it into a parking spot, and cuts the engine.

"Come on," he says.

I look around doubtfully. "Where are we going?"

He takes in my expression and laughs. "Not far. There's a trail right there, and a little ways down, there's the river. Don't worry, even you couldn't trip and fall."

Aidan is as good as his word. The trail is wide and clearly marked, and it opens up into a path along the banks of a meandering body of water—as much as water in Colorado ever meanders. On the other side of the river, the cliffs rise tall and imposing against the horizon. We are the only people there, which doesn't surprise me; it is nearing dinnertime on Saturday night, after all, and this place isn't easy to find.

We walk along the grassy bank of the river until Aidan locates a spot that is flat and relatively rock-free. He steps close to me, so that I have to look up at him to see his face. There is an expression in his eyes I've never seen there before; it takes me a moment to realize it is fear.

I'm about to ask him what he's thinking when he says, "I love you," and kisses me with a fierceness that takes me by surprise. His hands move in my hair, and his body urges me downward, onto the riverbank. He presses me into the grass.

"Aidan," I say against his lips. This doesn't seem like such a good idea, for about a thousand reasons. For one thing, I haven't been back on the Pill for a solid month, and we don't have any protection with us—as far as I know. For another, as isolated as this place seems, it isn't like we can hang up a Do Not Disturb sign.

"Please, Maddie," he says, reaching between us to unbutton my jeans and push them down to my ankles. He strokes me roughly, his fingers taking up an unmistakable rhythm as they slide inside. Then he kisses his way down the length of my body, replacing his fingers with his lips and then his tongue. He is very talented in this department, and it is all I can do not to scream.

"But what if someone comes?" I whisper, settling on propriety as the simplest excuse, while I still have the use of at least some of my higher mental functions.

"They won't," he says. He has his shorts unbuttoned now, and he kicks them and his boxers off. He slides my jeans and my underwear into the grass. "Let me be inside you," he says, and he pushes up my T-shirt, unhooks my bra, and lowers his head to my breasts. He bites me, hard enough to leave a mark. "Please," he says again. He is shaking.

The bite ought to make me angry, but it has the opposite effect. My body responds to it, arching into his mouth. He pulls away, and I try again. "But, Aidan, what about a condom? What if something happens?"

His hair brushes my cheekbones as he bends to kiss me. "If it does, it does. You're who I want." He runs his fingers over my thigh, then pushes them inside me again, hard enough so that if I weren't ready, it would hurt. But I am, and it doesn't.

I raise my hips, an invitation. "Okay," I whisper, even as a small part of my brain is trying to figure out where I am in my cycle, whether this is such a good idea after all.

He is inside me before I finish speaking. "Tell me you love me," he says, his mouth against my ear. He outlines my earlobe with his tongue, grazes it with his teeth, then covers my mouth with his. When I open my eyes to look at him, he is staring right back at me. He takes my face in his hands, holding my gaze all the while, and kisses me like he'll never have the chance to do it again.

"I love you," I say when he lets me breathe.

He rolls me on top of him and holds my hips. "Not as much as I love you," he says. "But I can deal with that." And then he starts moving me, faster and faster, and he doesn't talk anymore.

Afterward, we reassemble our clothes and sit on the riverbank, his arm around me. "Where did that come from?" I ask, leaning against him.

"I don't know. You make me feel good, Maddie. You center me. And I was feeling very uncentered, all of a sudden." He smiles, but I can see the apprehension in his eyes.

"Why are you so nervous?"

His arm tightens around me. "I don't like talking about my dad. Number one, when I talk about it it's like I have to go through it all over again, which is no fun. And number two, I'm ashamed."

"Is it that bad?"

"It feels that way to me. The only people who know about it are the ones who were close to me back then, like J.C. It's not exactly good party conversation." He takes a big gulp of air. I feel him steady. "All right," he says. "I'm ready now."

NINETEEN

Nicholas

We lie there for a while in silence. Grace gazes up at me with perfect trust, her hair spread out around her on the floor. She looks more like a mermaid than ever. And I feel like a prick. Fitting.

"Are you all right?" she says.

I force a smile. "Great." In my head I hear his voice: *I told you this was a mistake.* He isn't gloating. He sounds sad. And for the first time I don't fight him. I let him in. *I'm not arguing*, I answer. *But what else could I do?* I wait for him to say something else, but he doesn't. Looks like I'm on my own.

"I missed you so much," Grace says. Her voice is full of gratitude and something else—triumph, maybe? It strikes a false note, and I file it away to think about later, when I need ammunition to convince myself that I'm not the villain here. She seduced me, I think, and laugh.

"What is it?" She traces the small smile on my lips with one finger.

"Nothing," I lie. She waits for me to go on, and I expound with the first thing that comes to mind: "This whole situation is funny, I guess." I gesture at the trail of our clothes, at us on the floor. "Funny bizarre, I mean, not funny ha ha."

"In a good way or a bad way?" she says.

"What do you think?" When in doubt, answer a question with a question.

"Are you kidding? It's what I wanted more than anything, to be close to you again. Although I have to say, it was more energetic than usual." Her tone turns light; she is teasing me. Ah, safer ground.

"Are you telling me we'd grown stale in our old age?"

"Not stale, just . . . when you're with someone for a long time, you know, you fall into patterns. He does this, you do that. This was different."

I don't say anything, and after a minute she peeks up at me from under her lashes. "Did I offend you?"

"Don't be ridiculous, Gracie. It's not like I remember being boring with you. To me, you're all new."

"You still don't remember anything, then."

"No," I admit.

She plays with her hair. "It's stupid, I know, but I'd kind of hoped that if we were together, that maybe everything would come back. Isn't that dumb?"

"I don't think so. In fact, I'd kind of hoped the same thing. You know"—I do my best Huey Lewis and the News—"*that's the power of love.*"

She grimaces. "How is it that you can remember cheesy song lyrics from the eighties, but our entire relationship is just—poof!—down the tubes?"

"It's a mystery. I wish I knew."

Disappointment flashes across her face, but then she reaches for me. "In that case, let me remind you." She winds her arms around my neck and kisses me. What the hell, the damage is done. I pull her on top of me. Her hair comes down over us both, hiding us. Her skin is hot on mine. I close my eyes and let happen what will.

Afterward, we get up and I let Nevada out. He wanders around the backyard, peeing on an azalea, while I take stock of myself. Guilt has not yet set in. Instead, I feel relaxed and clear. The night is sultry and humid, just a slight breeze. I lean on the railing of the deck, waiting for him to finish up. My pack of cigarettes sits abandoned on the table; I light one and blow smoke rings into the night.

The deck boards creak behind me. Grace is standing there, a glass of water in one hand, wearing one of my T-shirts. "Boo," she says. She runs her nails down my bare back and I shiver.

"Hey." I twist away from her. "That tickles."

She gives me a quizzical look. "You were never ticklish . . . before."

I answer without thinking. "There are a lot of things about me that aren't the same, Grace."

"I know that," she says.

"Do you?"

"I'll take whatever version of you I can get," she says. "It doesn't have to be exactly like it was."

"Why do you want me, Gracie?" I have never asked her this so directly before.

She sinks into one of the green plastic deck chairs. "Jesus, Nicholas."

"I'm serious."

"I know you are." Irritation has crept into her voice.

"It seems like a fair question to me. I don't remember anything about our life together. I don't remember you. I'm lucky I know how to dress myself in the morning, for God's sake. I'm moody as hell all the time and I've done the best job I know how to push you away. Yet here you are."

"Here I am," she echoes, and she sounds rueful.

"Did you ever think you'd be better off giving up?" I try to say it gently, but it comes out like a challenge instead.

"Do you *want* me to go?" Her voice shakes.

This is my chance to end it once and for all, but I am too much of a coward to take it. "To be honest, Grace, I don't think it matters much what I want. You shouldn't settle for some guy who spends most of his time trying to figure out where he came from, so he can get a clue about where he's going. That's shitty."

"I'm not settling," she says, defiant. "You're who I want."

"But why? Are you sure it's not just . . . habit?" The word hangs there between us, heavy in the air. In the meantime, Nevada gets tired of marking every bush in the yard and wanders back up onto the deck. He comes over to me and jumps up, putting his front paws on the railing. I scratch behind his ears.

When I look over at Grace, her expression is set, her eyes angry. "Are you implying I don't know the difference between what I want and what I'm *used to*?" Frost drips from every \word.

"No, Grace. I'm implying that sometimes what you want and what you're used to are the same thing. It's human nature."

"What would you know about human nature?" she snaps.

Fair enough. "I'm learning fast," I retort before I can stop myself.

She is on her feet now, tears standing in her eyes. "I love you, Nicholas. I've spent the past two years loving you and I'm not about to stop now. I don't care what ugly things you choose to say to me."

This would stop a better man in his tracks; instead, it goads me on. "This is just what I'm talking about, Grace. Call it habit, call it stubbornness, call it whatever you want. You're so bound up in this idea that I'm the one for you, you won't even consider any other options."

"That's what love *is*," she says. "For better or for worse, for richer and for poorer, and all that jazz. Isn't that the whole point of choosing to be with someone forever?"

"I wouldn't know."

"Then take my word for it."

"We're not married, Grace. You can be with anyone you want."

"And I choose you," she says. Her lower lip juts out, and I can see what she must have looked like when she was five years old.

"Shit, Gracie," I say, grinding my cigarette into the ashtray. I am exhausted.

She looks at my face, then away. "We don't have to figure everything out right now. It's late. Let's talk about it in the morning."

The thought of going through this all over again makes me want to get in my car and just keep driving. I should have known better: Making love to Grace hasn't alienated her, it's just made her more convinced that we belong together. As for me, I feel more confused than ever. Perfect.

Nevada nudges my hand and whines. Poor guy. He probably thinks all of his people have gone crazy. "You tired too, buddy?" I say to him. "Wanna go inside?"

He leads the way, his feathery tail waving, and I follow, but Grace doesn't move. I turn around and she's motionless, her back to me, staring out into the night. "You coming?"

"Am I invited?" she says without turning.

"Don't be like that, Grace."

"Like what?" Hurt is clear in her voice.

Summoning all of my charm—or what remains of it at 4 A.M.—I walk up behind her and put my arms around her waist. She is stiff at first, but then she relaxes into me. "I'm sorry," I tell her, and that, at least, is truer than she knows. "This is just . . . it's hard for me. And sometimes I forget it's hard for other people, too. I don't mean to be selfish. I just hate to think of you waiting around for the guy you love to show up. I'm afraid he never will, and what then, Gracie? I feel like I should have a big orange warning sticker on me or something. You're taking a big chance, hanging around like this."

Like all lies, there is an element of truth within. I am afraid that the old me will never resurface—and then again, I am afraid he will. What will happen to my visions of the laughing woman when my memory comes back? What will happen to my compulsion to find her, the overwhelming feeling of rightness when I think about leaving my life here behind? Will I slide right back into being in love with Grace, right back into the rest of my life, as if none of this ever happened?

He has been silent for a long time, but now I hear his voice clearly. *Don't worry,* he says to me. *All will be revealed.* And then the motherfucker has the nerve to laugh.

I wish he were a real person, so I could punch him in the face.

What makes you think I'm not real? he parries.

Oh, a few thousand reasons, I say to him. *But this is hardly the time.*

Putting aside my mental malaise, I focus on getting Grace into the house so I can bring this endless night to a close and get some sleep. I dredge up a smile, run my fingers through her hair. "Please come inside, honey," I say to her.

By some miracle, it works. She follows me to my bed, where I fold back the covers and tuck her in, then lie down beside her until she falls asleep. I feel ill. "Asshole," I say to myself. I try to reassure myself with the thought that she wanted all of that to happen, that it isn't as if I raped her, for God's sake. I tell myself that I would have had to be a freaking monk to have turned her away. Then I get sick of my own macho bullshit and rummage around in my head for some other way to spin our little encounters. Nothing comes, not from me and not from the little companion who's taken up residence in my brain. His silence irks me—why can't he ever say anything when it would be useful?

I disentangle myself from Grace, careful not to wake her up, and lie back with my hands knotted behind my head. Now that sleep is a possibility, I am dreading it—what will Grace make of finding me on all fours by the side of the bed, soaked in sweat? I am not in the mood to offer explanations, and what would I say, anyway? I weigh my options: How rude would it be for me to pass out on the couch, claiming insomnia? Could I stay up for the rest of the night, and go to sleep after she leaves tomorrow morning?

I watch the lights from the occasional passing car drift across the ceiling and let my thoughts roam. After a while I play a slide show of random images, everything I can remember since waking up in the hospital: Grace's face, leaning over me; tossing the ball for Nevada on the beach; riding my bike; surfing with Taylor; dancing with Grace tonight; making love, if you could call it that. Grace would. Unbidden, more images come to mind as I slip down into sleep: *A snowy mountainside, dark before sunrise. The heft of my ice axes as I gather my gear to leave high camp. The burn of hot chocolate as I force myself to gulp it down—I'm more of an espresso guy, for one thing, and for another, eating at high altitude is no one's favorite activity—but I need the energy to take me through the hours ahead. I reach into the side pocket of my pack, rummaging until I find what I'm looking for. It takes me a while, and luckily I have on my leading gloves, or God knows how long I'd have to keep digging. I'm patient, though, and eventually I pull out a photo: the three of us, hiking in the Adirondacks last summer, when we visited Madeleine's parents. Gabe is on my shoulders, smiling so wide it takes over his entire face. His hands are looped around my neck. Maddie has one hand on Gabe's sneakered foot and the other around my waist. She is not looking into the camera, though. She is looking at me. And I am staring straight into the lens, with that focused, intense gaze that Maddie teases me about and that Gabe has inherited. Maddie calls it "climber's eyes."*

I flip the photo over. I have read the inscription so many times I have it memorized, but by now reviewing it before a day's climb has become a ritual, a good luck talisman. In her rounded handwriting, Maddie has written: Aidan, Madeleine and Gabriel. *And beneath that:* Come back to me.

It is a promise I intend to keep.

From outside the tent, J.C. calls me: "A.J., you ready? It looks good out here. Time to go." I can hear Jesse and Roma downing the last of their breakfast, sorting through the 'biners, ropes, harnesses, grip tape, picks, ice screws, and other stuff that's essential to our assault.

"Yeah, man," I call back. I kiss the photo and tuck it into my pack. Maddie and Gabe will make it to the summit with me today.

With the familiarity born of long-standing habit, I check my crampons, pull my balaclava and knit cap into place, and tug my glacier sunglasses over my eyes. I give my gear one last once-over, making sure I have my Deploy shovel—Madeleine would kill me for forgetting it, if an avalanche didn't do the trick—and that my leashes are attached to my harness. I'd be pissed if I lost one of my good axes in all this fucking snow.

Satisfied, I zip my pack and duck through the flap of the tent into the icy cold, metal clanking around my waist with a comforting sound. We have about two hours before sunrise. The weather is freezing but clear—perfect. Maddie was overreacting as usual, with her obsessive worrying about this climb. I've never seen a better morning for taking on a mountain. I allow myself a smile—she really had me going this time around.

I turn to J.C., who will be belaying me on the first pitch; I've got the sharp end of the rope this time around and I'm pretty psyched to lead. "Let's do it," I say. We high-five in the near darkness and I tie into the rope, grinning at the camera for Roma. Then I stick my hands through the wrist loops of my leashes and grab hold. My heart pumps hard as I sink my axes into the snow and ice that blanket the mountain, kick my left foot in for purchase, and up I go.

• • •

This time, when I open my eyes I am still in bed, but my own heart is racing as if I've just run a four-minute mile. Sweat sheathes my limbs.

I think about the picture, the three of them together, and shake so hard it's a wonder I don't wake Grace up. But no: She sleeps on, hugging a pillow, the quilt pulled up to her chin.

I know what I have to do, but I would really rather not. I would rather stay right here in bed, where I can pretend that the voice in my head is a delusion that will be quelled with some nice strong drugs, an alternate version of myself that was awakened by the accident.

My body has other ideas. Next thing I know I am on my feet, padding toward the office. I power up my laptop and shake some more, just for fun. My fingers are trembling so badly it's a wonder I can type the words into Google: Aidan. Climber. Avalanche. But type I do.

I tell myself I am doing this to prove once and for all that I am just plain garden-variety nuts. Then I tell myself that it's pretty sad if that seems like the better alternative.

I have high-speed Internet and it takes only a fraction of a second for the results to come up. But in that brief interlude I die the proverbial thousand deaths.

I click on a link and there it is, some kind of memorial on a climbing site:

On Saturday, June 7, noted alpinist and mountaineer Aidan James of Boulder, Colorado, was reported missing after an avalanche on Alaska's Mount McKinley. James and the other members of his climbing party, John "J.C." Cultrano, Jesse Hurley and filmmaker Dennis Roma, planned to reach the South Summit, attempting a new variant of the existing route. All three of the other climbers survived and spearheaded a substantial but fruit-

less search and rescue effort. James' body remains unrecovered. He leaves behind wife Madeleine Kimble and son Gabriel Ari James, four.

There is more, but I don't read it. I am too busy trying to remember how to keep breathing. Because to the left of the article there is a photo—the same photo from my dream. In it, Aidan stands straight and tall, his dark blond hair tumbling into his eyes, which are a shade of blue that mirrors my own. They stare into the camera with mesmerizing intensity. *Be here now,* I think. My stomach lurches. Next to him is my ivory-skinned, brown-haired laughing woman, only here she isn't laughing. She is holding on to her son's foot and gazing at her husband, not in a soppy, sentimental way, but with a peculiar tenacity that makes me think she wants to keep him grounded, by sheer force of will if need be. Completing the scene is the small boy, just growing out of the roundness of toddlerhood. He has inherited his father's dirty blond, unkempt hair and penetrating gaze, which looks out of place on a preschooler. His pale, heart-shaped face is his mother's, though, and the grin that illuminates his face reveals two dimples in his cheeks that are all his own. With a start I recognize his angular bone structure, the fragility of his small shoulders: This is the boy from the avalanche dream, the one that I only see from the back. Gabriel.

I think back to the man at the base of the cliff who belayed me up the mountain. Beneath his balaclava and his glacier glasses, it was impossible for me to see his features, or the color of his eyes and hair. Still, I am sure that this is the man from my dream, the one who has something to say. John Cultrano, I think. J.C.

A sense of heavy inevitability settles over me, knowledge combined with purpose. Beneath this courses a river of fear. The fear is mine, I know that—but the purpose? I feel it as strongly as I have ever felt anything in my life, but it is somehow *other*. And sure as shootin', as Taylor is wont to say, I know it is not mine.

It is his.

"Fuck," I say under my breath, and close my eyes.

I sit there, breathing in and out, my fingers spread on my knees. After a moment I feel something cold and wet nudge my hand: Nevada. "Hey, boy," I say to him. He leans against my legs and whines. I knead my forehead, behind which a headache is starting to bloom.

All this time, it's his voice I've been hearing in the back of my mind. At first he could get through only when I was dreaming, but tonight that changed. Does this mean he's getting stronger? Will he just keep going and going until he takes me over, until there's no Nicholas Sullivan left at all?

How is this even possible? And what the hell does he want from me?

Maybe I am dreaming *now*, I think in desperation. Soon I will wake up, and have some strong coffee, and make love to Grace, and this will all go away.

I force my eyes open, convinced that I will see my own bed, Grace lying next to me, my grade books stacked in the corner. Enough of the Edgar Cayce bullshit, I tell myself.

No such luck. I am still right here, in front of my Toshiba's trusty little screen. And just in case I wasn't freaked out enough, my eyes light upon the date of Aidan's accident again. This time it sinks in: June 7. The same day I smashed myself up en route to points unknown. My heart pounds in my temples, my wrists, my chest. I stare at the screen, at the words, at Madeleine's face, Gabriel's, Aidan's. He looks so vital, it's hard to believe he's dead.

Then again, the force of that avalanche—I don't see how anyone could've withstood that, unless they were extremely lucky.

Like me.

Aidan's luck ran out that day on the mountain, but I still had some left to spare.

Was it that simple?

In for a penny, in for a motherfucking pound.

I close my computer, get up from my desk, and walk into the kitchen. Somewhere, somehow, there has to be hard liquor in here, and I will find it. With shaking hands, I pull bottle after bottle out of the cabinet over the stove: olive oil, balsamic vinegar, peanut sauce, cooking sherry. Taylor was right—though I may not like to cook, the Original Nick Sullivan apparently had no such qualms. Finally—thank you Jesus, Buddha, Allah, Vishnu, whoever is listening—I find a dusty bottle of Jack Daniel's. I haul it out and take a shot straight from the bottle. *What is happening to me?* I think. *What has already happened?*

I hold the bottle by the neck, considering. Then, with some regret, I put it back into the cabinet where it came from. If I am going to drown my sorrows in alcohol, I would at least like it to be my own idea. I may not be able to control what I want to eat, drink, smoke, or dream, but I can at least be clearheaded about the impulses on which I choose to act. That much is up to me.

Opening the refrigerator, I forage around until I find the makings of a sandwich—turkey, some wilted lettuce, bread that's only a few days past its expiration date, some mustard. I pile it all onto a plate and head out to the deck, Nevada on my heels.

After I eat, I feel a little bit better. Actually, I feel like going running, but that seems ridiculous. It's almost 5 A.M. Instead I bring my plate inside, rinse it off, and put it in the sink, just like a normal person would do. Then I grab my laptop and walk back out to the deck. I open up a Word document, save it as "Aidan James," and write down everything I can remember from the dreams, the feelings I have, the habits that people tell me aren't mine. I find the memorial site again and copy the text and images. Then I sleuth around some more, collecting whatever details I can find. It's not too hard.

I was right—J.C. is, indeed, the dark-haired guy from my dream. Apparently he and Aidan ran a climbing company called Over the Top Ascents, which seems pretty successful. Over the Top's website has a bunch of links to talks both of them have given, YouTube clips of them pulling some crazy stunts, even films of their expeditions, some sponsored by The North Face. I bookmark these to look at later.

Then I hit the jackpot—a Facebook page with all kinds of posts from Aidan's friends and family, from fellow climbers. I read the comments, look at all of the pictures. In most of them, he is in a tent, on a rocky ledge, or wearing some kind of outdoor gear, hanging out with a bunch of friends and looking happy. He's got an unself-conscious, open grin.

There's one of him and Madeleine—Maddie, which she seems to go by—sitting outside at some restaurant and holding hands, which stands out from the rest. It's a candid shot, and in this one he isn't smiling. She's saying something, and he's concentrating on her face, giving her his complete attention. He's looking at her like she's the most important person in the world. For some reason, this is the image that stays with me.

I close the laptop, prop my feet on the railing, and think, trying to bring logic to bear on this crazy situation. But however I examine the facts, the end result is the same. My memories are gone. The only ones I have are his. And he is dead.

I ponder the implications of this dilemma, feeling more

disturbed by the moment, until the sun creeps over the horizon. The sky fills with light, and I sit still, watching. Then I walk back inside, climb into the shower, and prepare once again—for no one's benefit more than mine—to impersonate a sane, well-adjusted human being.

TWENTY

Aidan

"When I was growing up," I say to Maddie, "I thought my father was God." It is as good an opening line as any for a story I have no desire to tell.

Maddie asked me why I was nervous, and I told her it was because I don't like talking about my dad. This is true. I dislike talking about him almost as much as I despise the motherfucker himself. On top of everything else, I'm not in the mood to detail all the ways that J.C. and his family are vastly superior to me and mine. The timing could hardly be worse.

Still, I'd rather have a thousand conversations about Sebastian James than face losing her. She and J.C. are good with words, but that has never been my way. I believe in what is in front of me, what I can see. The truth is, I was staking a claim, the only way I know how. She is the one I want to be with, the only one. I won't lose her. Not for this.

God damn J.C., anyway. I would've told Madeleine about my screwed-up family when I was ready. He's forced my hand, and I don't like the way it feels. Comparing me to Sebastian—that was dirty, all right. J.C. knows good and well that my worst nightmare is to turn out like my father. For him to say what he did, he had to be supremely pissed. And for him to be supremely pissed, he'd have to be equally jealous. Which means that he didn't kiss Maddie to get back at me. He kissed her because he has feelings for her. This is a poor turn of events, not least because she kissed him back.

I have never been the type to brood about things. Sure, I've got a temper, but I don't usually hold a grudge. Staying mad at J.C. and Maddie will serve no purpose. It will drive a wedge between all three of us, and I'm not going to let that happen. If he loves her, so much the better. If something happens to me, he will look after her. But here and now, I'll be damned if he's going to take her away from me. I will do what I have to do. If that includes talking about my sonofabitching father, then I'll suck it up . . . but that doesn't mean I have to be happy about it. I might as well stamp *Caveat Emptor* all over myself and save us both the trouble.

"What have I told you about my family?" I ask Maddie. I'm sitting with my knees bent, rolling a blade of grass between my fingers. She leans against me, warm and solid and *here*.

"Not much," she says. "I know you're not close to your mom or your sister. And you never talk about your dad, so I hardly know anything about him, other than the fact that he's in the military and you two don't get along."

Suck it up, I think. "My father is a marine. He's an officer, and the last time we saw each other he was a brigadier general. He was a pilot first, and he's been deployed all over the world in combat. You name it, he's been decorated with it." I picture our living room in Pensacola, the rows of pictures with dignitaries, the framed medals. "When Ella and I were little, we thought he was the king of the world. Everyone saluted him, everyone asked his opinion. He was brave, he was a hero. When I grew up, I wanted to be just like him." The blade of grass is shredded now, ripped to bits. I open my hand and let it fall.

It's sunset and the light is fading, but I can see the curiosity in Maddie's face all the same. I can't think how to go on, and she doesn't push me. It is one of the many things I love about her. She waits while I dig for a cigarette and light it, while I figure out what I want to say.

I think back, to the big stucco house with the empty rooms, my mother drifting from one to the other like a planet orbiting a sun gone off course, waiting for my dad to get home. Again I feel that leaden sense of responsibility weighting me down. *Make her smile. Watch out for my sister. Be the best the best the best. Stay out of his way, say all the right things.* And his voice, as commanding at home as it was on the base: *Wipe those tears off your face, sissy boy. I didn't raise you to be a little pussy. Take it like a soldier, get over it, be a goddamn man.*

He ran that house like a squadron. Everything neat and organized, everything on a schedule. I'm sure this is the origin of my allergy to planned activities and paying the bills on time. People think I'm fun and spontaneous, but it's really PTSD in action. Just the sight of a daily planner is enough to send me running for the nearest exit. Bless J.C., is all I have to say. If it weren't for him, we'd be living in the dark with no running water and only basic cable.

Not Brigadier General Sebastian James, though. He operated according to military time, no matter where he was, and God forbid my mother didn't have dinner on the table when he got home. I can see her cooking his favorite meal—pot roast, and if I never eat it again, it will be too soon. I see her putting on her makeup, choosing a dress he said he liked, smiling her nervous smile as we sit down to dinner and she waits, we all wait, for him to take a bite. And I can see her face fall when he tells her there is some strange spice in there, why does she always do that, he can't eat it now, he doesn't want it. Why can't she just make it the way he likes it? Why does she always have to change things? I see her raise her napkin to her face, see her excuse herself from the table, see him push his plate away. Motherfucker. Small wonder I'll eat anything that someone's gracious enough to put in front of me—aside from pot roast, that is.

J.C. knows this. It's why he torments me with his überspicy concoctions. He's just waiting for me to cry uncle, but I'll never give him the satisfaction.

Especially now.

When I look back, I can see how skewed my relationship with my mom was, but then it just made sense. It made sense that she'd turn to me when things were going wrong with my dad, that she'd want me to sit with her and talk until three in the morning, mixing her drinks and wiping her tears, that she'd ask my advice on how her hair looked prettiest or model the outfits that she thought my dad might like best. I'd tell her she should go back to school, so she could get a degree and support herself and not have to depend on him. She'd just shake her head, say she married him straight out of high school and he was all she knew. And I thought, but never said aloud, that that was a real shame.

She was gorgeous, tall and blond and arctic-eyed, and she used it like a weapon to get her way. What charm I have, I learned from her. Hot Mama, my friends called her when they wanted to piss me off. She'd had me real young, and we looked more like siblings than mother and son. When we went places together, heads turned, and she loved it. We closed ranks, me and my mom, showing the rest of the world a perfect face. She was proud as hell, and she could be cold, but I knew the truth—she was fragile. One word from him, and she would break.

I tried to get in the middle, to stop him. God knows I tried. I thought if I could be good enough, if I could be what he wanted, he'd be happy and he'd leave her alone. So I was the perfect son. Wherever we were, I trained until I was as fit as he was. I kept my hair cut short and I had perfect manners—yes sir, no ma'am. We never called him Dad—it was always yes sir this, no sir that. I never knew things could be any different until I met J.C.'s family.

Once J.C. and I were messing around in their living room and we broke this little sculpture they had on an end table. I was sure his dad was going to kill us, but he just blew it off, told us to be more careful next time. Said he hadn't liked that statue much anyway, and now he had an excuse to get rid of it. I couldn't believe it. My dad would've had us doing laps until bedtime. I remember how J.C. looked at me when I mentioned that to him . . . like he felt sorry for me, almost. He said, "I hate to be the one to tell you this, A.J., but your dad's an asshole."

I was sweeping up the pieces of that little statue and I waited for him to burst into flame. It's crazy to think about it now, but that's how brainwashed I was. I started to argue with him, to tell him all the places my dad had been, all the rescue missions he'd been on and the lives he'd saved. And then I realized that had nothing to do with it. I looked back at him and I said, "You know, you're right. He is." It was like someone had pulled the curtain off Oz the Great and Terrible. But I had to go home and there he was, bitching about the pot roast and making my mother cry.

Ella had it worse, I think. He just ignored her. Me, it was always, "Try harder. You can do better. You're not focusing. You're not concentrating. You're better than this." If I got an A-minus or something, he hit the roof. But Ella, he just wanted her to be his pretty little princess. He never expected anything else from her. And look at us now. She's a pilot just like he was. She's still trying to get him to pay attention to her. And me, I'm this crazy climber who's spent half my adult life living out of the back of my Jeep.

When I think back on how hard I tried to please him, I have to laugh. I went out for every sport there was, and I was good. Hell, I was better than good. He came to all the games when he was home, and he sat in the bleachers, just watching. He never cheered. And at the end, he'd always tell me what I'd done wrong, what I could do better next time. He never said, "Good job, son," or "Nice pass," or anything. But I didn't give up. I just kept trying. The coach praised me left and right, recruiters started coming to my football games by the time I was a junior. I didn't care. I just wanted him to look at me like I was worth something.

What a goddamn joke. I could've run the Boston Marathon twelve times over without stopping and he wouldn't have cared. I don't know why I bothered. But bother I did, over and over again. It would be late, practice would be over. It'd be getting dark. Everyone else would be going home, and there I'd be, running laps around the track, trying to build up my endurance. I was exhausted, but I knew I wasn't supposed to quit. I ran until it was dinnertime, and then I ran home. And he'd look at me, and he'd say, "You're late. Go wash up."

So there we were, stuck in our nasty family dynamic, just cruising along. Ella was in eighth grade and I was a junior, marking time until I could get out of that house, and worrying about what would happen to my mom and my sister when I did. This one Friday night, my parents went to some type of fancy charity function. I'd stayed home to watch Ella, so I was there when they came through the door. My mom looked like she'd been crying. My dad was fuming. This sick aura surrounded him when he got mad, like Pigpen and his cloud of dirt. You could almost see it, dark and rageful and pulsing. It moved the air.

They stomped through into their bedroom. I could hear him screaming at her, something about how she had flirted with some guy, didn't she think he'd notice, how dare she make eyes at one of his officers like some common slut. (Like my mom ever had to "make eyes" at a man to get him to pay attention to her. All she had to do was show up, and they'd fall all over themselves to take her coat, open her car door, carry her bags.) I could hear my mother protesting that she would never, that she hadn't, could hear him accuse her of calling him a liar. Then I heard him hitting her and I busted the door open and he stormed out. As far as I knew, he hadn't come back, which was just fine with me.

At around two the next afternoon, the doorbell rang. I went to get it and there was a boy standing on the porch. He was about eight years old. The creepy thing was, he looked like me when I was his age—same hair, same eyes. Even his expression was like mine—trying to be brave on the outside, even when I was scared to death. He said, "Is my dad here?" I told him he had the wrong house, but he kept insisting that he didn't. Finally I said, "What's your dad's name?" And he said, "His name is Sebastian James. He's a brigadier general with the Marines." Then he said, "You must be Aidan. I've waited a long time to meet you."

I can still feel the shock of that moment, the fury that flared in my chest and shot through me like wildfire. It churns in my stomach now, acidic and dangerous. The nerve of him—to accuse my mother of looking at some dude, to use his fists on her, for God's sake, when all along he was screwing another woman, raising another family on the side.

It took me a second, but I found my voice. It seemed to be coming from far away, but it came nonetheless, and I was grateful. I asked the boy how he knew what I looked like, and he said, "I found pictures of you in my dad's wallet. You and Ella. She's pretty." I asked him how old he was. He said he would be nine in November. I asked him his name. He said it was Oliver James Baker. I asked him his mother's name. Olivia Baker, he said.

There in the doorway, the rage solidified in my limbs. A peculiar calm settled over me. Later, I would recognize it as the focus I attain when I am climbing, a state of pure, cold concentration. I told Oliver to wait. I called my mother.

I think on some level I knew she knew. But when I saw her face—there was no surprise on it at all. She told him to get off her porch and go home. She spat it at him, like this whole mess was his fault. Hell, he was just a kid. His eyes got all teary, but he got his bike and off he went. He waved goodbye to me.

My mom turned and went back into the house, like nothing had happened. I went after her, and I confronted her. And when she didn't want to talk about it, I started yelling. I told her she was a coward, that she should have kicked him out a long time ago. I screamed and screamed, and she cried. When she wouldn't look at me, I punched a hole in the wall. I kicked in the front of the dishwasher, I threw the kitchen chairs all over the place. My sister grabbed my arm, she tried to get me to stop, but she might as well have been a gnat for all the impression she made. I stood over my mother and called her the worst names I could think of until I ran out of steam, and then I left, slamming the back door so hard I broke the glass.

I ran the two miles to J.C.'s house. I didn't even knock, just slammed through the door like a crazy person and started swearing. He was sitting on the living room floor, playing his guitar. Calm down, he said. Take a breath. I can't understand a thing you're saying.

I stood. I breathed. I shook. And then the coldness came over me again and I laid it out.

When J.C. got what I was trying to tell him, he didn't say one word. He just stared at me, like he was trying to read my mind. And then he said, "A.J., don't do it. You can't go up against him over this. He'll kill you." I thought he was probably right, but it didn't matter, I was that furious. I stood in the middle of his parents' living room, where we'd broken the statue, wrestling. It seemed like a hundred years ago. And I said, "I don't care what he does to me. He's a hypocrite and a liar and I'm sick of it. He's stepped all over our family for the last time."

I remember that moment so clearly. I stood there, listening to J.C. try to talk me out of doing something crazy, and I thought: If my mother won't stand up to him, then I'll stand up for her, one last time. I'll stand up for my sister, and for myself. I'm not a child anymore. I don't owe him a damn thing. He made his choices. I will make mine. And I won't look back.

I went home to wait for my dad. I had to wait a long time. He didn't come home for hours, not until after midnight. I sat there and I watched the clock. My mom tried to get me to eat, she tried to talk to me, she tried to get me to go to bed, but I couldn't say one word to her. I was too ashamed. I sat there in the dark and I watched the numbers turn over on the clock and I waited for him to come home. And she and Ella went into their rooms and locked their doors.

I sat and I waited, and eventually I heard him come in. I stood up, and I said, "Semper fi, motherfucker." I hit him so hard he bounced off the wall and landed on the piano. It made an awful noise, and he came up swinging. And then it was on.

He was the one who taught me to fight, and I did him proud. I broke his nose. I tore all the pictures of him in his dress blues off the wall, shaking hands with politicians and getting his medals, and I smashed them over his head. I said terrible things to him, and he said some things right back. I didn't care what he said. I just kept coming. He broke my arm, he broke my jaw, but I didn't give a crap. I think maybe I would have killed him, if I could. But my mom called the police and they came and broke it up. They hauled me off him kicking and cursing. It took four of them to hold me back, I remember that. They stuffed me in a squad car and took me to the hospital. While they were putting me in the car my dad came out and he said, "Don't come back here. You're no son of mine." In the ER they told me he'd decided not to press charges, which made me laugh. And that was the last time I spoke to my father.

TWENTY-ONE

Madeleine

"That's quite a story," is all I can think to say when Aidan finishes speaking.

"So, do you hate me now?" he says, pushing himself up on his elbows and looking in the direction of the river. I can hear it below us, tripping over rocks and tumbling against the banks. He tries to sound casual, but he can't quite pull it off. It's as real in the dream as it was that night: the feel of the grass under my bare feet, the rush of the water, the brush of the wind against my skin. I feel the coming darkness like a weight.

"You're not the one who did something terrible," I say to Aidan, like I did then. "Your father is. Why would I blame you?"

"Because, Maddie. What if I'm a horrible husband? What if I'm just like him after all, underneath? I sure as hell was, that day. And you know the worst part? After all those years, there was something liberating about losing control like that. I think deep down . . . I liked it." He drums his fingers on his knees so fast they are a blur.

"But nobody's perfect, Aidan. And what your dad did, it was inexcusable. What were you supposed to do? Smile and go on like everything was fine? Not be mad at your dad for screwing over your entire family? Why wouldn't you be upset with your mom, anyhow? She knew, and she did nothing. She didn't even tell you the truth."

"What if I'm no good?" he says, as if he hasn't heard a word. He sits up in the grass and wraps his arms around his knees.

I shoot him a quizzical glance. "You're good to me. Sure, you screwed up big-time once, but I'm not going to hold that over your head forever. Just because you made a couple of mistakes, that doesn't make you a bad person."

Aidan is uncharacteristically silent and still, and when I look at him again, I see tears running down his cheeks. After a minute he puts his head down on his arms to hide his face.

I scoot a little closer to him and stroke his hair. "Hey," I say. "It's okay."

He shakes his head under my hand.

"Everyone's got some crazy shit in their past, Aidan. Maybe not quite as dramatic as this, I'll give you that much. But everyone has something. You're not responsible for what your family does. You're just responsible for you."

He makes a noise into his arm, like a laugh gone wrong. "Clearly you didn't grow up in the military. You're only as strong as your weakest link . . . which at the moment seems to be me. I've cried more since I met you than I have in the past ten years."

Silence seems like the best policy, so I peer into the dark, petting his hair like he's a small boy in need of soothing. There's something hypnotic about the sound of the water crashing over the rocks, like it has for centuries or even millennia. It makes whatever's going on between me and Aidan, whatever happened to him years ago, seem inconsequential. It gives me perspective.

"Tell me the rest," I say after we've listened to the river for a while. "You said the cops took you to the ER, and your dad decided not to press charges. But then what happened?"

His hand tightens around mine. "I told you he broke my arm and my jaw. That took a while for them to fix up. My mom, she never came to the hospital. I was a minor, and she gave them the release over the phone. J.C.'s parents came and got me, and they took me home. I lived with them until I graduated. I bet they wouldn't have let me, if they knew what they were getting themselves into." He gives a caustic little laugh. "I was a mess. I drank all the time, I started failing my classes, I slept around, I got a motorcycle and took some idiotic risks. J.C. tried to talk to me, and I blew him off every time. He would've been justified in throwing me out on my ass. But he was patient with me, him and his parents both. They saved my life, I guess." His voice is matter-of-fact, but I can tell he means it.

"So after a while you just . . . put it behind you?"

Aidan shakes his head, running his fingers back and forth over my knuckles. "Not exactly."

"What happened, then?"

He is silent so long that I think he isn't going to answer. Then he says, "My mother came to see me."

"You hadn't talked to her either, since . . . since that night?"

"Oh, I'd talked to her, but real utilitarian, you know.

I'm staying here, J.C.'s dad will be coming by to pick up my clothes and my toothbrush, that kind of thing. I told you she didn't come to the hospital, and she hadn't come to see me the whole time I was at J.C.'s., which had been about six months by then. My dad told her not to, and you didn't go against my dad."

He picks up a rock and tosses it in the direction of the water with considerable force. As usual, his aim is true, and a moment later I hear it hit. He searches around for another projectile as he goes on: "I acted like I didn't care, but inside it was tearing me up. I mean, she was my mother, for Christ's sake. I stood between him and her all those years, I stood up for her. He was the asshole, not me. I'd been a good son. Sometimes I felt like I'd spent my life taking care of her, instead of the other way around. But he gave the word, and she cut me off like I was nothing. I was angry, all right. And hurt, more than anything, not that I would've ever said that to her." Another rock hits the water, this one larger than the first.

"One Sunday morning, I was still hungover from the night before. I hadn't gone to sleep. And the more I drank, the madder I got. By ten o'clock I'd worked myself into a fucking frenzy. I got it in my head I was going to go to church and shame the hell out of both of them. J.C.'s mom did everything but lie down in front of the door to stop me. At least sober up, she said. At least put on some clean clothes. But I got on my bike in my shorts and my T-shirt, drunker than Elvis, and I took off down the road."

"Oh no," I say. Whatever happened next, it couldn't have been good.

He gives me a sidelong glance. "*Oh no* is right. Looking

back, it's like one of those horror movies where the whole audience is screaming *Stop, don't open that door,* but the moron goes ahead and does it anyway. And then the monster eats him." He snorts. "God, I must have been a sight. I'd let my hair grow out, and I hadn't shaved, and I was wearing these crazy skater shorts and a ratty-ass shirt. I was drunk off my ass, and righteous with it." He grins at the memory, and it isn't a happy grin.

"I pulled my bike up out front and I revved the engine. J.C. and his dad had followed me in their car, and they got in my face and started hissing like a couple of pissed-off cats. But I had it in my mind that I was going in, and you know me. I remember saying to J.C.'s dad, 'I appreciate your concern, Mr. Cultrano, sir. And maybe you ought to go home right now, because I think I'm about to make a scene.' We had a good laugh about that one, later."

"Did they leave?"

Aidan snorts again. "Oh, hell no. They looked at each other for a while, and then Mr. C. said, 'Son, if you're going to church then I guess we are, too. Too bad we're not dressed for it.' And in we went."

"Uh-oh," I say. The wind gusts then, as if for dramatic effect, and I brush my hair out of my face with my free hand. Aidan is so involved in his story, he doesn't react at all. I have the feeling that the entire riverbank could slide into the water and he'd keep going, treading water all the while. Or maybe he's just afraid that if he ever stops talking, he won't start up again.

"We stood in the back," Aidan says, "and we were early. Hardly anyone was there except the priest, and he looked like he had a few choice words he wanted to say to me. You gotta understand, church was really important to my family, growing up. I was raised Catholic. I was an altar boy."

"You never told me that," I say, trying to imagine Aidan in church for hours on end, doing whatever it is that altar boys do . . . carry candles around, maybe? Dress up in funny robes? I can't picture it.

"Yeah, we went every Sunday, no matter where we lived. My dad liked to parade us around, his goddamn perfect family." He lets go of my hand, lights a cigarette, and then goes on. "I was looking for my father, mainly. I figured no matter what he'd done, he was still showing up at church like the hypocrite he'd turned out to be. And sure enough, I was right. We waited about five minutes, and in marched the brigadier general with his shiny little family right behind him. My mom and my sister had their game faces on, just like I used to." He chucks another stone at the river.

"He saw me, all right, and he wasn't happy. J.C. and his dad put their hands on my shoulders, like they thought I was going to jump the pew and start beating on him, right in front of God and everybody. But you know what? They didn't even stop. Ella started to come over to me, but my mother grabbed her by the arm and pulled her back. And the way my mom looked at me, it broke something inside of me. It was like she was an animal caught in a trap." His voice trails off, and he swipes the back of his hand across his eyes, wincing as his fingers encounter the bruised flesh.

"Sorry," he says after a minute of silence. "Talking about this freaks me out more than I thought it would. It was so long ago, you'd think it wouldn't bother me anymore."

"Tell me the rest," I say in reply.

"It's a pretty short story. I saw them, they ignored me, I left and rode around on my bike for a while. Pretty anticlimactic for J.C. and his dad, I guess. I wound up in front of the address that Oliver had given me, where he and his mom lived. It was pretty nice, a cute little brick ranch. They had the blinds open and I could see in, but the way I'd parked the bike, they couldn't see me. I saw Oliver, and I saw his mom. She didn't look anything like my mother. She had brown hair and she was short and curvy. They looked happy."

"Did you go in?"

"No way. I'd seen enough. I didn't want to know anything else. I was just . . . done. I hated him, and my mother . . . I felt like she'd sold me out for his sake. I bought a six-pack, which was not easy to do on Sunday by the way, especially because I was underage, and I rode out to the beach and drank it, and then I bought another one and I drank that, too. I felt lower than dirt, like I was worth less than nothing. Like no one had ever cared about me and no one ever would, except for maybe J.C. and his family, and they probably just felt sorry for me, right? Because I was pathetic. I felt wrecked. And I promised myself no one would ever make me feel like that, no one would ever hurt me like that again. I wouldn't let it happen. I would keep moving." He leans back, bracing himself on his hands. "And I have, until right now. Until I met you."

"All those women," I say, almost to myself.

"Yeah, all those women. And Kate," he says, shooting a glance at me. "You scared the crap out of me. Hell, I ran halfway around the world to get away from how I felt about you."

I try to get us back on track. "You said your mom came to see you."

"Yeah, a couple of days after the whole church thing. She just showed up at J.C.'s house, like she thought I wouldn't have agreed to see her if she called. And she told me he'd left. She asked me to come home. Begged me, more like."

"And you said . . ."

"I said no," he says, staring up at the stars. "I wouldn't have lived in that house again if she'd paid me a million dollars. But we had a long talk that night. We worked it out the best way we could. At least my dad was gone, anyhow." He pulls up a handful of grass.

"And here I was wondering why you never took me home to meet your family," I say. I'm kidding, but he takes me seriously.

"J.C.'s folks have been more like family to me than anyone else, and I will take you to meet them, one day," he says. "If it hadn't been for them, I never would've gone to college, for sure. They took me to look at schools, they gave me money when I didn't have any. I almost dropped out about forty times. All I wanted to do was climb. But they wouldn't let me. Just hang in there, they said. And so I did. I busted my ass, for them. They came to see me get my diploma, and I thought Mr. C. would have a stroke, he was cheering so loud. But my dad . . . nothing. And after a while I found out they'd stationed him overseas. He divorced my mom and married Olivia, and last I heard, they'd had another kid."

I adjust my position. My butt is starting to fall asleep. "No wonder you got so angry when J.C. accused you of being like your dad."

"He was just trying to get under my skin, so he said the one thing he knew was guaranteed to make me lose my shit. But he should've kept his hands off of you. I don't know what he was thinking." He sighs. "Well, yes I do. But he shouldn't have been thinking it, even if you are pretty damn irresistible."

"Ha ha," I say uneasily. No one has ever described me as irresistible before. Smart, yes. Good at my job, sure. Pretty, even. But irresistible? Not so much.

"You are irresistible, at least to me," Aidan says. He leans toward me then, one hand on either side of my face. "I would do anything for you," he says. "When I'm with you, everything makes sense. I feel like . . . like you see me."

He is looking into my eyes with that piercing gaze that made me so nervous the first time we met. It still has the same effect; I feel like a butterfly pinned to a piece of cardboard, and I squirm to get out of his grasp. He won't let me. He braids his hands into my hair and holds me still.

"Of course I see you, Aidan," I say at last, irritated. "How could I see anything else? You won't let me move my head."

"Very funny," he says, but he doesn't relax his grip. The familiar confidence has crept back into his voice. Here is the Aidan I know. "I won't let you down, I swear to God," he says, his face coming closer and closer until it fills my field of vision. "I'll be steadier than a rock. I'll be anything you need me to be. And if we have kids, I'll learn how to be a good father. I'll call up J.C.'s dad and ask him to give me lessons. Please, honey. Please say yes."

I examine his face for a long time after his little speech, and he lets me. I can see the moonlight reflected in his eyes. He looks back at me with an even gaze. He doesn't blink. And as we regard each other I feel like for my whole life I've been heading toward this moment, like everything I've ever thought or been or done has been designed to lead me here, this moment in the dark on a riverbank. It is a scary thought, heavy with inevitability. It gives me pause.

Aidan loosens his fingers and runs them through my hair, making me shiver. "Tell me what you're thinking," he says, and his voice is so quiet I can hardly make it out over the rushing of the river, the wild beating of my heart.

I don't answer him at first, and he doesn't press me. On his face I see only trust, and patience, and hopefulness. And I know the time has come to make up my mind. What is the point in waiting?

As the night closes in around us, I hear Lucy saying that I've taken on more than I can handle, that I'm signing up for a life where the only sure thing is how much I stand to lose. Next in line is my mom, her voice seamed with worry, telling me that she trusts me to make my own choices, but that this isn't the life she would have chosen for me, if she could. I remember J.C. in the kitchen, telling me not to marry Aidan, that he will break my heart. My own personal Greek chorus of doubt.

I give that chorus its due. But then I hear Aidan, telling me I am who he wants, that I am beautiful. I hear his husky voice saying that he'll do anything for me, that he'll take lessons on how to be a good father and be steady as a rock—which is a pretty decent analogy . . . or not, depending on the rock in question. I hear him telling me that he loves me, that he won't let me down. Asking me to be with him that first night, saying that he wanted to promise me everything. Telling me to have faith.

And then I hear my own voice, clear and strong above the sound of rushing water, the drop of a small series of stones into the stillness of the night.

"I'm thinking . . . yes," I say, as much to myself as to him, and I feel his hands go still. A pure, uncomplicated smile spreads across his features like the sun coming out after a heavy rain. "Yes," I say, louder this time. "I'll marry you."

He laces his fingers around mine then, and kisses me for a long time. I can feel him trembling. He holds me by my upper arms, the ghost of that smile still on his face, and he says, his voice a low, sure promise: *"Thus, though we cannot make our sun / Stand still, yet we will make him run."*

TWENTY-TWO

Nicholas

Madeleine and I are kissing. It is dark, it is raining, and we are outside, but none of that matters—at least, not to me. My hands are inside her underwear, then under her wet shirt. She moves against me, and I want to peel the shirt off and see what her breasts look like in the moonlight, I want to feel her naked against me in the rain. We're in a semipublic place, but I don't care. I want to be with her, and I feel wonder and elation so great, it makes my hands shake as they pull her tighter against my body.

I lift her off the ground, onto a rough-hewn wooden railing, and step between her legs. "Be with me?" I ask. The voice that issues from my mouth surprises me; it's not Aidan James's dream voice, but my own.

"Yes," she says, and hers is the voice that sounds dreamlike, drugged. "Now please."

My fingers shake as I push her jeans down and undo the buttons of my shorts. The first time, I think, sliding into her, and I'm not sure what it means . . . is this the first time we've had sex, or the beginning of something else entirely?

I move inside her, and she holds tight to me, balanced on the railing. Then she is ripped from my grasp. I am falling. Above me I can see her face receding, a pale oval in the night, her lips an O of horror. I tumble ass over teakettle down a steep slope, I am pinioned. I see her face again but this time it's like a photographic still, the same old image, her head thrown back, her mouth open wide with laughter. I see the small boy, the dark-haired man, I hear the words. I can't breathe I can't breathe. My desire is ice, it is gone, I am gone.

This time when I wake up, the sheets are ripped from the bed, twisted around my body so tightly it takes me a few minutes to work myself free. By the time I unwind my limbs and crawl back into bed, I am more confused than ever. I can still hear Maddie's voice, I can smell her feel her taste her. And I can hear my voice, asking her to be with me. Mine, not Aidan's.

Speaking of Aidan, I'm pretty sure that I'm eavesdropping on some more of his memories, and I feel like a voyeur, a little bit. But I also feel jealous, which is ridiculous. After all, who would I be jealous of, in this scenario? A dead guy? My own misplaced fantasies? I can't figure it out, and maybe I don't want to. I pull the covers up to my chin, trying to get warm, and wait for morning to find me.

TWENTY-THREE

Madeleine

The memorial service is on a Saturday at three, after the farmers' market is over—otherwise, Boulder's Central Park would be way too crowded, with parking even more of a nightmare than usual—and J.C. is going to pick us up. I get Gabe dressed in a button-down shirt and khakis, and then stand peering into my closet for an inordinately long amount of time. I am so tired, even making a minor decision like this one looms large. I fall asleep fine, that's not the problem, but then the dreams start in. I can never tell whether they'll be bittersweet, a trip down memory lane, or if I'll end up dreaming about Aidan, trapped under the snow. On those nights, I wake up panicked and afraid. Then I look over to the other side of the bed, where he should be. Of course it's empty, the pillow plumped, the sheet pulled tight, which makes me feel lonelier than ever. It's gotten so that, if it weren't for Gabriel, I'd start sleeping on the couch. I don't want to worry him, though. I want him to think I am okay.

Eventually I settle on a dark blue dress that falls just below my knees and a pair of blue ballet flats. I debate whether to put up my hair or wear it down, and decide on the latter, letting it fall in loose waves to the middle of my back. I put on my makeup while Gabe sits on the bed and watches me. Then we go out to the front porch and wait for J.C. to arrive.

When he pulls into the driveway, right on time, and gets out of the car, I stare; I can't help it. I've never seen him dressed up before, not like this. He is wearing a navy pinstriped suit with a white shirt, despite the heat, and a sky-blue tie. We *match*, I think as he climbs the steps to the porch. "You ready?" he says to us.

"As I'll ever be," I say. Gabe takes my hand and we walk down the steps to the car.

J.C. parks the car on Thirteenth Street, as close as we can get. In the distance, by the park, I can see Aidan's mother and sister, and J.C.'s family as well. They are talking.

J.C. gets Gabe out of his booster seat and they stand together on the sidewalk. "Do you understand what's going to happen, buddy?" he asks Gabe.

"I think so. People are going to talk about Daddy, to say goodbye. Grandma Rachel will be there, and Nana. And your mommy, too."

"That's right," J.C. says. He ruffles Gabe's hair, and his voice is thick. "You got it."

"Do I have to do anything special?"

"Not unless you want to. You just stick with your mama, that's all."

"I will," Gabe says. He reaches up and holds my hand, and J.C. starts down the sidewalk, toward his family and Aidan's. I try to follow him, but my feet are frozen in place. I can't move.

"J.C.," I say, and he turns back to look at me. "I don't know that I can do this."

He walks the few steps back to me and takes my other hand, the one that Gabe's not holding. "I'm right here," he says. "I won't leave you."

He is as good as his word. We walk together toward the bandshell, rising white and scalloped toward the blue sky. The green benches are filled with people already, and as I watch, more trickle into the park, standing on the grassy strip behind the benches, finding their way through Central Park to stand on the grass next to the parking area. I clutch his hand. "Who are all these people?" I whisper.

He shrugs. "I don't even know all of them."

The three of us find a place near the front, where our families have already clustered. They've commandeered space on the benches, but I tell J.C. I would rather stand—it seems claustrophobic, everybody fitted next to each other like cards in an old-fashioned catalog. "Besides," I say as we approach our families, "what if we need to make a quick escape?"

He glances down at me, his eyes narrowed, but doesn't say anything, just keeps my hand in his as I hug Aidan's mother and sister, as I hug J.C.'s mother and father and his siblings. My parents find us in the crowd, and still he stays by my side. As person after person comes up to me—other climbers, friends of ours, clients, neighbors—he holds tight to my hand. Even when

I squeeze so hard that I'm sure I leave marks, he doesn't let go. I don't even realize that I'm crying until he reaches across and wipes the tears from my face with a tissue, which he stuffs into his pocket. "Hang in there," he says, next to my ear.

And I do. I hang in there as a steady stream of people come up to the front, onto the stage, and talk into the microphone, saying what they loved about Aidan, what they remember. I hang in there as, one after another, they lay a small memento beside the microphone; I can see CDs, and books, and photos, and equipment. Somebody brings a bottle of Johnnie Walker, somebody else brings a pack of American Spirits. A third person brings one of Aidan's drawings and lays it at the foot of the stage. And then J.C. says, "Sweetie, I'm gonna go say something. I'll be right back." He lets go of my hand and starts wending his way to the front of the crowd, and I feel weightless, somehow, like I might float away. Gabriel is leaning against me and I grip his small shoulders.

"It's okay, Mommy," he says, in a tone that sounds so much like his father's—protective, certain—that I shiver.

J.C. has made his way to the front now and there is a hush when people see who it is. Most of the people here know him; they know how close he and Aidan were, and they know J.C. was with him when the avalanche hit. They fall into a respectful silence.

He looks into the crowd for a moment, searching, until his eyes find mine. And then he says, "If he could have been here, A.J. would have gotten a huge kick out of this. There were few things he loved more than a good party, and I can see all of them from right here where I stand. He loved his family—his wife, Madeleine, and his son, Gabriel; his mom and his sister; he loved his friends, all of us here today; and he loved the mountains." He gestures beyond the benches, where the Flatirons rise above the city. "Everyone who knew A.J. knew that he was driven, powered almost, by what he had a passion for. He was never able to sit still. I could tell a lot of stories about the times he slogged his way to base camp and then lay down in the snow and did a hundred sit-ups, or the times he climbed a tricky run and then wedged a bar between two boulders and did a bunch of pull-ups. That's just how he was. When he cared about something, he never gave up. And all of us who loved him, we learned that from him. We learned what it meant to persist in the face of adversity, to not ever give up no matter what obstacles you faced." A murmur of assent rises throughout the crowd when he says this. He waits for it to subside before he goes on.

"When he and I started Over the Top, I had a lot of misgivings. I didn't know how we were going to find the money, or the sponsors, or even the clients. But A.J. believed in it, and he made me believe in it, too. He had faith that it would all work out, and look at us now. Sure, part of it's been luck, and a lot of it's been work, but without A.J.'s faith that we could do it, it never would've happened, not to the extent that it did—with The North Face getting behind us, and Roma's films, and all the rest of it.

"Aidan James was my closest friend from the time I was fourteen years old, and he was always an amazing guy. He went through some hard times in his life, but he weathered them with courage, and persistence, and above all, with grace. And so I'd like to sing something now—bear with me, if you don't mind—that makes me think of him. It's a song you all know, so feel free to sing along, if you like. God bless, A.J. I hope this sends you on your way."

He stands for a second with his eyes closed, and then his

voice rises, strong and clear, above the traffic on Canyon, the rustling of the crowd. *Amazing Grace, how sweet the sound . . . that saved a wretch like me . . .*

Next to me, I hear Aidan's mother stifle a sob. J.C.'s mother has her hand over her mouth; his sister is crying. And J.C.'s eyes meet mine as he sings, *Was Grace who taught . . . my heart to fear . . . and Grace, my fears relieved.* Layered and rich, his voice pierces the frozen hunk of ice that my heart has become. I've never heard it like this, outside a party or a casual gathering, and I'm willing to bet no one else here, except his family, has, either. And one by one, the crowd joins with him: *Through many dangers, toils, and snares . . . we have already come. Twas Grace that brought us safe thus far, and Grace will lead us home.*

I don't sing. I stand there, listening, and feel my heart crack apart, like it's shattering into a thousand pieces. Everywhere I look, people are crying and singing, often both at the same time. And still J.C. sings, staring over their heads, his eyes on me, until he gets to the last verse: *I once was lost, but now I'm found . . . was blind, but now I see.* The last notes float into the air, and then he closes his eyes again. "I love you, buddy," he says. "Rest in peace."

There is a pause. Then applause comes, and it is cacophonous, echoing in the open space. J.C. ignores it. He lays a photo next to the microphone stand, comes down from the stage, and walks back to me. He opens his mouth to say something and I bury my face against his chest. He puts his arms around me, shielding me from the crowd.

"That was beautiful," I say into his shirt, and the tears come, coursing down my face again. I seem to have an endless supply; by the time the memorial service is over, it will be a wonder if I'm not completely dehydrated. Gabe clings to my leg as J.C.

holds me, the three of us a triptych of grief, and—speaking of grace—I wonder if this day will ever have enough of it to end.

After what seems like forever, the memorial service draws to a close. Roma is videotaping it, for which I am grateful, because I don't think I'll remember much. The day has blurred into an endless stream of people speaking about Aidan, leaving an item that reminded them of him on the stage like we'd asked, hugging me, patting Gabe on the head, telling me they are sorry, so sorry, more sorry than I can imagine. At this last I want to take umbrage; I can imagine quite a bit, including hitting the next person who says that to me over the head with a large object. No, I want to tell them, I am sorrier than *you* can imagine. He was my husband, after all. This is our child, standing next to me, who will never see his father again. But my manners are better than that, or maybe I just can't summon the energy. I stand there, and grip J.C.'s hand like it's a lifeline, and say thank you. Over and over I say thank you, until my voice cracks and sinks. On my other side, my mother has a firm hold on Gabe, who has let go of my leg and is standing there, wide-eyed, accepting the pats on the head like a well-trained puppy.

A few centuries later it is over, and a much smaller group finds its way back to our house for food and drink. I have never felt less like eating, but I know this is what you're supposed to do. Patty, Jos, and Lucy have already gone back to set up.

By the time we get back to the house, our friends are filtering in. These are people I don't have to pretend for as much, but I still try to be a good hostess, partially due to habit and partially because it keeps me moving. I make conversation, I thank people for coming, I check on Gabe, and if periodically I vanish into the bathroom, sit on the toilet seat, and put a cold washcloth on the back of my neck, nobody needs to know about that, do they? The hours wear on, and finally it is dark outside and I am hugging people goodbye: Patty, Nathan, Jesse, Roma, Aidan's mom and sister, Mr. and Mrs. Cultrano, and then Lucy and Jos and my parents, who are all going home tomorrow. I thank them for everything, I promise to call, I tell them not to worry.

Eventually they are all gone and it is just me and J.C. and Gabe, who is rubbing his eyes and yawning. He asks me if he can watch TV, and I tell him yes, today is a special day and that's okay. I get him set up on the couch with his blankie and Teddy and *Harry Potter and the Sorcerer's Stone*. Then I make my way back to the kitchen, where J.C. is staring at the wreckage, figuring out what to tackle first. My mom and Lucy cleaned up the rest of the house, but I drew the line at the kitchen, because I dreaded having them leave and then sitting on the couch with nothing to do. The result is that the kitchen is trashed; it should keep us busy for a while. I dig under the sink for some 409 and some paper towels, pass them off to J.C., and start on the dishes. We clean together in silence until I say, "J.C.?"

"Hmmm?" He looks up from the kitchen table, which he's been working on for about five minutes, scrubbing it like it did something to offend him.

"Would you do something for me?"

"Anything," he says without hesitation. "What do you need?"

"Would you stay here tonight?"

He sprays some more 409 onto the table, and goes back to addressing what must be a particularly stubborn spot. "You mean, overnight?"

"Yes. Would you?" I say to his back, which is somehow easier than if I had to look him in the eye. "I wouldn't ask, but it's just—there's been so many people here, day in and day out, and I thought that all I wanted was for them to leave, but now they're all gone and the house seems so empty, with just me and Gabe. And I don't know how I'm going to feel when everything's all cleaned up and there's nothing left for me to do."

"You don't have to explain yourself, Maddie," he says, attacking the spot with renewed vigor. "Of course I'll stay, if that's what you want. I'm happy to do it. To tell you the truth, I don't feel like being alone, either. And if I go out and start drinking, the way I feel right now, there's no telling how the evening might end up. Just let me go home and get a change of clothes."

I walk around the table, dish towel in hand, so I can see his face. "Thank you."

"No worries," he says. Crumpling the paper towel into a ball, he tosses it into the trash can. "You got anything else that needs to be thrown out? Because I might as well take out the garbage, if I'm going outside anyway."

I look around the kitchen, which looks cleaner than it's been in a long time. The countertops sparkle, all of the dishes are put away, and even the front of the stove shines. It's amazing how death and cleaning are inextricably linked. I say as much to J.C., who says, "When you're cleaning, you don't have to think about other stuff, right? It's mindless work, and I don't know about you, but I could do with a little less thinking right about now."

"I don't know that I am thinking, to be honest. I feel kind of numb."

"You did great today," he says, tying the garbage bag closed. "He would have been proud of you."

"That's nice of you to say. But I don't know that there's any way to do well at this sort of thing, is there? You just muddle through somehow."

"You're doing a good job of muddling, then." He lifts the bag out of the trash can. "Let me take this out, and then I'll run home real quick. Unless you need me to do anything else around here?"

"No, I think we're about done. Go ahead."

So he does. When he comes back half an hour later Gabe and I have changed into our PJs, and we're snuggled together on the living room couch watching Harry Potter, my old quilt drawn up over us. J.C. drops his red duffel bag at the foot of the couch and sits down. "Hey, buddy," he says. "I'm going to stay over here, with you and your mom, tonight. Is that okay?"

"Sure," Gabe says, sounding drowsy. It's no big shock to either of us when he dozes off midway through the first Quidditch match. I gather him up, carry him down the hall to his bedroom, and tuck him in, turning on his Tasmanian Devil night-light. He doesn't stir.

J.C. and I watch the rest of the movie in silence, lost in our own thoughts. As the credits roll, he turns to me and says, "Where should I sleep? The couch, or your office maybe? You've got a futon in there, right?"

"Actually," I say, "I was wondering if you would sleep in my room."

He does a double take. "What, in your bed?"

"If you think it's too weird, forget about it." I wrap myself more tightly in the quilt. "I shouldn't have said anything. It's just that I've been having these crazy dreams, and I would feel better if someone else was there."

"If that's what you want," he says. "Sure."

"You would?"

"Absolutely, if it makes you feel better. Don't worry about it." He picks up his duffel. "I'll just go brush my teeth." And off he trots down the hall. When he comes out of the bathroom, he's wearing a blue Widespread Panic T-shirt and pajama pants. He goes into the kitchen and pours himself a glass of water, and I take my turn in the bathroom, peeing, washing my face, flossing and brushing. It seems so ridiculous to me: Aidan is dead, and still I have to floss. You would think the laws of the universe would be temporarily suspended, or something.

By the time I make my way into my room, J.C.'s already in there, lying on Aidan's side of the bed, on top of the quilt, his hands folded behind his head. I turn off the light and crawl under the covers on the other side.

"Thank you," I say into the darkness. "For everything."

"My pleasure. Good night, Maddie."

"Good night," I answer him, and slip down into sleep like someone pushed me, hard.

TWENTY-FOUR

Madeleine

The snow is heavy, and Aidan is buried under it. One moment he's standing on a ledge; the next he's hurtling through the air, and then he's pinioned under an unyielding, icy weight. He scratches at it, he kicks and claws, but nothing he does makes any difference. He is paralyzed, he is suffocating, and I am on the surface, digging as fast as I can with a shovel. The handle breaks off, and I start scraping the snow away with my bare hands. I dig frantically, ignoring the cold, but when I find him, it is too late. I uncover his face and discover that he is dead, his eyes frozen wide, his mouth open and filled with snow. I scream and scream, but no one comes.

I bolt upright, my hand over my mouth. The bed shifts under me, and I realize that I'm not alone. For a second I don't know where I am, or who's with me. Then reality filters in. It's the night after Aidan's memorial service. J.C. is here because I asked him to stay.

I can just make him out in the darkness. He is still lying on the other side of the bed, his hands folded on his chest. "You okay, Maddie?" he says as I sink back down onto my pillow, trying to slow the pounding of my heart. He sounds fully awake, like he's been waiting for something like this to happen.

"I had a dream," I say, but then I can't go on.

One of his hands reaches across the expanse between us and fumbles around until it finds mine. "I'm here," he says, squeezing my fingers.

We lie there in silence for a little while as I catch my breath. He doesn't say anything else or come any closer, just runs his thumb over the back of my hand in a comforting kind of way. I can hear him breathing, slow and even, and I try to match his pace without much success. Try as I might to purge the dream images from my mind, I keep seeing Aidan fall, seeing him trapped under a giant mound of snow, trying to claw his way out. It hollows me inside, makes me feel like I might fly into a thousand different pieces.

"Would you hold me?" I ask J.C. Maybe that's a mistake, but right now all I want is to feel someone's arms around me, someone who is grieving as much as I am.

"Sure," he says after a moment. "Come here."

I slide across the bed and lie on my side against him, one leg over his and my head on his chest. He puts his arms around me and strokes my hair. I can hear the regular thump of his heart—an athlete's pulse, like Aidan's. It feels very peculiar to be lying in bed with someone else, especially in the dark. It's oddly intimate, like maybe we just finished making love or are about to start.

J.C. must be having the same types of thoughts, because he fidgets under me and I realize he has what feels like an impressive erection. It presses against my leg and I don't know what to do—should I ignore it? Move away? Say something?

The second option is probably the best, maybe in some combination with the third, but I don't want to move, is the thing. It's peaceful, lying here with him, the first time I've felt like a human being in days. I feel safe with his arms around me, secure. With a start I remember Aidan asking all those years ago if I cared for J.C. as more than a friend, telling me that if something happened to him, he wanted to know that I'd be with someone who loved me. Back then I'd thought he was crazy, and I'd told him so. But now, in our darkened bedroom, that long-ago conversation seems prescient, and I shiver.

"I'm sorry," J.C. says in a rueful voice. "I can't help it."

I lift my head from his chest. "Do you want me to go back over there?" I gesture at the other side of the bed.

"No," he says. "Not unless it makes you too uncomfortable. I'm a big boy. Don't worry about me." His voice is so matter-of-fact that I lay my head back down on his chest, listening to his heart beat. It's picked up speed, belying his calm tone.

He strokes my hair again, running his fingers through it. "I might as well say something, Maddie. I wasn't going to, not now, but this seems as good a time as any."

"Maybe you shouldn't," I say. My own heart begins to pound. I'm sure he can feel it.

"No, I need to. Anyhow, I think it's something you already know. And if you don't, you should."

"Go on," I say despite my better judgment. My mouth is dry.

"I love you," he says steadily. "You and Gabriel both. I've loved you for a long time. I'm not trying to . . . to move in on A.J., or anything like that. But this"—he moves a little bit so I can feel him pressing against my hip—"it's not just the situation. It's because of how I feel."

"Oh," I say, which might win the prize for the world's most inadequate response. But truly, I am emotionally drained. Aidan is dead. Here is J.C., lying in my bed with his arms wrapped around me, telling me he loves me. The situation seems so surreal, so turned on its ear, that I don't have any idea how to respond. I don't think I could come up with another strong reaction to anything if my own life depended on it, and Gabe's, too. So I lie still, listening to J.C.'s heart speed along. I spread my hand out on his chest, feeling his body heat through the cotton of his T-shirt. No wonder he was so conscientious about sleeping on the other side of the bed.

"You don't have to say anything," J.C. says. He's worked all the tangles out of my hair and now his fingers run through it easily. "I don't expect you to. I just want you to know that I'll be here for you, no matter what happens. Any way you want it."

I let his words sink in. There is something so familiar about his touch, familiar and yet brand-new. I miss Aidan so much it hurts, like an ache deep in the pit of my stomach. Again I think about that conversation we had so long ago. It feels odd, as if he's given me permission to be lying here like this with J.C. As if it's what he would have wanted.

"Thank you," I say, and as I speak I realize that I'm thankful for much more than J.C.'s offer. I'm thankful for the way he stayed tonight, how he's acting like a gentleman right now instead of taking advantage of the situation. I'm thankful for how he held me when I had my little breakdown, and how he risked his own life to search for Aidan after the accident. How patient and loving he's been with Gabe. The incredible speech he gave at the memorial service, and the song, and how he stood beside me for hours, holding my hand while I cried.

I lift my head from his chest and look down at him for a moment in the darkness of the room, and then before I can lose my nerve, I kiss him on the lips. *You asked me to,* I think. *You wanted this to happen.*

J.C.'s hand stops moving halfway through my hair. There's a moment when his body is completely still. Then he unfreezes and kisses me back, lightly at first, then harder. His tongue slides between my lips and his hand tightens in my hair.

"Maddie," he says, and from the way he says my name, like a caress and a warning rolled into one, I can tell how much he wants this, how much he's been holding back. I've never heard J.C. sound like that before, without any of his usual cool logic tempering what he's got to say. It ignites something in me, a fierce surge of desire that is the last thing I expected. *Oh, Aidan,* I think, and my eyes fill.

J.C. slides out from under me, so we're both on our sides, and pulls me close. I can feel him pressing against my belly, but I don't move away, not then and not when he runs his hand over me from my neck to the curve of my hip, careful at first, like he's asking permission. When I don't tell him to stop, he does it again, and this time the flat of his hand brushes against my breast, sending electricity coursing through me. I gasp, and he makes a deep noise, almost like a growl. "Maddie," he says again, and then he's kissing me, and there's nothing gentle about it.

It is so strange, kissing someone who isn't Aidan. I'd forgotten how J.C. kisses like he's carrying on a conversation, waiting for me to answer before he responds. He moves his hand under my tank top in a questioning kind of way, and when I don't stop him he slides it up and cups my breast in his hand. "Oh," he says in a voice I've never heard him use. Then he jerks back as if I've burned him. He is breathing hard. "Maddie. What are we doing?" he says. "Is this what you want?"

I don't answer him, because how can I? What would I say? Instead I get up and lock the door. Then I crawl back onto the bed, where I take off my tank top. That seems to be answer enough, because he pulls his shirt over his head, then kisses me, his mouth greedy, running his hands over my bare back. He trails his tongue down my neck to my breasts, slower now, then follows it with his hands. I look down at his dark hair and I think, *This is crazy.* I wonder if I'm dreaming, but I know I'm not.

I trace his tattoos with the tips of my fingers, like I've wanted to do since I met him. Truth, and harmony. Then I reach over and turn the lamp off, plunging the room into darkness again. His arms go around me and he presses me backward, into the pillows. My pants are off, then his are, too. He makes a choked noise, and I wonder if he is crying. I run my hand across his face, and sure enough there are tears there. But before I can say anything about it, to ask him if he wants to stop—because surely we should stop this, this can't be good—he pulls me on top of him, so that my face is right over his. His fingers trail down my body, find me, and slide inside.

"J.C.," I say. "If the avalanche—if you and Aidan had both—I don't know what I would've done." My voice shakes.

"Hush," he says. "I'm here. I'm not going anywhere."

"Promise me."

His fingers move faster now. "I promise," he says. "I'm right here."

I reach between us and grab his wrist, pulling his hand away. I wrap my fingers around him. "Oh God," he says. He rolls us over then, so he's on top of me. He spreads my legs with his hand.

"J.C., please," I say, and I don't recognize my own voice.

His mouth covers mine, and then his hand is gone and he enters me, as smoothly as if we've been doing it for years. For a moment he doesn't move. He traces my lips with the fingers that were touching me. I open my mouth and taste myself on my tongue. "Please what?" he whispers, and I realize he is teasing me.

To my horror, tears start running down my cheeks again. "Please don't leave me," I say. Am I talking to him or Aidan? In the moment, it doesn't seem to matter.

I try to hide my face, but he's having none of it. He kisses away my tears, he strokes my hair. I wrap my arms around his neck, my legs around his back, and hold on tight. His hand slips under me and he lifts me off the bed, then pulls me up so I'm sitting on his lap, one leg on either side of him. I lay my head on his shoulder and he takes my hips to guide me.

"Look at me," he says, and so I do. My eyes have adjusted to the darkness now, enough so that I can see his face. His eyes are open, staring into mine. "I'm here," he says again. He encircles me with his arms and moves inside me, as if to eliminate any trace of doubt. "I'm right here, Madeleine. I'm not going any- where, I promise."

He kisses me again, and God help me, I believe him. In- side me something breaks away. I let him move me, and then

I'm moving him, pushing him backward onto the bed with a violence that surprises me. I bite his nipples, dig my nails into his shoulders, but he doesn't stop me. Instead he rolls me over and pins my wrists above my head. He kisses me until I can't breathe, and then he closes his mouth on my throat, on my breasts. "Open your eyes, Maddie. You stay with me," he says, and when I obey he pushes inside me, rough, then again. The pleasure that bursts through me then is so great that I scream, I can't help it, and he lets my hands go and claps his fingers over my mouth. Then he's burying his face in the pillow, biting it I think, so he won't make any sounds of his own. He shudders against me over and over. Then he is still.

I feel as if I've been hit by a truck. J.C.'s body is soaked with sweat, and after a moment I realize that mine is, too. I run my hand over his back, and it comes away wet. I wipe it on the sheets, which, I realize with some distant part of my mind, I am most definitely going to have to change.

We don't say anything for a long time. I lie there, listening to hear if we've woken Gabe up, watching the ceiling fan revolve, and waiting for the wave of guilt to hit. But all is quiet from down the hall, and though many emotions are coursing through me right now—in fact, I'm not sure that I could even name them all—guilt is not among them.

After several minutes J.C. rolls to his side, props himself on an elbow, and looks down at me. "You okay?" he says.

I nod, because in this moment at least, it is true. "Are you?"

"Hell yes," he says, with such vehemence that it makes me smile. "I've wanted to do that for years. And it was even more amazing than I'd imagined. So . . . yes."

He wraps his arms around me and kisses my neck, like the

period at the end of a sentence rather than a prelude of things to come. In the warm circle of his arms, I feel the last of the tension drain out of my body. I close my eyes and drift down into the first sound sleep I've had since he called me from Alaska to tell me Aidan was dead.

TWENTY-FIVE

Nicholas

I am running. The air rasps into my lungs, my heart thuds, my feet pound the loose dirt of the trail. I've always done my best thinking while in motion, and today is no exception: The harder I push myself, the faster my brain whirs. I run in the early morning, when there's hardly anyone out except hard-core lunatics like me. Usually I spend this time dreaming up new routes or planning how to raise money for an expedition that's already in the works, but today is different. Today, I'm trying to figure out how I got so motherfucking lucky.

More than that, I'm wondering how my definition of luck has shifted so drastically. If you'd told me a year ago that I'd be frolicking in my own personal Elysian Fields after I lost one good friend, almost lost another, and nearly died myself, then exported a chick halfway across the country to live with me, only to discover that

I'd knocked her up prior to tying the knot . . . well, let's just say I would've told you to put the crack pipe down. Yet here I am, all but pinching myself to make sure this is real.

I don't know what happened, but I do know one thing—I better not mess this up, like I've hijacked every other relationship I've ever had. Between Maddie, my Emotional Sherpa, and me, the Emotional Terrorist, we're bound to produce an interesting creature. I run and run and think about how not to be like Sebastian, how to treat her well and make sure my son-to-be knows I love him. I sure hope some of this parenting thing is instinctive, because if it's all based on experience, well then, I'm pretty much fucked.

The path ends at a flight of concrete steps and I jog up them, onto the sidewalk. Our house is across the street, and I'm quiet when I put the key in the lock. Maddie is probably still sleeping. I go straight into the bathroom and turn on the shower; I've run hard and I doubt I smell like a rose. Then I get out and crawl into bed with her, naked. She stirs and I run my hand down her belly, then back to her hip, learning her new topography. The baby kicks beneath my palm and I jump, startled. I won't let you down, I *whisper into her hair.* I promise.

But even as the words leave my lips, I can feel her slipping away. The bed tilts, the floor is gone, and she sleeps on, oblivious. I reach for her but there's only air, then not even that. It is dark. I can't feel my legs, I can't move. I can't see.

I've spent my life trying to suppress the rage that is my birthright, but it rises now, thick in my throat where air should be. No, *I think with the reserves of oxygen that feed my sputtering brain.* No! *But the word is useless, too little too late. I have already moved on.*

. . .

After I climb off the floor and towel myself clean of sweat, I walk onto the back deck with Nevada and light a cigarette. It's six thirty in the morning, but there's no way I'm going back to sleep. I have done some more research about Mr. Aidan James, as much as Google will yield and my sanity can stand. I know as much as I can handle about his life and his death. What I don't understand is what he's doing in my head, what he wants from me. I'd put money on the fact that if it weren't for him, I would've woken up from my accident with my memory still intact. Somehow, some way, he has done this to me.

I ought to be angry, and I am, sure; but I'm also filled with that sense of purpose, of determination, that first filled me when I sat in front of my laptop and saw his face, saw him in that photo with Madeleine and Gabriel. There's something fantastic about feeling like I have a direction, that I'm not just wandering around in the shell of my life, waiting for my memory to come back. The scary thing, though, is that every day that sense of purpose grows stronger, to the point that it's almost become a compulsion. There is something I have to do, something connected with Aidan James. I can feel it. I'm sure it has to do with Maddie and Gabe. When I think of the two of them, rightness settles over me, and comfort. For a moment, I don't feel like a stranger in a strange land anymore. Then the real world floods back in, and I have that sensation of being lost in time and space, of being in the wrong place at the wrong time, away from the people that matter.

Maybe I am crazy. But hell, I didn't ask to smash up my bike. I didn't ask to share my head—and my heart, for that matter—with a dead guy. And I sure didn't ask to break Grace's heart, like I'm on the road to doing. I've avoided her for the past few days, but I can't keep dodging her forever. She's already pissed at me, and who could blame her?

If she knew the truth, though, she'd be pissed about a heck of a lot more than my inability to return her phone calls. The truth is, it's not just that I don't have feelings for Grace—it's that I have feelings for someone else. Maddie is the one I want, and that's not something Grace could be expected to understand or forgive. I don't understand it myself.

The last few times, the dream has been different—at least before it devolves into the now-familiar plunge into oblivion. I think about how the arms I wrapped around Maddie were really mine, dark-haired and less muscular than Aidan's. The hands that caressed her belly had my long fingers, the voice that whispered to her was my voice. And the feelings I have now—that something infinitely valuable has been snatched from my grasp, that I'm wasting my time, standing here rather than pursuing the woman I love—those are mine, too. Because improbable as it may seem, impossible as it may be, I have fallen in love with Madeleine Kimble.

In a way, this seems crazier than the dreams themselves. After all, how can I love someone that I've never spoken to or even emailed, let alone met? How can she be the place that my mind wanders, every time, possessing me more surely than the spirit of the dead guy that introduced the two of us in the first place?

Just considering this dilemma makes me mentally ill—or more mentally ill, if you prefer. I feel like a stalker, or a spy. But I also feel elated. The question is, what do I do next?

I have no answer, at least not one I'm willing to act upon.

After all, no matter what else Aidan has taken from me, I still have free will. I can choose to find her, to go to her, or I can choose to stay here and attempt to participate in my life. My *real* life, is how I think of it, italics and all. No matter how inevitable it feels, it is a choice. I tell myself this night after night, as the images flash behind my eyes and the sweat drenches my body. The smart thing to do would be to wait for these feelings to fade, for the dreams to stop and my memory to come back. That's what I should want to happen, what any sane person would want, and if I am patient, if I don't give in, maybe it will. So I wait, and I miss her, and I tell myself it's for the best. And sometimes, I almost believe me.

TWENTY-SIX

Madeleine

In the morning, I wake to the sound of voices. I am lying in the middle of the bed, covered by the quilt, in a patch of sunlight, and I am alone. I'm also naked, which confuses me. I lie on my side, trying to puzzle it out, and then last night comes rushing back with a flood of images: J.C. kissing me, staring at me with his dark eyes and telling me he loves me. J.C. inside of me.

Now the guilt will come, I think. And it does, but not in the way that I'd anticipated. I feel guilty about being with J.C. so soon after Aidan is dead. I feel like an adulteress, like I've cheated on Aidan when he was on a climbing trip. But I also feel guilty that I'm lying here, thinking about Aidan the morning after I've slept with J.C., which makes no sense at all. And I feel guilty for having sex with J.C. while Gabe was sleeping right down the hall. Yep, I'm just a bundle of good feelings today.

Gabe, I think with sudden panic, and sit straight up in bed. But when I listen harder, I can hear his voice, coming from the kitchen, and then a deeper one, answering him. J.C. has gotten up to be with my son, so that I can sleep. I hear him saying something, I can't quite make out what, and then Gabe laughs, for the first time in weeks. Tears come to my eyes when I hear his high, sweet laughter.

I look over at the bedside table, searching for the clock. At some point in last night's festivities, we knocked it over, and I have to haul it back up by the cord. When I see the glowing blue numbers, my eyes go wide with surprise. It's almost 11 A.M., later than I've slept in years. Maybe since Gabriel was born.

Whew.

I stretch, feeling a pleasant soreness from last night. The bed smells like sex, and like J.C.—Ivory soap, with his own spicy scent underneath it. A warm feeling spreads in my belly and sinks lower. Oy vey, as my mother would say. I need to get out of this bed, and fast.

Maybe I should ask J.C. to leave, I think, but then I reject that notion. For one thing, it's a bit too late for that. The damage, what there is of it, is already done. For another, he's been looking after Gabe for me, playing with him and probably feeding him and God knows what else. Kicking him out would be a poor expression of gratitude. Not to mention, how would I explain it to Gabriel?

I look around for my clothes from the night before, expecting to find them on the carpet. Instead, J.C. has folded them and put them in a neat stack at the end of the bed. One of Gabe's blank index cards is on top, with a little smiley face drawn in red crayon. An artist, J.C. is not. But he is a phenomenally sweet guy, I think as I pick up the little stack of clothes. Not to mention exceptionally, unexpectedly good in bed.

And Aidan's best friend.

My eyes roam over the picture of Aidan and Gabriel on my dresser, and I have to remind myself yet again that I haven't been unfaithful. As I listen to J.C. and Gabe talk in the kitchen—all I can catch are snatches of their conversation, something about Optimus Prime and Bumblebee—I can't help but wonder what Aidan's friends would think of this situation. If there is a decent, acceptable mourning period that's supposed to go by before sleeping with another person after your spouse dies, I have definitely violated it. And J.C. has disrespected the hell out of whatever weird moral code guys go by.

Taking one last look at the photo on the dresser, I get out of bed, pull on last night's clothes, and head into the bathroom to take a shower—my go-to method for clearing my head. It works, at least kind of; by the time I emerge, exfoliated and conditioned to the nth degree, I feel much better. Heading back into my room, I get dressed in jeans and a black tank top, make a mental note to tackle the laundry later, and go down the hall in search of caffeine.

"Mommy!" Gabe says when I come into the kitchen. He's sitting at the table, drinking a glass of orange juice. His favorite blue plate sits in front of him, on top of his Transformers placemat, and on it is a half-eaten stack of pancakes, drowned in maple syrup. He's got a fork in one hand and his glass in the other, and wonder of wonders, he is smiling. "Look, Uncle J.C. made me pancakes," he says. "They have blueberries for eyes, see?"

J.C. is standing at the stove, his back to me, flipping what must be batch number two, wearing clean gray cargo shorts and a red shirt. He turns and gives me an easy smile. "Good morning," he says. "Coffee?"

My heart rises into my mouth when I see his face and I can't say a word. Luckily he takes my silence as affirmation and pours me a cup, which he doctors with cream and sugar before handing it to me. "Here," he says. "Go sit down." He turns back to the stove and slides the spatula under one of the pancakes, lifting it onto a plate.

I wrap my hands around the mug and take a sip of my coffee. It is perfect.

"Mommy," Gabe says again. "Look. This one has blueberry fangs, like a vampire."

"When did you see a vampire, Gabriel?" I ask him.

"On *Scooby Doo*. See? Isn't it cool?"

I lean over him to check out the vampire pancake. "Awesome. J.C., I had no idea you were so gifted."

"I have many hidden talents," he says, and he winks at me. That warm feeling spreads in my stomach again, and I have to look away.

When I look back, J.C. is standing in front of me, all business. "Pancakes?" he says.

I start to tell him that I'm not hungry, which has been my de facto response over the last few weeks. But then I look at Gabriel, who has maple syrup all over his hands and face, and I change my mind. "Sure," I say. "Thank you."

He sets the plate in front of me with a flourish. "Enjoy."

I sit down in the chair next to Gabriel and regard the humongous stack of pancakes. "What are you going to eat?"

"I'll make another batch."

"Have some of these. I can't possibly eat them all."

"Don't be so quick to judge. You haven't had my blueberry pancakes," he says. "They're in a league of their own."

"They're really good, Mommy," Gabe says with his mouth full.

"I see that." I snag the chair next to mine, pushing it out so J.C. will sit. "Please eat some of these, J.C. If I finish this whole thing, I'll weigh five thousand pounds and it will be all your fault."

"I'd like to see that," he says, but he grabs another plate and an extra set of silverware, and neatly slices the giant mound of pancakes in half. "Happy?" he says as he deposits the precarious pile on his own plate.

"Ask me once I've had some more coffee," I say, taking another sip.

He grabs the syrup and pours it over his pancakes. "Want some?" I nod and he douses my plate, then sits back with his arms folded.

"Why aren't you eating?" I ask him.

"I might ask you the same question."

I groan. "Fine. I'll try them." I spear a forkful of syrup-laden pancakes and take a bite, then another. "Wow," I say. "These are incredible." They taste good to me, which seems miraculous. I've gotten so used to food tasting like sawdust.

"I told you so," he says.

"Don't gloat. It isn't polite. And Gabriel, honey, don't put your hand in your . . ." My voice trails off. "Hair," I say as five sticky fingers make their way behind his ear.

"Too late," J.C. says, sotto voce.

Gabe tries to pull his fingers free and fails. "I had an itch," he wails. "An itchy itchy one. And now I am syruped to myself."

I reach over and tug his hand loose. "It's okay, buddy," I say.

He looks from me to J.C., who is doing his best not to crack up. "No harm done, little man," he says. "It's all good."

Gabe's face starts to crumple. "My hair is ruinded," he says. Big tears form in his eyes and threaten to fall into what remains of his pancakes.

This is so unlike him, I hardly know what to do. Gabe rarely cares what he looks like or what substances he's covered in, and he hates to cry. Even worse, he hates for other people to see him upset. It embarrasses him. I sit frozen for a second, trying to figure out how to avert disaster.

Then J.C. says, "Hey, check me out." We look over at him, and he has poured a handful of syrup into his palm.

"You wouldn't dare," I say.

"Watch me," he says. "I need a shower, anyhow." And before I can stop him, he's dumped the entire handful on his head. He grins at Gabe and starts working the syrup into his hair like it's styling gel. "Is it a good look for me, buddy? What do you think?"

Gabe's eyes widen, and he stares at J.C. as if he's gone crazy. "Oh, you are going to be in so much trouble," he says in such an accurate imitation of me that my jaw drops and I start laughing. A moment later, Gabe and J.C. join in. We sit there, two of us covered in maple syrup, and giggle.

Across the table, J.C. catches my eye and smiles. I mouth "Thank you," and he inclines his head, his dark eyes warm. With that look, the ice around my heart softens, melts. And for the first time in weeks, I know one thing for sure: No matter how much syrup J.C.'s poured into his hair, the person at this table who's in the most trouble is me.

TWENTY-SEVEN

Madeleine

The three of us spend the day together, and it's the best one I've had in a long time. After breakfast (which is really lunch, if you think about it), J.C. and Gabe take a shower. I stand outside the bathroom door for a minute, and hear Gabe giggling as J.C. tries to rinse the maple syrup from his hair. "Out, out, damn spot!" he says, loud and clear, and I put my hand over my mouth. I know what's coming next.

Sure enough, Gabe scolds him. "You said a bad word."

"Yeah, well, I'm going to say a lot more if this stuff doesn't start coming out soon," J.C. says, and Gabe laughs harder. I can hear his giggles all the way down the hall to the kitchen, where I unload the dishwasher and take out the trash. By the time I'm finished with that and ready to start on the dishes, J.C. appears with Gabe wrapped in a towel like a burrito. "One clean boy," he says. "Syrup-free."

"Uncle J.C. said a bad word," Gabe tells me.

"I know. I heard."

"You'd say a bad word, too, if Aunt Jemima had welded your hair follicles together. And you weren't supposed to tell. Now you're really in trouble." He starts tickling Gabe, who shrieks. "And you!" he says to me over Gabe's squeals. "What do you mean, you heard? What were you doing, listening at the bathroom door?"

"Oops. You got me."

J.C. gives me a mock glare. "Your mother is a spy," he tells Gabriel. "I hope you know that."

Gabe has stopped laughing and he looks me over with his big blue eyes, like he's taking my measure. "She is very, very sneaky," he says to J.C., as serious as it's possible for a four-year-old to sound. "She is a sneaky one."

"Thanks for the tip," J.C. says in a tone that matches Gabe's. "I'll keep that in mind. Hey, sneaky one, you wanna take a walk with us? We're going exploring."

"Sure," I say. "As soon as I do these dishes."

"Don't worry about them. I'll get them later. Come on."

"Yeah, come on, Mommy," Gabe says.

So we go for a walk along Boulder Creek. We've done this plenty of times, but as a foursome. Aidan was always with us, racing J.C. with Gabe on his shoulders, making elaborate plans for some crazy adventure. Walking along the trail without him, there's no pretending. The three of us are all that's left. I know that J.C. and I need to talk about what's happened, that I need to make sure he knows it can't happen again, but I don't want to.

That sense of peace, of safety, that I felt last night, falling asleep in his arms, is still with me. I am selfish, I am the worst kind of coward, but I don't want to give that up. I keep waiting for J.C. to force the subject when Gabe is out of earshot, but he never does. He doesn't even reach for my hand, even though we're strolling along next to each other and he has plenty of opportunities. He is a perfect gentleman.

By the time we get home, it's almost 3 P.M. and Gabe is yawning. I tuck him into bed for a nap and read him two of his favorite stories—*Slowly, Slowly, Slowly Said the Sloth* and *Henry the Explorer,* which is so old, I can remember my mom reading it to me. It's kind of sexist, when you read it closely, but Gabe loves it and I figure there's no need to indoctrinate him with feminist politics this early on. His eyes are at half-mast by the time I walk out of his room, closing the door quietly behind me.

When I go back into the kitchen, J.C. is already hard at work as promised. He's cleared the table and is loading the dishwasher. As I come in, he's sliding Gabe's blue plate into one of the bottom racks.

"You don't have to do those," I say, and he gives me a smile over his shoulder.

"No big deal. I'm almost done." He closes the dishwasher door and turns to face me, wiping his hands on his shorts to dry them. "Gabe go down okay?"

"Yeah, he was fine. He wanted a couple of stories, and then I lay down with him. His eyes were closing when I left."

J.C. doesn't say anything. He leans against the counter, waiting for me to go on, his arms folded over his chest. His posture is as unthreatening as it could possibly be, but I am suddenly aware of the fact that we are alone for the first time since last night. I feel afraid—not of him, but of myself, what I want, what I might do.

I try to look away before my feelings show on my face, but it's too late. He's always been able to read me well, maybe better than anyone else. He tilts his head, pushes off the counter just a little, like he's getting ready to come toward me. "Hey," he says.

I take a step backward, mimicking his posture, my arms folded over my breasts. "Thanks for getting up with him," I say. "You're a trouper. I didn't even hear a thing."

His eyes narrow, and I can see him decide whether to press the issue. In the end he lets it go, easing back against the counter and letting his hands fall at his sides, palms open, as if to show me he means no harm. "It wasn't that big a deal. I actually never went to sleep."

"You . . . what? Just lay there, all night long?"

"There wasn't that much of the night left," he says, making an effort not to sound lascivious. "Besides which, sleep isn't working out too well for me lately. The few times I've dropped off, I have these horrible vivid dreams. So."

"There's a lot of that going around."

"Feel guilty?" he says, and it isn't a non sequitur.

"In a way."

"I do. Not so much about this"—he gestures between us—"but about the fact that I'm still here. I mean, why him? It could just as easily have been me leading that pitch. Maybe it should have been."

"How can you say that?"

"Come on, Maddie. What do I have? My car, a good job, some friends, that's basically it. But A.J., he had a family. You and Gabe were everything to him. What kind of sense does this mess make?" His voice cracks.

"None," I say, even though his question doesn't really call for an answer. "It makes no sense at all. But it wouldn't make any more sense if it was you buried under all that snow instead of him."

He looks at me then, hard, like he's trying to see if I really mean it. "Thank you," he says. "I wish I could let myself off the hook that easily."

"For what? I don't understand."

"I had him on belay, Maddie. I had him on the fucking rope. If he'd decided to anchor in differently—if there hadn't been all that slack in the rope, or if I hadn't fed it to him so quickly—if there'd been wind or something, and I hadn't heard him the first time around—maybe he'd still be here." He rubs his jaw. "Maybe it's just survivor's guilt, but I keep feeling that if I'm still here, then there's got to be a reason. Or that I have to be worth it, somehow. And the only thing I can think to do right now is to take the best care of you and Gabe that I can."

Leave it to him to play the hero. The last thing I want is for him to feel bound to us by some twisted sense of obliga-tion. This situation is complicated enough as it is. "What about Roma and Jesse?" I ask him. "They were there, too. You think they're walking around wondering why this didn't happen to them, or figuring out how they're going to . . . I don't know, pay Gabe's college tuition?"

"That's different," he says, leaning back against the counter. He looks exhausted.

I take his hand. "It wasn't your fault, any more than it was when Ellis died. These things happen. I know that. I knew it when I married Aidan. I took a risk. It doesn't make it any easier, but it's the truth."

His mouth twists down in a grimace. "If this is the cost of doing business, then maybe I'm in the wrong business." He looks down at our fingers, joined together. "Plus, Jesse and Roma didn't want to be with A.J.'s wife."

"No," I say. "I guess they didn't." My heart is pounding again, like it was last night.

"They didn't sit there and feel like they were being gutted every time he put his arm around you, or kissed you, or held your hand. They didn't imagine what it would be like to sleep next to you every night, instead of him." His voice is so low I have to strain to hear it. "I've wanted to be with you for six fucking years, Maddie. I've wanted it and ever since that afternoon way back when, I've kept my thoughts to myself. But that doesn't mean I didn't have them."

"J.C.—"

"No, let me finish," he says with sudden insistence. "I wanted you, sure. But I sure as hell never meant for it to happen like this." He raises his head then, and looks at me directly. His dark eyes are filled with tears, and it strikes me that he's been trying so hard to hold up for my sake, he hasn't had a chance to process how he feels at all. And I've been so wrapped up in my own grief, I haven't really asked him. *Selfish*, I think, and I put my arms around him. He lowers his head onto my shoulder and speaks into my hair.

"The way he fell, with all that slack, he took this massive whipper, Maddie. It unzipped all his protection and he fell all the way past me. It shook me, bad. If I hadn't had such a god-damn bomber anchor system, I probably would've been swept down the mountain with him. And then when it was over, all I could think was, *I held the break. I didn't lose him.* I had hope, you know?"

I nod. I do know, all too well.

"But I pulled on the rope and it came right out of the snow, without him on the other end. I don't know if a piece of the glacier got it or what, but the rope was sliced, just like with Ellis. And I knew he was gone. I knew we'd never find him in time." His face is wet, and his arms tighten around me so it's hard to breathe. "I lay in my tent that night and I thought about how I had to tell you, how you'd hate me now. I thought I'd lost both of you. How it felt . . . there aren't words." The length of his body shakes where it presses against mine. We stand there in silence, holding each other, until his phone rings.

I step back and he grabs for it quickly, so it won't wake Gabe. His voice comes out hoarse, and I hear him telling whoever's on the other end that he's fine, just tired. I roll my eyes. He's such a damn private person. Or maybe it's just that he's a guy. Either way, he wipes his eyes and manages to sound almost normal. The caller turns out to be Beth, calling about this welcome-back shindig she's throwing at the Walrus for the search and rescue team tonight. They've rented out the bar, so it's kid-friendly.

I'd forgotten all about it, probably because at the time, it sounded like a nightmare. Now, though, I've changed my mind. For one thing, if I don't go, J.C. probably won't, either, and he deserves to be recognized for trying to bring Aidan home. For another, the idea of being here alone with him tonight terrifies me. What good can come of this? The last thing I want to do is hurt him. I've done enough of that. I don't know how he can stand to be around me, really. Maybe he's just a glutton for punishment.

So I tell him I'll go to the party. He looks surprised, but he relays the message to Beth. He flips the phone shut and shoves it back into his pocket. Then he yawns, covering his mouth with one hand.

"You need to get some rest," I tell him. "Especially if we're going somewhere tonight."

"I told you. I can't sleep."

"I'll sit with you, if you want. If that will help."

His eyes flash to my face, startled. "You would?"

"Sure. If you want me to."

He regards me for a long moment, and then he looks away. "All right," he says to a point somewhere above my head. It occurs to me that he's embarrassed.

I take his hand again. "Come on," I say, and I tug. He follows me down the hall and into my room, where he stretches out on the bed. I cover him with the quilt and he yawns again.

"Lie down with me?" he says.

"You're supposed to be sleeping."

"I am. I mean, I will be. I just want to hold you," he says. "You asked me to last night, and I kind of screwed that up. Let me make it up to you." He sounds sincere enough, so I lie down next to him, my head tucked under his chin. He puts an arm around me and kisses my neck. His lips are soft, his stubble rough where it rubs against my cheek. Something twists down low in my stomach. I take a deep breath, trying to steady myself, but that doesn't help. I breathe him in, and suddenly I am hyperaware of all the places where his body touches mine. Luckily for me, he is half-asleep already.

"Thank you," he says, his voice drowsy.

"For what?" My voice comes out defensive, almost hostile. He ignores it.

"For being here. For doing this." His arm tightens around me. "Wake me up at six," he says, and then he is gone.

TWENTY-EIGHT

Nicholas

I lie outside by the fire, hands behind my head, one leg bent so my foot rests on my knee. In the light of the flames I can see J.C., sitting with his backpack guitar in his hands. We've just finished guiding a group of clients up Devils Tower. We took them up the Durrance Route, which is a 5.6 and thus not too bad. J.C. and I are camping in the national park, staying on to see if we can try out some of the others. I have my eye on a few choice routes—Adventurous Daze, Burning Daylight, *and* Spank the Monkey (*just because I like the name*). J.C. *is pulling for* Lovely Liana, *which is fast but tricky.*

I look over at him, picking out notes on his guitar. "How'd you think it went?" I ask.

"What, the group? Awesome. It was cool to see that girl and her dad, doing something together like that. And Edward . . . shit."

"I know," I say. And I do. Jenny and her dad have climbed together all over the country. Everyone else in their family thinks they're crazy, but they love it. Maybe one day Gabe will want to come cragging with me. How sweet would that be?

As for Edward, he's an Iraqi Freedom vet who lost an arm and a leg when the Jeep he was riding in drove over a roadside bomb. He was a rock hound before he went to Iraq, but nothing too serious. Now he's got these crazy prosthetics and no route's too gnarly for him to take on. I was a little worried about bringing him on this trip—I haven't worked with many disabled climbers—but he put the rest of us to shame. I'd like to do some more routes with him and his buddies, if they're into it. The irony doesn't escape me: I've come back around to the military, after everything, and I wonder what my father—Mr. God and Country—would say if he could see me now.

"A.J.," J.C. says.

"Huh?"

"You thinking about your dad?" he asks, like he can tell.

"Yeah, I guess. Just wondering if he'd . . . I don't know, what he'd think of this."

J.C. is silent. Then he says, "He'd be proud, if he had a lick of sense."

"Yeah." I grab a beer out of my pack, crack it open, change the subject. "Hey, how're things going with Elise?"

J.C. extends his hand, and I toss him a bottle. He says, "They aren't. She wants marriage, the white dress, the whole nine yards. And me, I'm still debating whether I want her to keep a toothbrush at my place. We're not exactly on the same page."

"Sorry, man," I say. He makes a noncommittal noise, and I take a gulp of my beer. I'd bet my life on the fact that there's nothing wrong with Elise, per se. It's not who she is, it's who she isn't.

He's never going to find what he's looking for, because the person he's looking for is married to me . . . and I sure as hell am not giving her up.

I know this, and he knows I know. There's no need to discuss it, so we drink our beer, he plays his guitar, and we talk about other things.

This time, when I wake up, I'm in my bed, not on the floor. It's ridiculous, but I am jealous. I sit up, trying to make the feeling go away.

To distract myself, I think about the rest of the dream, about the clients they were guiding up the mountain. That girl and her father . . . that's pretty cool, to have something you share with your old man, even when the rest of your family thinks you've gone around the bend. And the Iraq vet—wow. I can't imagine caring about anything so much that I'd strap on a couple of prosthetic limbs and go hightailing up a gigantic spire of rock. Impressive.

I fall asleep again thinking about what it feels like to have everything you want, only to lose it . . . and to know what you want, but not have it. In that way, Aidan James and I are opposites. We differ in another vital way, too, of course: I am still alive.

TWENTY-NINE

Madeleine

There are about a thousand things I need to do—laundry, for one; pay bills, for another—but instead I just lie there and watch J.C. sleep. After a while I slip out from underneath his arm and sit next to him, looking down at his face. His dark lashes cast shadows on his cheeks, and he needs to shave. He sleeps sprawled out, one arm flung above his head, like he's been dropped from a great height and has landed on my bed.

After a while he mutters something, too low for me to hear. Then he says it again, sounding agitated. I make out, "Watch it," and then, "Damn it, Roma." There's more mumbling, and then he says, "Try harder." His eyes snap open and he stares straight ahead, but I don't think he's seeing this room.

I take his hand and hold it, like he did for me last night. "It's okay," I say. "Go back to sleep." I smooth his hair away from his face. He's sweating.

He grips my hand, so hard it hurts, and then he blinks once, twice. He takes a deep shuddering breath, and his eyes shut. He is asleep again. His fingers loosen, and I slide my hand free. About fifteen minutes later he starts mumbling again, louder and louder. He says, "Look out!" and his hands come up in front of him, as if he's trying to ward something off. His eyes fix on me, and I tell him again that it's okay. "I'm here," I say, like he said to me the night before. "Nothing is going to happen to you." And this time when his eyes close, they stay that way.

He sleeps for a long time, long enough that Gabe wakes up. "Is Uncle J.C. still here?" he asks when I come to get him.

"Yes," I say. "He's sleeping."

"Like me?"

"Yep."

"Where is he sleeping?" It's a reasonable question, but it sends guilt shooting through me.

"In my bed," I say.

"Can I see him?"

I start to say no, but then change my mind. "You know what? Would you mind if I set you up with a movie on my laptop, in there? I could give you some headphones so the movie wouldn't be loud, and we could sit with him."

"Sure," Gabe says. "What movie? Can I pick?"

"Go ahead," I tell him, and he runs into the living room, trailing his blue blanket behind him. He settles on an *Aladdin* DVD, and together we tiptoe back into my room, laptop in hand. Gabe climbs up on the bed and I place the laptop next to him. We plug in the headphones and he puts his finger over his lips. I smile at him and we are conspirators.

"Mommy?" he whispers.

"What, Gabriel?"

"Can I have some chocolate milk? In a cup with a top, so I don't spill?"

"Sure." I walk back to the kitchen to get it, stopping to grab something from the bookshelf on the way—Marisa de los Santos's *Belong to Me*. I haven't been able to concentrate on reading anything lately, but I don't think I can stomach watching *Aladdin* again. And if I'm going to sit next to my son and a sleeping J.C., in the bed where we had sex last night, when the sheets still haven't been changed, I'm going to damn well need a distraction.

It's another forty-five minutes or so before J.C. stirs. This time when he opens his eyes, they're tired but clear. "Hi," he says, looking over at me and Gabe.

Gabe takes off his headphones. "You woke up!" he says. "We've been waiting and waiting. You were pretty sleepy, huh?"

"Yeah, I guess I was." He reaches out and tousles Gabe's hair. "Whatcha watching, buddy?"

"*Aladdin*. Mommy said I could watch it in here, if I was really quiet, so I have her headphones on. See?" He holds them up for J.C.'s inspection.

"Cool deal."

"I took a nap, too. But I woke up before you did. Mommy gave me chocolate milk. Do you want some?"

"No thanks," J.C. says. "But thank you for the offer."

"You're welcome," Gabe says with gravity, putting the headphones back on just in time for Aladdin to kiss Princess Jasmine.

J.C. sits up and looks over Gabe's head at me. "You stayed."

"I told you I would."

"What time is it?" He stretches, and the muscles in his arms flex.

"Six thirty. I thought you deserved some extra rest. Beth won't care if we're a little late."

"I can't believe I slept."

"You woke up a couple times. Don't you remember?"

He shakes his head. "Did I say anything to you?"

"Not to me, directly. But you were talking in your sleep, about the accident, I think."

"Oh God. What did I say?"

"Not much," I say, striving for nonchalance. The last thing I want is to make him feel bad. "Just—you told someone to watch it, and to try harder. I think you said, 'Look out,' too. Oh, and then you swore at Roma a little bit."

"I'm sure he deserved it," J.C. says. "I'm sorry, Maddie. I'm sure you don't want to listen to a freaking reenactment of what happened out there. It can't be pleasant."

"It's not your fault," I say. "Give yourself a break. What could you have done?"

"I could have listened to you, all those times you told us not to go. I could have taken you seriously. And what do I do instead? Go up on that bastard and get A.J. killed, and then come home and make you sit next to me so I can get some sleep, like a damn baby." His voice is heavy with self-disgust.

I glance over at Gabe to make sure he's still ensconced in the movie before I reply. He's busy watching Jafar toss Aladdin into the ocean; headphones cover his ears and he's paying no attention to us whatsoever. He hasn't heard a word we've said, which is a good thing. Under normal circumstances, J.C.

wouldn't swear in front of Gabe—much less twice in one sentence and three times in one day, if you count his Lady Macbeth impersonation—and he definitely knows better than to talk about the accident like this.

I can't bring myself to chastise J.C., though, because when I turn back to him, he's regarding Gabe, too, his eyes suspiciously shiny. I don't think I can take seeing him break down. One of us has to be on solid emotional ground, and at the moment, I guess that person is me.

"J.C.," I say, but he doesn't reply or shift his gaze from Gabe. I try again: "Give yourself a break. You're not a murderer, for God's sake. You almost died yourself." I shake his knee, trying to get him to listen. "You've been there for me every second since you got home, including last night, after I had that horrible nightmare. And I slept better than I had since . . . since you called me from the satellite phone, because you were here. So . . . what goes around comes around."

He looks at me closely, and then his face breaks into a reluctant smile. "We're a messed-up pair, you know that?"

I smile back at him. "At least we have each other."

"Oh, yeah. Because that's not messed up at all, in and of itself. But this is most definitely not the time to talk about that." He stretches again, yawns, and pulls the headphones off Gabe's ears. "Hey, man. You ready for a party?"

Gabe considers. "Is it bad to go to a party, when Daddy is in heaven?"

I have to hand it to J.C. He swallows hard, but then he says, "I don't think so, little man. Not this kind of party. It's a welcome home for me and Jesse and Roma, for coming back from the mountain."

"And for trying to save my daddy?"

J.C.'s hand tightens on the fitted sheet so hard it pulls loose from the mattress, but there's no hint of tension in his voice when he answers Gabe. "Yeah," he says. "That, too."

Gabe absorbs this. "Okay," he says. "Can I bring my *Star Wars* guys?"

"Sure you can. Come on, I'll help you pack them up." He picks Gabe up and throws him over his shoulder in a fireman's carry, and they disappear down the hallway, leaving me with rumpled sheets, the laptop, which is still playing *Aladdin*, an empty sippy cup, and a very muddy state of mind.

THIRTY

Madeleine

It's seven thirty by the time we get to the bar, and the party's in full swing. Beth is the first person we see, and from the looks of it, she's already had a fair amount to drink. She grins at the three of us like it's Christmas, Hanukkah, and Kwanzaa all rolled into one. "Well, hey!" she says. "We were beginning to wonder when you were going to get here."

"Sorry," J.C. says. "I fell asleep."

"No big deal. You're here now. Come in, come in." She steps aside, stumbles, and catches herself on a table in the nick of time. J.C.'s lips twitch.

Gabe tugs on her sleeve. "Are there any other kids here?" he asks.

"Sure," she says. "There's a whole room set up just for you

guys, with hot dogs and burgers and everything. I can show you, if you want."

"Can I go, Mommy?" Gabe asks.

"Sure," I say, and he reaches for her hand. They wander away together, into the crowd.

J.C. and I stand there for a moment, nonplussed. Then he starts laughing. "She's totally wasted," he says.

"No kidding," I say, just as we're accosted by Nathan, all six-foot-three, skinny red-headed inches of him. He's got a shot glass in one hand, and he downs the contents before he speaks.

"What's up, home chicken?" he says to J.C. "Hey, Maddie. How you doing?" He puts an arm around each of us, and I flinch. He smells like he's been rolling in a vat of marijuana.

"We're okay," J.C. says, raising his voice over the noise in the bar. "Damn, boy, what've you been smoking?"

"Roma's got some kind bud, if you're in the mood. He's out back." He winks at J.C., who says, "Fanfuckingtastic. Why am I not surprised?"

I am mildly annoyed by this development. "I thought this was supposed to be a kid-friendly deal," I say to both of them.

"It is," Nathan says. "The kids are in that little side room. Aspen got Lego Batman for his Wii and they've got it hooked up in there. Patty's girls are here, and Aspen of course, and a bunch of other kids. Gabe'll have plenty of things to do far away from us sinners."

Aspen Sutherland is eight, and both his parents guide for Over the Top. Aspen himself climbs, and snowboards, and mountain bikes. Gabriel idolizes him. If he's here, that will make Gabe's night.

"You mind if I borrow him for a sec?" Nathan says, and it takes me a moment to realize he's talking to me. After all, it's not like J.C. is mine to lend. Finally I say, "Of course." J.C. mouths, "I'll be right back," as Nathan pulls him in the direction of the bar.

I glance around the crowded room—lots of faces I recognize, plus some I don't. There's a long table with platters of food—the hamburgers and hot dogs Beth mentioned, plus wings, veggies and dip, and what looks like cheese sticks. Beyond that is the small dance floor, and I can see Roma doing his best to cozy up to a pretty girl in a low-cut shirt. Good luck, Roma.

I spy Patty, and have started to make my way over to her when someone grabs me in a big hug. "Maddie!" a woman's voice says, next to my ear. The scent of patchouli overwhelms me, and I pull away to see Sarah, a friend of Aidan and J.C.'s from way back. "I am so sorry," she says, taking my hand in hers and peering into my eyes. Sarah is all red hair and swishy skirts and amber jewelry, and she is very New Age. I shudder to think what she might say to me next—something about Aidan's eternal soul, or my aura. Whatever it is, I am ill-prepared to handle it.

"Thank you," I say, looking around for an excuse, any excuse whatsoever, to extricate my hand from hers.

"I can't believe it," she says, her eyes downcast now. "It's hard to imagine all of that energy, gone to a different plane. My prayers are with you."

I am torn between bursting into laughter and saying something truly cutting. Luckily, the cavalry arrives in the form of Patty, who puts her arm around my shoulders. "Excuse us," she says to Sarah. "I need to talk to Maddie about something." And she guides me through the crowd, toward the food, without waiting for Sarah's reply.

"Thanks," I say to her.

Patty tucks her short brown hair behind her ears. "Don't worry about it. After Jim died, people used to say the most awkward things to me. It was horrible. The look you had on your face—it was how I used to remember feeling inside. I figured I'd better save you before Sarah what's-her-name lost a limb." We share a smile, and then she asks, "How are you holding up?"

"Okay, considering. It hits me at the oddest times. I'm so used to him being gone, on some crazy trip or whatever, that this just seems like—normal, somehow. But then I have to remind myself that he's never coming home."

"I get it," she says, and I know she does. "I'd go along for days, being fine, and then I'd see, or hear, or even just smell something that reminded me of Jim, and I'd go all to pieces."

"You know, on some level I've been preparing for this to happen for years. But now that it has, I don't know how I'm supposed to feel."

She takes this in. "You feel how you feel," she says. "You've got to go through it, is the thing. I kept trying to go around it, or under or over or whatever. Then I'd wake up every morning, and there it would be, staring me in the face: Jim is dead. It got so I had to repeat it to myself everywhere, in the shower, in the car, wherever no one could hear me. I had to say it over and over so I would believe it with my heart, not just my head."

"Do you still miss Jim?" It's a personal question, and she and I have never really been on that type of footing, but I ask it anyhow.

"Every day," she says simply. "I miss him every day. But, Maddie, maybe it won't be as bad for you. Jim and I were together since high school. He was the first guy I ever got serious about. When he died, it was like he took part of me with him. At least you had a whole life before Aidan came into it. And you'll have a life again. You will be okay," she says, squeezing my shoulders.

"That's what J.C. says," I tell her. "But he's a wreck himself, so half the time I think he's just saying things to try to make me feel better."

"He's a good guy. After Jim died, he looked after us, made sure the house was in good shape, the car ran, all the stuff Jim used to deal with. Usually he wouldn't even tell me about it. I'd just come out and the walk would be shoveled, or there'd be chains on the tires. And he always picks up little things for the girls' birthdays, even still. Jim respected him, which carries a lot of weight with me."

"Yeah, he's been a rock," I say, since she seems to be waiting for a response. "He's been looking out for me ever since he got back. I don't know what I would've done without him."

She gives me a sharp look. "It's a wonder some lucky girl hasn't snapped him right up."

Uh-oh. I like Patty, but she's not known for her discretion. "Yes, it is," I say, with what feels like the world's most fake smile. "But I bet the right one will come along someday soon. He deserves it."

She opens her mouth to say something in reply, but before she can get a word out, Beth climbs up on a chair right next to us and starts clapping her hands over her head to get everyone's attention. "People!" she yells. "People, listen up!"

"Oh no," I say. "What is she doing?"

"God only knows," Patty says, regarding Beth like she's a car wreck in progress.

Someone turns the dance music off, and into the ensuing quiet, Beth says, "As most of you know, this celebration is a welcome home for the search and rescue team that made it back from Mount McKinley. We're so lucky to have Jesse, Roma, and J.C. safely home. Even though A.J. can't be with us tonight, he loved a good party, like J.C. said . . . and I'm sure he's with us in spirit. To A.J.," she says, raising her beer in a toast.

There's a chorus of "To A.J." and "Here, here." I look around at everyone's faces—people who have climbed with Aidan and partied with him, people we have known for years—and his absence hits me harder than ever. Missing him isn't a specific feeling, one I can slide in and out of like happiness. It's something I feel in every part of me, centered in my heart and sinking to my stomach, spreading outward to my arms and legs, my fingers and toes. It fills my throat when I try to speak, it clouds my eyes. I feel like it will always be there, like the way your back's never quite right after you throw it out; some days it's so bad you can hardly move, and others it's just in the background, giving you a warning twinge if you pick up something too heavy or make a sudden lunge for a dropped piece of paper.

"Excuse me," I say to Patty, and I weave through the crowd and onto the street with no particular direction in mind. I just know that I have to get away. Patty doesn't follow me, for which I am grateful.

I stand outside the bar, practicing my yoga breathing and working on being honest with myself. I don't like what I see. No matter what Aidan told me he wanted, how can I justify turning to J.C. for comfort? What does it mean that being with him feels so natural, so easy? And how can I even be thinking about something like this, with Aidan's body still unrecovered and less than a month passed since the accident?

I am lost in this sticky moral thicket, feeling sick to my stomach, when the door opens and closes behind me. "Hey," J.C. says. "What are you doing out here?"

"Thinking," I say, giving him a small smile. He isn't fooled.

"Don't let Beth get to you. She means well," he says, coming to stand next to me.

"She didn't, not really. It was just . . . a lot, all of a sudden. I needed air."

"You want to go home?"

I shake my head. "Not yet. I'm just taking a break. But I should probably check on Gabe."

"He's playing Batman. He couldn't be happier. I went to see him before I came out here."

He is such a gentle guy, such a good guy. "I don't deserve you," I say.

"What? That's bullshit, Maddie. Come on."

"I don't. Why aren't you with someone, J.C.? Anyone would be lucky to have you."

"Feels like we've been having this conversation for years," he says. "And you know why. You know better than anyone. What would be the point? I'd just be thinking about you. You think I haven't tried? You think I like feeling this way?"

"No," I say. "I know you don't." And it's the truth.

"Besides," he says, "even if it doesn't go any further, even if it doesn't last, I feel like I am with someone. I'm with you. And you know how that feels? It feels like coming home, like I'm where I'm supposed to be. If I ever find that with someone else, you'll be the first to know."

"Oh, J.C.," I say, and my voice is sad.

"Come inside." He takes my hand. "Dance with me."

"You think that's such a good idea?"

"Why not?"

"You know why not," I say, echoing his own words.

His hand stiffens in mine, and I look over at him. His expression is troubled. "I'm not stupid," he says. "I'm not going to do anything that embarrasses you, or me either for that matter. What do you think, I'm gonna undress you right in the middle of the Walrus? I know how to behave. I just want to be close to you, is all." He turns to face me, taking my other hand in his.

We're still standing there, looking at each other, when the door opens and Beth comes outside. Even in the half-light, I can see the surprise that comes over her face, followed by what I would swear is jealousy. It dawns on me that she used to have a crush on J.C., which I can't remember whether he ever returned.

Apparently it's still very much alive, because when she speaks, her tone is as bitchy as it gets. Her eyes go from J.C.'s face to mine, then linger on our joined hands. "Excuse me," she says. "I didn't mean to interrupt anything."

"You're not interrupting—" I start to say, disengaging my hands from his, but she has already shut the door and gone back inside.

I look to J.C. for support, but he's eyeing me with a blend of disappointment and resignation. "I'm not ashamed," he says, his voice low. "I think it's a beautiful thing."

I want to tell him that I'm not ashamed, either, that Beth just took me off guard. I also want to tell him that all she saw was two good friends holding hands, two good friends who made a mistake. I want to tell him that he shouldn't hurt himself by believing that we're together, not even for a little while, but then I think about the fact that telling him that will hurt him just as badly as his illusion of couplehood. In the end, the words pile up in my throat and nothing comes out.

J.C.'s eyebrows lower, his jaw tightens, and finally he says, "I'll be inside if you need me." He walks away, closing the door behind him a little more forcefully than necessary, and I stand there, wondering how many more ways it's possible for me to screw up. Maybe I should start spanking Gabriel, or drowning puppies, or eating bacon sandwiches in a synagogue on Yom Kippur. Or maybe I should just figure out how not to hurt J.C. any worse than I already have. Maybe I should fix this, no matter how much I need him. Maybe I should let him go.

THIRTY-ONE

Nicholas

It's 10 P.M., a few nights after my little indiscretion—make those indiscretions, plural—with Grace, and Taylor is at my house. We're drinking whisky. Ostensibly, we are also playing poker. But what I am really doing is watching him get wasted, and trying to postpone the moment that he leaves and I fall asleep.

For the past month, I've kept all of this insanity to myself—the not-dreams, my obsession with a dead man's wife—on the grounds that a) maybe if I don't mention it, it will go away, and b) if I tell anyone, the little men with the white jackets will come and cart me off. But tonight I feel like I need another person's perspective, someone who will hear me out. Someone who knows me, or at least the me I used to be.

"Taylor," I say.

He looks up from his hand of cards. "Huh?"

"I have to tell you something," I say. "It's going to sound completely wacko, and I know that. I want to get that out there, right up front. But I just need you to listen."

"What's going on, Nick?" He puts the cards facedown on the table.

"Maybe we should go outside." Sitting still seems like a bad idea; the walls are closing in on me, and the ceiling is getting lower. Air would be a good thing. That, and space.

"You okay, bud? You look like you've seen a ghost," he says, which is such a peculiar choice of words given the circumstances, I almost drop my tumbler of whisky.

"No. Okay is one thing that I am most definitely not." I stand up, grabbing my cigarettes and my lighter off the coffee table, and head for the back door, Nevada in my wake.

Taylor's right behind me. "You've got me scared now," he says.

"Not half as scared as I am," I tell him. And then I unload the whole story, from before I woke up in the hospital to tonight. The dreams, the laughing woman, the man and the boy, the voice in my head. The cigarettes, the whisky, the smoke rings, the way Grace said I was different when we had sex. Everything I found on the computer. The sense that Grace is the wrong person for me, that where I belong is with Maddie. The compulsion to find her, to make things right. By the time I finish, I have chain-smoked five cigarettes and drained my glass. I don't feel well at all, and from the way Taylor is staring at me, I probably don't look all that well, either.

"Damn," he says when I am done, which about sums it up.

"I knew about some of it, but the rest . . . that is some seriously freaky *X-Files* shit."

"You're telling me."

"Don't tell Grace. She'd freak."

"I wasn't going to. But thanks." I flip my lighter in the air and catch it. "I haven't told anyone, except you. For obvious reasons."

"Yeah," he says. "Don't."

"Do you think I'm crazy?"

Slowly, he shakes his head. "I don't know what to think. I'm a real estate lawyer, not a psychiatrist. But you don't seem like a crazy person to me. More like a person caught up in crazy stuff."

"What do you think I should do?"

"Now that, I have no idea. You've hung around here for a month, and you haven't gotten any of your memories back yet, right?"

"Not a one."

"But this guy Aidan, you said that these dreams or whatever they are, just keep getting stronger."

"Stronger, and more detailed."

"You don't think that there's a possibility you read about him somewhere, before your motorcycle accident, and your brain's just spinning stories around it? That that's where all of this is coming from?"

"Given that all my memories are wiped, I wouldn't know. But for one thing, why would I read all of these details about some random mountain climbing guy? It's not like I was into climbing before all of this happened, was I?"

Taylor shakes his head again. "Nope. Surfing and biking, yes. Climbing, no. What are you going to climb around here? A dune?"

"So there you have it. And for another thing, it doesn't feel like that, for what it's worth. It feels . . . like memories, not like some shit I made up."

"You can't know that for sure, Sullivan," he says, and his voice is gentle. I don't care for the way it sounds, not at all. It sounds like he pities me.

"No," I admit, petting Nevada, who's leaning against my legs. "I can't. But that's how it feels."

"Did you tell any of this stuff to that shrink they made you see?"

"Some. Not all of it. I didn't want him to think I was crazy." Which is pretty ironic, considering his choice of profession. "Plus, I hadn't slept with Grace back then."

"You still seeing him?"

"Nope. I went three or four times, but it just seemed . . . I don't know, pointless. How many times can you talk about how your brain's a blank? He even tried to hypnotize me, but no dice."

Taylor's eyes are wide. "He tried to hypnotize you?"

"Yep. I wasn't a very cooperative subject." I remember my urge to impersonate The Notorious B.I.G., and smile. "The whole thing seemed like a waste of time, so I quit going, which he wasn't happy about either. AMA, he called it. Against Medical Advice. So here I am."

He ogles me for a moment, at a loss for words. Then he says, "Where are Mulder and Scully when you need them?" He's trying to lighten the mood, but it doesn't work. And I realize that telling him was pointless after all, that the best I can hope for is that he's too drunk to remember any of this tomorrow.

"Come on," I say. "Forget about it. I'm sure you're right. Let's go back inside and finish the game."

"You sure?" He looks at me with concern, and I realize he's not so far from calling the little men with the white jackets after all. In fact, that's probably a best-case scenario. I'm lucky he hasn't gone shrieking into the street, waving his hands above his head: This way to the Delusional Dude.

"Yeah," I tell him. "No worries." I give him an ain't-this-shit-something kind of grin. "Let's finish up the game. You want another shot?"

"Okay," he says. He looks dubious, but he and Nevada follow me back inside, where I proceed to get him blitzed, in the hopes that I can engage in some creative memory-wiping of my own. I feel like a frat boy, trying to take advantage of a sorority sister who won't put out. I also feel like an asshole. But then again, what are my other options?

Eventually he passes out on the couch. I toss a blanket over him and go back outside, leaning on the railing. I close my eyes and see Aidan's face, then Madeleine's, then Gabe's, then J.C.'s. Sadness sweeps over me, and regret, and a sense of loss so profound it leaves me shaking. Mine? His? Both? Who knows? One thing's for sure, I have to do something. I can't just sit here and let life happen to me, spend the rest of my days having nightmares, waking up on my hands and knees, afraid to tell anyone what I'm really thinking. I can't run scared forever.

The thing is, I don't even know what to hope for. I know I should want my memory back. And I do, I do. But right now, this is all I have, all I know. In its absence, what would there be?

On the one hand, it would be fantastic to be rid of my little deceased companion. On the other, my feelings for Maddie are the best, the strongest element of my life right now. They're what drives me from one day to the next, what pushes me forward.

It can't be too hard to find her, and maybe once I did, whatever happened would restore some kind of balance to my life. Then again, what makes me think she would even speak to me? She'd probably think I was some kind of bizarre stalker. Most likely, she'd call the police.

Or maybe I'd get lucky, and she'd hear me out. Maybe, in some freakish turn of events, she'd believe me. Then what? What am I supposed to do? Tell her I love her? Yeah, that would go over really well.

"What do you want from me, Aidan?" I ask out loud. But nobody answers, in my head or otherwise. In fact, I haven't heard anything from him since the night Grace was here, at least not while I'm awake. The nights, of course, are a different story.

I sit on the deck, smoking one cigarette after the next, lighting them off each other until the pack is almost gone. They taste disgusting, and I curse Aidan for my newfound nicotine habit. Nevada sits at my feet and I look into his wise doggy eyes. I kiss his muzzle. Then I close my eyes again.

I am tired now, my defenses aren't at their strongest, and the mountain swims into view almost immediately. This time I'm in a small plane, which is swooping low over the glacier. "Check it out," someone says next to me. I turn and see J.C. peering out the window, his dark eyes narrowed. "I don't care who you are. That's one tough mother."

"You got that right," I say as I watch the snow blowing off the summit. "And three weeks from now we're going to be able to say we kicked her ass."

He laughs, and the image fades as I open my eyes again. I smoke the last of my cigarettes, and I peer into the night, and I know what I have to do.

I have to leave.

THIRTY-TWO

Madeleine

J.C. and I don't say a word to each other all the way back to my house. After five minutes in which he excitedly informed us about the ins and outs of Lego Batman, Gabe has fallen asleep and so the drive is completely silent. J.C. clenches the wheel so hard the tendons in his arms stand out, and once or twice he opens his mouth like he wants to say something. Then he closes it again, once with a snap so loud I'm afraid he's bitten his tongue. It would be funny if the atmosphere in the car weren't so tense. I look over at his face several times, hoping to get a clue about what he's thinking, but his expression is blank, his eyes fixed on the road. My stomach churns. If he's going to lose his temper, I wish he would just go ahead and get it over with. Then again, he hates confrontation as much as I do. A fine pair we make.

After an eternity, we pull into my driveway. J.C. cuts the engine, goes around to Gabe's door, and lifts him out of the booster seat as if it's the most natural thing in the world. He waits for me to unlock the front door and then he carries him into the house, like Aidan has done a hundred times.

In Gabe's room, I pull the covers down and J.C. settles him on a pillow. He turns Gabe's night-light on as I pull off his shoes and socks. It's as smoothly choreographed as if we'd planned it. Together we stand by the side of the bed and look down at Gabriel, and then J.C. leans over and kisses him on the forehead with a tenderness that takes me off guard. "Night, buddy," he whispers, and we tiptoe out of the room, shutting the door behind us.

We have walked all the way down the hall and are back in the living room before J.C. breaks the silence. "So," he says. "If you want me to go home, I'll understand."

His voice mirrors his face—empty, careful. There's no anger in it, but there isn't any love in it, either. If I didn't know him so well, I'd say he was calm. It's a good act. Most people would buy it.

I sink down on the couch, fingering the quilt that's draped over one arm. "I don't want you to go home," I say. This is true. Selfish, but true all the same. I remember my vow outside the Walrus—to fix this, to set J.C. free—and I intend to honor it. Still, that doesn't mean I have to evict him. We are adults. We can sit in my living room and talk about this like grown-ups. "I think we got ourselves on Beth's bad side, though," I tell him. "You, especially."

"Like I give a shit. That's just because she wants to get in my pants, you'll excuse the expression, and I keep not letting it happen." He sits down next to me, making sure to keep his hands to himself. "I don't care what she thinks, babe. Or any of the rest of them, either. It's none of Beth's goddamn business, or anybody's except ours."

He sounds so sincere, it breaks through all my defenses, and I ask him the question that's been bothering me since last night, the one that I honestly don't know the answer to. "Are we evil people, J.C.?"

"No, baby. Of course not. How can you even say that?"

"Look at what we're doing!" I say, and a tear makes its way down my cheek, quickly followed by another.

He looks stricken. "Don't cry, sweetheart. Don't cry. It will all work out, I promise."

"How? How will it work out? Because from where I'm sitting, I've got to tell you, things look pretty messed up." I rub my eyes, wipe the tears from my cheeks.

"I don't know how it will work out. However it's supposed to, I guess."

"Is that meant to reassure me?"

"I'm not an oracle, Maddie. But I do love you, and I know you care about me. As far as I'm concerned, that's a pretty decent foundation for whatever happens next."

"I do care about you," I say. "A lot. But this . . . J.C., I just can't . . ." My voice trails off and dies.

He swallows, so hard I can hear it. "Maddie, do you want me to back off? You want to quit this, go back to the way things were?"

"We can't go back to the way things were," I say, raising my head to look at him.

"Okay, but the way things were between you and me, before this." He gestures between us.

He is giving me an out, and I should take it. But instead I

hear myself say, "I don't know what I want, exactly. I miss Aidan, all the time. I'm not sure how I feel about what happened last night. And I'm worried about Gabe."

"Of course you miss him. I miss him, too. But you know what, as crazy as it sounds, I don't think he'd be angry about this. I don't think he'd mind."

"I know he wouldn't," I say before I can help myself.

"What do you mean?"

"I mean, I know he wouldn't. He told me so."

"What are you talking about?" J.C. says. He leans closer, peering into my face.

"I wasn't going to say anything about this. It just seemed too weird."

"What, for God's sake?"

I gather the material of the quilt between my fingers, crumple it, and release it again. "It's just odd, J.C. It's awkward, is what it is."

"That'll be a change," he says, and he smiles, though it seems forced. "Just tell me, Maddie." He pats my hand where it lies on the quilt, a brotherly gesture. Then he takes my hand and holds it.

I look at our intertwined fingers. His are broad, with dark hair dusting the knuckles, and capable-looking. I think about all of the times I saw him swing a hammer, the times I watched him cut a piece of wood to size, his eyes narrowed in concentration and the tip of his tongue between his teeth, one big hand holding the wood steady while the other guided the jigsaw along the lines he'd traced. I think about him standing waist-deep in the creek, tossing Gabe into the air and catching him before he hit the water, about him standing in my kitchen the day he came home from Alaska, slicing avocados for our burritos. About the time he climbed the third Flatiron with Aidan and Gabe that first time; how he cheered when Gabe reached the top, and hoisted Gabe onto his shoulders and did a silly victory dance. About him standing under a streetlight, the night that Aidan kissed Kate, telling me that he didn't like drama, but he liked me just fine. Oh, I think dismally, he is going to be so pissed off.

J.C. squeezes my hand. "Hey," he says. "Earth to Madeleine."

"Um." I turn to look at him, and he gives me an encouraging smile. One of his bottom teeth is chipped; I never noticed that before. "I feel kind of strange talking about this," I say, running my fingers over the stitching of the quilt. "But you know the day you and Aidan had that fight?"

"Of course. Not one of my finer moments."

"Right. Well, he asked me if you . . . if there was any weight to what you said, about how I wouldn't marry him because I had feelings for you." I wad the corner of the quilt into a ball, then smooth it out with the tips of my fingers. I can't look at him.

J.C. is quiet. His silence is a solid thing, an object that settles between us on the couch, taking up space. After a bad little moment, in which I shudder to imagine what he is thinking, he says, "And you said . . . ?"

Gathering my courage, I glance at him out of the corner of my eye. His face is inscrutable. I bite my lip. "I told him most of the truth."

"Which was what?"

"I told him that I liked you a lot, that I thought you were kind and interesting and great to talk to, that you'd been there for me when he messed around with that girl Kate. Some other stuff, too, I can't remember all of it. But basically that was what I said." Grief twists in my stomach when I think about that night, and I reclaim my hand.

"You said you told him most of the truth," J.C. says, spreading his palms on his thighs. "What was the rest of it?"

Heat creeps over my face. I duck my head, trying to hide behind my hair.

"You're blushing," J.C. says with some surprise.

"I am not."

"You are so. How come?"

"It's embarrassing," I mumble. Truly, I wish I'd never brought up this entire subject; but it's too late to turn back now.

"So? This is me, right? How many times have I put myself out there for you to stomp all over? Come on. Play fair." He raises my face and looks into my eyes with a wicked little grin I've seen a thousand times. "Give," he says.

Maybe it's this flash of the familiar, the way the old J.C. blends with this brand-new one, that gives me the fortitude to blunder on. Either that, or it's the realization that he'll pester me until I tell him what he wants to know. Whatever the reason, I surrender. "Fine," I say. "Sometimes I used to think about how it would be if we were, you know, together."

His smile widens. "Together, like, dating? Or together, like, in the biblical sense?"

"The latter," I mutter, tossing dignity to the wind.

"Really," he says, making it into a three-syllable word. His eyes narrow. "What did you think about, specifically?"

"Oh no," I say when I see the way he is looking at me.

"'Oh no,' what? Come on. Tell me."

"Use your imagination."

"Babe, I've done enough of that where you're concerned to

last me a lifetime. Now spill." He folds his arms over his chest and stares me down.

I give a big, put-upon sigh. "I used to think a lot about your hands," I say, so quietly it's a wonder he can hear me at all.

"My *hands?*" He looks down at them as if he's never seen them before. "What about them?"

"I like them, that's all. They're very . . . oh, Jesus, J.C., do we have to talk about this?"

"Yeah, I think we sure do. I've never seen you so uncomfortable. I'm having a great time." He grins at me to demonstrate just how much he's enjoying himself.

"Fine. I think you have sexy hands, and I used to think about what it would feel like if you . . . if you touched me with them." I am now as red as the tomatoes Jos used to grow in her backyard every summer. My cheeks burn.

"And were you disappointed?" he says.

I shake my head, flushing redder still.

"My hands, huh? Anything else?"

"I did think about kissing you, in a fair amount of detail. Satisfied?"

"Not even close," he says, looking me up and down in a speculative kind of way. "But that's neither here nor there at the moment. We were talking about your conversation with A.J."

"Right." I might as well get it over with. "He said if anything happened to him . . . that he would want me to be with someone who cared about me, like you. That you would be good to me. He would have said more, but I didn't give him the chance."

J.C.'s eyes widen, and his jaw drops. "That motherfucker," he says. "I should have known." And then he laughs, but it's not a happy sound. "Is that why you had sex with me, Maddie? Because A.J. told you to?"

"No," I say, studying my own hands. "But it's why I don't feel like a total harlot."

"What a goddamn mess," he says. "This would have been nice to know, before."

"You're mad at me, aren't you," I say to my hands. "For not telling you."

"No, baby. I'm not mad. I'm confused. I've been feeling pretty guilty, myself, for making a pass at you given the circumstances. I mean, the last time the topic came up, A.J. and I wound up beating the crap out of each other. But now it turns out he was okay with it all along. So now I'm not real sure how to feel. Used, maybe. Or maybe relieved. Maybe both."

"I'm not using you," I say.

"I wasn't talking about you." He lifts my chin, so I have no choice but to look at him. "I don't expect you to ride off into the sunset with me, or anything. You know that, right?"

"What do you expect, then?" I ask him. "What do you want?"

"Which? Because they're probably mutually exclusive."

"Both," I say. "Either."

"I've given up having expectations right now. It seems pretty pointless, given that I could never have predicted everything that's transpired in the past few weeks, much less last night. But what I want . . . God, I don't know that I'm even ready to talk about that. I want to be happy, Maddie. I would like to try being happy with you, if that's a possibility."

My heart picks up speed, thudding against my rib cage. This is where I should stop him, tell him that what he wants is not an option. But I don't, and he goes on, each word measured. "I know you're dealing with a lot. And so am I. I wouldn't want us to do things for the wrong reasons. But I feel like . . . well, I don't know that I can be with you halfway. And if you don't feel the same, then maybe we shouldn't keep this up. Then again, it's not like this is a good time to make any major decisions. Like you said, it's hard to see clearly. So, maybe we should just take this one day at a time and see how it goes."

"I don't know if I can do that," I say. "It's too soon. And I'm such a mess. It's not fair to you."

"Why don't you let me decide that?" He leans forward so he can see my face. "We're still here, Maddie. We have to go on somehow. If we can make each other happy, is that so wrong?"

"I don't think so. But I can't just turn my heart off and on like a faucet."

"I don't expect you to," he says, taking both my hands in his. "Just give me a chance, that's all I'm asking. Give me a chance to let this be something real, instead of some stupid interlude we're both going to regret."

He waits, and when I don't say anything, he slides closer to me on the couch. He runs his fingers over my hair, turning my face toward his. The look in his eyes is so serious, it scares me a little bit. But all he says is "Dance with me," and it isn't a question.

"To what music?"

"Surely you've got something decent. Or if all else fails, you can choose a song and I'll sing it. It's handy, having a human jukebox."

I tell myself that it is just dancing. What harm can it do? "Come look through my iTunes, then."

"Is that a yes?"

"Yes," I say, and he pulls me to my feet.

* * *

My iPod dock is in the bedroom. J.C. sits on the side of the bed, takes off his sandals, and gives a lot of serious consideration to his song selection, during which time I drink a glass of water, pee, check on Gabe (fast asleep), and brush my teeth. After much deliberation, he settles on a remix of U2's "Mysterious Ways." He turns off the overhead light and flips on the bedside lamp. Then he sets the volume low, in consideration for Gabriel, and presses play. The music fills the room as he says, "Close your eyes."

"What? Why?"

"Don't argue with me. Close 'em," he says, so emphatically that I do. His arms come around me, and his hands spread out on my back. He dances like he kisses, like he talks . . . conversational, a natural give-and-take. But he also dances like he makes love, confident and questioning, tender and rough.

The music fills the spaces between us, driving us forward, Bono telling us that to touch is to heal. This makes me smile—J.C. is such a deliberate person, and tonight I guess he's decided that subtlety isn't the better part of valor.

There's something about having my eyes closed like this that intensifies the heat between us, pushes it to the next level. I should back away, I know I should, but instead I press against him and he makes a small sound. Then his lips force my mouth open, his tongue finds its way inside. His mouth is hot, his hands are everywhere. "Sweet Jesus," he says. "What you do to me, girl. You don't even know."

"I'm beginning to get an idea," I say, and my voice is as uneven as his.

"You ain't seen nothin' yet," he says, backing me against the door. He removes my shirt, then my jeans, then my bra, taking his time with each of them. He takes my underwear off with his teeth.

I try to pull him up, but he won't let me. "Slow, baby," he says. "Slow." He runs his hands over me like he's trying to commit the lines of my body to memory.

"J.C., come here," I say. I have my hands in his hair, and I tug.

"What's your hurry?" He lifts his head and smiles at me.

"You're a tease," I tell him, and he laughs.

"Remember I told you I had many hidden talents? Well," he says, his face against my belly now and moving lower with each word, "this is one of them." His tongue is inside me then, his hands on my bottom, pulling me closer. Somehow he can read my body; he anticipates what I want before I know it myself. There's no awkwardness, no need for direction. It's uncanny, is what it is, and erotic in a way I've never experienced before. By the time he backs me onto the bed and takes off his clothes, I am digging my nails into his shoulders so hard it's a wonder he isn't bleeding. His eyes don't leave mine as he slides inside.

"My mama always told me anything worth having was worth waiting for," he says, his voice hoarse, "and damn if she didn't know what she was talking about." Then he starts to move, and this time when I close my eyes, he doesn't stop me.

THIRTY-THREE

Madeleine

We lie together afterward, stretched out on top of the quilt, letting the air from the fan cool our bodies. I catalog how I feel. Disappointed in myself, that's at the top of the list. That, and guilt. I imagine what Beth would say if she could see this, what Roma would think. Probably that the whole grieving-widow thing is a front, that we were just waiting for disaster to strike so that we could hop into bed together and fornicate our little amoral hearts out. On top of which, as bad as J.C. probably feels for lusting after his best friend's widow, I feel equally crappy for taking advantage of him in a misguided attempt to assuage my own loneliness. In this moment, it doesn't matter what Aidan said he wanted. I might as well pin a big scarlet A to myself and be done with it.

It would be so simple if that was the sum total of my emotional state. Shitty, yet simple. But I'm introspective—or maybe masochistic—enough to look a little deeper, and what I see confuses me, badly. I think about J.C.'s confession the night before, the way he looks at me when we're alone, and I have to suppress a shiver. Regardless of how much I care about him, I'd figured that in the light of day, our little indiscretion would seem more or less like an accident, a little grief-stricken sex between friends, at least for me. I expected to feel self-conscious, for us to be awkward together. Instead, we're like we were before, just—more, I guess. It doesn't feel strange. It feels right, or at least like one possible version of right, if that makes any sense. Lying here with him, I feel sated, content, safe. Peaceful, even. My heart aches for Aidan, but it feels separate from this moment, like one has nothing to do with the other. My head throbs, right behind my eyes.

"J.C.?" I say with sudden conviction.

"Hmmm?" he says, slow and lazy. He's tracing a figure eight on my back.

When I don't respond, he slides out from under me and leans on his elbow, so he can see my face. His eyes sharpen then, and he sighs. "It's like that, is it," he says.

I don't know if it's easier or harder that he isn't going to make me say it. Easier, probably, except now I can add cowardice to my list of transgressions. I attempt anyhow, opening my mouth—most probably to put my foot in it, but I have to try. I owe him that, at least. I am vacillating between *It's not because I don't love you* and *You deserve so much better* when he places a finger across my lips. His eyes are sad.

"Don't," he says. "I'll just go." He sits on the edge of the bed and pulls on his shorts, then yanks his shirt over his head.

I'm relieved and alarmed, all at once. "It's the middle of the night, J.C. You don't have to leave."

"Yes, I do." He slides his feet into his sandals.

"I'm sorry," I say to his back. It's not much, but it's something. And at least it's sincere. I'm not sure about a lot of things, but I am sorry for hurting him. It's the last thing I intended.

"I know that better than you do," he says, reaching down to the foot of the bed for the extra blanket. He shakes it out, tucks it around me like he's putting Gabriel to bed.

"You know I love you, right?" I say, putting my hand on his arm. I don't want to make a bad situation worse, but he looks so unhappy, I can't help myself.

"Sure," he says. "I know. But that doesn't mean you want to do this."

While I'm thinking of a good rejoinder, he leans over and kisses me on the forehead. "Good night, Maddie," he says, and those three words are full of emotion, like he's saying something else.

I resist the urge to reach out to him, to make this better. *Stop*, I want to tell him. *Stay.* But I say nothing, and he walks out the door.

THIRTY-FOUR

Madeleine

You would think that asking J.C. to leave would make me feel better, or at least more morally upright. It does, and then again, it doesn't.

After he left, it took me a long time to fall asleep. If I'd been less exhausted, I probably wouldn't have slept at all. But somewhere close to dawn, I passed out, only to have a nightmare about Aidan, struggling underneath the snow. I shot upright, sweating, with the weirdest sense that Aidan was in the room watching me, and that was it for sleep. Instead, I took a shower, made coffee, and then sat down on the couch to assess what to do next. And what I did was nothing, at least until Gabriel got up and I had to go through the motions of being a functioning parent.

I wish I could be angry at J.C., that he would pressure me to be with him or at least talk about what happened, but nothing could be further from the truth. Instead he is back to being his normal helpful self. He calls the next afternoon like nothing's amiss, asking if I need anything from the store. His timing is perfect: I've been scrubbing the kitchen floor while Gabriel builds a Lego fort for his *Star Wars* guys, periodically opening the refrigerator and examining the empty shelves. After we threw out the leftovers from the memorial service, not much was left. I need cereal for Gabe, milk, eggs, fresh fruit, the basics.

It shouldn't be a big deal, but the thought of going to the grocery store, traversing the aisles, and having to make decision after decision floors me. I can't even decide what to wear in the morning. Choosing between five brands of granola, followed by seven types of apples, is out of the question. I'd probably wind up abandoning my cart in the middle of the cookie aisle—Oreos or Chips Ahoy? Who can tell?—and fleeing, Gabe in tow, for the relative safety of my car.

"How did you know I needed food?" I ask J.C.

Over the phone, I can almost hear him shrug. "I just did. You want to give me a list? I can come by and pick it up. Or you can email it to me."

I am tempted to take him up on his offer to send the list through cyberspace, but then I think better of it. Not even I am that big of a wimp. "Come by," I tell him. "I'll give you my debit card. And thanks."

"No worries," he says. He arrives. He gets the list and the card. He shops, he returns, he unloads the groceries, he helps me put them away. Then he stays and plays with Gabriel, who is thrilled to see him. He is careful with me, so careful—back to how he was before the avalanche, except now I know what's behind the distance he keeps.

The odd thing is, the more appropriately J.C. behaves, the more I feel for him. I am floored by the simplest things—how he sits on the carpet with his eyes focused on Gabe's face, nodding intently like the world is no bigger than this small boy and his pillow-fort-in-progress, the long, lean line of his back as he stretches to put the spaghetti sauce in the cabinet above the stove, where I can't reach. Watching him, I find myself thinking of the amethyst cathedral geode that Aidan brought me from Brazil, the time he and J.C. climbed Tres Picos. I remember cradling the hollowed rock in my hands, its unremarkable gray exterior transformed through some strange alchemy to conceal a mysterious, glittering heart: clusters of progressively purple quartz crystals, translucent lavender to deep shadowy violet, an alien landscape in miniature. Amethyst, for healing, restful sleep, meditation, and peace. And also, as the little card that came with the geode attested, for awakening the soul, bridging the gap between this world and the next.

If J.C. notices how I look at him, he doesn't acknowledge it . . . but I know, which is bad enough. Here he is, treating me exactly how you should treat your best friend's widow—running errands, helping out around the house, entertaining Gabe—and here I am, wanting to feel his big hands trace my body, wanting to hear him say my name the way he did that first night. Then he leaves, and I spend the hours until he comes back missing Aidan, cleaning my house obsessively, and trying to be a good mother to Gabriel, or at least a competent one.

It is all beginning to overwhelm me, and I begin to think that maybe I need a geographic cure. Maybe if I go home for a little while, to stay with my parents, I'll find myself again. Gabe and I will spend some quiet time together. I will figure out what we are going to do next, when I'll be ready to go back to work.

I'll return phone calls and emails, I'll do yoga, I'll let myself miss Aidan, and life will begin to make sense.

I say as much to J.C. the next time he comes over. It's night-time, and Gabe is already in bed. J.C. made dinner, gave him a bath, even put him in his pajamas and read him stories. "Relax," he tells me, and I try, but serenity eludes me. When J.C. comes out of Gabe's room I am at the sink, scrubbing the pot he'd used to make couscous.

He walks up behind me and takes the sponge out of my hand. "You are not a good listener," he says, his tone light. I try to take the comment at face value, but I can't. I am too aware of the way his fingers don't brush mine when he removes the sponge from my grasp.

"I know," I tell him. "I'm a disaster area."

I wait for him to contradict me, but he doesn't. Instead he squirts more soap on the sponge and finishes off the couscous pot. He starts on the cutting board next, like I haven't said any-thing at all.

"I think Gabe and I need to leave town for a little bit," I say into the silence. "Maybe go see my parents in New York."

His hands stop scrubbing for a moment, then resume their motion. "Why?" he asks, and if I didn't know him so well, I wouldn't be able to detect the slight edge to his tone.

"I just need a break from all this. I need to get my life in per-spective, so I can figure out what to do next. And I need to do it somewhere that doesn't remind me of Aidan everywhere I turn."

He puts the cutting board on the drying rack and turns to face me, wiping his hands on his shorts. "You running away, Maddie?"

"I don't think so," I say. "Just trying to see clearly."

"Don't leave because of me," he says in the same even voice.

"I'm not," I say back, which isn't a total lie.

He regards me for a moment, studying my face like he's try-ing to decide whether to believe me. And then he says, "Okay then. Let me know when you're leaving and I'll take you guys to the airport," and turns back to the sink. He runs water into the asparagus pan.

I don't know what I expected him to do or say—to argue with me, maybe, ask me not to go—but that's not his style. If he'd given me a hard time, I would have gotten angry, told him to mind his own business. So why do I feel disappointed?

There's no good answer to that question, or at least no an-swer I'm willing to accept. I watch J.C. do the dishes, giving them his complete attention—perhaps no dishes will have ever been so clean; they could give my overscrubbed kitchen floor a run for its money—I wrap my arms tight around myself so I won't touch him, and I plan my much-needed escape.

THIRTY-FIVE

Aidan

Nicholas is awake. I am cast out, at least for the moment. Sometimes this happens, sometimes it doesn't. I take advantage of the opportunity, coalescing in Gabe's room. I miss him so much. I'd give what passes for my existence right now to be able to really hold him, to put my arms around Maddie and have her know I'm here.

If my plan works out, if Nick and I can come to an understanding, I'll get my wish. He's a stubborn son of a bitch. He is fighting me. But I am stronger. I'm tethered here by sheer force of will, by a promise I need to keep. He can fight me all he wants, but he won't win. I'm sorry for co-opting his life like this, but not sorry enough to try to undo whatever metaphysical shit binds me to him. I don't know how it works, what I'm doing, but if it means getting to see Maddie again, getting to see my son, I'll keep it up.

Gabe is lying in bed, tucked under his soft blue blanket, a copy of *The Velveteen Rabbit* next to him on the pillow. I think he's asleep, but his eyes open and when he sees me, a smile spreads across his face. "Daddy!" he says. He jumps up on his knees and his old white teddy bear goes flying. Without thinking about it, I put up my hand. I expect the stuffed animal to go right through me, but wonder of wonders, I catch it. For a second I just look at it in my hand, matter and antimatter, or whatever the hell I am right now. Then I hand Teddy back to Gabe.

"Hi, monkey boy," I say. "How's it going?" I don't expect him to hear me—last time, he couldn't—but he does. His eyebrows pull down, like mine do when something confuses me.

"But you're dead, Daddy," he says. "Aren't you?"

How do you answer a question like that? "Looks that way, champ," I say. I run my hand over my jaw and feel stubble.

"But, Daddy, I don't get it. How can you be here and dead at the same time?"

"That's a good question," I tell him. I wish I had the answer. "If I figure that one out, I'll let you know."

"I miss you a lot," he says. His eyes swim with tears, and I watch him fight them back. He hates to cry.

"I miss you too, Gabe. You and your mommy both." Tears prick my own eyes when I think of Maddie. Can ghosts cry? I don't want to find out.

Gabe has moved on to another topic, a determined set to his face. "Mommy doesn't believe that you came to see me before. She thinks it was just a dream. I told her and told her and she got all mad."

"I can see why." I smile at him, just a little bit. "I don't understand it myself."

"Are you real, though?"

"What is real?" I say back to him, courtesy of *The Velveteen Rabbit.*

He shrugs. I don't know how much time I have, so I figure I'd better cut to the chase. "Gabe, this is important," I tell him. "A man's going to come to see you and your mommy. His name is Nicholas. He has black hair, and blue eyes like yours and mine. The stuff he says, it may sound crazy, but you need to get your mommy to listen to him, okay?"

Gabe knits his eyebrows again. "When is he coming? Because Mommy says we're going to New York."

"To see Grandma and Grandpa Kimble?"

"No. They're going on a trip. We're just . . . going, I guess. Mommy says she needs to think about stuff."

I run one hand through my hair. This could be complicated. I'll have to figure out some way to reroute Nicholas, to let him know where Maddie's going and make him think it's his own idea. I'm not the best at manipulation; I'm more of a head-on kind of guy. But I'm lucky to be here at all, in whatever capacity. I'll take what I can get. "How is your mommy?" I ask. The answer's bound to hurt, but I need to hear it anyway.

"She's sad," Gabe says. "She cries a lot. But when Uncle J.C. is here, she's happier. He makes her smile."

Shit, fuck, and damn. I would say my body's not even cold yet, but I know better; wherever I am, physically speaking, I am a Popsicle. I know I gave her permission, I all but pushed her into it, but . . . damn. I never expected to be around to deal with the consequences.

Gabe's looking at me like he thinks I'm going to start yelling. "I know you told me to take care of her, Daddy, and I'm trying, honest. But it's hard. And he . . . well, he's a grown-up. I guess he's just better at it than me."

"I'll bet he is," I say. "Tell me something, Gabriel. Does Uncle J.C. stay overnight? Like, for sleepovers?"

"Sure, sometimes," Gabe says, confirming my suspicions. "He's here right now."

This is just wrong. Please tell me I am not trapped in this room with my son, while my wife is fucking my best friend down the hall. I close my eyes, try to hold my breathing steady. I wanted this to happen, I tell myself. I told her to. And him, what did I expect he would do?

I remember that moment in the tent, right after . . . well, after. What did he say? *I'll take care of your family. I won't let you down.* This wasn't exactly what I had in mind, motherfucker.

I can't blame him, though, much as I want to. He has loved her for years, not just lusted after her but really, truly loved her. I saw it in the way he looked at her, the way he never touched her unless she initiated it first. He locked himself down like Attica so he wouldn't break the trust between us again. I know J.C., and if I think I'm conflicted right now, he's got to be feeling ten thousand times worse. He's got that whole savior complex going on. I'm sure he's found a way to blame himself for what's happened, and that every time he puts his hands on her, it's threaded through with guilt.

Still, it hurts to think of him kissing her, touching her. I picture his olive skin against her paleness, imagine his body inside the woman I still think of as mine, and feel a spark of rage so intense it makes me dizzy, even in this altered state.

"Damn," I say finally, letting my breath go in a low, whistling sigh.

"Daddy?" Gabe asks. "Why can't you go see Mommy yourself? How come you can only see me?"

It's more like the other way around—he's the only one who can see *me*—but that seems too complicated to explain to a four-year-old. "I wish I knew, buddy man. It would sure make things simpler, if I could talk to Mommy right now." I roll my eyes. What would I find if I materialized in the room with Maddie? Her and J.C., talking? Making love? Or dancing maybe; he loves to dance and he's good at it. Roma and I used to tease him, call him the sex machine. I don't know that I could handle seeing him dance that way with my wife. Nope, better to stay here, with Gabe and Optimus Prime.

"Do you want me to go get her, Daddy? I will. You can stay right here and I'll bring her back to see you. Then she'll believe me, for sure." Gabe is excited now. He's so much like me—once a solution comes to mind, then it's full speed ahead, and damn the torpedoes.

"I don't think it works that way, buddy," I say, and watch his face fall. "You'll just have to keep trying. Maybe I can come up with an idea, to convince her. And in the meantime, you tell your Uncle J.C. to behave himself."

Gabe thinks this over. "Okay," he says. "Will you still come see me when we go to New York?"

"If I can, I will. I promise, and you know I always keep my promises, right?" It's true, I've always kept my promises to Gabe. When he wanted the new Boba Fett figure for Hanukkah—we always celebrated that and Christmas, too, just to cover all the bases—and every frigging place was out of stock except for one little store over the Utah line, I put the chains on the Jeep and drove way the hell out to bumfuck to get it for him. When I got home, cursing bad drivers, snow, and ice six ways from Sunday, Madeleine asked why I hadn't just ordered the damn thing online. I told her the truth: It wouldn't have gotten here fast enough.

"I know," Gabe says to me now. "Like with Boba Fett."

"Yeah, like that. So if I don't come, you'll know it's because I couldn't, okay?"

"Okay, Daddy."

"Do you remember the name of the guy I told you about?"

"Nicholas," he says, slow, to make sure he has it right. "And he has blue eyes like us."

"Nicholas Sullivan," I remind him. "From North Carolina. Can you remember that?"

"North Carolina," he repeats. "Where is North Carolina, Daddy?"

"A long ways from here. Get Mommy to show you on a map. It's where I met her."

"Okay. But why is he coming? Does Mommy know him?" Gabe leans forward, propping his elbows on his knees.

"No, buddy. And chances are, she won't want to talk to him, either."

"Why not?"

"Because people run away from what they don't understand. They see what they want to see. And I doubt your mom will want to see Nicholas Sullivan. She may even say bad things about him, like he's crazy or not nice. But you'll know better, right? You'll know I sent him."

"Yes, Daddy," he says. "Nicholas Sullivan. From North Carolina."

"Good boy," I say. I lean close then, to kiss him. He throws his arms around my neck, but just like last time, his hands lock around air where my neck should be. I see him sitting there, his arms empty, his eyes filled with tears. More than anything, I want to hug him, tell him it will be okay. But that would be a lie, and besides which, I couldn't tell him anything, even if I wanted to. His room fades away. There is a tunnel, and I am inside it. Someone is calling me. Nicholas slips down into sleep, pulling me with him, and I can't break free. I slide down the length of the tunnel, into Nick's body, and wake up in his dreams.

THIRTY-SIX

Nicholas

I have learned quite a bit about myself since what I've come to think of as the Great Awakening. For instance, I used to like wine, and now I prefer whisky. I never touched a cigarette, but now I could take out stock in American Spirit. I am a decent dancer, I have eclectic taste in music, and I can't cook worth a damn. Also, apparently I am a coward.

This is not a nice thing to discover about oneself, but it's the truth. Because otherwise, I would have called Grace to let her know I was leaving soon. After all, I told Taylor, the victim of my successful memory wipe, when I asked him if he'd watch Nevada for me while I was gone. He wanted to know where I was going, of course, which was tricky. Since I discovered Aidan's Facebook memorial, I've been checking it every day; it helps me focus, makes me feel less insane. Maddie hasn't posted anything before, but yesterday she wrote a note thanking everyone for their support, and saying that she and Gabe are going to New York to visit her parents for a while. I guess they live in Brooklyn, and that is where she's staying. Which is nice to know, because it's not like Aidan has been dropping any little hints. Ever since that night with Grace, he's been completely silent when I'm awake, leading me to wonder if the voice I heard was really my own. This decreases my fear that he's going to take me over, *Exorcist*-style, but ups the ante in terms of the insanity factor. Oh well, you can't have everything, right?

Speaking of having everything, I'd give a lot to have a nice little face-to-face palaver with Aidan James. I mean, for real. But since this doesn't seem likely to happen anytime soon—given the inconvenient truth that he's dead, and all—I've been forging ahead on my own. Madeleine kept her maiden name, Kimble, and her parents are listed. Presto, I have their address. Nicholas Sullivan, private eye extraordinaire, that's me. Next I make a plane reservation, find a Brooklynite on Craigslist who's off to the Hamptons for the summer and is renting out their place week by week, arrange for Taylor to watch Nevada, and I'm all set . . . except for a Grace Robinson–shaped wrinkle in time.

Who knows what Grace would've said if I told her I was leaving? Maybe I could've passed it off as a vacation, like I did with Taylor. Or maybe Grace and I would have had a nice dinner, complete with anxiety and miscommunications, which I would have suffered gladly because I am, after all, leaving the state for an indeterminate amount of time after having sex with her not once, not twice, but three times in a twenty-four-hour period. Yes, that would have been appropriate, if awkward as hell. It would be the least she deserves.

But I don't tell her that I'm leaving, or invite her to dinner. What I do instead is, I write her a note, and I stick it in her mailbox when I know she'll be at work. And then I console myself with the fact that I didn't send her an email. Yep, *coward* is the word for me, and I'm willing to bet Grace will have several more colorful ones in mind when she gets home and reads my note. And she'd be right, because aside from the guilt that's become so habitual I barely notice it anymore, my predominant emotions are excitement and relief. *Now,* I think. *Now everything begins.*

THIRTY-SEVEN

Aidan

I come to myself next in our bedroom, watching Maddie sleep. Given what Gabe told me, I half expect to see J.C. lying next to her—or, hell, on top of her for that matter. I brace myself for it. But no, she is alone.

Like before, she fights the pillows, pushing at them. *Aidan,* she says, and *why,* and *I'm sorry.* Her hands clench the blanket and she says my name, she says to hold on, she says she's coming. *Wait for me,* she says, clear as if she knows I'm here beside her. Then her breath comes faster, and she says *No.* Over and over she says it, until the syllables blur together into a wordless shriek. Her eyes snap open then and she sits up, panting. Into the silence of the room she says, *You were gone. I didn't mean to.*

It doesn't take too much imagination to figure out what she means. I wait for that spark of rage to burn me up again, but it doesn't come. Instead I think, *He will take care of her. He promised. She doesn't have to be alone.*

For a while she stares at the ceiling, expressionless. Then her gaze shifts left, and in the dim light of the lamp I see what she's looking at: the photo of me and Gabe on the dresser. Sadness comes over her face, so immediate and deep, it transforms her features like a mask. She wipes at her eyes. *Fuck*, she mumbles, and I grin. It sounds like something I'd say when under duress. Maddie is usually more eloquent than that.

She glances at the neon numbers of the clock—3 A.M.—then gets out of bed and walks into the kitchen. She pulls open the cabinet where we keep the cups and glasses, and at first I think she's going to get some water, but that's not what she's after. Instead she takes out the plate and the mug Gabe and I made her at that pottery place last year. She cradles the plate, looking at the heart-shaped faces. Tears slip down her cheeks.

I look at her standing there, wearing one of my Ouray T-shirts, her hair loose down her back. The shirt is way too big for her; it falls off her shoulder on one side, exposing the pale curve of her neck. I am close enough to smell the salt on her skin.

Gabe said J.C. makes her smile, and for a moment I am so jealous, I could deck the guy. It rips me up to watch her fall apart this way night after night, because of me. It breaks me into pieces inside. She's suffering, and I can't do anything about it. But maybe he can.

Goddamn it, if he can make her happy, then let him. I don't have to like it. No one would. But I love her enough to show her I meant what I said, I love her enough to open the way. I stand there in our kitchen, looking at the plate Gabe and I made for her together. She cries, and I decide.

THIRTY-EIGHT

Madeleine

We leave for New York three days after I tell J.C. we're going, courtesy of Aidan's frequent flyer miles. My parents are out of town for a few weeks, visiting relatives in San Diego. They offer to postpone their trip, but I won't let them. They've been planning this for a long time, and I think it will do me some good to be on my own with Gabriel. We've been surrounded by people since the accident—well-meaning, loving family and friends, but still. If Gabe and I are going to be a family of two, we might as well start figuring out what that feels like.

It takes a while, but I finally convince them to leave their keys with a neighbor and let me look after the house for them while they're gone. They own a brownstone on Union Street in Park Slope, which they bought back when such things were affordable, renovated it top to bottom, and divided it into apartments. Now they live on the bottom two floors and rent out the top. My dad wants to sell it and get something more practical, but my mom won't let him. The neighborhood is fantastic for kids, and I think Gabriel's enthusiasm whenever we visit is one of her primary motivations for keeping the place. As for me, it's my childhood home. It will be a sad day for me when they sell it.

J.C. drives me and Gabe to the airport, as promised. He doesn't say much, and with his sunglasses on, it's hard for me to tell what he's thinking. Then again, maybe I don't want to know.

He unloads our stuff at the curb and makes sure we get checked in. Then he kneels down to Gabe's level and hugs him. "Take care of your mama, little man," he says.

"I always do," Gabe says, his small voice serious.

"Good." He holds his palm up for a high-five. Gabe slaps it, hard, and J.C. grins. "Catch you on the flip side," he tells Gabe.

"Later, skater," Gabe says right back, the way his daddy taught him. Then he looks into J.C.'s face, his blue eyes as intent as I've ever seen them. "Be good," he tells J.C., like he's channeling E.T.

J.C. looks puzzled and amused, all at the same time. "Right back at you," he says to Gabe. Then he stands up and turns to me. "So," he says.

"I'll be back," I tell him.

"You better be." He pulls me to him, holds me close. "I love you," he says in my ear. And before I have a chance to react—to say anything, or to read his expression—he lets me go, gets back into his car, and pulls away from the curb.

When I open my wallet to retrieve my driver's license, so we can negotiate security—no joke at DIA—I find a small piece of paper inside. I've only seen J.C.'s handwriting a few times, but it's distinctive and I have no problem recognizing it now. On the white page, which looks like it was torn from a notebook, he's printed four words: *Just think about it.* It's what he said before he kissed me that first time, standing in his and Aidan's kitchen, before all hell broke loose. I know he knows I'll remember.

I fold the paper and put it in my pocket, where it feels like it's burning a hole. All the way to Charlotte, where we have to make our connecting flight, and from there to LaGuardia, I reach in and touch it, like a talisman, like a map that can show me the way home.

THIRTY-NINE

Madeleine

It is strange to be in my parents' house when they're not there. To make matters worse, I can't remember the last time I was here without Aidan. I keep expecting to encounter him on the stoop, smoking a cigarette, or in the library, sprawled full length on the couch, a book of poetry in his hands. It's as if my mind is playing tricks on me—surely he's only dead in Colorado! Here in New York, all will be as it once was—and every time I realize that's not the case, I have to fight off a dangerous sensation of vertigo. To combat it, I fill our days with activity. We visit the aquarium and the beach at Coney Island, we watch the boats come in while eating Thai food in Sheepshead Bay, we take the train into the city and hang out at the Museum of Natural History, looking at each and every dinosaur skeleton. Aidan used to climb at Chelsea Piers whenever we were in town, and at Gabe's request we go back there, just to check it out. We spend a lot of time walking. I don't have a jogging stroller, and it crosses my mind that most almost-five-year-olds would balk at trekking long distances in the New York sun, where the heat bakes up from the asphalt and down from the buildings—but not Gabriel. He's used to hiking with his dad and J.C., and he never complains.

In fact, Gabe's behavior is almost preternaturally good on this trip, which worries me a little bit. He's never been a complainer, but he is stubborn—wonder who he got that from?—and he's been known to sink into spectacular bouts of sulking when he doesn't get his way. He doesn't throw tantrums; he's not that kind of child. Instead, he broods. Since Aidan's accident, though, he's been sweet and helpful to a fault. There's clearly something on his mind; he watches me all the time, his jaw set and his eyebrows knitted like Aidan's used to be when he was trying to figure something out. And he asks strange questions. One time he asked me if I believed in ghosts; another time he asked me to pull out my parents' atlas so I could show him where North Carolina was. But when I ask him why he wants to know, he just shrugs, looking as mulish as his father. For a four-year-old, he is good at keeping secrets.

I always thought that Aidan's tendencies to "keep himself to himself," as he described it, were a function of growing up in a skewed family system, but now I am beginning to wonder whether they are genetic. It's a little frustrating, and if I didn't have so much else on my mind, I would press Gabe to tell me what's going on inside his little head. As it is, though, I just answer his questions—no to the ghosts, and as for North Carolina,

I show him where I used to live, where I met Aidan, but that doesn't seem to be what he's after. He thanks me, and then he goes off to play with Luke Skywalker, Han Solo, and company, his source of endless entertainment.

The end result of all this is that during the first week we're in New York, I spend some quality time worrying about Gabe. He's always been an observant, selective child—my genes at work—though when he wants to, he can pour on the charm. Now he is so quiet, it scares me a little bit. He seems like he's waiting for something. On our visits to the musical playground in Prospect Park, our excursion to the Park Slope puppet theater, our dinners at the Pit Stop—a fabulous restaurant on Columbia Street where Gabe eats mini-burgers with gusto, I pick at my mussels marinière, and we watch a group of progressively drunken people mangle game after game of pétanque—he glances around like a fugitive on the run. Whenever I ask him what he's looking for, he gives me an innocent smile and says, "Nothing, Mommy. Just seeing what's going on." If I had any extra emotional energy, it would probably manifest itself in the form of irritation.

As it is, when our adventures for the day are done and Gabe is tucked into bed, the sadness and bewilderment that I've held at arm's length come rushing in. I've put J.C.'s note—*Just think about it*—on my mom's bedside table, and it might as well be my mantra. Those long nights during our first week in New York, I don't do anything *but* think. That and cry, my other new pastime. I could give lessons in the fine art of sobbing without making a sound.

I think about J.C., like he asked me to. Was it wrong, being with him like that? In my heart, I don't feel that it was. It felt good and calm, an oasis. When we were together, it felt right. But my head is a different story. How could I do that to Aidan, no matter what he'd said about J.C. taking care of me?

If being with J.C. is something I decide to entertain, it has to be just that—something *I* decide, something I want and take responsibility for. And that's where everything falls apart. I feel guilty for sleeping with J.C., guilty for wanting him. I feel guilty for asking him to leave, guilty for thinking about asking him to come back. How can I miss Aidan so badly and think about being with someone else, no matter that I've known J.C. as long as I've known Aidan, that he can tell what I'm going to say or do before I've figured it out myself? After six days of this vicious cycle, I'm no closer to figuring out whether we should try to be together—an idea that, by turns, terrifies me and makes me feel like I can finally breathe—or whether it would be for the best to call the whole thing off, for good.

Then there's the issue of money. Aidan had what he called a bitch of a time finding life insurance, since few companies wanted to insure a guy who took his life in his hands on a near-daily basis. His predilection for extreme sports resulted in an exorbitant premium, and Aidan swore in particularly colorful fashion every time he had to write a check to the company that deigned to take him on. The end result is that, now that he's gone, Gabe and I have a sizable chunk of change coming our way—or we will as soon as I finish wrangling with the insurance company, an activity that I relish just slightly more than stomping on the huge cockroaches that used to invade my house in Durham, no matter how many times I sprayed. What to do with the money, though? Invest it for Gabe's college fund? Use it to live on while I gather my powers of concentration enough to start writing again? Start a memorial fund in Aidan's name? I spend a substantial amount of time tossing and turning, trying to determine the best route to take.

When I'm not worrying about Gabe, J.C., or my finances, I lie in my parents' bed and grieve. I could get a job missing Aidan—his exuberance, his crooked smile, the way he looked at me like I was the only person in the world. I feel like I've been hollowed out, like I can't breathe. I try and try, but my lungs won't fill. I wish that Aidan was next to me, holding me, and because I know that's impossible, I wish for the best alternative, the one I can have—J.C. Then I feel terrible for a whole variety of reasons, most of which lead me right back to worrying about whether J.C. and I have any right to be together . . . and the whole process begins anew.

This is the frame of mind I am in on the seventh day of our sojourn in New York, as Gabe and I make our way back home from Barnes & Noble. We're wandering along the tree-lined streets of the Slope, checking out the stoop sales, watching the squirrels scoop up the acorns that have tumbled from the trees. Then Gabe's head goes up like a hunter who's sighted the first buck of the season, and he points. "Mommy, look," he says.

I look where he's pointing—toward my parents' brownstone, three houses away. There is a man sitting on the stoop. This far away, all I can see is that he has dark hair, and my heart skips a beat. Surely J.C. wouldn't have followed me up here, when I told him I needed space?

Before I can stop him, Gabriel takes off. He runs toward my parents' house as fast as he can, skidding to a halt right in front of the iron gates that enclose the front yard. I run after him.

"Wait, Gabe!" I yell, but there's no need. He's not approaching the man. He's just standing there.

When I catch up with him, I can see why. We don't know this guy; he's a total stranger. His hair is darker than J.C.'s, almost black, and longer. He looks at me as I come up behind Gabe, and I take in breath so quickly I start coughing. His eyes are the same blue as Aidan's, as Gabriel's, and they're filled with recognition.

"Hi," he says. "Sorry if I scared you. I didn't mean to."

FORTY

Nicholas

Now that I am sitting here, on the stoop of Maddie's parents' house, looking at Maddie and Gabe in person, I don't know what to do or say. It's beyond strange to see them in the flesh, after all the dreams, the pictures, the images on Facebook. Here are his dimples, his lanky limbs, his blue eyes like his father's, his pale skin and heart-shaped face like his mother's. Here is her wavy chestnut hair, her wide-set eyes, her slender build. And here is her voice, unhappy, threatened.

"What are you doing on my parents' stoop?" she says, looking at me as if I might be closely related to Son of Sam.

I smile, in part because she's as bristly as a mama cat whose kitten is in harm's way, and in part because I am so happy to be talking to her, it doesn't much matter what she says to me. "Waiting for you," I tell her.

Panic fills her features, and I realize that I've said the wrong thing. Now she's eyeing me like I'm a stalker who's laid a trap for her and her son. To buy time, I light a cigarette. Her eyes go from the pack on the stoop to me, and now they're not just alarmed; they are sad, too. "What do you mean, you're waiting for me?" she says.

This is, of course, the million-dollar question, and not one that can be tackled in thirty words or less. I'd hoped that Aidan would provide me with some magical words to say, something that would instantly persuade her of my identity (or, rather, of his) but surprise, surprise—this doesn't happen. So instead I just tell her the truth. "It's a long story. I'd love to tell it to you, Maddie," I say, blowing smoke rings over the railing.

She follows the progression of the smoke rings with dismay. And then she gets very defensive, very quickly. I'd hoped that using her name would relax her, but it's had the opposite effect: It's made her suspicious, and pissed. She starts firing questions at me, too fast for me to answer. "Who are you? How do you know my name? How did you know where to find me?" Then she sticks one hand in her pocket, like she's got a weapon in there . . . pepper spray, maybe, or a cellphone, in case she needs to call the cops about the crazy man on her porch who talks in riddles and won't go away.

Sighing, I put out the cigarette. All I want to do is hold her, but that would go over about as well as a lead balloon. So I just say, "It's all part of the same long story. I know your husband, is the shortest answer I can give you."

She draws herself up to her full height, which is maybe only five four. "My husband is dead," she says, each syllable like a bullet.

"I know that, too," I tell her. Boy, do I. "Maybe better than anyone."

Now she thinks I'm certifiable. Her face shuts down, like someone has pulled the curtains for the day. "I don't know who you are, but if this is a practical joke, it isn't very funny. I'm going inside. If you're not off my steps in the next five minutes, I'm calling the police. Come on, Gabe," she says, and she grabs his hand.

Now what? I can hardly jump up and block her way, nor can I blurt out the truth—*I channel your husband while I sleep! The only memories I have are his! He made me come find you! And I love you! But I'm not crazy, honestly!* I sit there like an idiot, my mind going a million miles an hour, feeling desperate. And then Gabe saves me.

"Wait, Mommy. Don't get mad. I know him," he says. He plants his feet, refusing to let her pull him.

You do? I think, just as Maddie says, "No you don't," in a tone so definitive, it could slice diamonds.

"I do too," Gabe says. "You're Nicholas, right? Nicholas Sullivan?"

Dumbfounded—although why I should be, I have no idea; it's not like anything else that's going on makes sense—I nod. "That's me."

"You came all the way from North Carolina to see us?" Gabe asks.

Again, I nod. That strange feeling of *purpose* is sweeping over me again. "I sure did."

"How do you know that, Gabe?" Maddie says, and she sounds freaked-out. I can't blame her. I'm a little freaked-out myself. Not to mention, I would also like to know how he knows who I am and where I'm from.

Gabriel takes a deep, deep breath. Then he says, real slow, "Daddy sent him. He said you might think he's crazy, or call him names, but I'm supposed to make sure you listen to what he says."

Thanks, Aidan, I think. Couldn't do anything the straightforward way, could you? A four-year-old and an amnesiac. The ideal believable duo.

Maddie grabs Gabe's shoulders like she's getting ready to steer him up the stairs. "I don't know what you're talking about. How could Daddy send him? Daddy is dead, remember?"

A less self-possessed child might back down, but Gabriel stands his ground. "I told you he came to visit me. I told you it wasn't a dream. He told me Nicholas was going to come see us. And here he is." He disengages himself from his mother's hands and steps toward me, and in that instant I can see what he'll look like as a teenager, as a man. "I've been waiting for you. I was beginning to think you weren't coming at all," he says.

"Here I am," I tell him. "I got here as fast as I could."

"You do have eyes like mine and Daddy's. He said you would, but I wasn't sure."

I smile at him, trying to look nonthreatening. And I guess I succeed, because he says, "It's dinnertime. We're having mac and cheese, with hot dogs all cut up. Plus, carrots and ranch. Are you hungry? You could eat with me and my mommy."

When I am brave enough to look at Maddie, I see that she has gone even whiter than she was to begin with, which is quite an accomplishment. On a crazy whim I hold up my hands, palms out. "I come in peace," I say. "I swear."

"Don't move," she says to me, and she takes Gabriel by the arm and tugs him under one of the oak trees on the sidewalk. Then she kneels in front of him and says something, in a voice too low for me to hear. He says something back; they look like they are arguing. She gesticulates; he shakes his head. This goes on for about five minutes, or maybe an eternity. Eventually they walk back over to the bottom of the stoop and she says, as if someone is holding her feet to the fire (or maybe a gun to her head), "Would you like to join us for dinner?"

"I would love to," I say, and I get to my feet. As they walk by me, up the steps, Gabe looks over his shoulder. Though I wouldn't think it was possible, coming from a kid his age, he winks.

Over dinner, we make small talk, avoiding the elephant in the room. Maddie leaves her cellphone on the table, just in case I turn out to be a serial killer, I suppose. She opens a bottle of red wine and pours each of us a glass; Gabe has milk. Then he goes into the living room to eat a bowl of ice cream and watch TV, and I help her clean up.

"So," she says. "How about that long story?"

"It really is long, Maddie. And it's going to sound crazy to you. I mean, it sounds crazy to me, and I'm stuck in the middle of it."

"Try me," she says, her hands on her hips.

I fumble around, trying to figure out where to begin. "Okay. Well, back in June—June seventh, to be exact—I was in a motorcycle accident. I woke up in the hospital, and physically I was fine. But otherwise, mentally speaking, I had some issues."

I see her register the date of Aidan's accident, file it away for consideration. "Like what?"

"My memory. It was—it *is*—just totally wiped. I can remember cultural stuff, like music and movies and books, but not anything personal."

"That's terrible," she says. "But I don't get what that has to do with me. Or Gabriel."

"Here's where it starts to get crazy. Before I woke up in the hospital, I had a dream. In it, I was climbing a mountain. The sun was rising, and I had stopped to look at it when I heard a horrible noise. It was an avalanche, and next thing I knew, it had swept me down the mountain. I got buried under the snow. And while I was under there, I saw these images—of you, and Gabe, and this guy. J.C., I guess he is. And then there was this poetry."

She has gone white again. "What poetry?" she says.

So I recite the words that have been rattling around in my head for the past month and a half: *Thus, though we cannot make our sun / Stand still, yet we will make him run.*

Her hand goes up to her throat, and her fingers close around the necklace she's wearing—a small white turtle whose shell glimmers in the light. She doesn't say a word.

"Anyway," I go on, when it doesn't look like she has anything to add, "at first it was just that avalanche dream. I dreamed it every night. Then I started doing things, like smoking and drinking whisky, that apparently I didn't used to do. And then I started to dream more stuff, too, about that morning at high camp, and this picture, with you and Aidan and Gabe in it. On the back, it had your names, and the date, and it read, *Come back to me.* So when I woke up that time, I was able to look up Aidan's name . . . and that's when I realized."

"Realized what?" She is bracing herself on the back of a chair now, her expression blank. I can't tell if she's getting ready to pass out or toss me into the street.

Here goes. I suck in air, then say, "Well, that the only memories I have . . . are actually Aidan's. After a while I started dreaming about other things . . . like when you met, I don't know how to say this without sounding rude . . . but I know the two of you were together, outside. It was wet and raining, and there was this railing . . . I dreamed about him running, thinking about how lucky he was, how he was determined not to turn out like his father, how he didn't want to mess up your relationship somehow. And then I dreamed about him and J.C., up on this monument, Devils Tower, it's called . . . they were talking about Aidan's dad, and he was thinking about how J.C.'s relationships with women never work out because you're the one he really wants."

She is now so pale, I could use her to light my way on a darkened road. This makes me both gratified and sad; gratified, because it means that what I'm saying is resonating with her, and sad, because I don't want to upset her, and that seems inevitable. "A lot of the habits I have now, they're his, too," I continue. "Ever since I woke up, I've had this compulsion . . . to come find you and Gabriel. It's gotten stronger and stronger. I just feel like I know you, like this is what I'm meant to do." That's as far as I'm willing to go; there's no way I'm going to let her know how I feel about her, the weeks I've spent obsessing, seeing her face. That would end with me getting forcibly ejected from her apartment, for sure. "I don't know why, I don't know what I'm supposed to do now that I'm here," I conclude. "But here I am."

"You're right," she says, her lips barely moving. "It does sound crazy."

"Any crazier than Gabriel knowing my name?" I challenge her. "Or you thinking Aidan shouldn't climb McKinley?"

"How do you know that?" she says.

"I told you." Shrugging my shoulders, I fold myself into a chair.

"This is insane." She reaches for her glass of wine and downs it, then pours herself another.

"I couldn't agree more," I tell her.

Our conversational impasse is breached by Gabriel, who has brought his empty ice cream bowl into the kitchen. "Here, Mommy," he says. He smiles at me.

"Thanks, buddy," she says, taking the bowl from him. "It's your bedtime, I think."

Unlike most children, he doesn't whine. "Okay," he says. "Will you read to me?"

"Of course."

"Read me three stories."

"We'll talk about it after you're in your PJs. Hurry up and get changed." He trots off down the hallway, and she turns to me. "After he goes to bed, we'll talk more. Do you mind waiting?"

"Not at all." I try to sound casual, but my heart speeds up, and I feel blood rushing to my cheeks. After all, what have I done for the past month and a half but wait, presumably for her? The hell of it is, I don't know for sure if it's me or Aidan who feels this way . . . but after weeks of confusion, grief, and anger, I don't think I care. It's nice to feel certain about something for once; whether they are his emotions or mine, I'll take them.

Over her shoulder I see Gabriel, wearing blue flannel pajamas with rockets printed on them. He is half-in, half-out of the shirt, his head stuck just inside the opening like the world's most recalcitrant turtle. She goes to him and kneels, pulling the shirt into place. His head emerges, dirty-blond hair standing up all over. "I picked our books," he announces.

"Good," she says.

"But I want Nick to read them." His gaze goes beyond her, finds me.

"Really?" I say. He nods.

"If your mom says it's okay," I say, looking at her.

"If that's what he wants," she says. "But first go brush your teeth and pee." She follows him into the bathroom to supervise. I stand there and look around the apartment—books, books, and more books; African soapstone sculptures; Oriental rugs. Then Gabe is out of the bathroom, and it's story time.

Maddie has tucked Gabe in, and the books are stacked neatly on the bed next to him. A worn white teddy bear is under one of his arms. "I'll be right outside," she says to both of us, which I realize is meant to reassure Gabe and warn me. She kisses Gabe and then walks out of the room, leaving the door partially open. She stands there like a sentry, her arms folded; I can see her through the half-open door.

"Which book do you want to start with?" I ask Gabe.

"You don't have to read me anything," he says. "I just want to know . . . did you know my daddy?"

"Not when he was alive," I say, weighing each word.

"Then how did he send you?"

I think about this for a moment. "You know how you told your mom that you had dreams about your daddy?"

"Sure. But they weren't really dreams."

"What do you mean?"

"I'm awake when he comes. He sits on the end of my bed and he tells me things. And when he leaves, everything is all cold."

I shiver, despite myself. "What does he tell you?"

"That he misses me. And he asks how my mommy is. And you were coming, he told me that." Gabe's tone is defensive, like he expects me to contradict him.

I wrestle with what version of the truth to share with a four-year-old. In the end I say, "Well, my dreams are really dreams. I'm asleep, and everything. And in them, your daddy told me to come here, to find you and your mom."

"Does my daddy come to see you a lot?"

"It's hard to explain. But pretty much . . . yes."

"You're lucky," Gabe says, hugging his teddy bear. "He's only come to see me twice."

"I guess he hasn't come to see your mom at all, huh?"

Gabe shakes his head. "He says he wishes he could, but he can't."

"Maybe one day he will," I say, although I don't believe it. If Aidan could talk to Maddie himself, he would have done it by now.

"I don't think so," Gabe says. He scoots back against the pillows and looks at me. "I'm glad you came, like Daddy said. It was a big secret to keep."

"You did a good job," I tell him. "Are you sure you don't want a story?"

He shakes his head again. "Go talk to my mommy," he says.

I ruffle his hair, then get up and leave, closing the door behind me. Maddie is still standing just outside; I wouldn't have expected anything less. "You heard all that?" I say to her.

"Yes. Although I won't pretend to understand it."

"Don't worry. I don't understand it, either."

"Tell me all of it," she says. "Tell me the rest."

So we go into the living room and sit down on opposite

ends of the couch, where I go through the entire story, leaving out nothing, not even Grace. She doesn't offer any comments, just stares at me like I'm a mirage. And finally I work up the courage to allude to how I feel. "I know it sounds insane," I say. "I know you don't know me from Adam. But I just—I mean, I really—I know you're missing him, and everything, it's way too soon—but maybe one day you would consider—I'm not a bad guy, I swear, and there's the advantage that I get to reinvent myself every day . . ." I'm trying to make a joke out of it, but it falls flat, and mercifully, I wind down and shut up. She's still quiet, and rather than deal with the skeptical expression I'm sure is on her face—or worse, out-and-out disgust—I employ my signature sneaker-gaze.

"Nicholas," she says, and I hear the couch springs give.

I raise my head. She is six inches away from me, looking into my eyes as if she's trying to see my soul—probing, direct, and searching. It's uncomfortable, but I don't look away. In the space between us, the air seems to heat and waver, as it does in the desert.

My eyes on hers, I reach my hand out and run my index finger along the length of her cheekbone. It seems incredible to me that I am touching her, that she is real. "Maddie," I say, and I have the eerie sense that the words are Aidan's, that he is speaking through me. "Have faith."

Her eyes widen, filled with an impossible amount of light. They shine, then fill with tears. Under my touch, she trembles. "How?" It is a whisper. Tears spill over, run down her cheeks. I trace their path as Grace did with mine that night, then place the palm of my hand against her cheek. The salt water seals our skin together, and she doesn't pull away.

"He misses you so much," I tell her. I can't shake the feeling that Aidan is here, in the room with us. I can't see him, but I feel his happiness, his grief, and an undeniable sense of triumph that he was actually able to pull this off. It could just be my imagination, but from the way Maddie is looking at me, disbelief and hope clear on her face, I don't think I'm the only one.

"He told me not to worry," she says, her voice breaking. "He wanted me to say everything would be all right, but I couldn't do it. I knew he wasn't coming home."

"I am so sorry," I say, without thinking. It doesn't sound like me. "Jesus, Maddie, I am."

She just looks at me. I sit there, feeling that strange electricity, that sense of Aidan's presence. Here I am, in a Brooklyn brownstone, touching another man's wife. My head is full of someone else's memories, and only a few of my own—many of them featuring Grace, whom I have treated abominably despite my best efforts. I'm not sure why I'm here, except for the compulsion that drove me forward each day, haunting my dreams until not acting was no longer an option. I have no inkling of when my personal history may choose to make a reappearance, if at all, and no idea what will happen next. Yet somehow, none of that matters.

I love her, I think, and emotion floods me. There's no room for anything else but how I feel. There's no need to analyze it, to take it apart. It simply *is*: exultation, lust, anticipation, and tenderness, all rolled into a wave that I'd expect to swamp me. Instead, it buoys me up, lifting me on its crest.

Slowly, slowly, she slides closer still, closing the distance between us. The air hums. It crackles. The urge to touch her is so strong it eclipses desire; it is a need, like food or water or air.

Equally slowly, I lift my other hand to her face. And then I kiss her, not the awkward, getting-to-know-you kiss of two people who have just met, but an intense kiss, intimate and familiar. I feel the electricity in the air flowing through me into her, like a circuit is closing. She kisses me back, and that is when I know she feels it, too.

FORTY-ONE

Madeleine

It's impossible, but sitting there on my parents' couch, look-ing into Nicholas's eyes, which are so much like Aidan's—that layered, vibrant blue—I recognize my husband. I've seen that single-minded, incisive look a thousand times, when Aidan was trying to figure out a new route or convince a donor to fund an expedition. I saw it when he was coaching me through labor with Gabriel, holding my hands and telling me I could do it, that I was strong. And I saw it when he kissed me for the first time, when he asked me to marry him, when he held me on a Colo-rado riverbank and pleaded with me to say yes.

I stare back, trying to figure out how this can be. I blink, hoping that will fix things. But it doesn't, and when Nicho-las lifts a finger and traces my cheekbone, feather light, I feel

Aidan's touch. "Maddie," he says, his voice lower, huskier than it was before. "Have faith."

The tears come then, filling my eyes and making their way down my cheeks. "How?" It isn't a rhetorical question. How can he know what Aidan would say to me, what he said all those years ago and again, right before he left? And if Aidan is really here, how can he expect me to have faith when everything's gone so horribly wrong?

Nicholas doesn't answer. Instead he lays his palm against my face, like Aidan used to do. "He misses you so much."

"He told me not to worry. He wanted me to say everything would be all right, but I couldn't do it. I knew he wasn't coming home," I say, as if Nicholas knows what I'm talking about. Maybe he does.

"I am so sorry," he says, pain clear in his voice. "Jesus, Maddie, I am."

I don't know what comes over me then. I know Aidan is dead. I stood at his memorial service, I mourned him with J.C. But something in Nicholas's tone, in his touch, moves me. So I slide closer to him, even though part of me thinks this is a bad idea. The air feels heavy, full of the pressing potential energy that precedes a storm. It's hard for me to breathe.

For a second Nicholas just looks at me with those foreign, familiar eyes. And then he lifts his other hand to my face. He kisses me, and that is when I fall apart. His lips touch mine, and I can feel Aidan's urgency, his fear, his tenderness. I feel him all around me, and when my eyes close and I kiss him back, he shakes so hard, it shifts the couch.

"Tell me you love me," he says, an eerie echo of the conversation that we had the night before he left for Alaska. "Say it now so I can hear."

"I love you," I say, just like I did that night. My voice breaks. "I love you more than you know."

He moves his face down to my neck, inhales like he used to when he'd come home after an early morning run and climb in bed with me. He always said I smelled like bonfires and choco- late, which made me giggle. *Basically*, I'd tell him, *you think I'm a s'more.* He'd chase me around the room, pin me down, and kiss me all over. *Yup*, he'd say, licking his lips, *Hershey's finest. But don't worry, Maddie. S'mores are some of my favorite things.* And then he'd kiss me some more, until Gabe stared at us like we were a couple of zoo animals gone rogue, and I made Aidan behave.

"You do what you need to," he says now, "and don't you feel guilty. Don't you wait for me, because I'm not coming back."

"What do you call this?" I retort, and he laughs. It's Aidan's belly laugh, loud and contagious.

"This?" he says. "This is an illusion, honey. An irresistible blend of stubbornness and mad freaking skills."

It's just like him to crack a joke in the midst of our per- sonal Hiroshima, and for a blissful second I let myself forget what's happened, why we are here. I smile despite myself, and he returns the favor, his lips curving against my skin. "That's it. That's my girl."

I stiffen in his arms. "I told you not to go. I begged you."

"I know. I know you did." His hands are on my back now, running over my shirt, but not in a sexual way. It's more as if he's trying to reassure himself that he is holding me, that this is real. "I'm so sorry," he says again, and his mouth closes on mine.

I fix this moment in my mind—the sound of his voice, the feel of his lips. And then I lift my own hands, touch his hair, his face. I half expect to feel Aidan's dirty-blond waves, the fine stubble that covers his high cheekbones. But of course I don't, and when I open my eyes I see Nicholas sitting next to me, just like he was to begin with. This is so disorienting, given everything that's come to pass, that I have to fight a wave of dizziness.

He looks at me then, like he can feel the weight of my gaze, and I have to accept the truth. This is not Aidan, no matter how much I want it to be. This is a strange man, and an even stranger situation. Until I figure out what's really going on here, I have no intention of doing something I'll regret, especially not with my son in the next room.

My palms come to rest on his chest, and I press against him, push him back. We consider each other, Nicholas and I. I don't know what he's looking for, but I'm searching the depth of his blue eyes for the spark that was Aidan, the one I was so sure I saw before. He allows this, sitting patient and still, his hands in his lap. He doesn't try to touch me again.

We sit there for a long minute, me figuring out what to do next, him letting me make up my mind. Now that we are not talking or touching, common sense rears its well-coiffed head. I'm alone in my parents' house in the middle of the night, kissing a stranger who's claiming to channel Aidan. And the bizarre thing is, I just might believe him. I know I should be frightened, but I am not, and that scares me more than anything else.

It must be eighty degrees outside, but a chill sweeps over me nonetheless. I shiver, clutching my upper arms. One thing's for sure—I have to think, and that's not going to happen with Nicholas perched on my couch. I clear my throat, imbue my voice with as much determination as I can muster, given the goose bumps that have risen all over my body, the smell of him on my skin. "You have to go," I say.

I expect him to protest, but he doesn't. Instead he nods,

stands in silence, makes his way to the door. When he turns to face me, I don't see Aidan there at all, and it occurs to me that I've lost my mind. Wordless, I close the door behind him, lock it. I lean against it, listening, until I hear his footsteps retreat down the steps and onto the sidewalk, hear them fade away.

Once I'm sure that I'm alone—except for Gabriel, that is—I wander aimlessly from one room to the next, trying to process what has happened, to make sense of it. And finally I realize there's only one person I want to talk to. I take my phone off the kitchen table and dial J.C.'s cell. It's not until the phone is ringing that I realize what time it is: three in the morning my time, which means it's 1 A.M. in Colorado. It rings three times, then four, and I'm considering hanging up when he says, "Hello?"

At the sound of his voice, relief rushes through me, like I've been holding my breath for a long time and have let it out. It takes me by surprise, so much so that I don't say anything in response.

"Maddie?" J.C. says. "Everything all right, sweetheart?"

"J.C.," I say, which is all I can manage.

"Yeah? You okay, babe?"

"Sort of," I say, since I don't know the answer.

"Did something happen?" His voice is sharper now, alert.

"Um. Did I wake you up?"

"Not hardly. I'm at Roma's." I can hear background noise now, voices and what sounds like a television.

"What are you doing?" I ask, just to keep him talking.

"Drinking beer and playing *Lego Star Wars*," he admits, and I hear someone—it sounds like Roma—laughing.

"*Lego Star Wars*? Really?"

"I bought it for Gabe, as a birthday present for when you guys come back. But then I thought I better learn how to play it, in case he needs help or something. And Roma just happens to have a PlayStation 3." He pauses, and I hear Roma laughing again.

"You are coming back, aren't you?" J.C. says, his voice pitched lower, more serious. "You didn't call to tell me you're moving there permanently."

"No. That's not why I called."

"Oh," he says. "Good." I hear more background noise, and then he says, "Roma says hello."

"Tell him hi," I say, and he relays the message.

"Why did you call then, Maddie?" he says when he comes back on the line. "Not that I'm not glad to hear your voice, but still. It's three in the morning for you, right?" He sounds wary, and I can hardly blame him.

"Something happened. Something really weird. I don't even know what to think of it. But I didn't know who else to call."

There's a pause, and then he says, "Tell me."

"Are you drunk?" I ask. The last thing I want is to have to repeat this story.

"Hang on a second," he says, and I hear bottles clinking. "Roma, how many beers have I had, you got any idea?" he shouts, away from the phone.

"Since you got here? Eight? Maybe nine?" Roma yells back. For a second I imagine them—J.C. must be in the living room, since that's where the flat-screen is, and Roma is most likely in the kitchen, hunting through the refrigerator for reinforcements. It's a scene I've witnessed more times than I can count, at dozens of parties and late-night hangout sessions. I can even see Trek, Roma's huge black Lab, sprawled at J.C.'s feet on the off-white Berber carpet.

"Did you hear that?" J.C. says to me.

"Uh-huh."

"You make the call. I don't feel wasted, or anything. But I probably shouldn't drive, and I might say a couple things I'll regret when I'm sober. So it's up to you, just like usual." He chuckles.

I turn the situation over in my mind. Then I say, "I'll take my chances."

"Fine. Hold on. Yo, Roma," he calls.

"Yeah?"

"You wanna try, or should I pause this?"

"I got it," Roma says, sounding closer to the phone. "Here. This is the last one, anyway."

"Did he give you another beer?" I ask.

"Yep. That a problem?"

"No. I'm just trying to picture what you're doing."

"You miss me? Never mind, don't answer that," he says. "Let me help you out. I'm petting Trek, and now I'm walking outside, and I'm sitting on one of Roma's crappy chairs. I am opening my beer, and I am looking at the stars, and I'm wondering how many of them you can see, where you are. I'm guessing not that many." He pauses. "I'm also thinking that I'd like to ask what you're wearing, but that would be inappropriate, so I won't. And now I'm kicking myself and wishing I would shut up already. Maybe I am drunker than I thought."

"Maybe so," I say, smiling even though he isn't here to see it. "And sorry to disappoint you, but I'm wearing black pants and a pink tank top. Nothing too exciting."

"I bet you look beautiful, anyway. You look beautiful no matter what you wear," he says, and the humor has faded from his voice. "Or what you don't wear, as the case may be. Okay, note to self: nine beers, and I lose my ability to keep my mouth shut. You have the floor."

"I don't know where to start."

"Why don't you start at the beginning," he suggests. "That usually works for me."

So I tell him everything that happened, from the moment I saw Nicholas on the stoop of my parents' house to our discussion on the couch. I leave out the very end, when he kissed me good night and I asked him to leave, since I can't imagine that that will sit too well with J.C. He interrupts a couple of times to ask questions, but other than that, he lets me tell it. It takes about fifteen minutes, and in the end even I can hear how crazy it sounds. If it weren't for the extra dishes in the sink, the second wineglass on the table, I might be inclined to think I'd made the whole thing up.

"Ohhhhh, shit," he says when I'm done. "Where is this guy now?"

"He left. He went back to . . . well, wherever he's staying."

"Did he touch you?"

So much for leaving out that part of the story. "He did kiss me," I say. "But it wasn't him, not entirely. It was Aidan. I know how nuts that sounds, but it's true. He looked at me like Aidan used to, and he said the things Aidan said, and the way he kissed, it freaked me out completely."

There is an ominous silence on the other end of the phone. Then J.C. says, "I'll kill him," in such an un–J.C. kind of voice, it chills me to my core.

"Why?" I say, startled into bluntness.

"Because, Maddie. This guy is either some kind of con artist, or he's psycho, or there's something going on that I'm not nearly sober enough to consider. Or drunk enough, one of the two. Either way, he came into your house, and he fed you a bunch of lines, and then he put his hands on you. He could have hurt you, he could have hurt Gabriel. He knew you were alone, and he took advantage of you. If he comes near you again, I will fucking kill him." He pauses. "Do you want me to fly out there? I will. I'll get Roma to take me to the airport and I'll be on the next plane out."

"He would never have hurt me," I say. "And I believed him. I know how that sounds, but it's true. You would have believed him, too, if you'd been there. It was . . . it was eerie." I shiver. "And the really bizarre part is that Gabe knew him. He knew who he was, he recognized him. He told me he'd dreamed about him, that Aidan told him Nick was coming. Gabe asked Nick to read him his bedtime stories."

A second silence falls, this one even more ominous than the first. Then J.C. says, "That's it. I'm booking a flight."

"J.C., it's all right. Really. I'm fine."

"It is most emphatically not all right. This situation may be many things, most of which I am poorly equipped to judge, but 'all right' isn't one of them."

I don't know how to respond to this, and silence falls between us. J.C. is the one to break it. "Goddamn it," he says.

"Goddamn it, what?"

He takes his time in answering. I can hear him breathing in and out. I can picture him sitting out on Roma's deck, his legs crossed at the ankles, staring up at the stars like he said. Then he says, "I can't do this. I'm sorry but I can't."

"What can't you do?" I sound like a parrot.

"For one thing, I can't sit here and listen to you tell me how you kissed some other guy, and how incredible it was," he says, and his voice is cold.

"I never said it was incredible. I said it freaked me out."

"Because it reminded you so much of A.J. Come on." He lets out a long, slow breath. "What do you think I'm made of? You call me at one in the morning and get me all worked up over the idea that something horrible's happened to you. Then I'm dumb enough to think that you called because you want to talk to me, like you miss me or something. But instead you want me to listen to some cock-and-bull story about this guy who shows up like some kind of reincarnation of A.J., there's more things in heaven and earth than are dreamt of in your philosophy, blah blah blah. How twisted is that? And then you tell me that you let this guy kiss you, and it freaked you out, and you expect me to just listen and—what, console you? Make it better?" His voice is growing louder and louder. I have never heard him yell before. "You don't want me to come there. You don't want me to take care of you. Hell, maybe you don't want me at all. Or maybe you do. Who knows?" I hear him inhale again, get hold of himself. "I could've gone home with about three different women tonight," he says, quieter now. "But do I want them? I do not. And why? Because I am hung up on your sorry ass, lovely as it is. So instead I'm sitting here, getting drunk in Roma's living room and playing a video game I got for your son to put a smile on his face, and you call and I'm thinking that we have a chance, that maybe you're calling to say that you're coming home. But no. Of course that's not it. When will I ever learn? God fucking *damn* it," he says, and I hear something slam, loud. "What do you want from me, Maddie? How much more can I give? Because I'm telling you now, baby, I don't have anything left. You want sympathy, I am fresh out. You call me when you've made up your mind, sweetheart. Because I can't take any more of this shit." There's a hitching noise, like a sob, and then it cuts off midstream. The phone goes dead.

FORTY-TWO

Aidan

I watch Nicholas walk out the door, see Maddie lock it behind him. Good girl. I can still taste her in my mouth, feel the texture of her hair between my fingers. God, I've missed her. I can feel it now: My time here is short. I've done what I came to do, almost. Just a little bit more, and then I'll be free.

I watch her lean her forehead against the door, but I don't touch her. What if she can't feel me? Or worse yet, what if she can, and it repulses her? So I stay back, watching her wander from room to room. Eventually she picks up her phone from the kitchen table and sits down on the living room couch. I sit next to her, waiting. She dials. "J.C.?" she says.

It makes sense that she'd call him. I get it. But I don't want to listen to their conversation, either. I get to my feet, pleased with my newfound mobility, and walk down to Gabe's room. My fingers close around the knob. I push the door open and step through.

"You came!" Gabe says when he sees me.

"I promised I would, monkey boy." I walk over to his bed and brush his hair back from his forehead. Wonder of wonders, he can feel my hand; my touch makes him shiver, but he doesn't back away. Instead he leans into me, like a cat.

"Nick was here, Daddy. And I did what you said."

"I know you did, buddy. You did a great job." I sit down next to him, tuck the blanket tighter around him so he won't be cold, and drape my arm over his shoulders.

"Then why do you look so sad?"

"I'm sad because I miss you and Mommy," I say. "And because we're not going to get to see each other anymore."

He squirms out from under my arm, so he can face me, and grabs my sleeve. I look down at myself and realize I am wearing blue jeans and a white T-shirt. Interesting. "Why, Daddy?"

"You know why, little one."

"Daddy, no. I won't tell anyone else, I swear. I'll tell Mommy I made it up. Just don't go away." His eyes well up, and this time the tears fall. They freeze before they reach his chin, and I brush them away. Bits of ice fall onto his blanket.

"It's not you, Gabe. You did just right by telling Mommy. And there's nowhere I'd rather be than here with you. I wish I could stay, buddy. But I just can't."

"Where will you go? To heaven?"

"Why not? Heaven sounds good to me." In truth I have no idea what my next stop will be. Something's waiting for me, I can tell. It doesn't feel bad, though, or scary. It feels . . . welcoming.

"Where is heaven, Daddy? Is it on top of a mountain?"

"Darned if I know. Get your mommy to show you on a map," I say. Let her deal with that one. I'd probably just fuck it up. "I love you, buddy. So much. You be good, and you take care of Mommy. I'm . . . so proud of you. You're going to grow up to be a great man. I just wish I could've been around to see it."

I hug him then, and kiss the top of his head. Whatever's waiting, its pull is growing, getting stronger. With the time that's left to me, there's something I still need to do. "Bye," I say into his ear, and as much as it pains me to do it, I unwind his fingers from my sleeve.

My breath must be icy, because he shivers all over. "No, Daddy," he says, tugging on me. "Daddy, wait. Draw me a picture." He climbs down from his bed, gets crayons and paper and a book, and hands the lot to me. "Here."

I don't want to leave him, either. Whatever is waiting will just have to be a little patient. I sit on his bed and draw. When I'm done, I write something at the bottom, then hand him the piece of paper. "Show this to Mommy tomorrow," I say. "Maybe then she'll believe you, if she doesn't already."

"What does this say?" he asks me, but I can't answer. I am hovering above him now, looking down. I can see the dent in the pillow where I was leaning against it, see Gabe sitting there in his favorite rocket ship pajamas, holding the drawing I made him in one small hand. Tears drip down his cheeks, but he ignores them. Carefully, as if he's handling one of Maddie's mom's Swarovski crystals, he places the picture against the pillow. He sits back then and looks at it, his lower lip trembling.

"Bye, Daddy," he says.

FORTY-THREE

Nicholas

When Maddie asks me to leave, I don't argue. For one thing, I am stunned by the feeling of electricity, of rightness that flooded through me when I kissed her. From the shocked look on her face when she pushed me away, the way she responded to the things I said, I'm pretty sure she felt it, too.

For another, I am overwhelmed by the conviction that whatever I've come here to do, making love to her is not a part of it. I don't know where that conviction comes from, but it is there and it is strong. So I get up from the couch and I leave without another word. I hear her lock the door behind me.

I'm staying in an apartment on Eleventh Street, and I don't have far to walk. This is a good thing, because I'm not sure that my legs would hold me. Everything looks different, more real somehow. I run my hands over the bark of trees, I kick pebbles along the sidewalk, I peer up at the starless sky. Probably anyone who sees me thinks I'm tripping, but I don't care.

Back in my borrowed apartment, I sit on the edge of an overstuffed chair and go over everything that happened tonight, from the moment I saw her standing at the bottom of the stoop to the time I walked out the door. I feel more confused than ever. I should be ecstatic that I kissed her, but instead I feel detached, like I checked something off a list. I look inside myself; where that powerful sense of purpose that's driven me since I opened my eyes should be, there's a void. I can no longer tell how much of what's happened was of my own making, or how much of it was Aidan's doing. The two of us are all muddled together somehow so that I can no longer tell one from the other. It makes my head spin.

For want of a better alternative, I try talking to Aidan. *Here I am. I did what you wanted. Now what?* But nobody answers, and I'm left sitting in the living room of an apartment in a strange city, conversing with the furniture. It's not like I haven't become used to living in the moment, but still.

I put my head in my hands, trying to focus, to force my memory to come back. If I can't figure out what I'm supposed to do, it would at least be nice to know who I am. But nothing happens, and I stretch out in the chair, no more knowledgeable than I was before. I close my eyes, and the exhaustion of the day catches up with me. If you'd asked me, I would've told you there was no way I could fall asleep after my conversation with Maddie, after that kiss. But after all, I'm no expert on myself, and the next thing I know, I am dreaming.

I know it's a dream, because I don't see the living room of the apartment around me anymore—green overstuffed chair and couch with darker swirls, mahogany coffee table and book-cases, Japanese lanterns and prints on the walls. Instead I'm outside, on a deck. There's a grill, and a pair of weathered deer antlers, and two Adirondack chairs, one of which I'm sitting in. When I turn my head, I see Aidan James sitting in the other chair, wearing jeans and a white T-shirt. His legs are stretched out in front of him, and he's got a pair of sunglasses pushed up on top of his head. "Hi, Nicholas," he says in that husky voice I'd know anywhere, and he smiles.

"Hi, yourself," I say to him. "It's about time."

He just goes on grinning, so I say, "Where are we?"

Aidan looks around. "Oh. This is the backyard of my house, in Boulder. Not sure how we ended up here."

"It's charming, in a *Pet Sematary* kind of way," I say, gestur-ing at the antlers.

"You're funny. I like that about you."

"A laugh a minute," I say, deadpan. "What are we doing here?"

He drums his fingers on the arm of the chair. "I wanted to thank you for what you did. I know it wasn't easy."

"You didn't exactly give me a choice," I say. "Plus, I think I scared the hell out of your wife several times over."

"She'll be okay. Maddie's tougher than she looks."

"I'm confused," I tell him. "All of this time, I was so sure that I was falling in love with her. I felt it more strongly than anything else. And in her parents' apartment, I felt that way, too. But now . . . I don't know what I feel."

He bites his lip. "I'm sorry," he says. "It was sort of necessary, at the time."

"What was?" I have a horrible feeling that I know what he's getting at, but I am going to make him say it anyhow.

"You felt what I felt," he says. "How could you love Maddie? You don't even know her."

"So everything . . . it was all fake? How can that be?"

"Not fake. Just . . . not yours." He fidgets, crossing and uncrossing his legs. "If you didn't feel that way about her, why would you come all the way up here?"

"You manipulated me," I say, trying it on for size. Anger shreds the edges of my voice.

"She didn't want me to go," he says. "She begged me not to go. I was so arrogant, so stupid. I told her there was no way she could know that anything was going to happen. I laughed at her. And all the time, she was right." He shakes his head. "The night before I left for McKinley, I promised I would come back. I told her she and Gabe were my life."

"From what I could tell, they were," I say. "But does that give you license to take over mine?"

"I kept my promise," he says then, his eyes on mine. "I told her I would come back, and I did. Even if it wasn't quite in the way I'd planned."

"You could say that again," I mutter, and he laughs, a low, humorless sound.

"I just wanted to be with her one more time. I'm sorry you got caught up in it, but I didn't know what else to do. It's not like I had a lot of options."

I put aside the morass of conflicting emotions with difficulty; I don't know how long I'll have with him, and there are some questions I desperately want to ask. "How did you do it?" I lean toward him, my palms on my knees.

"I don't know, Nick. I've always been a stubborn guy. If there's a way, I'll find it. I'm not sure what happened. I made up my mind, is all. And the next thing I remember is waking up in that hospital bed, with you."

"So you've been with me, all this time?"

"Sure," he says, his eyebrows drawing down. "Where did you think I was?"

"How the hell am I supposed to know, Aidan? It's not like you came equipped with a manual."

He laughs again. "I was trying to give you some privacy. Also, you're pretty guarded, most of the time. It was a lot easier for me to get through when you were asleep."

I take a deep breath, then ask him the burning question. "Why me?"

"You were . . . how can I say this? Empty, it felt like. Like you'd lost your way, kind of. There was lots of room for me."

I think about that one. "Empty, huh? How do you mean?" But I think I know what he means: the sense that my life has no larger meaning, that my career is a trap, that the days are just hours strung together like beads on a chain. The scary thing is, loving Maddie was the bright spot in an otherwise hazy existence. Without her, what will I go back to? And what have I done to Grace?

"I don't know how to describe it any better than that." His fingers are drumming on the arm of the chair again. "It happened pretty fast. One second I was on the mountain, and then I was there, with you. I'm pretty sure we were just in the same place at the same time, metaphorically speaking. I was dead. You were unconscious. And voilà." He waves a hand.

"My memory?" I say, raising my eyebrows.

"I'm sorry about that, too. I'm sure it's been frustrating."

"*Frustrating?*" My voice rises. "Try disorienting. And terrifying. And infuriating. And embarrassing. And God knows what else."

"Okay, okay. All of those things. But how else was I supposed to get you to listen to me?"

"How did you do it?" I ask again.

"I'm not sure. You were empty, like I said. I just filled in the crevices." He laces his fingers together and stretches his arms out in front of him, cracking his knuckles.

"So . . . what? This whole thing was just some sort of cosmic coincidence?"

"Maybe at some level," he says. "On another . . . probably not."

Well, that clears it right up. "Fantastic. Could I have my memory back now, please?" I sound petulant, like a five-year-old asking someone to return his favorite Power Ranger.

Now he looks abashed. "I don't know how to give it back."

"What the hell do you mean? You took it, didn't you?"

"I think so. Maybe it would have been gone anyhow."

"Not like this!" I say, and now I am yelling. "Not everything I've done, everything I am."

"It'll come back, Nick," he says. "It'll come back when you finish what you're supposed to do."

"Cut that crap out. What do you mean, what I'm supposed to do? I did what you wanted me to, didn't I? I fucked up my relationship with Grace, I tracked your wife down, I humiliated myself to get her to listen to me. I thought I loved her, for Christ's sake." A thought occurs to me. "You were there, weren't you? When I kissed her? All those things I said, that weird feeling I had, that was you?"

"Did you have a weird feeling?" he says. "What kind of feeling?"

"Like electricity," I say. "Like . . . like a circuit closing."

"I just wanted to say goodbye." His voice is sad. "I wanted her to know I kept my promise."

I'm poised to fire another series of questions his way, but the look on his face stops me. "It's not fair," he says, and rage is clear in his voice. "To find what I want, after all these years, and have it snatched away like that. It's not right." He swipes a hand under his eyes. "But I want her to be happy, no matter what. You tell her I meant what I said, about J.C. Make sure you tell her that, okay?"

"Okay, Mr. Mysterious."

"She'll know," he says. "No need to burden you with the details. And tell her to tell him . . . the universe isn't so fucked-up after all. Or if it is, the joke's on me. Tell him he deserves to be happy. You tell him to take care of her, or I swear to God I will find a way to haunt his sorry ass with every step he takes."

"What do you think I am, Western Union?"

"Remember," he warns me. "Or here, write it down." He grabs a pad and pen off the picnic table. I could have sworn they weren't there before, but hey, in dreams anything can happen, right? "On second thought, I'll write it myself," he says, flipping the pad open to a blank page. "Or . . . wait. I have an even better idea."

"Why can't you talk to them yourself, Aidan?" I say as I watch his pen fly over the paper. He's got it tilted toward him, and I can't see what he's writing. "Why did you have to do it this way, with me and Gabe?"

"I don't know," he says. "I tried to talk to them. I tried over and over, but . . . nada. So here I am." He turns his attention back to the pad of paper. "X marks the spot," he says, and chuckles. I consider asking what he means, then decide I don't want to know.

"I'm sorry you died," I say to him after a few minutes.

"I'm sorry you lost your memory." He turns the paper around so I can see it. It's not a note at all; it's a drawing of Maddie, Gabe, and J.C. Behind and above them is an incredibly detailed mountainside. I would know it anywhere. It's the mountain from my dream. As I stare at it, the background transforms so that I'm looking at Aidan's face. He fills the spaces between the three of them, he holds them close, he surrounds them. I blink, and there's the mountain again. On the bottom of the drawing, he has printed, *Not as much as I love you.*

I feel my mouth fall open. "I didn't know you could do this."

"Give this to her, please," he says. "And then go home. Clean up your life, starting with your office. That place is a mess. Who knows, you just might find what you're looking for."

"What do you know that I don't know?" I ask him.

"How to be happy, for one. Took me a while, but I learned that." He flips his sunglasses down, over his eyes. "Give this to Maddie, and I won't bother you anymore. And tell her what I said, okay? Don't forget."

"I won't," I say. "Don't worry."

"You did good, Nick. I owe you, big-time." He stands up and stretches. "And now I really do have to go."

"Where are you going?" I stand up, too, and he reaches his

hand out toward me. We shake. His fingers close around mine, calloused, rough. His grip is firm.

"On," he says, wearing a cryptic grin. "You tell J.C. . . . peace out." He lets my hand go and strides toward the back door of the house. Then he opens it, turns and waves, and steps through. He doesn't close it behind him, but when I walk to the doorway and look inside, he is gone.

FORTY-FOUR

Madeleine

To say that I have a difficult night would be putting it lightly. Between what happened with Nicholas and my unsettling phone call with J.C., I am beside myself. I don't know what to think, or what to believe. I spend a lot of time pacing the length of the living room, debating whether to call J.C. back and then deciding against it. I crack Gabe's door to peer at him several times, but he is fast asleep. By the time the street starts to lighten and people start trotting by on their way to the subway, I've all but convinced myself that J.C. was right—that Nicholas was psychotic, or at the least some kind of crazy con artist who gets his kicks out of preying on widowed women. I must have imagined the things he said. Wishful thinking and sleepless nights aren't exactly conducive to mental health, after all, and I've been doing a lot of both.

But then there's the matter of how Gabe knew who he was, and then there are the details of Nick's dreams, which I don't understand how anyone could know unless they had been on the mountain that day, or spying on me and Aidan at Wildacres. Or unless he's telling the truth. But that's not possible, is it? Is it?

If anyone could will their way back from the great beyond, it would be Aidan. Then again, he wouldn't have had much patience for this kind of story himself. If Nicholas had showed up on our doorstep selling this song and dance about Jim Ellis, Aidan would have handed him his ass on a platter, right before he showed him the door. He wouldn't even give my little premonition the time of day, for God's sake.

But there was the premonition, wasn't there? And Gabe's dream the night Aidan died. And the kiss, which was one of the weirdest things I've ever experienced. I wasn't lying when I told J.C. it freaked me out. When you're married to someone for almost six years, you know how they kiss, how they hold you. And if I hadn't known it was Nick on the couch, I would've sworn Aidan was there with me.

I feel like I'm going crazy. I debate calling Jos or Lucy, but first it's the middle of the night and then it's horribly early in the morning, and that hardly seems fair. Desperate for some air, I open the door and step outside. And then I let out a shriek, because someone is sitting on the stoop again. He turns, and of course it is Nicholas. Of course it is.

I sink down onto the stoop's top step and try to slow the jagged rhythm of my heart. "Jesus," I say, except it comes out more like a squeak, because I am minus most of my oxygen supply.

"Sorry, no," he says. "Just me."

FORTY-FIVE

Nicholas

I didn't expect to see Maddie come out of the house like that, not so early. I figured I'd have more time to gather my thoughts. But here she is, wearing the same clothes she had on last night. She collapses on the top step like I've scared the crap out of her. Which, I realize, I have.

"What are you doing here?" she says.

"I had to give you something. And to tell you something, too." I show her the piece of paper. "Here," I say, coming up the steps to hand it to her.

"What is it?"

I don't reply—honestly, what am I going to say?—and she takes the paper from me and looks at it. Her eyes widen, and the blood drains out of her face as if someone is siphoning it away. "Where did you get this?" she asks, without looking up.

"I had another dream," I tell her. "Last night, after I left here. But this one was different. Before, it was always like I was Aidan, or he was me, or whatever. This time, we were sitting down next to each other, talking. We were outside, on a deck. There was a grill, and a picnic table, and these totally macabre deer antlers. He said it was your backyard in Boulder."

"Go on," she says, staring at me with those wide brown eyes. It's strange, but the compulsion to be near her, to touch her, is gone. Like Aidan really has left, for good.

"We talked," I say. "About a lot of stuff."

"And?" she prompts. She is holding the drawing so tightly, she's crumpled one of the corners.

"He thanked me for coming to see you. He said that he was arrogant and stupid for not believing you, when you asked him not to go to Alaska. He said he promised you he'd never let you down, and that the night before he left, he told you he'd come back." I eye her cautiously, assessing her reaction. "Does any of this make sense to you?"

She looks ill. "Go on," she says.

So I tell her the rest of the dream, if that's what it was—everything Aidan said, everything he asked me to pass on to her and to J.C. "And then he drew this," I say, pointing at the drawing. "He told me to give it to you, that he wouldn't bother me anymore. And he left."

"Left where?"

"Through the back door of your house. I went after him, to see where he'd gone, but he'd just disappeared." I fold my arms over my chest. "Needless to say, I didn't get much sleep. I figured I'd just come over here and wait for you."

She glances down at her hands, realizes she's crushing the

drawing, and smooths it out with shaking fingers. "How is this possible?" she whispers.

"I don't know," I say. "He tried to explain, but he didn't do a very good job."

"I don't understand how you could know these things," she says. "Or this." She points to the line at the bottom of the page, the one he's written. "Unless you got this drawing from him somehow, before he died."

I shake my head. "I never met him, not really. Not unless you count last night."

We sit in silence, there on her parents' stoop. Then she says, "Suspending disbelief for a minute . . . do you feel like he's gone? Assuming, of course, that he was there to begin with."

"Yes," I say. "That's how I feel. Those things I said to you about you and me . . . don't worry about any of that, okay? It was just—it was him, I guess. I don't feel that way, anymore." What I do feel is hollow, and bewildered, and lost. But that isn't her problem, and I'm certainly not going to lay it at her feet.

Relief flashes across her face. "So what will you do now?"

"I'll go back to North Carolina," I say. "Try to make things right." And to figure out what Aidan meant when he said I was empty, that on some level this wasn't just a coincidence. Not to mention trying to reclaim my memory and patching up the wreck I've made of my life, chasing after a dream that wasn't even mine.

She bites her lower lip, like Aidan did last night. "That doesn't sound like something a crazy person would say."

"I'm not crazy. Not much, anyway."

"But if you're not . . . then this . . ." She waves the drawing, gestures at the two of us. "What am I supposed to do with this?"

"The right thing," I tell her. "You'll do the thing that's right for you." I fish in my pocket, pull out the other piece of paper I've brought with me. It's folded into fourths, and on it I've written my name, my email address, and my phone number. "Here," I say, handing it to her. "Keep this, just in case."

She unfolds it, looks it over. "In case what?"

"In case you need it," I say, and she nods as if this makes sense, folds it back up, and puts it in the pocket of her jeans.

And then, because that seems to be all there is to say, I turn to leave. Western Union, that's me after all. My work here is done, and I have business elsewhere. Like, getting my memory back. Like, reclaiming my life.

I get all the way to the bottom of the steps before I hear her calling me. She is crying and making no effort to hide it. "Nick," she says, so I wait. She clears her throat, wipes her eyes, and tries again. She smiles through her tears, and I can see why Aidan fell in love with her, why he would do anything to be able to say goodbye.

"Nick," she says again. "Thank you."

FORTY-SIX

Madeleine

I watch Nicholas walk down Union, a green duffel bag slung over his shoulder, and wrap my arms around myself for comfort. *You tell her I meant what I said, about J.C. You tell him to take care of her, or I swear to God I will find a way to haunt his sorry ass with every step he takes.* That sounds like Aidan, all right, like something he'd say. And what about this drawing? *Not as much as I love you.* Maybe I'm the one who's going crazy, and none of this is happening after all.

I am a mother, I admonish myself. I need to pull myself together. A nervous breakdown is a luxury I can't afford right now. I finger the necklace I'm wearing, a paua-shell turtle that Aidan brought home from New Zealand. Then I make myself get up and walk back inside. I put the drawing on the kitchen table, I lock the door behind me. I grind coffee beans and start the machine. Then I splash some cold water on my face and go to check on Gabriel.

"Hi, Mommy," he says when I push the door open. "Where did you go?"

"Just outside. I didn't realize you were awake, buddy. Sorry."

"It's okay," he says. "I was just looking at this picture Daddy made me. He said to give it to you." And then he extends a piece of paper in one small hand.

My heart starts pounding again, as if it might jump out of my chest and take off down Fifth Avenue, leaving me behind. Feeling like I'm moving through a vat of molasses, I make my way over to the bed, over to my little boy with the sleep-mussed hair and the rocket pajamas and his daddy's blue, blue eyes. I take the paper from him. And then I sit down on his bed, hard. It's lucky the bed is there, because otherwise I would have fallen to the floor.

The picture Gabe has given me is drawn in crayon, but other than that, it's an exact replica of the one Nicholas handed me on the stoop, down to the angle of the sun, the height of the mountains. Other than the medium—and the fact that this drawing is done in several colors, not just blue pen—the only difference is what's printed along the bottom, in Aidan's spiky writing, with its mix of capital and lowercase letters, its angular m's and w's.

Thus, though we cannot make our sun
Stand still, yet we will make him run.

FORTY-SEVEN

Nicholas

I fly into Wilmington more confused than when I left, if such a thing is possible. The dreams are gone, as is the bizarre sense that I am sharing my body and thoughts with someone else. This, of course, is a blessed relief. On the other hand, I am still minus all of my memories, which is inconvenient, to say the least. Also, losing Maddie has messed with my mind. You could argue that I'd never had her to begin with, that I wasn't in love with her, and you'd be right—but I thought I was, and as irrational as that is, it feels as sorry as if I'd lost the real thing.

Maybe I am just grieving the idea of being in love. And maybe I ought to give Grace another chance; maybe in the absence of being possessed by Mountain Boy, my feelings for her will come back in, loud and strong, like a signal that's no longer made fuzzy by bad reception.

The more I think about it, the more likely this seems. *Empty*, my ass. I have a job, I have friends, I have a dog and a house and a girlfriend. That doesn't seem so damn empty to me. We can't all spend our days clambering up teetering piles of rock and ice. Next to that, whose life wouldn't seem devoid of excitement?

I do know one thing—if I'm going to find any answers, they won't be in New York, with Madeleine. So back home I go, as per Aidan's instructions—although it pisses me off that I'm still doing what he says. I pick up Nevada from Taylor's house, dodge Taylor's questions about what went on in New York, and then humble myself to beg Grace's forgiveness. Armed with roses and a bottle of wine from the Fresh Market, Nevada and I drive over to her house and knock.

She opens the door, and when she sees me her jaw drops. "You're back," she says.

"I'm back," I echo.

"Where've you been, Nicholas?" Her tone is measured.

"You wouldn't believe me if I told you." Lord knows that's the truth.

"Try me," she says.

"I went to New York."

"I knew that."

"Taylor told you, huh?"

"I forced it out of him," she says. "Or maybe *coerced* would be a better word. What were you doing in New York?"

"Would you believe sightseeing?" I ask her. There's no damn way I'm going to tell her the truth. Maybe one day, when all of this is far behind us.

"Nope." She blocks the doorway so I can't enter. "How's your memory?"

"Still a tabula rasa. I thought the New York trip would help, but it didn't. Oh well, nothing ventured, nothing gained."

I'm blowing off her question, but Grace lets it pass. "Are those for me?" She gestures at the roses, at the bottle of wine.

"Hopefully," I tell her, and smile.

"And if I don't want them?"

"That's easy. I'll give the flowers to the first girl I see, and then drink the whole bottle myself. You know, drown my sorrows. But I'd much rather share it with you."

"I didn't think you liked wine."

"I don't. Or at least, I don't think I do. But maybe I could learn."

She shuts her eyes. "You are horrible!" she says. "You take off and I have no idea where you've gone. That note you left was useless. Then you show back up with flowers and wine and expect me to forgive you, just like that. And you haven't even said you're sorry."

"I'm sorry, Grace," I say. "And not just because you mentioned it. I really, truly am."

"Did you find what you were looking for?" she asks, eyes still closed.

"I don't know. Ask me again in a few hours, and I'll have an answer for you."

Now her eyes open, and she looks up into mine. She's a tall girl, and she doesn't have to look that far. "You hurt me, Nicholas," she says. "Give me one reason to let you do it again."

"Because you love me," I say. "Isn't that reason enough?"

She glares at me for a moment, but then she caves. "Come in," she says. And so I do.

. . .

One thing leads to another, and Nevada and I wind up spending the night. In the morning I wake up, restless. Grace is asleep naked next to me, her long red hair streaming down her back, and I don't want to disturb her with my fidgeting. She'll have to get up soon enough for work, anyway. More than that, I am disappointed. Being with her felt just like it had before I left. I don't know what I'd expected—not a lightning bolt or bells ringing—but I sure as hell expected something. Instead, I got zip, which befuddles me further.

In the end I grab Nevada's leash and take him for a walk on the beach. My intention is to grab two coffees and some breakfast sandwiches from Robert's, but I find myself ordering coffee for one and then heading to my car as if my feet have a mind of their own.

I slide behind the wheel, then text Grace, tell her I didn't want to wake her up, that I'll see her later—all of which is true, as far as that goes. So why do I feel guilty all over again?

I drive home and unlock the door to my house with a sense of profound relief, like I've gotten away with something, or at the very least escaped. This puzzles me, since it wasn't like anyone was holding me captive. Dismissing the anxious, not-right feeling in the pit of my stomach, I open up all the windows; the place is musty after the days I've spent away. After I get Nevada some food and water, I decide that what I need is organization. If I am going to have to start over, I might as well figure out what I'm working with. And after all, Aidan did tell me to clean out my office.

Just to be obstinate, I start in the kitchen instead, hauling out Tupperware containers and tossing the ones that are mismatched. I sort through the bills that have come in my absence—Taylor has been collecting my mail—and pay them. I do some serious yard work. Then I look through my clothes and bag up whatever I don't want for Goodwill. I scrub the floors, I wash the front of the kitchen cabinets, I sort through the freezer and toss some frostbitten items that look like they've personally experienced the Ice Age into the trash. What with one thing and another, it's almost three in the afternoon before I get to my office.

I'm feeling pretty virtuous—not to mention tired—by the time I sit down at my desk and open one of the drawers at random. There's no rhyme or reason to what's inside: magazines, some file folders, a box of staples, some empty CD jewel cases. I dump it all out on the floor and start sorting.

Stuck between two of the magazines is a blue spiral-bound notebook. I snag it and toss it to the side for future consideration. It lands open, though, and I can see writing inside. Curiosity gets the better of me, and I pick it back up. I look at the top of the page. It's dated June 7—the day of my accident. That gets my attention, all right. My hands go cold as I start reading.

There's got to be more to life than this, I'm sure of it. That sounds so melodramatic, and I don't mean it that way. It's just, I'm tired of doing the same thing day after day, tired of talking about the same things with the same people. The kids are great, but I'm getting burnt out, I can tell. And Grace—what am I supposed to do about her? She doesn't say it, or at least she hasn't said it yet, but I'm sure she expects me to ask her to marry me soon. We've been dating for over two years now, and I know she thinks I'm The One. She says it often enough. The shitty thing is, I don't think I'm in love with her anymore, if I ever really was. I'm just going through the motions. But every time I try to talk about it with her, she avoids me somehow. It's driving me nuts. We have a date tonight and I think I've worked up the balls to tell her I don't think we should be together anymore, flat-out. It's not fair to her, that's for sure. I'm just treading water. I need to end this. I'm writing it down this time, so I won't chicken out. Tonight, I am going to break up with Grace.

The entry ends there. I sit with the paper in my hands, staring at it. And then, as if it's burning my fingers, I tear it out of the notebook, crumple it into a ball, and throw it across the room. It lands in the corner, looking as inoffensive as any piece of trash.

I planned to break up with Grace before the accident? Below the surprise, I feel a rush of relief. It wasn't just Aidan pushing me toward Madeleine and away from Grace. There was some of myself in there the whole time, telling me that my relationship with Grace didn't feel right. That it wasn't where I belonged.

I am still in here somewhere, after all.

A headache blooms behind my eyes, and I get up and fetch two Advil. I wash them down with a glass of water. Then I walk out to the back deck, where I settle on the steps that lead down into the backyard. I put the glass down next to me and rub my eyes so hard, entire constellations explode behind the lids. Nevada noses my face, worried.

My head pounds, and I feel dizzy. I rub my eyes again, watch the laser light show play out. I dip my fingers into the cold water, rest my hand on the back of my neck. And then, with the rush of the avalanche, the same sense of being swept off balance, the same lack of air, my self comes rushing back to me. The force of it knocks me sideways. From far away I hear the glass tip over on the step, fall all the way to the ground. I hear it shatter. But none of that matters now, because the fireworks behind my eyelids have been replaced with a flood of memories.

Me at six, blowing out candles on a birthday cake. Sitting at the kitchen table with my dad, tracing the contours of the globe with my finger, telling him where I want to go one day. At ten, trying so hard to complete my math homework that I snap my pencil in half. My mom, presenting me with a homemade cake—vanilla with chocolate frosting, my favorite—for my twelfth birthday. Opening my present—a Nikon with all the bells and whistles, which I take with me everywhere that year, prepping for my future as a National Geographic *reporter. Talking with the exchange students that my family's always hosted, looking at the pictures of where they live, staying up late to make a list of the places I'll go someday, with a flashlight under the covers so I won't get in trouble. Getting my driver's license, and taking off down the highway in my first car, a two-door Honda Civic that had seen better days. At sixteen, the first time I slept with a girl—Steph Kramer, a pretty redhead; I seem to have a thing for them. Walking across the stage to accept my college diploma a few years late, after catching the waves in Costa Rica and working the tourist boats in the Virgin Islands. Thinking that the next step will be the Peace Corps, for sure—and two weeks later, getting the news of my parents' death. Sitting with my arms around Nevada, who was just a puppy then—I'd picked him out for my mom as an anniversary present—burying my face in his fur and sobbing. Deciding the hell with the Peace Corps, my parents had always wanted me to make a steady living and I owed it to them to listen. The conclusion that teaching global studies seems the least of all evils. My first day in a classroom, and how scared I was that I'd screw everything up. The next day, and the next and the next and the next, until they blur together. My first date with Grace, my second, my third. Wondering why I don't love her, knowing I should. Feeling more and more like my job is nothing, my relationship is nothing, my life is nothing. My growing sense of dissatisfaction, my desire to do something, anything, to break out of this rut I'm in, to feel something for once. Writing the note that's now crumpled in the corner, riding my Harley to Grace's house, telling her it's over. Her arguments, my refusal to listen, her tears. Getting on my bike just for the sake of riding, with no particular destination in mind. Feeling happy, feeling free, knowing I've had a little too much to drink but just not caring. And then the glare of oncoming headlights, the sound of brakes, the awful realization that the driver is not going to be able to stop in time.*

I open my eyes, stare down at the fragments of glass. I haven't moved, but somehow everything looks different.

All this time, she knew I didn't want to be with her, and she was just stringing me along, messing with my head? Thinking . . . what, that since she believed we should be together, she'd make it so, even when she knew it wasn't what I wanted? She let me believe that everything was just peachy between us, let me punish myself for feeling that something was wrong. For Christ's sake, she told me we were getting married. *Goddamn it*, I think. I say it out loud, and Nevada noses me again, whines.

I think back over the past couple of months, how lonely I felt, how adrift, eager to cling to any fragment of my original self. And now it turns out that even the few things I thought were true, the things I thought were solid ground, have turned out to be lies. Award-winning works of fiction, crafted by the master storyteller Grace Robinson. She ought to win the Pulitzer Prize. She's got a gift.

I am furious with Grace. I feel betrayed. But all of that fades into the background, paling next to the realization that I am myself again. For the first time since I woke up in the hospital two months ago, I can access any memory I choose, from the most insignificant to the most important. I know my favorite color, the name of the first girl I ever loved, how I like my steak (medium-rare), the fact that my mom used to call me Nicky. My sense of helplessness, of suspension over an unknown abyss, is gone. I know who I am, plain and simple.

But I also know who I am not. Unlike Aidan James, I am not someone who knew what he wanted and then went after it—Maddie, climbing, whatever else came to mind. I am someone who turned his back on what he cared about, telling himself it was childish and silly, and pursued a life of mediocrity. Or, as Aidan put it, I was empty.

And he filled me.

He reminded me what it was like to feel passionate about what I did, who I was with. He made me believe I was in love with Maddie—but he also showed me what it was like to love someone the way he did, with his whole self, holding nothing back. He terrified me by having me fall off a mountain again and again, night after night—but he let me know what it felt like to be so devoted to what you did, you'd risk your life for it.

If I were a cartoon character, a lightbulb would be flashing over my head.

I wasn't in love with Aidan's wife; but I *am* in love with the idea of caring about someone like that, so you'd alter the pattern of your life and become a better person. I have no desire to climb mountains, but I do want to travel the world, my Nikon in my hand, like I always dreamed I would. I want to teach kids somewhere far away, learn their language, eat their food, take their picture. I want to reduce my possessions to what I can carry on my back and hike through the rain forest somewhere that cellphones and emails can't find me, and the trees are filled with animals I've never seen outside of books. I want to find someone who will travel this path with me, so we can discover hidden places together and make each other happy.

I think back to the dream, what I felt when I cupped my hands to my face under the snow. I felt hope, and I realize now that it was mine, not Aidan's. He gave that back to me. He gave me back the small boy who pored over maps and watched the Discovery Channel like it was the gospel, who dreamed of exploring with only my camera for company, capturing blue-footed boobies in the Galapagos and sifaka lemurs—those balletic little primates—in Madagascar.

He gave me back my self.

I sit for another moment, getting my balance, adjusting to this new version of reality. Then I go back inside and walk through every room of my house, touching objects like a blind man, seeing them with my new eyes. I look under the bed for the book I dropped back there five months ago and pull it out, covered in dust bunnies. I rummage in the kitchen drawer for the vegetable peeler that used to be my grandmother's and has somehow ended up with me. I pet Nevada on the head, thinking about when I rescued him from the shelter, how I chose him out of all the puppies in the litter because he didn't bum-rush me, just sat there staring with his big, hopeful doggy eyes.

Finally I sink down on the couch, looking at the floor where Grace and I made love that night before I left. I remember how we met, where we went on our first date, our little private jokes, what I bought her on our first anniversary. Then I hear her telling me that she'll take whatever version of me she can get, that it doesn't have to be exactly like it was. And I realize the irony of this whole situation: In finding Grace, I have lost her again.

FORTY-EIGHT

Madeleine

After Gabe shows me his drawing, I sit for a few long minutes with my head between my knees. Gabe comes up behind me and hugs me. After a while, I feel something soft poking through the space between my upper arm and my ribs: Teddy. I take him and concentrate on continuing to breathe.

"What does it say, Mommy?" Gabe asks after he's figured out that I'm not going to keel over anytime soon. "I asked Daddy to read it to me, but he disappearded, like in Harry Potter."

I make myself raise my head. My little boy's face is next to mine, squished together with worry. "Did Daddy write something bad?" he asks.

"Where did you get this?"

"Daddy drew it for me, when he came last night. He said maybe it would make you believe me. What does it say?"

So I read the lines of poetry out loud for Gabe, who looks baffled. "I don't get it," he says. "What does it mean?"

"It was something special your daddy used to say to me," I tell him.

"Oh."

"Gabriel, when you say Daddy came to see you . . . how many times?"

He counts on his fingers. "Three," he says. "The first time, with the accident. The second time, when he told me Nick was coming. And last night. But he said he wouldn't be coming anymore. He said you should show me heaven, on a map. Do you have a map of heaven, Mommy?"

I shake my head. "Tell me the truth, Gabe. Where did you get this picture?"

"I am telling you the truth!" he says, piqued. "Daddy drew it, and he told me to give it to you. So I am. I think it's pretty. Look, it's got Uncle J.C. on it and everything. Daddy was a little mad when I told him Uncle J.C. came for sleepovers, but he must not be mad anymore, because look." He touches J.C.'s face.

"You told Daddy what?"

"He asked if Uncle J.C. slept over. So I told him yes. Because he does."

"And what did Daddy say?"

Gabe's jaw tightens up. "I can't tell you that."

"Why not?"

"Because it's a bad word," he says, his small face obstinate.

"I won't get angry. Just tell me."

Gabe folds his little arms over his chest. "Fine. He said, 'Damn.' And then he told me to tell Uncle J.C. to behave himself. So I did. I told him to be good. At the airport, remember?"

I do remember. Except at the time I thought Gabe was

channeling E.T. the Extraterrestrial, not his dead father. I shiver, and rub my upper arms to warm myself.

"Why did he say that, Mommy? I think Uncle J.C. has very good manners. Don't you think so?"

"He does have good manners," I say. "Better than mine." Which is the truth.

"I miss him," Gabe says, peeking at my face as if he thinks I'm going to explode. He could be talking about Aidan, but I know he isn't. He's talking about J.C., and I feel a wave of guilt sweep over me. J.C. is the closest thing to a father figure Gabe has left. I never stopped to think about the fact that taking off for New York would rob him of that sense of security. I thought I would be enough. But looking into Gabe's face, I realize I was wrong. The nights that J.C. stayed over, maybe Gabe felt as safe as I did. After all, I haven't exactly been a bastion of mental health. And here I am, shipping him halfway across the country, without even his grandparents to turn to. Some mother I am.

I run my fingers over the texture of Aidan's drawing, tracing our faces, feeling the contours of each word. "I'm sure you do," I say to Gabe. "I miss him, too." And with those words, my world settles into place, at least one small corner of it. To hell with decorum, propriety, and all the rest of it. We will go home to Colorado, and celebrate Gabe's fifth birthday with his friends, the people who love him. I'll show J.C. these drawings, and I'll tell him what happened, the part he doesn't know. I'll deal with whatever anger he needs to direct my way. And whatever comes next, whatever the future holds, we will face it together.

One way or another.

FORTY-NINE

Nicholas

I sit on the front steps of Grace's beach cottage, waiting for her to get home. The driveway is full of her upstairs neighbors' cars; there's just one spot left for Grace, and I leave it empty out of some misplaced sense of chivalry. My Honda is parked a couple of spots down.

It occurs to me that maybe waiting on Grace's steps isn't the best idea. It's an eerie echo of how I waited for Maddie, plus if I really want some answers, I am unlikely to gain them through public humiliation. Oh well. Too late now.

I check my watch. It's five fifteen, and Grace should be here any second. Sure enough, her blue Jetta rounds the corner. The windows are open, and I can hear music blaring from inside—Madonna's "Crazy for You." Grace is kickin' it old-school, and the symbolism of her song choice cuts a little close for comfort.

She kills the motor and gets out of the car, slinging her messenger bag over her shoulder. Then she sees me, and a smile spreads across her face. "Nicholas!" she says.

I can't bring myself to smile back. Instead I just regard her until her own smile freezes, fades. I see the truth break over her face, fill up her eyes. She stops at the bottom of the steps, sets the bag down.

"You said we were getting married. That I proposed to you, and you said yes." Why this is the opener I go with, I have no idea. It's just what comes out. "I trusted you," I say, and to my surprise, my voice breaks. "I had nothing—less than nothing—and you lied to me."

She doesn't try to deny it. "I'm so sorry," she says. "I am."

I reach into my pocket, pull out my cigarettes, and light one. I'd hoped regaining my memory would negate my addiction to nicotine. So far, this has not proved to be the case. "Why did you do it?" I ask, but that's not exactly what I mean. What I mean is, *How could you do it?* I doubt she has a good answer, but I ask anyway. Unsurprisingly, she doesn't respond.

"I felt so guilty," I say. "I went around flagellating myself all the time. *Why don't I feel this? How can I treat her this way?* I felt like a complete asshole. And then yesterday! You let me come back here, with those stupid flowers and that bottle of wine, and grovel like an idiot." My nails dig into my palms.

She takes a step back, away from me. "Nick—"

"Did you enjoy your little trick? I hope so, because I believed every word you said."

"I just . . . I felt like it was a fresh start," she says, and her voice is less confident than I've ever heard it. "A chance to start again."

"Right. Because I didn't have enough of that going on."

"I meant for us." She reaches out to touch me, and I draw back without thinking. I don't want her hands on me.

She has the nerve to look hurt when I flinch back. "I loved you so much, Nick. I still do. I couldn't understand what was happening to us, why you wanted to break up. And when the accident—I know I took advantage of the situation. I know it was wrong. I just thought maybe—if you couldn't remember that we were supposed to be done—that you'd want to be with me."

"I beat myself up about those times we were together," I say, my voice even. "I felt like a total shit, leaving after that. And the whole time, you were using me."

"I wasn't—"

"I hope it was worth it," I say.

She grabs the porch railing, like she needs the support. "What are you saying?"

"I think you know."

"Don't," she says, and she is pleading with me.

I look down at the steps, take a deep drag of my cigarette. "Give me a break, Grace. You don't expect me to just get over this, do you? Sweep it under the rug, like your Gram used to say?"

She gapes at me. "Gram?"

I sit up straight then. I look right at her. "I remember," I say. "I remember everything."

For a moment she says nothing. I mistrust her enough to wonder if she's calculating her odds, trying to figure out if I'm bluffing. Maybe she is planning her next move. But in the end I decide she's simply trying not to cry, because when she speaks, it sounds like she's forcing her voice past a giant lump in her throat. "I'm so glad."

"I can't imagine why you would be." Now that's the God's honest truth.

"I know what I did was wrong," she says. "I just didn't know how to take it back."

"Lucky you. You didn't have to go to the trouble," I say, grinding out my cigarette. I stare over her head, at the widow's walk of the house across the street.

"Nicholas, please," she says in a small voice. "I am sorry. I don't expect you to believe me, but I didn't do it to be malicious. I made a mistake, a bad one, but I made it out of love."

She is so pathetic, standing there, that some of my anger bleeds away. "God, Grace," I say, rubbing my temples. "A mistake is when you forget to pick up the milk. A mistake is when you add wrong on your deposit slip. It implies a lack of premeditation."

"I didn't plan to do it," she says. "It just . . . piled up."

"Now *that* I believe," I say, and I force a rueful smile. It doesn't cost me anything. This will end the same way, anyhow. I can do my best not to make it ugly. Well, uglier.

Relief sweeps her face when she sees me smile, and I sigh. She eyes me cautiously, like she's waiting for me to snap at her again. "I hope one day you can forgive me," she ventures, and because I hope that, too—who wants to walk around dragging grudges behind them like the chains on Marley's ghost?—I nod my head.

"I'll work on it," I tell her. "But shit, Gracie. You can't *make* someone be with you, even if it's what you really want. There's this little thing called free will."

"Every time I thought about saying something, I just—I couldn't," she says, tracing the railing with one long finger. "How do you tell somebody you've lied about their whole life?"

"Don't exaggerate," I say, rolling my eyes. "Not my whole life. Just your part in it."

"Same difference," she says, smiling a little, and I know why. I used to get after her for saying that; it drove me crazy. Like saying *most unique.*

"You liked me better when I was lying," she says.

"Not true. I like you better now. You make more sense."

"Were you ever happy with me?" She's back to that small voice.

"I wasn't happy with myself. It had nothing to do with you. I just wasn't brave enough to admit it."

She considers that, digests it. "So what will you do now?"

It's the same question Maddie asked me, and I have even less of an answer for Grace. I told Maddie I'd go home, try to make things right. And I am, insofar as I know how. I'm being honest with myself, and honest with Grace. But after this, it's anyone's guess. Maybe that should frighten me, but it doesn't. It fills me with anticipation.

"I have no idea," I say, watching a seagull swoop down to the widow's walk and land on the railing. I try to make the next part come out gentle. "But whatever it is, I wouldn't worry too much about it, Grace. You don't really love me, or you never would have treated me like you did. You were just afraid of letting me go." There's a difference, and no one knows that better than I do. We were both afraid—her of moving on, me of what I really wanted. It brought us together, it bound us, but no longer. I am done with making decisions based on fear. "You deserve to be happy," I say. "And so do I."

"Nick," she says, and now she is begging. "When you woke up—and you looked at me—I felt like it was a miracle. First, that you were alive at all . . . and then that I would have another chance to make it right between us. I just . . . I couldn't face losing you twice."

I look away from the seagull and focus on her face, but there's nothing there for me to see. "Make that three times," I say. And standing, I leave Grace behind.

FIFTY

Madeleine

We've been back in Boulder for almost fifteen hours before I work up the temerity to face J.C. At last I call Jill Sutherland, Aspen's mom, and ask her if she wouldn't mind taking Gabe for a little while, so I can get some stuff done. I don't specify further, and Jill doesn't ask. Luckily she's free, and Gabe is over the moon, which he thinks Aspen hung. So I drop Gabe off at their house, and he runs inside, heading straight for Aspen's Wii.

"I'll bring him back at one, after lunch," Jill says. "That'll give you about three hours. Does that work?"

"Perfect," I tell her, and I mean it. I give her a hug—she always smells so good, like apples—and yell goodbye to Gabe. Then I get back in my car and drive down Arapahoe Road toward J.C.'s little house.

On the front porch, I hesitate for a moment, the drawings clutched in one hand. I take a deep breath. And then I knock.

"Coming," I hear J.C. yell. "Hang on." The door swings open, and then he's standing there in front of me, shirtless, wearing the drawstring pants he slept in at my house. His hair's a mess, his cheeks and chin are covered in dark stubble, and he's wearing his glasses, which I've hardly ever seen him do. They're round and silver-rimmed. He gapes at me like he's not sure I'm real.

"Hi," I say, when it's clear he's not going to say anything.

He's got his hand on the door frame, his arm blocking my passage, and he doesn't let it drop. "What are you doing here?" he says, in a tone that borders on hostile.

I knew he was mad, but I didn't expect a reception quite this chilly. "I came home," I say. "Like I said I would."

"You said a lot of things." The expression of surprise has faded from his features now, replaced with a blend of suspicion and defensiveness.

"Can I come in?"

"If you want." He folds his arms over his chest and stands aside to let me pass. His house isn't a wreck, but it's not as neat as usual, either. His Vans are underneath the coffee table, his blue fleece is draped over the arm of the couch, and his guitar is lying across the cushions. There's a half-finished TV dinner on the coffee table, which surprises me more than anything else. In all the time I've known J.C., I've never seen him eat a frozen dinner.

He follows my gaze and gives me a tight, humorless grin. "Sorry it's not up to my usual standards. I haven't been in the mood to clean."

"What mood have you been in, then?"

"Reflective," he says. "Realistic." He sits down in the middle of the couch and grabs the guitar, pulling it into his lap. As I contemplate whether to take a seat on the floor, squeeze in next to him on the couch, or not sit down at all, he starts strumming some chords. "So," he says. "What can I do for you? Did you come back to drag me over the coals some more?"

This is not what I expected him to say, and I don't have a good rejoinder. In the silence that follows, he starts humming, then singing—not loudly, just sort of as background music. The words sound familiar—something about how the days are gone when the ladies said please—but I am not paying that much attention.

"I live here," I say. "And I came over to talk to you."

"About what? Kissed any new guys lately? Care to share?"

"Don't be like this, J.C."

"Like what?" he says, looking up from his guitar.

"Like you hate me," I say, biting my lip.

"I don't hate you, sweetheart," he says, and the way it comes out of his mouth, it sounds more like an epithet than an endearment. "I've just opened my eyes a little bit, that's all. I've got a clearer view of the way things are."

"And how are they?" I try to keep my voice level, but it's hard, because I'm shaking. Whatever's going on here, it isn't good.

"We should never have . . . done what we did. It was a mistake," he says. "You were a mess, and I took advantage of that. I don't know what was in my head, thinking we could be together. Let's just chalk it up to survivor lust and leave it at that, what do you say?"

Now it's my turn to gape at him. This is so close to what I planned to tell him before I left that I can't think how to respond. While I stand there, eyes wide, he fills the silence with another verse of the damn song—this one about brown-eyed women and red grenadine. I still can't place it, although I'm sure I've heard it before.

"It wasn't like that," I say.

"Sure it was. And that's okay. You can go home. No strings."

"What if I don't want to go home?" I say. My stomach is churning, and my hands are like ice. Of all the ways I imagined our reunion scene would play out, this version wasn't even in the running.

"Then I don't know what to tell you." He strums some more. "It wasn't meant to be, Maddie. We had our chance six years ago. Now, it is what it is. No point trying to build a fire from ashes, right?"

"Don't I get a say in this?" I ask him. "What about what I want?"

For the first time I see anger glint in his eyes. "Haven't you said enough?" he says. "You got something to add?"

"Actually, I do." I hold the drawings out to him. "I need to show you something."

"What are those?"

"They're pictures."

"Yeah, I can see that. Pictures of what?"

"They're pictures of the same thing. Drawn by two different people."

"You gonna fill me in, or do I need to drag it out of you?"

"You could stop that for a moment and look. It wouldn't kill you." I gesture at the guitar, at his fingers on the strings.

"Nope," he says, impassive. "I've been working on this song all week."

I am tempted to snatch the guitar out of his hands and smash it to bits on the coffee table. "Fine. Gabriel drew one of the pictures. The other, Nicholas drew. They were in totally separate places, but they drew the same thing, at about the same time. And if you would just look at them, I think you'd see how incredible this whole thing is. First, that Gabriel could draw something like this at all. Second, the drawings look just like the ones Aidan used to do. And third, there's stuff written on them that I think you'd be pretty interested in, if you'd just take a look."

"Jesus Christ, Maddie. Not this ridiculous *Tales from the Crypt* bullshit again." He strums the guitar so loudly, I jump. "I'm thrilled your new boyfriend drew you a pretty picture, and that he and Gabe have so much in common. Take 'em home and frame 'em, why don't you, instead of showing them to me?"

I haven't lost my temper in so long, but I am close to it now. "Damn it, J.C.!" I say, and my voice is sharp. "Nicholas is not my boyfriend. We kissed. Once. Which I wish I had never told you about, based on your psychotic reaction. And now he's gone back to North Carolina, where he came from. I don't expect I'll ever see him again, for your information. Nor do I need to. I came home to see *you*, among other things, which I am now beginning to sorely regret."

Silence follows my outburst. Then J.C. says, "He's gone?"

"Yes," I say. "Is that what your problem is? Are you *jealous*?"

"Of course not," he says after a pause. "I told you, you and I were a mistake. Why would I be jealous?"

Why, indeed. "Then what is wrong with you?"

"Nothing is wrong with me, Maddie. I'm fine, just like always."

"Yeah," I say, waving my hand at the messy room, the TV dinner, his less-than-stellar ensemble, his unshaved face. "You're doing great."

"What can I say? We can't all go gallivanting off to the Big Apple to have a fling every time our lives fall apart. Some of us need to stick around town and deal with it."

"That's not fair," I say, so loudly it cuts across the strumming. Rage bubbles up in my throat.

"All's fair, apparently."

"Cut it *out*, J.C.!" I am now so infuriated that I stamp my foot, like a toddler having a tantrum.

"I thought I had."

"You're obviously angry at me," I say, and my voice is as level as his. "Why don't you say what you're really thinking? Why do you have to be so damn calm all the time?"

"I did say what I'm really thinking, Maddie. You just don't want to listen."

I glare at him so hard it feels like my eyes are throwing sparks, but he is unimpressed. Instead, he launches into the next verse of the song, taking his time with each syllable.

There's no talking to him when he's like this, and moreover, I don't want to. "You're being a jerk, and I'm leaving," I tell him, tossing the drawings on the coffee table.

"Take those," he says. "I don't want them."

"Why don't I leave them here, in case you change your mind?"

"Suit yourself," he says, and when I turn to walk out the door, he doesn't get up. Like Orpheus, I refuse to turn around; I'm afraid that if I do, I will start begging him to believe me, to look at me the way he used to. So I gather my dignity around me like a cloak, trying to make it as impregnable as the air of detachment and resolution that surrounds him, and I turn and walk away. I can feel his eyes on me now, and I hope he'll come after me or call my name, but he doesn't. Instead he just sits there on the couch, playing his damn guitar. And that is where my resemblance to Orpheus ends. I keep walking and I don't look back.

It's not until I slam the front door behind me that I remember: The night Aidan kissed Kate, when J.C. followed me outside and we were standing on the sidewalk, we heard a guy singing this song. It's "Brown-Eyed Women," by the Grateful Dead. I even remember being surprised that I recalled the lyrics, since it had been such a long time since I'd heard them.

I'm sure J.C. remembers this, too, and I'm equally sure that he's chosen this song on purpose. It occurs to me that maybe he's trying to tell me that we've come full circle, back to where we started. That we've gone as far as we can, only to find our way back to the beginning.

Through the door I can still hear him singing. I force myself to stand there and listen. Finally the song ends and there is only silence. There's nothing left to do then but get into my car, crying so hard I can barely see, and drive home to face the mess I've made.

FIFTY-ONE

Madeleine

Once I get to my house, the only thing I want to do is curl up in bed and pull the covers over my head. I don't do this, though, for several reasons. First of all, it would be childish, not to mention unproductive. And second of all, if I crawled under the quilt, only to discover that the sheets and pillowcases still held J.C.'s scent, there's no telling what would happen to my already fragile emotional state. So instead I sit on the edge of the mattress, watching the numbers flip over on the alarm clock and wondering what I will do if I have to face losing both Aidan and J.C. in such a short period of time. Anger wells up in me—not just for the way J.C. acted today, but because I remember what he said to me the first night we were together—*I'm right here, Madeleine. I'm not going anywhere. I promise.* Even though I know it's ridiculous to hold him to something he said in the middle of sex, I realize now that I counted on him to keep his word. I needed to believe that he would always be there for me, no matter what. Now he's reneged, and I feel not just furious, but abandoned and betrayed.

I sit with that feeling for a minute, there on the edge of the bed. And slowly it dawns on me that I took J.C. for granted. The more I think about it, the more I realize how unfair it was for me to call him that night after Nicholas left. I should have called Jos, Lucy, my mother, anyone else, if I needed to speak to someone so badly. It doesn't matter that he was the only person I wanted to talk to, the only one whose voice I wanted to hear. I think about the time we stood in my kitchen, when he told me that he wanted me, sure, but he never meant for it to happen like this. I remember the way his dark eyes filled with tears, and how hard he fought to hold them back so I wouldn't see. The feeling of selfishness that filled me then sweeps through my body with renewed intensity. It settles in my stomach, a gut-wrenching guilt. I was so overwhelmed by the things Nicholas said, the way he touched me, the way he looked at me, that I never wondered how hearing about what happened would affect J.C. I wonder if he thinks that I turned to him after Aidan died only because I was lonely, that anyone would do and he just happened to be there. After all, how could I expect him to believe what transpired, with Nicholas's appearance and Gabe's dreams? I hardly believe it myself, and I have the proof. Of course, now so does he—not that he's willing to consider it.

When I think back on all of my memories of J.C.—and there are so many; in almost all but the most private memories of me and Aidan together, he is there, climbing, joking, telling stories, helping Gabe build a fort for his *Star Wars* guys from scrap wood off one of his jobs, teaching me to bake bread from scratch at high altitude—I recall only one other time that he sounded so aloof, so cold. The day he kissed me in the kitchen of the old house, and he and Aidan got into that fight, his tone had the same taunting edge, that same indifference that sidestepped into cruelty. I haven't heard him sound that way before or since, and never when he was talking to me. *Selfish*, I think again, and lower my head into my hands. It's a good thing that Gabe is over at Aspen's, because I don't want him to see me like this. Tears streak down my face, slip between my fingers.

Of course, the moment that I entertain this thought, I hear a car pull up in the driveway. I figure it's Jill, bringing Gabe back early, and I rocket to my feet, heading to the bathroom to splash water on my face. A quick glance in the mirror shows me that there's no way to hide the fact that I've been crying. My eyes are red-rimmed, and I look as desolate as I feel. Still, I give it my best shot; I pat my face dry, pull a brush through my hair, and head toward the door just as someone knocks.

"Just a second," I call, tugging my clothes into place. I open the door wide—and then I just stand there, stunned by a sudden sense of déjà vu. On my porch is J.C., and he doesn't look a whole lot better than I do.

"Um," he says.

I step outside and close the door behind me. Then I take a good look at him. He's changed clothes, into shorts and a forest-green T-shirt with Arete Films printed on it in white, above the peak of a mountain. He's tamed his hair and put in his contacts, but he hasn't shaved. And just like last time, he looks exhausted.

He's got the drawings in one of his hands, dangling down by his side. Maybe he has come to give them back? But that doesn't make sense. Why would he drive all the way over here just for that? I force air into my lungs, down my throat so I can speak. "What?" I say.

He shifts from one foot to the other. "I need to talk to you."

"Oh no you don't," I say. "You've said plenty. Really." The rage I felt before is simmering below the surface, just waiting for a target. "If you came here to tell me how not-meant-for-each-other we are, don't bother. I got your point, loud and clear."

"That's not why I'm here," he says. "At least, not entirely."

"Why, then?" I do my best to keep my voice from trembling and giving me away. I'm trying to sound icy, like he did this morning—which I'm normally good at; it's my default mode when angered or wronged—but somehow I can't summon the necessary grit.

J.C. takes a step back anyway, and he flinches like I've hit him where it hurts. "Where's Gabe?" he asks.

"At Aspen's. He'll be back pretty soon, so whatever you've got to say, go ahead and get it over with." I struggle to imbue my tone with some bravado, and have what feels at least like moderate success.

He rubs the flat of his free hand over his shirt. "Just let me talk to you, Maddie." When I don't say anything he steps closer again, so we're almost touching. "Please," he says, and I can hear the pain in his voice. I've never heard J.C. beg before, but that's what he's doing, all right.

"I don't know if I want to hear anything you've got to say," I tell him, lifting my chin. "Where is there to go, conversationally, after telling someone that they were a mistake?"

"Okay, I deserve that. I owe you an apology." He's still an inch away from me, and the door is at my back, so I can't retreat.

"I'm sorry," he says, his eyes locked on mine. "I shouldn't have spoken to you like that. It was inexcusable, no matter how I felt. I was wrong and I'm sorry."

"Okay," I say. "You apologized. So now you can go."

"No, I can't." There's an odd finality to his tone.

Gabe will be back soon, and I have no desire to be embroiled in this discussion when he arrives. "What do you *want*, J.C.? Just spit it out already."

Wordlessly, he holds the drawings up so I can see them. He shakes them a little, then harder, so I'm afraid the paper will rip. "What the fuck are these? Is this just you messing with my head?"

"No," I say. "It happened like I said. Nicholas drew one, and Gabe drew the other."

"I'm listening."

"It was the next morning. After we talked, you know? I went outside to get some air, and Nicholas was sitting on the stoop. He handed me the drawing, and he told me he'd had another dream about Aidan, that he sat and talked with him, in our backyard in Boulder. In the dream, Aidan said to tell you that the universe wasn't so fucked-up after all. That you deserved to be happy, and to take care of me." I decide to leave out the rest of it, about Aidan's threat to "haunt his sorry ass." "He said Aidan drew this." I gesture at the picture of me and Gabe and J.C., set against a detailed mountain scene. J.C. is still holding the drawing up, and I watch as the plateau, the crags, the sun all shift to form the features of Aidan's face. "Where is it?" I ask. "Do you know?"

"McKinley, en route to the South Summit," J.C. says in a wooden voice. "That's how it looked, the morning he died. Just like that. You look close here"—he points—"you can even see the fracture line."

"Oh," I say, and I can feel the blood draining from my face.

"And this"—he points at something I hadn't noticed—"what is this supposed to be?"

I lean in closer, and see something that, at first glance, I'd mistaken for part of the mountain's upper slope. "It looks like an X. Or a cross, maybe. Why, what do you think it is?"

"I don't really want to say."

"Oh, for God's sake, J.C. Just tell me."

"Fine. That spot, right there . . . it's where we thought A.J. should've ended up, after we took a good look at the fall line. The team dug there for hours. We didn't find anything, but I still thought . . . well, anyhow." He shifts his weight. "It's where I would've started looking, when we went back next year. It's the first place."

"Oh," I say again, and even though it's August, a chill sweeps through me. "You think that's where his body is?"

He shrugs. "How should I know? It would make sense though."

I am still trying to process this gruesome, miraculous bit of information when J.C. plows onward. "What does this mean?" He taps the line of text, written in Aidan's handwriting.

"It's just . . . something he used to say to me. Something private."

For a second I think he's going to ask me to explain, but he thinks better of it. "And this?" he says, switching the pictures around so I can see the one Gabe drew, with its bright Crayola colors.

"Nicholas left, like I told you, and I went back inside, to

check on Gabe. He'd been sleeping when I went out. When I came back he was awake, and he said he had something for me. And then he handed me that picture."

"You expect me to believe that Gabe drew this?" He shakes the picture again. From the look on his face, he'd prefer to be shaking me instead.

"I don't expect you to do anything. But it's the truth." I clear my throat. "I told you he had that dream, before Aidan . . . before you called me that night. And then I guess he had two more . . . and he drew this. Or someone did, anyhow."

He underscores the lines of poetry. "What about these?"

"Hold on a second," I say, and I pull the door open.

"Where are you going?"

"I'll be right back. Just wait."

"Out here?" He sounds exasperated.

"Just hold on." I go inside, into my room, and locate the drawing Aidan did all those years ago at Wildacres. It's pressed between two books on my bedside table. Then I smooth it carefully and carry it outside for J.C. to look at.

He frowns when I hand it to him. "I could've done without erotic imagery of you and A.J."

"Forget about that for a minute," I say. "Look at what he wrote."

His eyebrows drawing down in displeasure, J.C. complies. I see the shock come over his face when he reads the lines of poetry at the bottom of the page. "Oh," he says. "Oh, hell."

"My thoughts exactly. And I'll tell you something else. Nicholas wrote down his name and his phone number for me before he left, and his handwriting looks nothing like Aidan's. Not only that, but the piece of paper he wrote it on looks just like the other one he gave me, with the picture. They've both got that red margin, those wide lines, like they were torn from the same pad."

"He gave you his phone number?" J.C. says, looking more displeased than ever.

I sigh. "Yes, he did. Are you going to have a conniption about that, too? We had a really weird experience. It would've been even weirder for him to disappear into the ether, like none of it ever happened."

J.C. opens his mouth, shuts it again, and finally decides to let the subject drop. "When did A.J. do this?" he says, tapping the drawing of the tree.

"The night we met. I guess it was his way of asking me . . . well, you know." I blush. "But anyway, he wrote those lines on there. And then when I told Aidan I'd marry him, he said them out loud to me. They're from a poem by Andrew Marvell. I don't know if you know it."

"'Were there but world enough, and time,'" J.C. says. "Sure. A.J. and I read it in English class our senior year. You would've thought the teacher had passed out *Playboy* or something. He liked that poem. I remember."

"Gabe can't even read, J.C., not beyond super-basic stuff like *See Spot Run*. How he wrote this . . . much less how he drew the same thing Nicholas did, with the details, and the picture of the mountain . . . I have no idea. He said his daddy did it, and it looks just like Aidan's handwriting. Either way, it made a believer out of me. And it made me decide to come home."

"I don't believe in any of this shit." He bites out each word. "I was raised Catholic, just like A.J., sure. But I never . . . I don't understand."

"Maybe you don't have to," I say. "Maybe you just have to accept."

He puts the three drawings together, flattens out the wrinkles. "Can I ask you something, Maddie?"

"Go ahead."

"When you say he kissed you like A.J. did . . . did you mean that?"

"Yes," I say after a pause. "Just like him. Like he was saying goodbye."

"You weren't just bullshitting me?"

"I wouldn't do that. Not about something like this. And I don't just kiss strange guys out of the blue, J.C. I would never . . ." My voice trails off.

"I don't know what to make of all this," he says. "But I'm willing to be open-minded."

"That's a start."

"Which brings me to the other thing I have to say."

"I'm all ears." I lean back against the door.

"Can I please come in, Maddie? I'd prefer not to have this discussion on your front porch. It won't take long."

I swing the door inward and gesture for him to enter. "Thanks," he says as he steps over the threshold, careful not to touch me. He walks into the kitchen and sinks into one of the chairs, pulling the other one out for me with his foot.

"I'll stand," I tell him.

"Don't be silly. Sit down," he says, rolling his eyes up to meet mine. "I'm not going to bite you."

Grudgingly, I sit across from him. "So talk."

He cracks his knuckles. "Okay. Look. When you called me from New York—I'd been drinking, like I told you. I didn't have the—I don't know what you'd call them—the defenses, I guess, that I normally have in place when I talk to you. I was just happy to hear your voice. And then when you said what you did, about kissing that other guy—I just lost it. I know that must seem ridiculous, after all those years you were with A.J. But him—that was different. You loved him, you had a child together. I could handle that a lot better, I could force it to make sense in my mind. But for you to hook up with some random dude, after all those years I spent wishing that we—well, never mind. Suffice it to say, it just killed me. Made me feel like the times we were together, they meant nothing to you. Like I could've been anyone. It tore me up." He meets my eyes across the table, and I can see his true self in them, the J.C. I know.

Having my suspicions confirmed doesn't make me feel any better. "That wasn't it," I say. "Being with you—it was special, J.C. It scared me how natural it felt, how easy it was, especially coming right after the accident. It petrified me, if you want to know the truth."

"So you ran. You ran like A.J. did, when he fell in love with you."

"No!" I say, indignant.

He just waits, his hands folded on the table, his eyes on mine. Finally I say, "Well, maybe. But not on purpose. I just couldn't think in a straight line. I don't understand how the two can coexist, the way I hurt over losing Aidan, and the way . . . the way I feel about you."

"How do you feel?"

"Right now? I feel confused."

"That's a shit answer," he says, and there is heat in his voice. "I can't do this by myself, Madeleine. Don't ask me to. You think this isn't a risk for me? You think this is easy?" His voice shakes. "I told myself that when you came home, I was going to shut the door on this whole thing, for good. But then you show up with these damn drawings, looking beautiful like you do, and it just wrecks me. I don't know whether to hold you or hate you. You tell me. What am I supposed to think?"

"I'm sorry I've been so selfish," I say, which is the best answer to his question that I can give. "I'm sorry I took you for granted."

He inclines his head in acknowledgment. Then he says, "You remember before, when you asked me what I wanted?"

"Of course I do."

"I want a family," he says. "I want a life. I'm thirty-three years old and when I look into the future, all I see is your face. I told you I didn't expect you to ride off into the sunset with me, and I don't. But what I expect and what I want, they're not the same thing. I want you, and I'm tired of making excuses about it. I want a life with you. And if there's no possibility that I can have that, which I completely understand, then I need to cut my losses and move on."

I try to swallow and give it up as a bad job. "What are you asking me, J.C.?"

"I asked you to give me a chance for this to be something real," he says. "Can you? Be honest with me, please. Whatever the answer is, I need to hear it. Even if the answer is no."

His face is still, expectant, as he waits for my reply. Only his hands, pulling at a loose string on one of the placemats, give away how he feels.

I take a deep breath, then another. I picture Aidan's face. Then I see the drawings, both of them. I remember the words. And I do what Aidan asked all those years ago, I have faith. At the edge of the cliff again, I do what is so unlike me. For the second time in my life, I look into the unknown, and I jump.

"You'll have your chance," I tell J.C.

"For real?" he says. "No hiding, no keeping secrets? Like a real couple, out in the world?"

I shudder at the thought of what our friends will make of this development. It won't be pretty, and I can just imagine the vicious gossip that will spread. But I know that if I act ashamed of whatever's between us, I will ruin it. J.C.'s pride will never be able to sustain a relationship like that, and as for me, I can't stand the thought of living a lie. Plus, I think, looking at the drawings that J.C. has placed on the table, this is what Aidan wanted. To hell with what other people think.

"For real," I say with conviction, and he smiles.

"I thought you were never coming back," he says, taking my hand. "I was going crazy, baby. Really."

"I know. I could tell."

"I was a total ass earlier. I'm sorry. But I was sure you could see right through me, anyhow."

"So you *were* jealous."

"Of course I was. What did you think?"

"I didn't know what to think. You were so distant, it was like talking to a wall. I'd never seen you act that way. You did an excellent impression of a first-class jerk."

"Sorry about that. I have lots of practice hiding how I feel when I'm talking to you. Plus, I was mad. And tired of putting my heart out there for you to kick around like a football on Super Bowl Sunday. Not to mention, between the goddamn avalanche nightmares and obsessing over you, I'm running on a minimum amount of sleep. Like, hardly any."

"You were very convincing," I tell him. "I bought every word you said."

A shadow crosses his face. "You did, huh? You really believed I thought what happened between us was a total mistake?"

"You can be pretty persuasive when you want to be."

"Yeah?" He still has my hand, and now he leans across the table, pulling me toward him, slow, so I have every chance to draw back. "Let me show you how I really feel," he says, and then he is kissing me. He lets go of my hand and winds his fingers into my hair. His other hand is on my face, cupping my jaw, stroking my cheek. There's nothing careful about it, nothing hesitant. I kiss him back the same way, and when we separate, both of us are out of breath. My heart is pounding, hard.

"When did you say Gabe was coming home?" he says, cradling my face in his hands.

"By one. Any minute now."

"Damn. Otherwise, I'd be happy to persuade you some more, if you think it's necessary. Or even if you don't." He frees one hand to rock the table back and forth, and I realize he's trying to judge its ability to withstand our combined weight.

"Seriously? Right here?" I can't help but smile.

"Honest to God," he says, and from the look on his face, I can see he means it. "But if we've got to wait, we've got to wait." He comes around the table and puts his arms around me. I feel safe, like this is where I belong. Maybe that should scare me, but it doesn't. I lean against him and breathe him in.

"Welcome home, baby," he says, and then he kisses me again. He's trying to be good, I can tell, but it doesn't quite work out that way. After a minute he picks me up and sets me on the edge of the table, anyhow. I wrap my legs around him and he slides his hands under my shirt.

"We should probably stop," I whisper to him.

"Uh-huh," he says, his lips against my neck, not stopping in the slightest.

"Seriously, J.C." I struggle to marshal my wits. "It's not a good idea to unveil our couplehood by having sex on my kitchen table in front of Jill and Aspen and Gabriel."

"Not even a tiny bit of sex?" He presses against me in a way that nearly undoes my resolve.

"Not even that," I say, pulling my shirt down.

"If you say so," he says, and with reluctance, he backs off. The expression on his face is such a comical blend of disappointment, lust, and happiness that I burst into laughter. He eyes me quizzically but sets me on the floor, and just in time, too. The front door opens, and Jill calls, "Knock knock!" in her cheerful throaty voice.

"Oh shit," J.C. says, and he bolts for the bathroom, presumably to hide the state of his shorts. This doesn't do a great deal to help stifle my laughter, and I am still giggling when Jill comes into the kitchen, followed by Aspen and Gabe.

Jill raises her eyebrows—the last few times she's seen me, I've either been in tears or close to it—but all she says is "I can't stay long. This one has soccer practice."

"Another time," I assure her, getting my giggles under control. "Thanks for watching Gabe. Was he okay?"

"He was fine," she says. "Like usual. They talked about *Lego Batman* the whole time. I lost about thirty brain cells, just listening."

"I know the feeling."

"Mommy," Gabe says, tugging on my sleeve. "Can I go get my Batmobile out? And my action figures?"

"Sure," I tell him, and he runs out of the kitchen and down the hall to his room.

Jill puts her bag on the floor, between her feet. "I thought I saw J.C.'s car outside. Is he here?"

"He's in the bathroom," I say just as J.C. emerges, looking none the worse for wear.

"What's up, home slice?" he says to Aspen, and they bump fists. "Hey, Jill."

"You're alive," she says. "I've been trying to call you for, like, three days."

"Sorry. I was off the radar for a little while there. What did you need?"

"Business stuff. I don't have time to go into it right now." She reshoulders her bag. "I'll call you later, if you'll answer your phone."

"I'll answer," he says.

"You'd better," she warns him. "Come on, Aspen. Time to kick some butt." She hugs us goodbye, Aspen waves, and off they go. They cross paths with Gabe, who comes running into the kitchen.

"Mommy, look!" he says. Then he sees J.C., and he skids to a halt.

"Hi, little man," J.C. says. He gets down to Gabe's level, the same way he did at the airport. "Thanks for taking care of your mama, like I asked."

"You're here," Gabe says, and, his small face alight, he leaps into J.C.'s arms.

FIFTY-TWO

Nicholas

After my little tête-à-tête with Grace, the pieces fall into place like they're part of a master plan. My mom always told me that when you're doing what you're supposed to do, the universe will help you out. It may throw you a few curveballs, but they're all in the name of a good cause. Once you leave your path behind, that's when you start swimming upstream. It's good advice. My parents may have wanted security for me, but more than that, they wanted me to be happy. They would be proud of me right now. I'm sure of it.

I drive home from Grace's house. Back home, I put the key in the lock, filled with the sense that a loop has closed. It's the same feeling I had when I kissed Madeleine, and when I think about it for a minute, I realize that if I hadn't gotten hit by that car, this is what I would have done on June 7—come home after my little joyride, unlocked the door, taken Nevada for a walk. My life is back on course, just with a few extras, and I intend to take full advantage of them.

That's how I come to find myself in the window seat of a plane, headed across the Atlantic Ocean, on the first leg of a twenty-three-hour transcontinental flight. It's 6:30 A.M., Mountain Standard Time. Somewhere in Colorado, the sun is rising. Maybe Gabe and Maddie have gone home. Maybe he is waking up, maybe she is nursing her first cup of coffee. Or not. Somewhere in Alaska, Aidan James's body lies under a massive amount of snow, waiting to be discovered. Or not. Somewhere in Wilmington, Grace is driving to work, cursing my name. Or not.

I've quit my job, rented my house, sold my furniture, broken up with my girlfriend for the third time, and gotten Taylor to look after my dog, which wasn't a tough sell. And aside from having to leave Nevada behind, I've never been happier in my life.

I'm on my way to India, to teach English at a school in Dharamsala. I didn't set out to choose a location surrounded by mountains—much less the awe-inspiring peaks of the Himalayas—but this is how it's worked out, and somehow I'm not surprised. Though Aidan's spirit is gone, I can still feel him with me somehow, guiding my way. That's one reason I chose to go to India; maybe through yoga, meditation, and spiritual studies, I can make sense of what happened to me. Or not.

In the meantime, I am struggling manfully to quit smoking, and I still prefer whisky to wine. Aidan may have moved on, but traces of him are still here, within me. Somehow I find this comforting. After all, without him, I doubt I would have the nerve to do what I'm doing right now. He gave me back to myself, even if that wasn't his primary purpose, and I will always be grateful for that.

As my plane soars higher, the sun breaks out from behind the clouds, outlining them in orange, then red. I think back to the avalanche dream, how we refused to look away from the light even when it made our eyes tear, how we confronted what was coming head-on. That confidence is with me now, as I speed across the Atlantic toward an uncertain future—but this time, instead of a warning of dire things to come, the sun's rays are a beacon, lighting my way. Once again purpose fills my soul and courses through my limbs, but this time it is accompanied by an unmistakable presentiment of peace. Even though I've never done anything like this before, even though I have no idea what will happen, I recognize the path I've chosen. It is foreign, but familiar; it is scary but so right, there's no room for doubt.

It is the way home.

EPILOGUE

Aidan

Below me the mountain falls away, an infinite stretch of snow and rock and ice. Above me it rises, magnificent and cruel. I survey its pitches and angles, the quality of the lines. This is not a route I recognize, and I'm free-soloing it; there's no ropes, no partner to back me up. By rights, I should be worried, but I'm not. I feel strong, and confident. There is nothing to fear.

Either the sun hasn't risen yet, or it's just set. Alpenglow fills the sky as far as I can see. The view is awesome, but there's no time to linger over it, not now. It's not that I'm in a hurry, precisely—more like I've got somewhere to go, and there's no point in waiting.

As I scale the next pitch, the sun breaches the horizon, shooting prisms of color across the ice. Something about this sight arrests my upward motion, and I almost remember—There is something I ought to know about this climb, an element that makes it especially significant. It bothers me that I can't figure it out. The memory dances just out of reach, tantalizing me.

Puzzled, I look down the mountain again, then up, searching for the source of my unease. I see black rock, glittering ice, snow-covered peaks bathed in light. There is no noise except for my breathing, quick and even, and the sound of distant seracs breaking free, crashing into the valley below. I am at home in this world, as comfortable as I ever am, unless I'm lying in Maddie's arms.

Suspended halfway up this spectacular column of ice, I open my eyes and gaze upward, into the rising sun. Though I could have sworn I was alone, I hear a voice calling me from the top of the pitch, just out of sight. At this distance, I can't tell whether it's male or female. What I do know is that it's warm, and full of the kind of enthusiasm I've always found hard to resist.

"Climb on," the voice tells me—a dare, a directive, an unmistakable invitation.

And so I do.

ACKNOWLEDGMENTS

Writing may be a solitary process, but publication is a team effort. My deepest thanks go first to Caroline Leavitt, my extraordinary mentor, who was the first person to glimpse the world I created in these pages. Her unflagging belief in Madeleine and Aidan's story means more than I can say.

I owe a debt of gratitude to my indefatigable agent, without whom the book might never have found an audience. Felicia Eth, you are the best advocate a fledgling writer could ask for. Thank you for finding my imaginary friends a home. And to Linda Marrow, my editor—your keen insights and thoughtful comments made all the difference. I am so lucky that you took a chance on me.

On the home front, thanks are due to Anne Firmender, who read every draft of this book—and there were many. Thank you to Jessica Whaley, who did me the great service of listening as I talked my way through sticky sections of the plot. Jess, if you were secretly crafting your grocery list as I rambled on, you never let it show.

Big hugs to my parents, for entertaining Lucas while I gallivanted across the country, and to Neil, for putting up with me when I had one foot in his world and the other one in Maddie's.

Walter Scott Kiesling was the best climbing consultant an acrophobic girl could ask for. Thanks for reading, and your invaluable suggestions. Any mistakes that remain are my own.

I owe a shoutout of epic proportions to Chamisa Wheeler for introducing me to Colorado, to Russ and Linda Criswell for welcoming me into their home, and to an anonymous group of Outward Bound instructors in Rifle Canyon who were kind enough to share their expertise with a stranger. Thank you to the crew at Port City Java for caffeinating me with such tender care, and to my book club ladies for cheering me on. You know who you are.

ABOUT THE AUTHOR

EMILY COLIN lives in North Carolina with her partner, their son, and two reprehensible canines. In her other life, she serves as associate director at DREAMS of Wilmington, a nonprofit organization that provides multidisciplinary arts programming for youth in need. *The Memory Thief* is her first novel.

ABOUT THE TYPE

This book was set in Transitional 521, a Bitstream version of Caledonia, designed by William A. Dwiggins in 1938. He described the face as having "something of that simple, hard-working, feet-on-the-ground quality" as well as a "liveliness of action in the curves—the way they get away from the straight stems with a calligraphic flick, and in the nervous angle on the under side of the arches as they descend to the right"